Twisted Lace
A.M. McCoy

"Time to learn another party trick."
— Lex

Am.
Ammy

COPYRIGHT

Copyright © 2024 by A.M. McCoy

All rights reserved.

No part of this book may be reproduced in any form or by any electronic or mechanical means, including information storage and retrieval systems, without written permission from the author, except for the use of brief quotations in a book review.

This is a work of fiction. The names, characters, incidents, and places are products of the author's imagination and are not to be construed as real except where noted and authorized. Any resemblance to persons, living or dead, or actual events are entirely coincidental. Any trademarks, service marks, product names, or names featured are assumed to be the property of their respective owners and are used only for reference. There is no implied endorsement if any of these terms are used.

The author acknowledges the trademarked status and trademark owners of various products referenced in this work, which have been used without permission. The publication/use of these trademarks is not authorized, associated with, or sponsored by the trademark owners.

This book is intended for mature audiences.

Contents

Warnings		V
Description		VII
1.	Attention!!	1
2.	Chapter 1 – Lex	3
3.	Chapter 2 – Lex	7
4.	Chapter 3 – Lex	11
5.	Chapter 4 – Hannah	19
6.	Chapter 5 – Lex	25
7.	Chapter 6 – Hannah	37
8.	Chapter 7 – Knox	49
9.	Chapter 8 – Brody	61
10.	Chapter 9 – Lex	69
11.	Chapter 10 – Hannah	81
12.	Chapter 11 – Brody	93
13.	Chapter 12 – Hannah	105
14.	Chapter 13 – Lex	113
15.	Chapter 14 – Knox	123
16.	Chapter 15 – Hannah	129
17.	Chapter 16 – Lex	137
18.	Chapter 17 – Brody	145

19.	Chapter 18 – Lex	155
20.	Chapter 19 – Knox	163
21.	Chapter 20 – Hannah	169
22.	Chapter 21 – Lex	185
23.	Chapter 22 – Brody	191
24.	Chapter 23 – Hannah	197
25.	Chapter 24 – Lex	213
26.	Chapter 25 – Knox	223
27.	Chapter 26 – Hannah	233
28.	Chapter 27 – Knox	237
29.	Chapter 28 – Brody	257
30.	Chapter 29 – Lex	267
31.	Chapter 30 – Hannah	273
32.	Chapter 31- Knox	281
33.	Chapter 32- Lex	295
34.	Epilogue – Brody	303
35.	Epilogue – Hannah	317
36.	Epilogue – Knox	323
37.	Epilogue – Lex	333
38.	Bonus Scene	343

Warnings

Twisted Lace isn't a particularly dark romance, but it does have some elements that may be disturbing to some readers.

Triggers include but are not limited to:

CNC/Dub Con

Detailed Sex on Page

Profanity

Tattooing

Gambling

Violence

Alcohol

Blood

Death of Family Members (not on page)

Talks of Suicide

Mental Health

Sexuality Changes

Pregnancy

Spanking

Restraining / Bondage

Degradation

Other BDSM Elements

If you have any concerns or questions ahead of time, please do not hesitate to reach out to A.M. McCoy's team at a.m.mccoybooks@gmail.com to discuss.

Description

They call me Emo Barbie. And they're not far off, though I consider myself a little more alternative than that. I just so happen to do everything in six-inch heels and blood-red lipstick.

I like it when people stare. I like the attention.

I've never been drawn to the meek or mild. At least, not until I met Hannah Kate, the journalist hired by Dallin to do a story on Twisted Ink and feature me as its best artist.

Even her name screams good girl next door. And that's exactly what she is.

Sweet. Innocent. Pure.

Everything I'd ruin if I had even a small taste of her.

The problem?

The two hulking neanderthals she's linked herself to in a surprisingly sexy throuple.

Brody and Knox are the epitome of dark, brooding, alpha holes that ooze testosterone and scream bad boy in charge.

They're everything I've always competed with as a dominant lesbian. Yet when I see them with her, I'm fascinated.

Drawn in and unable to walk away.

So tell me why I was a no-strings-attached kind of girl when I met Hannah, determined to use her newly discovered bisexuality to steal her from her men for some fun, yet now I'm aching to fall to my knees and suddenly be a good girl for Brody and Knox with Hannah at my side?

<u>Attention!!</u>

I said it with Twisted Ink, and Twisted Lace is no different.
Leave your expectations for world-class literature at the door and worry more about if your batteries are charged, or if your partner is free for the next few hours.
This one is for the sluts 2.0.

Chapter 1 – Lex

"You fucking rusty, worthless piece of shit. If you don't let it go, I'm dropping you off at the scrap yard, Sally. I swear to God, you'll get chopped up into tiny little scrappy pieces if you don't cooperate with me right the fuck now!" I stomped my feet like a spoiled child as frustration got the better of me.

"You okay under there?" A random voice asked from above and scared the shit out of me, making me lurch forward, banging my forehead off the undercarriage of my car where I was laying under it. "Jesus, sorry."

"Ouch." I cursed, holding my head and sliding out from under Sally, my broken-down muscle car on the side of the road to see who interrupted me and instantly got blinded by the sun as I tried to look up that high.

"Here." The voice said as he stepped in front of the blazing sun, casting a shadow over me and held his hand out to help me up. "I didn't mean to scare you."

"You didn't." I snapped, taking his hand and letting him pull me from the dirty shoulder. Even on my feet, I had to look way up to see his face. I admitted, "I was just too busy shit-talking my car to notice that someone had stopped." His motorcycle was parked behind Sally on the shoulder, and it freaked me out that someone had gotten that close to me without even noticing him. Again.

"I heard that." He grinned and finally let go of my hand as his eyes roamed down my body. I knew my style was over the top, so I was used to getting stares, but there was something more to his gaze as he took in my appearance. "Nice boots." He nodded to my black chunky combat boots.

"I'd say thanks, but I don't think you actually like them." I retorted, raising my brow at him in a challenge. Even though I had no fucking clue who he was, there was something about him that just... pissed me off.

"I don't." He shrugged and then nodded to the flat tire I had been trying to change. "Want some help?"

"Want?" I looked down at the shredded rubber. "No." I sighed and kicked the useless tire iron I'd been trying to get free of the jack. But it was as rusty as my soul and stuck inside the joint. I couldn't change the tire without getting the tool free to take the lug nuts off. "However, I think I don't have a choice."

He squatted down, and I moved to the side as he twisted the iron twice and then pulled it free from the rusty jack holding my car up. He made it look impressively easy. Which was also impressively annoying.

I rolled my eyes at his back and leaned against the trunk of my car as he loosened the nuts. I took a deep breath as I fought the urge to tell him never mind and to get lost, because I had an appointment I was already running late for as it was and I didn't feel like making it worse by shooing away my only help at the moment.

He worked silently, removing the lug nuts that hadn't budged even when I stood on the handle of the iron ten minutes ago before it was stuck in the jack. Once again, making it look annoyingly easy. I observed him working silently, matching his silence, and had no choice but to admire his appearance.

It wasn't the tight Wrangler jeans that hugged his massive thighs that caught my attention. It wasn't even the way his biceps flexed under the hem of his white t-shirt as he worked.

It was his ink.

Ink was my love language. Sometimes, it felt like the only way I could connect with any other human on Earth. I was usually too unconventional for most people to relate to, but tattoos were universal. Most everyone in the United States had at least one these days or could admire the art behind them instead of judging the person wearing them.

Except for people like me. Because I was covered in them. Literally from head to toe. I had one above my right eyebrow and a large one covering my entire neck down over my chest. Both arms and legs had them, and mostly, I was just *too much* for people to handle.

But the stranger had them up both arms too, and it was some sort of common ground.

My phone rang in the back pocket of my cut-off shorts, distracting me from the black ink swirls above his left elbow and I answered it. "I'm on my way."

"You're late and your appointment is here," Dallin replied. Neither of us were big on pleasantries on a good day, and the morning had already started out royally wrong.

"I have a flat tire," I stated, cutting off his retort.

"I thought you knew your way around that car well enough to change a tire."

"I do." I snapped, "And if the piece of shit jack wasn't so rusted, I would have been done an hour ago."

"I'll send Parker to come help you."

"No need." I rubbed my forehead as the stranger looked up at me from his crouch, remaining silent. "This random dude on a Harley pulled over to help. If I disappear, start there. It's always the bikers that are the weirdos."

"Not funny." Dallin deadpanned. "You safe?"

"Yes, Daddy." I droned on, annoyed, and the stranger's hand slipped off the tire iron, hitting the ground and busting his knuckle wide open, making me cringe. "I have to go; the biker dude is trying to bleed all over Sally's rims." I hung the phone up and pocketed it, reaching into the back window and grabbing a towel from my gym bag. "Here."

"Thanks." He grumbled, not making eye contact as he wrapped his hand in the towel and then went back to work. He worked so fast that I hardly had time to worry about my now very late start to my day before he was wiping his greasy hands off on the towel and standing up. "You're all set. Don't drive over forty-five on that spare and get it replaced ASAP."

"You sound like a professional." I grabbed the tools from the shoulder and tossed them in the trunk as he lingered next to the car. He didn't make any move toward leaving, so I paused, "What?"

"Why didn't you call for help before I came by?" He looked up and down the road, which sat empty. No other car had passed in the time it'd taken him to change the tire. "Why struggle?"

Closing the trunk, I shrugged my shoulders. "I'm not a damsel in distress kind of girl. I would have gotten it eventually if you hadn't helped."

He scoffed and shook his head, walking back toward his bike. "Sure."

"Whatever." I brushed it off. He was a grumpy asshole, and he didn't deserve my time, even if he'd helped me out in a jam.

"I think you were looking for, *thank you*." He slung his leg over the bike, and I found myself way too interested in the motion as he rocked the bike forward, adjusting himself on the seat.

I tilted my head and clasped my hands together, attempting to appear overly sweet. In a breathy Marilyn Monroe voice, I gave him what he wanted. "Thank you, Mr. Biker Man, for assisting me in changing my stubborn old tire. However, can I repay such a favor?" Then I rolled my eyes and flipped him the bird. "Better?"

"Much," he smirked, and his devilish grin on his dark face took me aback. "But you're not my type, so that wouldn't work either." He looked me up and down one last time and then started his bike. The roar was deafening, but not worse than the sound of my blood pulsing through my ears as embarrassment bloomed in my chest. He rode away without another glance and I stared after him, utterly shook.

How did that man push my buttons so well that he made me feel insecure?

"Fuck you!" I screamed after him, flipping him the bird again and then flying the other one just for good measure before stalking back to my car. "I hate men."

Chapter 2 – Lex

Trey glanced up from his magazine at the breakroom table as I walked into Twisted Ink, an hour and a half late. "Well, look who decided to show up."

"Don't start." I snapped, blowing past him.

"Oooh, somebody's in a mood." He stood up and followed me to my suite, but I turned and blocked his path as he tried to follow me inside.

I held my fingers up in front of his face, pinched so tight there wasn't a paper's width of space between them. "I'm this close to knocking someone's teeth out. If you want it to be you, then keep it the fuck up. If not, get lost. I have a client to see."

He scoffed and leaned against the doorjamb, dramatically keeping his toes from crossing the threshold. "Actually, you don't. Dallin canceled your appointment."

"What?" I whirled on him. "Why?"

"Uh, you're almost two hours late." He widened his eyes like it was obvious.

"Ugh!" I screeched, throwing my purse at the wall and huffing. "I'm so not in the mood for your shit today, Trey!"

"Whoa," Parker's calm voice sounded from the doorway, and I glared over my shoulder at him as he pulled Trey back. "That's enough poking the bear, buddy." He shoved him back toward his own suite.

But Trey was too dumb to leave with his safety intact, "Let's be real. We all know that little Lexi-poo isn't dangerous." He added. I snatched the first thing within reach, which turned out to be a metal paperweight, and prepared to strike.

"No!" Parker barked, grabbing my arm and stopping me, sliding my door closed behind him as he went. "Down girl, he's not worth it."

"I'm not in the mood to be bothered right now, Parker," I warned, tossing the heavy metal weight down onto my desk and putting my hands on my hips as I fought for control of my temper.

"What's going on?" He asked, sitting on my stool, and staring at me, giving me no choice but to talk. Parker was probably the closest thing I had to a best friend. Typically levelheaded, he had a knack for understanding women's thoughts, making him an easy person to talk to. But I still wasn't in the mood.

"I hate men," I answered like that was any answer at all.

"Yep, you're a lesbian. That tracks." He nodded like a therapist would for me to continue.

I glared at him for good measure and then threw myself down into my comfy chair, where I sketched most days and deflated altogether. "Sally blew a tire this morning. And I missed my first appointment because Dallin canceled it when I was late."

His eyebrows rose. "Why didn't you call me? I would have changed it for you."

"Because I'm not some helpless ninny!" I huffed. "I can change a tire. But my jack was so rusted and stubborn it ate my tire iron and left me stranded."

"So how'd you get here?"

I pursed my lips. "Some asshat pulled over and changed it for me."

He cocked his head to the side with a stupid smirk on his face. "A man, I presume."

I flipped him off, "I've flown this bird so many times this morning, it's going to fall off my hand."

He fake cried, "Not the pussy pleaser three thousand!" His pretty boy grin was almost enough to make me crack a smile, but not quite. After settling down again, he went on. "So what was it about the asshat man that got you so pissed off?"

I shook my head and pulled at a thread on my shorts. "Fuck if I know. He just instantly rubbed me the wrong way and gave me some toxic masculinity vibes, as he assumed I should throw myself at him in thanks for helping me out. And then," I pointed at him, "He criticized my appearance."

Parker gasped dramatically. "Is the ALT girl crying because someone turned their nose up at her over-the-top style? I thought that was kind of why you dressed so crazy some days."

"It is," I admitted. "But more than that, I do it because I like it."

"Then what does it matter if he didn't?" He leaned forward on his elbows.

"I don't fucking know. I think that's half the problem."

"Were you attracted to him?" He asked, and I could hear the caution in his tone.

"I don't do dicks, Parker. You know that."

"You haven't done dicks, Lex. That doesn't mean you can't change your mind, though." He rubbed his hands together excitedly. "Do you think maybe you were attracted to him and that's why his snub affected you? Have you felt attracted to men before?"

"Yes," I admitted. "I can appreciate the male form and the differences between men and women. But that doesn't mean I want to fuck them. It's like admiring a tattoo, even if it's nothing you'd ever want on your body."

"But did you want that man on your body?" He raised one brow with a smirk. "You're avoiding my key question, which I think answers it in reality."

I squinted at him but didn't respond.

"Interesting." He mused, sitting upright. "I'm going to let you reflect on that for a while."

"You're a pain in the ass, you know that?"

He nodded his head easily. "I do know that. I think you still love me either way, though."

"Debatable." I threw back, but he just laughed and left my suite, leaving the door closed behind him as he went.

I hated that he zeroed in on the problem at hand.

I *was* attracted to the biker.

And that was befuddling because, besides some mild appreciation for the male body before, I had never experienced active attraction towards a man before.

Leave it to me to suddenly find myself attracted to a man for the first time with one who had a disposition as prickly as mine.

Good thing I'd probably never see him ever again.

Chapter 3 – Lex

"Your four o'clock is here." Paisley, the receptionist for the shop, popped her head in my room, surprising me and dragging me out of the headspace I'd been in while sketching the giant backpiece I had scheduled to tattoo tomorrow morning.

Scowling at her, "I don't have a four o'clock. I have a five, but there's no way she's early."

"Not a tattoo." Paisley walked in and leaned against my wall. "The journalist for the Nashville paper."

"Ugh." I groaned, tipping my head back in impatience. "I forgot all about that."

"Dallin didn't." She tapped her fingers on her arm. "He told me to make sure you were on your best behavior. Seems like he knows her and she's doing him a favor by letting the story be about you, not him."

"Hmm." I laid my tablet down and stretched my sore neck. "How kind of him to pass off his responsibility onto my shoulders and then demand I behave."

Paisley smirked and rolled her eyes. "It's like he knows you or something." She peeked out the door to the reception area and then lifted her shoulder in a shrug. "And I'm guessing he wants to protect her innocent little soul from your wild side as much as possible."

"Innocent?" I cringed. "I taint innocence for the fun of it. Why would he sign me up for the assignment, and not Parker, if there was so much at risk?"

She tittered and backed out of my room, "I don't know, but I'm going to enjoy the show."

"Give me a minute to put my cloak of goodliness on." I joked and then cleaned up my design space.

I mentally counted to ten and then ten again before looking in the mirror on the wall, taking in my appearance.

My wavy black hair was long and the bleached money pieces in the front highlighted the black ink on my face and neck. The piercings in my cheeks that accentuated the deep dimples there added a bit of femininity to the rest of my edginess. My black crop top band tee and cut-off jean shorts with silver chain embellishments set the look paired with the black combat boots that the biker commented on.

I loved every bit of it. I'd spent years figuring out my style and identity, and I didn't regret a single piece of it. But I didn't have any illusions about what vibe I gave off either. Nor could I figure out why Dallin would want me to be the 'face' of the shop for his big article.

"Well, here goes nothing." I mused and walked out after Paisley to the reception area.

I clocked the journalist immediately. She stuck out so much that it was almost painful to see her in the edgy tattoo shop. She was probably in her late twenties, but she had one of those faces that would always leave her looking young and fresh.

Untouched.

She had light strawberry blonde hair, tied back in a tight knot with a few wisps blowing in the fan's breeze. She wore a business-savvy white dress that collared at her neck with sleeves down to her elbows. It just touched the tops of her knees as she stood by the front door and her sensible black flats screamed middle-aged mom.

But what stood out the most to me was every inch of her blank, untouched skin visible around her modest dress.

A virgin.

Tattoo virgin at least. I'd bet money that she didn't have a speck of ink on her soft white skin and something about that—called to me. God, I was the worst.

"Ah, here she is." Paisley nodded to me, catching the journalist's attention. "Lex, this is Hannah Kate. Hannah, this is Lex."

"Hi!" Hannah walked toward me with her hand extended and a bright cheery smile on her face. "It's so nice to meet you! I feel like I've spent the last week stalking you and your work so extensively that I know you inside and out by now." She laughed at her joke while I raised my brow in surprise. "Sorry." She grimaced. "I'm a blabber."

"I'll keep that in mind." I nodded, shaking her hand and staring straight at her as she shrunk a bit. We were probably the same height, but with my heeled boots on, I towered over her slight frame. Everything about her was small. Dainty, even. "Come on back and we can get started."

She fell in step behind me as we went deeper into the shop, passing rooms where tattoos were in progress. As we neared Parker's room, she glanced inside and her step faltered when she saw the massive man in Parker's chair, getting his stomach tattooed. "Ouch." She murmured to herself, before running to catch back up with me.

I motioned for her to walk in ahead of me and then slid the door closed behind her, expecting and then catching the feminine floral scent as she brushed past me.

Predictable.

Yet not in a bad way.

"Thanks so much for making the time for me in Dallin's absence," Hannah said, looking around my private room. "This is so stinking cool." She had an awe-struck look on her face as she took it all in, and I tried to imagine seeing my space through her eyes. The room had a cool vibe with matte black walls and fancy gold accents on the chairs, lighting, and décor. The floor glowed with pink up-lighting, and an ivy plant with light pink petaled flowers completely covered one wall. I only kept the plant alive because it pissed Trey off the most. He hated plants in any form and took personal offense to the small ivy plant when it was in a lattice pot on the floor. So of course I let that bitch free to grow up the wall. I even went as far as having Parker help me hang a support lattice for her to twist around, simply because I could. And it made one hell of a photo backdrop for the before and after photos of my clients. And let's be honest, social media presence was everything. "I feel so unworthy of being in here." She contemplated and then shook her head with a goofy grin on her face. "But I'm totally loving it."

"I'm glad." I motioned for her to sit in the comfy black chair in the corner that I sketched in and then took my office chair and turned it toward her. "You'll have to forgive me; Dallin was pretty vague on the details of this piece and what you needed from me, exactly."

She smiled and rolled her eyes, waving me off. "I'm not surprised. This piece is a feature piece on the shop itself as well as on you," she motioned to me before placing her hands in her lap, all prim and proper. "My plan when I had originally gotten the okay to do it with Dallin, was to interview him, then shadow for a few appointments, get some up close and personal photos of his work, throughout the process, and then do a feature shoot here at the shop and in a studio." She grabbed her laptop bag off the floor and pulled a tablet out, flipping the cover off and showing me a cover of Inked Magazine. It was an edition from a few years ago that I recognized because the woman on the cover was one of the most successful women in the tattoo industry. "After he switched and told me I'd be following you, I dove deep into researching ways to highlight not only your strengths as an artist, but also as a woman. And this is the vibe I was going for. Something fun yet powerful." She bit her bottom lip and waited for a reply, like she was afraid I'd veto the entire thing.

"I'll admit, I'm impressed." I leaned back in my seat, as my head spun with the details she shared in such a short amount of time. "And intrigued."

"You're one of the most sought-after tattoo artists in all of Nashville, and you're a woman. Those two titles rarely pair up in any industry, but especially in one that would rather the women be the canvases and models, instead of the designers."

"You did dive deep into the research." I praised her and she blushed a little as her shoulders sagged in relief.

"I never do anything half-assed. And if I'm being honest, which I always am," she giggled at herself and I smirked, "I'm truly looking forward to this piece far more now that it revolves around you and this angle than when it was about Dallin." She held her hand up. "As great as he is, which as Reyna's friend, I know he's great. Even so, I like this far more."

Pieces started fitting together as I found out that Hannah was a friend of Rey's. As much as I loved the wife of Dallin, Trey, and Parker, she was still a cute little vanilla girly girl in public, and the pairing made sense.

"Well, I'm at your mercy then, I suppose. Interview away." I held my arms out and crossed my leg over my knee.

Hannah smiled brightly and flicked through some pages on her tablet and then pulled a voice recorder from her bag and held it up. "Is this okay?" I shrugged, giving her the go-ahead, and she turned it on and set it down on the table next to her. "Okay, so how about we start with how you decided tattooing was the medium of art you were interested in?"

"Geesh." I thought back and smirked. "It wasn't so much that I decided on tattoos, as much as it was tattoos chose me. My dad is a tattoo artist. A damn good one, too. And when I was a kid, I used to love watching him tattoo and wanted so desperately to get one of my own. He, of course, had the opinion that my skin would never, ever feel the sting of a tattoo gun if he had anything to say about it."

Hannah listened intently, like what I was saying was the most interesting thing in the world, and I hated how it warmed my frigid heart to feel important in the moment. "Let me guess, Daddy's girl?" She asked knowingly.

"Very much so," I admitted. "And he was going to preserve me as the sweet little innocent baby girl as long as he could."

"Uh oh," she grinned, "So you rebelled."

"Hard." I shook my head, remembering those years when my dad and I butted heads over what my future would look like. "One night, when I was fourteen, I snuck down into his studio after bedtime and tattooed my leg, intent on proving him wrong."

"You did not!" She gasped with wide eyes, looking thoroughly scandalized. "What did you tattoo?"

"A rainbow." I fiddled with a ring on my finger. "It's the one tattoo from my early years that I never went back and touched up or covered."

"Can I see?" she asked, biting her bottom lip.

Keep your shit together, Lex.

She was a fucking good girl, and she meant nothing sexual by it, but there was no way I could resist corrupting her and overlook such a sexual mannerism.

I nodded, and she walked over to me with that stargazing awestruck look on her face, I raised the frayed edge of my cut-offs to the spot where my leg and hip met and watched her face as she saw the squiggly, black-lined rainbow with little puffy clouds on each end.

"No way." She whispered and flicked her big green eyes up to mine and my entire body heated like some schoolgirl. "That's so cool." She went back across the room to her chair, and I smoothed my shorts back down. "Did your dad find out?"

"I didn't plan it very well because we were going on vacation the next week and two days in, he saw it while I was in my swimsuit." I shook my head. "He was so mad, he refused to even speak to me for two days. Which was unhinged because we were best friends, so that silence did far more than any screaming or discipline could have. After some self-reflection and a few really long late-night conversations on it, he concluded that he exposed me to that life, and he could either nurture my interest in it, or I could do shady back-alley style tattoos on myself as I honed my skills. And neither of us wanted me to look like some bathroom stall, graffitied with messy work. So he started teaching me and I ended up in this life."

"Wow." Hannah sighed, mystified by it all. "That's incredible. Does he still tattoo today?"

"He does." I nodded, "He owns a big-name shop in Las Vegas, and has big name clients."

She cocked her head to the side. "Why don't you work there?" She hesitated and cringed slightly. "If you don't mind me asking. I should have prefaced this whole thing with you are more than welcome to tell me to get lost at any point if you aren't comfortable."

I waved it off. "There isn't much in life that makes me uncomfortable at this point anymore, Hannah. Don't worry. My dad is wildly successful and talented, and with that comes a gigantic shadow to stand in. And I didn't want to always live the life of following him, never making it for myself. So eight years ago I packed up and moved, first to LA, and then a few years later I moved here to Nashville, and I knew pretty much right away that this was where I was supposed to be."

"Incredible." She licked her lips, blinking rapidly as she focused on her task. "How long have you been here at Twisted Ink?"

"Five years." I crinkled my nose. "I never planned to stay in one place this long after leaving Vegas, but the thought of leaving now makes me anxious. So I'll stay a little longer, I think."

Hannah was about to say something when there was a knock on the door, and Paisley appeared. "Sorry to interrupt, but your five o'clock is here." I caught the pointed look on her face as she mentioned my next client, reminding me of the awkward situation I was about to find myself in.

"Right. Thanks." I stood up, hating the way I was actually kind of bummed to have the private interview interrupted when an idea came to mind. Considering the warning I had been given about being on my best behavior around Hannah, I should have shut it down instead of speaking my idea into reality. I just wasn't ready to end our interview.

Hannah stood up and looked from Paisley to me and back.

"Well, do you want to see what a coy fish on a spine looks like?" I asked, and her eyes rounded excitedly.

"Heck yes!"

Paisley and I chuckled as I motioned for her to follow me out to the reception area to chat with my next appointment.

I never allowed spectators during appointments outside of the client's personal entourage, but I was far from ready to end my time with Hannah.

Even if I had no fucking clue why I was entertaining the innocent little church girl any longer than I needed to.

Chapter 4 – Hannah

I was sweating. Thank god for clinical strength deodorant, or I was pretty sure Lex would have kicked me out for stinking up her studio.

She was majestic and regal in every way possible, leaving me feeling like a mere spectator amongst greatness the entire time I was in her presence.

Yet I wanted it to never end.

When I first received the assignment to interview Nashville's hottest tattoo artist, I felt overwhelmed and completely out of my comfort zone. Luckily for me, my very best friend Reyna was married to not one, but three of the biggest names in the game. So, of course, I phoned a friend and got the inside connection for the piece.

Then Dallin canceled, using an upcoming expo as the reason behind the last-minute change of plans. I thought maybe Parker or Trey would step in since they were wildly successful at Twisted Ink, too. But Dallin had emailed me with the name of another artist to do the piece. His email had been brief and vague, leaving me scratching my head as I tried to figure out his angle on it. Before long, the why behind it didn't matter. I was hooked.

Lex Donovan.

Or, as I later discovered, Alexi Faith Donovan, was hands down the most talented female tattoo artist in all of Nashville.

Yet hardly anyone outside of the tattoo world knew her name. An injustice that should have been criminal. A crime I was guilty of as well until a week ago.

My experience with tattoos was minimal, having never gotten brave enough to get one myself. But even as a novice who only admired other's work before, it took me almost no time at all to realize just how incredible Lex was.

Her art was phenomenal, and after learning who the artist was, recognizing the femininity and sensuality of it was no hard task. I felt like an enthusiast getting to study one of the world's greatest artists only through textbooks for years and then finally seeing the work at a gallery in real life. It was world-changing.

And then I got to meet the paradox herself, and I was no less blown away by her in person.

She was insanely nice to me when I interrupted her day with my nosey questions and novice take on her world. And it was an oddity, given her appearance, that I would feel so comfortable around her.

Well, mostly comfortable.

There was something about her I couldn't quite put my finger on yet. Something in the way she watched me when I spoke or the look in her eyes when she glanced up at me while she was tattooing. It was almost unnerving. And not in a bad way, but in a voracious way. I felt like a rabbit, sitting on the edge of a meadow, watching a fox in all her majestic wonderfulness, too entranced to run away in self-preservation, and lost to the allure she cast over me as she neared me. Would the spell wear off and leave the little rabbit the fox's dinner in the end? Would the rabbit go, accepting its fate, knowing she was in the presence of something greater than herself?

Was I thinking too deep into the entire situation?

Of course, that was my specialty after all.

"What got you into journalism?" Lex asked, glancing up from the back of her client where she was outlining the coy fish that covered every inch and breaking me out of the trance I'd been in watching her work. Her body moved in sync with her brain as she tattooed, curving and bending around her canvas to create the art. It was art in its own way, watching her.

I smiled fondly, "Journalism kind of chose me, much like tattooing did you. I have always been an overthinker type. And as a kid I used to drive everyone nuts asking a million questions about every topic on the face of the earth, and my teachers were so over it by middle school that they made me join the yearbook club." I shrugged a little with a smirk. "I quickly overwhelmed them and then they pushed me into the newspaper club, which, to be honest, rarely accepted middle schoolers, since high school students primarily ran it. But it did the job, because I finally had tasks that could keep my inquisitive brain busy long enough to keep my mouth shut."

"You make it sound like curiosity is a bad thing." Lex wiped some ink off and kept going. "I think it's an outstanding trait to have, especially in a child trying to figure out the world."

"I'm still trying to figure the world out." I joked. "The zest for knowledge is something I never want to lose."

She looked up at me and her brown eyes held mine for a moment that felt longer than polite before she blinked and gave her attention back to her tattoo. I didn't know if it was her standard practice or not, but when her client got to her appointment, she almost seemed disappointed to find out that she wouldn't have solo time with Lex for the tattoo. And then there had been some weird tension to begin with, but it had faded as the hours wore on, filled with small talk between Lex and me, and the buzz of her tattoo gun. At one point, I even thought, perhaps her client had fallen asleep. She had a few other large tattoos, so she was obviously no stranger to the pain.

"Well, that about wraps it up for today." Lex sat up straight and stretched her neck as she tilted her head to look at the art. "Take a look and let me know what you think."

Her client, Ashley, stood up, holding the skimpy tie back shirt she wore over her chest as she all but ran to the mirror to look. She gasped as she caught the delicate black outline in the reflection. "Oh my god, Lex." She covered her mouth with her hand and widened her eyes. "It's so much more than I could even have imagined. And it's just the line work. Oh, my god!"

I watched as Lex brushed off the over-the-top excitement with a small smile and prepped the after care supplies for her client. "Do you think I could get a picture of that?" I interjected before Lex covered the fresh tattoo with the plastic barrier.

"Am I going to make it in the article?" Ashley batted her eyelashes at me, and I chuckled at her obvious attempt to persuade me to make her art appear.

"There's a very good chance, given how beautiful of a piece it is." I nodded, and it was all the affirmation Ashley needed, as she twisted her back to me, standing in front of the pretty green ivy-covered wall in Lex's room. I snapped a few different pictures with my phone and had to force myself to back up and let Lex continue her job afterward, because I could have spent hours looking at the different parts of the tattoo. There was so much detail in the fine line work and I knew when it was all done, with color and shading, it would be a phenomenal piece.

"Stop out there with Paisley to schedule your next session in a few weeks, Ash." Lex told her as she removed her gloves and washed her hands. I couldn't help but notice the firm dismissiveness in her tone, even if there was a level of professionalism in it.

"Thanks Lex." Ashley replied, lingering at the door of the room, quickly glancing between me and her artist. "Uh, actually I was hoping—" Ashley started, and Lex cleared her throat, wiping her hands off.

"I can't." Lex cut her off before she could finish her sentence. "I have a ton of sketching to catch up on and back-to-back appointments tomorrow. But thanks."

I felt like a total lurker, standing in the room while the mysterious conversation played out with the total lack of actual words being used. The tension between the two of them had been high since the appointment started, but I hadn't been able to figure out what it was from exactly. But I was getting the idea.

"I can give you two a few—" I said apologetically, grabbing for my bag to leave the room so they could finish whatever needed to be said.

"That'd be great!" Ashley gushed appreciatively, moving to the side so I could leave the room, but Lex stopped me with her hand on my arm.

"It's unnecessary." She said firmly, staring right down at me before turning back to her client. "Like I said, Ash, I have a ton of work to do."

"Lex—" Ash chuckled awkwardly, and I wanted the floor to open up and swallow me whole.

"Have a great night, and make sure you drink lots of water the next few days while that piece pushes the ink."

Lex had a dominance about her, it wasn't necessarily in her tone or her appearance, but it filled the space around her like air thick with power. There was only one other person I'd ever encountered with that same supremacy that just forced you to comply without conscious thought.

And I had fallen in love with him because of it. Brody.

So it was a paradox to be in the presence of it with someone else that was the opposite sex of him, yet just as alluring.

"Right." Ashley brushed it off like the obvious rejection did not affect her, glancing briefly at where Lex's hand still held my arm, before turning and leaving the room in a huff.

"That was—" I murmured in surprise.

"I'm sorry." Lex sighed, releasing me. "I thought we were going to get all the way through the session with no issues. I should have known better. Ashley is never professional."

"No, no worries." I shook my head, trying to reassure her, but then my curiosity got the best of me. "Was she trying to ask you out?" Lex's dark eyelashes fluttered as she snapped her eyes to me. "Sorry. That was unprofessional of me. I can't believe I said that out loud." A blush cover my entire face and neck as I once again hoped the floor would swallow me whole and spit me back out on the other side of town. "I'm grateful for the time you have given me today; I'll get out of your hair." Grabbing my bag hurriedly, I tried to leave.

"Stop." Lex's voice was firm and demanded obedience. Something in me ached to be a good listener and follow along. She tilted her head to the side just the slightest bit as she regarded me, making the blush burn even warmer on my skin. Walking over to the chair I had been sitting in, she grabbed my forgotten tablet off the table next to it and brought it over to me.

It felt like the room got a million degrees hotter with every step she took, closing the distance between us until she stopped right in front of me and slid my tablet into the open pocket of my bag.

She held direct eye contact as she leaned down to put my tablet away, and it brought our faces only inches apart.

God, what was it about her that made me so overwhelmed?

I could admit to myself that she was hands down the most sensual woman I'd ever met before in my life. She was breathtaking, even with the thick black eyeliner and dark red lipstick. I felt like a boring brown duck in the presence of an elegant swan.

There was more than just being in awe of her beauty and presence, though I couldn't define it.

"I have a ten o'clock appointment tomorrow, I want you to see it." She stated with that velvet voice of hers, not asking, yet I would have agreed even if she did.

"Okay." I whispered, nodding my head slightly. Was my mouth hanging open like a freak? I closed it and swallowed, shaking myself out of her spell.

"Have a good night." She took a step back and leaned her butt against the tattoo bed behind her, just watching me with that powerful gaze.

The same gaze Brody gave me all the time. It was watchful and said so many things without using a single word.

"You too." I backed up, knocking into the doorjamb and wincing before correcting my course and making it through the door. "See you tomorrow."

Chapter 5 – Lex

"You're all sorts of twisted up tonight." Parker eyed me over the top of his beer bottle with a raised brow. "Care to share the cause with the class?"

I tossed back yet another shot and licked my lips, savoring the taste of the liquor on them. I didn't reply to him, though, and instead turned my head to look out over the crowd of Mav's tavern. The place was packed for a Wednesday night, but that was Nashville for you. The party crowd was always in town and the bars were always open.

"Damn." Parker mused humorously. "She must be something special." He cocked his head to the side and pointed at me with one finger off the hand still holding his bottle. "Unless it's that grumpy biker that's still got you all messed up."

"Don't you have a wife and husbands to get home to?" I finally quipped back, trying to express how unwilling I was to chat about it.

"I was due back an hour ago." He sat his now empty bottle down and raised his hand to our waitress for another round. "But I can tell when a friend needs me more than they do and I'm choosing to sit this one out for a while."

"I don't need you." I retorted, hating how aggressive it came off.

"Okay." He droned on, ignoring my tone the way only a best friend could. "Then what do you need?"

"Nothing you can help me with." I replied, hoping he'd catch my drift and leave.

"Sex." He nodded and looked out over the bar. "Any prospects?"

"None with you lurking around."

"Gah." He gasped theatrically. "You wound me. I'm always the best wing man on taco nights."

I snorted, "You're disgusting, you know that, right?"

He smirked and leaned on the table between us. "But it got you to smile." He cocked his head, "And that's the first time that's happened since you walked in. So spill. What's going on in that dark and twisted little mind of yours?"

"Nothing." I flicked my hair over my shoulder as I played with the label on my beer bottle.

"Couldn't have anything to do with your journalist visitor today, could it?" Parker watched me like a hawk. I felt heat ignite across my skin at the mention of Hannah while I tried to play the entire thing off.

"No."

"Interesting." He crossed his arms and waited, knowing I'd fold if he was right. We'd been friends for years now, and he had seen more than an indecent number of women come and go through my front door to read into things a little too easily. "She doesn't strike me as your type."

"She's not." I scoffed. "She could apply for the role of the Virgin Mary." I didn't meet his eyes as I kept my face trained out over the crowd, like I'd find the answer to my problems out there.

He snorted, "Hannah is anything but virginal. Quite the opposite, actually."

I snapped my head back to him and he raised his eyebrows at me, and I knew I'd given myself away. "What does that mean?"

"Not my story to tell." He mused, "But remember that her and Rey have been friends for years, so believe me when I say she gives off good girl vibes, but she's not innocent." I opened my mouth to contradict what he said, but he held his finger up, silencing me before he continued. "Tell me the truth."

"I don't know what the truth is, Parker." I admitted, holding his gaze.

"And that's the problem, isn't it? You're attracted to her and can't figure out why. Twice in one day with two different people totally out of your normal type."

I rolled my eyes, hating how on point he always was with my emotions. It was aggravating, to say the least. "I want to ruin her." Leaning forward on the table, giving it to him straight. "I want to ruin her perfect little outfit and hairstyle and show her exactly how good it can be to be bad." I challenged him to argue with me. "And that's fucked up, because a girl like that isn't the type of girl to be single or into women. Which means she has a man at home, and I have a list as long as my arm of women willing to let me do that to them, yet I'm thinking about little Susie Q and what she would taste like when she came."

"Then find out." He challenged, and a darkness that didn't take root in his eyes often clouded the normal clarity. "Maybe the only way to find out why she's got a hold on you is to give into it."

I scoffed, angry that he was purposing the one thing I couldn't do. "Dallin told me to be on my best behavior. Ruining the good girl doesn't exactly fall in line with that objective."

He chuckled and stood up, grabbing a wad of cash from his wallet and handing it to our waitress as she laid his beer down on the table, paying for it. He pushed his beer my way and when I reached for it, eager to add to the alcohol content in my stomach, he held onto it, making me meet his gaze. "Something I learned a long time ago is that Dallin Kent always plays the game better than anyone else could ever dream of. He's always in charge and always five steps ahead of everyone else. If he paired you up with Hannah, knowing full well what your tendencies were, there was a reason." I didn't reply and he let go of the beer. "I'll see you tomorrow."

He walked away without another word, leaving me alone in the bar with only my thoughts and his words to entertain me.

"Good girl." I praised, watching her head tip back as she gave into the ecstasy I was providing. "Just let go of everything else and feel it for what it is." I laid leisurely, slow kisses along her neck, dragging the edge of my teeth over the sensitive skin as her hands tangled in my hair, pulling me closer.

"Lex." She moaned my name, and I'd never heard it sound better coming off anyone else's lips before. Not until her. "I don't know—" She was unsure, nervous even. Something about being the one to lead her through it put me on a power trip.

"Pleasure is pleasure." I reminded her, "It doesn't matter if it's new or different, it's still good."

"God, it's so good." She moaned, arching her back as I got to her chest and twirled my tongue around one of her hard nipples. I'd always been a big fan of breasts, nipples especially, and she had a pair to worship. I could just lay with her all night and make her come from the worshiping I'd do to her perfect tits without even needing anything in return.

But tonight, I wanted more.

"Your touch is so different." She moaned, arching her hips as I kissed that space between her belly button and panty line. "Soft."

"Sensual." I added.

"Erotic." She panted. "It's so fucking good."

I smirked against her skin, damp with perspiration from the pleasurable torture I'd been putting her through. "What a dirty word on such pretty lips." I teased, closing the distance and blowing directly on her exposed pussy. She was soaked, I'd been edging her for days and she was finally in my bed and ready for me, making it worth it. "Say it again."

"Fuck." She screeched as I flattened my tongue and pressed it flat to her clit before sliding it down to her pussy. "Fuck. Fuck. Fuck." She moaned on repeat as I slid my tongue inside. God, she tasted so good. I wanted to taste her orgasm on my tongue. I needed it.

"So pretty." I twirled my tongue around her clit and slowly pushed one finger inside of her slick entrance. She was needy and rocked against my hand, taking me deeper and then rocking her hips. "Tell me what you want."

"You." She pleaded. "I want you to make me come, and then I want to do it to you."

"You want to make me orgasm?" I teased her with the dirty talk, knowing she was all about words. "Tell me what you want to do to me." I added another finger and sucked her clit as she opened and closed her mouth like a fish out of water, desperately trying to form a sentence. You didn't have to be a male to lose the blood flow to your brain when your sex organs were aroused. It was universal across mankind, and she was no exception. "Are you going to taste me?" I rocked my mouth against her clit and bent my fingers forward until she gasped and widened her legs even more.

"Yes." She nodded rapidly. "I don't know what to do, but I want to try. Fuck, I want to do it so bad."

"I'll teach you, baby." I flicked her clit again and then toyed with her nipple with my free hand. She curled forward, grabbing my wrist and holding onto me as I pleased her. "But I want you to come on my face first. Then I'll show you everything you've been missing."

"Please." She begged. "Please Lex, I'm going to explode if you keep talking like that."

"Do it." I challenged, "Come for me, Pretty Girl, and I'll let you play with me."

"God." She gasped, curling forward even tighter, and I could tell she was close. I rocked my hand faster and faster as she started coming undone above me, crying out and pleading to come.

And then she did.

"That's it. Such a good girl coming for me." I prolonged it, sucking her clit and slowly thrusting my fingers into her as she relaxed into my bed, sated.

But I wasn't done with her yet. I needed to make her do that again and again. "Oh my god," She moaned, looking up at me through her thick lashes and smiling a sweet and sultry grin. "I can't believe I just did that."

"I can't believe it took me this long to taste you." I slid up her body and softly slid my tits over hers, stimulating us both as our nipples brushed. Lifting my fingers between our faces, I slowly sucked one into my mouth right in front of her, moaning at the combination of her orgasm and my skin flavor mixing.

"Have you ever tasted yourself?" I questioned, tapping the end of my middle finger against her plush bottom lip. "Have you ever sucked your orgasm off of your partner before?"

She shook her head and then slowly parted her lips before sliding her tongue out and over my finger. I pushed it into her mouth, sliding it over the bumps of her tongue until I hit the smooth part in the back of her throat and she stared up at me, eyes hazy with arousal and desire as she sucked it clean.

"Do you like it?" I asked, struggling to focus as she gently took it deep into her mouth again.

"Only because it's on you." She admitted, and I rocked my hips forward as her dirty words tantalized me.

"I want more of it on me." I straddled one of her thighs and lifted her other leg, holding it to her chest as I rocked forward, rubbing my clit against her wet pussy. "Mmh." I moaned, feeling the pleasure roll through my body from one cell to another. I knew it would feel good with her from the moment we met. But it was otherworldly.

"Oh, my god." She gasped and put her hand on my hip, rocking me back and forth, grinding against each other. "Lex. Oh, my god."

"I know." I palmed her breast, playing with her nipples as I edged myself, desperate to fall over the edge of bliss but wanting to wait until she was crashing through that experience with me. "I'm right there with you." Leaning forward, I kissed her, and she clung to me, like she was breathing directly from my lips and I was her lifeline. "Use my body for your pleasure. I want to be the only thing giving you satisfaction. Think only of me."

Her eyelids fluttered open, and she stared directly into my eyes. "I'm with you." She whispered, leaning up to bite my bottom lip and suck it into her mouth as she started playing with my tits like I had been with her. She was so bold when she was stripped down and free. "I'm coming." She gasped, "Lex, you're making me come."

"Good girl, Hannah." I moaned, right on the edge of my orgasm, shook by the fact that Hannah Kate was underneath of me in my bed, about to make me come. "That's my good girl."

"Yours." She panted, digging her nails into my chest, marking me, and it was all I needed to crash over the other side of bliss. "Lex!"

Beep. Beep. Beep.

My eyes flew open in confusion and I panted as I tried to figure out what was going on and what that noise was.

My alarm.

It was a *dream*.

Reality crashed down onto me at the same time the disappointment and shame burned.

I just had a sex dream about Hannah, and I felt ill from it. Not because she was a bad pick for a wet dream partner, but because it felt like I took advantage of our professional relationship by dreaming about her. Like I somehow violated her.

"Fuck." I groaned, throwing myself out of bed and directly into an ice-cold shower, trying to get my electrified body to calm down and forget how fucking good it had felt to be with her, even if it was only in my head.

The tallest coffee in the world would not be enough to get me through the day, but I had no choice. So I drank it anyway and tried to convince the turmoil in my gut to settle as I parked at the shop with ten minutes to spare before my first appointment.

I never walked in that close to appointment time, but I didn't know what time Hannah would show up for day two of our interview and I couldn't bring myself to be alone with her for any length of time.

I had tried everything imaginable to get my mind under control after spending the afternoon with her yesterday. First with alcohol and then with a nameless stranger in the bar bathroom.

Despite that, all I could think about was the attention she paid to me. The way she watched and wondered at everything I did. And sure, she was there for an article and it made sense she would pay attention to the minor details for her article, but it was more than that. I was sure.

I read people easily and comprehensively. My entire life, I could almost hear people's innermost thoughts without them opening their mouths. And

Hannah was no different, she wore every emotion on her sleeve and couldn't hide a thing.

"Hey." Reyna came around the building toward the parking lot and forced me to get out of my car so I could pretend to function like an adult. "Are you okay?"

"Yeah, perfect." I adjusted my dark sunglasses and grabbed my bag of snacks and drinks I packed.

"Hey." She called again as I tried to walk toward the back door to the shop, "Thanks for letting Hannah tag along with you in Dallin's place." She smiled sweetly, and it was impossible to not give into her effortless charm. Next to Parker, Reyna was one of the easiest people to talk to and we had gotten close over the years. "It means the world to her to do a piece on someone so dynamic and different."

"Different." I nodded, smiling through that same stupid feeling I got in my gut when the shitty biker said I wasn't his type, like there was something wrong with me. "Right, no problem."

"I didn't mean you were different in a bad way." Her eyebrows pinched together in confusion, but I waved her off.

"I get it." Smiling, I hoped to lighten the entire situation so I could escape. "I have to get ready for my first client."

"Okay." She hesitated as I left her in the parking lot and went inside.

Different.

Dynamic.

I'd been called every name under the sun in my life, and it never bothered me before. So I couldn't figure out why I was so conscious of the labels the last few days. I wouldn't change a thing about me and my lifestyle even if I had a gun to my head, but I had never noticed the difference between me and most of the world before, either.

Until now.

"Oh good, you're here on time today." Trey deadpanned as I walked through the employee lounge in the back of the shop. "I was starting to worry I'd be stuck with Hannah today." He grimaced as I ignored him, dropping off a few items for the main fridge. "I think I scare her."

"You scare everyone." I deadpanned.

"Not as much as you do." He threw back in our normal insulting fashion.

"True." I shrugged him off and grabbed my bag to leave.

"Don't run into any garlic out there." He yelled as I walked out, making one of his usual vampire references.

"Watch out for those silver bullets." I lobbed back with my usual werewolf dig, though mine was accurate because he had a Little Red Riding Hood kink and he just scoffed at me in return.

I ignored everyone else, going straight to my room and mentally preparing for my first client. His name was Jack, and he was a Nashville cop who lost his K9 officer two months ago in the line of duty. He was getting a full sleeve dedicated to his partner, Arlo. It was an emotional piece, and it meant a lot to more than just Jack. Arlo's other partners on the force and his family, including Jack's kids, loved him, and his loss had a wide impact.

If I was going to get praise about my art and featured in some article, I wanted Arlo's piece to be at the forefront of it all. I wanted to be known for something that mattered.

"Your appointment is here. And so is Hannah." Paisley popped in with a mug of coffee in her hands and a hung overlook on her face. Something I could sympathize with completely. We were lucky to not open until ten in the morning, but most of us led lifestyles that left us out on the town until the early hours, anyway.

"Be right there." I took one last look at my room, making sure I was all prepped before heading out. Luckily, I made sure most everything was ready last night before leaving for the bar with Parker, so the morning would be easier. Before leaving my room to grab Hannah and Jack, I took a glance in the mirror and tried to see myself through fresh eyes.

I looked like a punk rock version of Sandy from Grease. An off the shoulder black blouse that showed off my chest piece, with a pair of black leather pants that hugged my ass and legs like a second skin down to the leopard print red bottoms that were as tall as skyscrapers, gave me the confidence to accomplish anything.

I had my hair up in a fun and flirty up do with a matching leopard print bandana to tie it all together.

I looked hot, that I knew. Sexuality was easy to understand when it was so commonly talked about in society. What was less known, however, was the why behind being openly sexy for others to see. If you did it for someone else, you were desperate. If you did it for yourself, you were conceited.

So was desperation or conceitedness to blame for my outfit?

They called me *Emo Barbie*, and it worked for me. Feminine and powerful all wrapped into one kick ass, steal your girl, doll. Yet in the moment, it felt like a costume.

"Hey." Hannah cautiously walked in my room, catching me mirror gazing. "I hope you don't mind, Paisley told me to come back." She looked so fucking cute in a pair of baby blue capris, a white boat neck shirt and matching white flats. She tied up her strawberry blond hair in a slick-backed ponytail, accentuating her bright green eyes. Hannah looked like the complete opposite of me standing there in black leather and Louboutin.

"Not at all." I gave her an easygoing smile to reassure her. Before I even got out of bed today, I promised myself I'd be welcoming and accepting to Hannah. Because she didn't need to suffer because of whatever mental breakdown I was going through the last few days, even if I could still taste her orgasm on my tongue from my dream. "Thanks for coming in."

"Oh, I'm so excited." She gushed relief as she eased into my welcomeness. "I can't wait to see what masterpiece you create today."

"Come on in and set your stuff down and I'll show you the sketch." I grabbed my tablet to show her the three-hundred-and-sixty-degree 3D rendering of the piece, complete with Jack's beefy arm wearing the art. "Today's piece is important."

"Oh, my god." She whispered in awe, leaning against my arm to see the tablet better. I tried to ignore how being that close to her felt and focused on the tattoo. "Is that K-9 Arlo?"

"It is. Good eye."

"I did a piece on him." She said, mystified, before shaking her head. "I sobbed at the ceremony they did when they laid him to rest."

"You went?" I asked, lowering the tablet.

She took a deep breath and looked up at me. "My dad is the Police Commissioner of Nashville." She shrugged nonchalantly. "I go to all those hard moments with him."

"That can't be easy." I deduced.

"It's harder for him. My mom passed away years ago, the least I can do is to be there in silent support for him while he supports all of his men and women in uniform."

"I don't think I've ever met someone like you before." I admitted, hating how deep that felt to say, but it needed to be acknowledged. Like her specialness needed to be recognized. She blushed and twisted her fingers together, clearly uncomfortable at the praise. I didn't want to keep her as the center of attention if she was uneasy, so I moved on, nodding for her to follow me out to get Jack.

"Lex." She said, putting her hand on my arm and stopping me before I made it out of the room. Instantly I flashed back to my dream and the way her hands felt on my tits. "Thank you for inviting me to be a part of today." She stared up at me with that pureness in her eyes. "This is the kind of thing that sets you apart from the rest."

I shook it off because I wasn't doing anything special. I was doing a piece that was special to my client, just like all the others. But I understood how it was important to a lot of other people, so I just nodded and led her to the reception desk.

Chapter 6 – Hannah

"Is he asleep?" I whispered, leaning over Lex's shoulder as she bent her head nearly upside down to tattoo the inside elbow of her client, Jack Potter.

"Probably." She whispered back, sitting up straight and stretching her neck and shoulders out. "He's slept through other appointments with me."

"Wild." I shook my head, backing up to give her space as she turned her head the other way, trying to stretch it further. "Can I get you anything?" I asked quietly.

"A sip of my water would be divine." She pointed over to her desk where her bottle of water sat. She hadn't taken a break in hours, working on the tribute piece to K-9 Arlo without stopping while his handler snoozed on and off. He was no doubt still dealing with the fallout of Arlo's passing and something told me he didn't find peace often, so neither of us could bring ourselves to disturb him.

I grabbed the mug and went to hand it to her, but realized that she couldn't take it with her sterile gloves on. "Oh, here." I tilted it to her and held her straw out.

I'm not exactly sure why, but as she leaned over and wrapped her bright red painted lips around the tip of the silicone straw, I had incredibly indecent images running through my head. She wasn't doing anything particularly sexual; it was just that natural sensuality to her that made it look seductive and alluring.

Standing next to her also gave me the opportunity to be taller than her, when her warm brown eyes fluttered up at me, with her lips still on the straw,

I finally understood why men loved when women looked at them during oral sex.

Like I really *got* it.

"Thanks." She sighed, leaning back and licking her lips. "Keep it up, and I'll make you stay with me for every appointment." She joked.

"Hmm." I hummed, overwhelmed with something akin to arousal warming my body.

Jesus, what would the guys say if they knew a woman as alpha as Lex turned me on? Would they truly be shocked by it?

It was one thing for me to be taken seriously in a polyamorous relationship with two men. But add in the fact that for months now I'd been battling random intrusive thoughts leading me to believe I could be bisexual too. God, what would my father say?

"You okay over there?" Lex's velvet voice brought me back to the present, and I snapped out of my stupor, setting her bottle down on the desk and turning back to her.

"Yeah. Sorry." I smiled. "Lost in thought."

"What about?" She asked, focused on her work.

"Uh—" I wracked my brain for an answer that didn't include, *oh, just imagining what it would look like to see you looking up at my boyfriends with your bright red lips wrapped around their cocks as you gave them blow jobs.* Or, how freaking hot that idea made me. "The layout for the pictures of this project." I lied.

"Does your art play out in your mind like mine does?" She asked, bending around Jack's arm again and getting the work done that was necessary. "Is it like a movie?"

"Yeah," I rubbed my hands down my pants and sat back down in my chair, "I can feel the flow of the article and the images mentally long before I even write a word down."

"I think all mediums of art are so cool. I love how different they all are, yet the end goal is always the same. Expression."

"I'll be honest, some pieces are more enjoyable than others," I joked, "They put me in the obituary section when I first started and that kind of sucked."

She grimaced, glancing over at me. "That sounds brutal."

"The worst." I shrugged, "But everyone has to start somewhere."

"True. I started in my dad's shop, sweeping floors and running across the street for cheeseburgers." She laughed. "Looking back, I still believe I learned the most in those years because I learned about the business and the art."

"That's fundamental. Have you ever thought about opening your own shop?"

She scoffed lightly and then froze when Jack snorted, "Lex is a lot of things, but organized isn't one of them."

"Hey." Lex cried, sitting up and pulling her hands free of the man. "I thought you were sleeping."

"Impossible with your heavy hand." He cracked one eye open and smirked, giving himself away to his lie.

"Anyway." Lex rolled her eyes and looked over at me. "He's right, I can't imagine keeping all the moving parts of a business in line and running smoothly. I manage a lot around here, but Dallin's mind is always working at hyper speed." She shuddered, "It's exhausting just thinking about it."

"I feel that in my soul." I relaxed back into my seat, "My boyfriends own a garage, and they primarily work on custom design jobs, and I used to run the books and do the admin stuff when they first opened and my brain literally melted by the end of the day." I paused when I noticed Lex and Jack both stared at me, silently just blinking for a moment. "What?"

"Did she say boyfriends?" Jack raised one bushy brow as he leaned toward Lex like they were having a private conversation.

"They, to be exact." Lex added with a wicked smirk on her face. "And now it all makes sense."

"What does?" I scowled suddenly on edge.

Lex shook her head and then turned back to Jack's arm. "You're all done." She cocked her head, looking down at it. "I think it's my favorite piece that I've done to date."

"You say that to all the boys." Jack pursed his lips, joking as he got out of the chair and went to the mirror.

But I knew without a doubt that she was telling the truth, because the piece was so moving and meaningful. There was a large portrait of Arlo, dead center of Jack's upper arm, and the detail was insane, right down to the reflective light in his eyes from the flash of the camera taking the picture. Then, all around the centerpiece, from his shoulder to his wrist, on all sides of his arm, there were pieces of his life and journey as a police K-9.

Pictures of him as a pup, dragging a toy twice his size. One of him laying upside down sleeping in the middle of a bed. There was one of him riding in a motorcycle sidecar with doggie goggles on and Jack driving, and one of him licking an ice cream cone out of a little boy's hands as he giggled and grinned back at the pup. Then there was the police badge for his department with a significant black band across the center, symbolizing the loss of an officer. The dates of his first night of duty and his end of watch date, also the date of his death.

"I'm at a loss for words, Lex." Jack blinked rapidly to keep the moisture in his eyes at bay. "There's never been a more beautiful tribute to all the different roles Arlo had in his life. He was so much more than just an officer and you really captured that. I'll cherish this for the rest of my life."

"It was an honor to be a part of." Lex smiled sadly, rubbing her hand over his back affectionately. "I hope your boys love being able to see their buddy whenever they see your arm now."

"They're going to love it." Jack agreed, pulling lex in for a big hug and holding onto her for a minute.

It was beautiful to witness the exchange of such a gift between artist and canvas. The weight of being responsible for something so powerful mystified me.

I hated to interrupt the moment between them, but I couldn't stand the thought of not getting pictures of the piece in complete detail, to share with the world in honor of both K-9 Arlo and Lex's talents.

"Do you mind if I document this?" I held my camera up, fully prepared to capture the tattoo today unlike yesterday, and Jack proudly stuck his arm out for me.

"How do you want me?"

"Just like that." I nodded to the beautiful backdrop behind him as Lex adjusted the lighting for me in the room.

It photographed amazingly, and as I worked, Lex watched over my shoulder, approving, and recommending different angles and shots until we were both confident we got them all. "Thank you so much, again Lex."

"I wouldn't have had it any other way, Jack. Come back whenever you want more." She patted his shoulder as he headed out.

"You know me, every couple of months I darken your doorstep." He joked, saluting us once as he left.

With him gone, the room instantly felt smaller and sadder, like the weight of the day and the meaning behind it was heavier to burden without Jack's charismatic presence there to buffer it. He was the one grieving, yet he had joked and lightened the mood for us, as though our feelings were important.

Lex collapsed into the black wing-back chair I sat in all day and sighed, and I knew she felt it too. "I'm not really sure what to do with myself now." She admitted before looking up at me where I stood by the wall. "It seems wrong to just go on with my day, even if it is already evening."

Jack had been a trooper, sitting through nearly eight hours of tattooing with only one brief lunch break and a few stretch breaks, more for Lex's well being than his own.

And Lex, dang. The endurance and stamina to tattoo that long was extraordinary and magical to watch.

"Do you have any other appointments today?" I sincerely hoped she wasn't booked for anything else; she deserved a break.

"God no," She scoffed and then stood up and started stretching her body out, bending over to touch her toes and then folding her arms over her chest. "I knew even if I physically could tattoo after that, which I can't, I wouldn't want to mentally. I think clearing a whole day for Arlo was the only way to handle his tribute."

"I agree." I warmed at her tenderness for an animal she never met. Her exterior was hard, yet her personality was soft and thoughtful whenever she showed me a piece. "How about you let me buy you dinner?" I asked, not even processing my words before they were out of my mouth. "You hardly ate anything all day, and it's the least I can do for your hospitality today." She watched me with that penetrating stare, making me wonder if I once again overstepped the boundaries of this professional arrangement like I had last night when I asked her about her relationship status with her client. "You can say no!" I hurried on, "I just thought maybe—"

"I'd love to." She cut me off, taking pity on me as I started rambling and back peddling so fast, I was sure to land on my ass. "But not because I feel you owe me anything. But mostly because I'm starving and if I don't eat soon, I'll turn into a wild, angry monster." Her eyes widened dramatically as she curled her lip up and pretended to show me her claws.

I giggled at her animation and felt a little more confident about my invitation. I turned around to grab my things. "We can't have that. There's this fantastic Mexican place down the street if you're up for some tacos?" When I faced her again, there was that predatory look in her eyes that instantly sucked all the air from the room like it had last night when we were alone.

Then her red lips curled up again into a grin that made my knees weak. "I love tacos."

Something about the way she said the word, made me think she wasn't talking about food anymore, but instead of embarrassing myself by asking for her to clarify, I swallowed down a gulp of anticipation and silently nodded for her to grab her things and lead the way out of the shop.

She meant food, right?

What on earth else could she be talking about?

I thought watching Lex tattoo was a sight to behold with her movements and grace, but it didn't hold a candle to watching her eat. She was one of those people who ate with their entire soul.

She closed her eyes and groaned when she took the first bite and danced in her seat on the high-top chair where we sat against the wall in the back corner of the busy place. Not an inch of red lipstick was out of place as she ate her first taco either.

I tried not to stare, but I couldn't take my eyes off her.

"Sorry." She smirked, holding her napkin over her mouth as she chewed. "I was starving."

"No." I blinked, focusing on my own untouched food, "I love it." I picked up my own shredded chicken and guacamole taco and took a bite. She was right, the food was damn good and deserved to be praised after a long day. "Gosh, I have to come here more often."

"How'd you find it?" She looked around before taking a sip of her margarita. It was an old industrial space made to look like a trendy garage, with big overhead glass garage doors that opened up to let the two environments inside and out mingle while patrons visited. "I didn't know it was even here."

"Knox found it by total accident one day." I grinned at the memory. "He was meeting Dallin for something after work one night and stopped in here for a drink before." I shrugged, "He came back the next night because of how good the food was."

"And Knox is—" She paused, raising one perfectly manicured eyebrow.

"My boyfriend." I blushed because I was so absolutely in love with him, that I couldn't help but go full schoolgirl anytime I talked about him. Even if we'd been together going on ten years.

"One of two—" She left the ending open and grinned at me. "I need to hear that story."

I opened my mouth to talk about Knox and Brody, but for some reason, talking about them with Lex made me feel slightly guilty. I felt as if I had been caught with my hand in the hypothetical cookie jar, and I knew I was going to get in trouble.

So I blew it off as best as I could, "Knox, Brody and I were all best friends in high school and eventually we kind of morphed into a new dynamic and haven't looked back since."

"I didn't mean to pry." She straightened up, wiping her hands on her napkin. "If anyone in the world knows what it's like to be unconventional,"

She waved her hand over her appearance, "It's me. So I should have thought better about digging into it. I'm sorry."

"No!" I sighed and smiled at her. "I didn't mean it like that. I guess I haven't always gotten the warmest responses from people finding out I'm in a polyamorous relationship. Often people think I'm a sister wife in a weird cult and even after they find out I'm the luckiest girl in the world who is loved by two men equally with zero competition or love triangles included, I'm left feeling icky from it all. So I'm naturally reserved, but I don't need to be with you. Because I know you'd never make me feel odd for it."

"You're not odd for finding love, no matter the label." She asserted, taking a sip of her drink.

"What about you?" I asked, toeing that line of weird comfort I'd felt in her presence. "Are you in a relationship? Or two?" I joked, trying to lighten the conversation.

"Ha." She chuckled, "I'm most definitely not a relationship kind of girl. It took me a long time to figure out what I was in life, but I knew pretty early what I wasn't. And monogamous or straight, wasn't it."

"So you're poly?" I questioned with surprise.

"Opposite actually." She shrugged, "I can't stand the idea of being committed to anyone ever, let a lone multiple people." She leaned forward on the table. "How do you do it with two?"

Now it was my turn to laugh, "I'd like to say it's hard, given that Brody and Knox are both over the top sometimes, but it's really not. We all kind of have our role, and it works."

"What's your role in the throuple?" She asked and then held her finger up, "Wait, are they together? Or just with you?"

"We're all together." Taking a bite of food, I went on, "I guess, in technical terms, I'm the submissive one. I more naturally follow their lead without hesitation." I hesitated for a second, "Brody's the alpha if I had to put a label on him. He's always in charge. Like always." Feeling the effects of the margarita, I giggled and relaxed the day away. "And Knox kind of falls in between those two roles somewhere. Some days he's in charge with Brody and taking the lead, and other days he falls in line with me and is easier going. He balances Brody and I out in a way." I shrugged. "God, I never really looked at our relationship from the outside like I am right now, but it's kind of cool."

Lex widened her eyes, "You mean you're enlightened by what you see?"

"Yeah, in a way I am. I always go to Knox as mediator when Brody's pissing me off and I think Brody does too, and it makes more sense now, because Knox is the levelheaded one."

"He's the switch." She mused, with a smirk on her face. "In my experience, relationships always work best when there's a switch involved."

I contemplated that. "Why do you think that?"

She shrugged, chewing a bite and then washing it down. "I guess it makes it easier for everyone to get what they need from the partner when that partner can fill multiple roles." She waved her hand toward me, "In your case, when you need someone soft and reasonable, Knox is that person for you. Or when Brody needs someone to challenge him and put him in place—"

"He's that person for him." I finished for her, completely enlightened. "Interesting. Did you think you'd be dissecting a poly relationship over tacos tonight?"

She snorted and covered her mouth, "Can't say it was on my bingo card at all."

I tipped my head back and laughed, loving the easiness of her humor.

"Well, that's a laugh I haven't heard in a minute."

I whipped my head around to find Knox himself walking toward our table with a beer bottle in his hand and a mischievous grin on his face. God, he looked so freaking good. Tall and built like a man who used his body every day for work, with tight blue jeans on and a dark green t-shirt that hugged his enormous arms, showing off his tattoos.

Tattoos I had a much bigger appreciation for after watching Lex spend hours crafting ideas into permanent art.

"Hi!" I gushed, flinging myself off my stool and into his arms. "Hi. Hi. Hi." I repeated as he caught me and held me tight to his chest. He smelled so good after going so long without him. "What are you doing here?"

"I just got back into town, found the house empty, so I came to get some food until you got off work." He glanced at Lex over my shoulder and then raised a brow at me. "Or until I found you in a bar, drinking and eating tacos with someone I don't know."

"Lex," I turned back to the table and found Lex watching us with a mask of indifference on her face that wasn't there a minute ago. "This is Knox. He's been out of town for the last two weeks. I had no idea he'd show up here. Knox, this is Alexi Donovan, the tattoo artist I'm interviewing for the paper. She works with Dallin."

"Nice to meet you." Lex held her hand out to him with a blank smile on her face and Knox took her hand, shaking it.

"Pleasure's all mine. I've heard a lot about you." He said thickly, and the hair on the back of my neck stood up at his tone. I looked up at him, confused, but they both just gave each other a lingering stare.

"I thought you weren't coming back until Saturday." I drew his attention back to me, catching the way his nostrils flared slightly before he smiled and put his arm around my shoulders, pulling me tight to him.

"I missed you. I didn't want to spend another night apart." He leaned down and kissed me, sliding his hand over my cheek and around the back of my neck, anchoring me to him so I couldn't pull back. Not that I would have, because I missed him so much, I ached for him. But I also was super aware of where we were and who was sitting a few feet away, watching us. I just didn't understand the feelings burning inside of me.

"I missed you too," I pulled back, creating just enough space between our lips to speak. "Pull up a chair, I'll go order your favorite."

"I was thinking more like we could get the hell out of here and go home." He slid his hand down my back to my ass and squeezed. "I missed you, Han."

"I know." I sighed, blushing from his unusual display of affection, and feeling torn about what I was going to do.

"You can have my chair; I was just about to leave." Lex interjected, forcing Knox to acknowledge her again. Something ignited inside of me as she pushed her mostly uneaten meal to the edge of the table and tossed back the rest of her drink.

TWISTED LACE

"No." I panicked, hating how anxious the thought of her leaving because of Knox's arrival made me. "Stay. You haven't even finished. And you were starving when we got here." I smiled, hoping she'd change her mind.

"It's all good." She gave me a nod and stood up, turning to Knox again. "I've taken up enough of her time the last few days." She glanced my way. "Have a good night."

"Well, wait." I chuckled, running my hand over my hair as I fought to come up with something else to say. "What time do you want me at the shop tomorrow?" I paused, waiting for her reply, but she hesitated too long, and I knew what she was going to say.

"I think you've got enough to write the article. You interviewed me non-stop today."

"I don't." Cutting her off, "Not near enough. I need more pictures of your art and more about the impact being here in Nashville has made on you, and how you're dealing with the growing concerns amongst public officials that someday the appeal of vacationing here will fizzle out and it will be a ghost town—"

"Hannah." She spoke firmly, with a stern look on her face. That same damn look Brody gave me when he was about to give me a command. "It's okay." She walked around us and then turned back before she left. "If you need anything else from the shop, give Dallin a call. Have a good night."

Chapter 7 – Knox

I watched the sexy brunette walk away, unable to stop myself from appreciating the way her long legs gracefully moved with each step. I knew that was exactly why she wore leather pants and heels, but I didn't dwell on it too long.

My attention immediately returned to my sexy girlfriend, who was also staring at the tattoo artist as she walked away. And if my eyesight was right, she was staring at her ass too.

"Hannah." I spoke, and she jumped, blinking rapidly and looking back up at me with a weak smile on her face. "What the fuck just happened?"

Her face fell and her shoulders sagged as she glanced back toward the door one last time, like she was hoping for another glimpse of Lex.

"I don't know." She finally said and looked back up at me. "I think I just want to go home."

"Let's go." I grabbed her hand and led her through the crowd. There was something going on in her head, making her act strange, and I was desperate to get to the bottom of it. That entire interaction at the table was the most bizarre dealing I'd ever witnessed with Hannah, and I needed to get some answers.

"My car—" She pointed to the lot out back of the restaurant where she had parked it, but I just shook my head and pulled her toward my bike on the street.

I took her bag and cinched it up, before sliding it into the saddlebag that held her gear.

"Knox." She tried one more time, but I shook my head again, holding onto the anxiety inside of me by a thread.

I wrapped my hand around the back of her neck and pulled her forward, flush with the front of my chest, and bent down to press my forehead against hers. "I don't know what just happened back there, but there are two things I *do* know, Hannah."

"What?" She whispered like she was almost afraid of my answer.

"One; I'm going to get to the bottom of it. And two, if I don't feel your body wrapped around mine, even from just the back of my bike for now, I'm going to lose my mind while I try to figure out yours." I kissed her roughly, pushing my tongue into her mouth and she welcomed it, surprising me when she bit it and whimpered against my lips. "Now get on my bike."

"Okay." She whispered as I threw my leg over the motorcycle and pulled the stand up, holding my hand out to help her on.

The moment her body pressed against mine and she wrapped her arms around my stomach, some of the unease settled in my gut.

"Hold on tight, baby." I warned as I started the engine, revving it a few times to tell the surrounding cars I was pulling out, my turn or not be damned.

"Always." She replied over the roar of the pipes and tightened her hold, sliding her fingers inside of the metal buckle of my belt, which was her favorite spot to hang on.

I moved us through the downtown traffic, splitting lanes and taking alleys until the congestion opened up and we hit the rural route leading us toward our house and with each minute that passed, leading us further from the city and closer to our slice of paradise, she settled and relaxed into me more and more.

As I drove through the winding blacktop driveway, the trees blocked the house, but I could see the glow of the porch lights before we broke through into the clearing. I drove the bike directly into the open garage bay and turned it off as my ears rang from the sudden silence. She slid off the back of the bike, grabbing her work stuff, but I took it from her hands and carried it for her as we left the garage, heading for the house.

She was silent.

Alarm bells rang in my head as my normally chatty girl held all of that chaos inside of her head instead of sharing it with me like usual.

Halfway up the steps of the front porch, Brody walked out of the screen door wearing a pair of low riding jeans and nothing else. "When did you get back?"

"Earlier." I said, grabbing him for a quick hug as Hannah lingered at the top of the steps, still silent. "I ran into Hanny at T's." I glanced back at her, and she was wringing her hands together in front of her. As Brody noticed the tension between us, his demeanor changed, and I accused, "What the fuck happened while I was gone?"

He snapped his head to me with a scowl. "What do you mean?"

I leaned back against the porch post and crossed my arms, nodding to Hannah, whose eyes were wide as they flicked between the two of us.

"I mean, did you know our girl was on a date with a centerfold model, who had enough big dick energy to put you in your place like a good little boy?"

"I wasn't—" Hannah started and then wilted a bit when Brody turned her way.

"You said you were going to dinner with the tattoo artist."

"*Lex*." I interjected for him and raised my brows at him. "Big, big dick lesbian energy wrapped up in a shiny leggy package."

"Will you stop it?" Hannah cried, looking at me with a look on her face I'd never seen aimed my way before.

Brody, sure. But not me, and her hurt look and teary eyes cut me deep.

"Hannah—" I froze, feeling like I'd landed in some twilight zone since returning home. "What's going on?"

"I don't know!" She yelled as those tears fell over her lashes. "But don't you dare stand there and insinuate I was doing anything improper in the middle of the damn restaurant because I wasn't!" She ended in a scream.

"Then what were you doing?" Brody asked calmly, which was odd.

Hello, twilight zone.

"I don't know!" She shook her head as her bottom lip quivered.

"But it wasn't platonic. Not completely, was it?" A rage I didn't recognize built inside of me as I finally understood what I was seeing at the bar, and I recognized the fear in her eyes.

"I—" She hesitated and swallowed. "I think I'm bisexual."

The entire world stopped spinning and everything around us drifted away as gravity no longer grounded us. "You're what?" Brody scowled, shaking his head.

"For a few months now I've wondered," She closed her eyes in pain. "I think meeting Lex confirmed it."

I walked away from her as panic burned in my heart.

You're not enough for me anymore.

I want something different.

This isn't working.

I imagined hearing her say one of those things next, putting the nail in the coffin of the only life I'd ever wanted; her and Brody.

"I'm sorry." She cried, but I couldn't stop. Seeing the hurt in her eyes, my world flipped and I couldn't stand it. "Knox! Please don't leave." I could hear the tears in her voice and my feet stopped moving as my need to comfort her battled with my need to digest what she just said. "Please don't leave me." She sobbed. "I won't do anything. Ever. I just wanted to understand what my mind and body were mis-communicating. I'll just turn it off. I'll figure out how to make it stop, please. I'm so sorry!"

My chest cracked open as I turned to face her. Tears streaked her face and her skin turned red and blotchy as she panicked. Brody stared at me with so much uncertainty in his eyes. I was positive I'd never seen him so unsure before. Since I met him in kindergarten, he radiated confidence every day, but her revelation left him shaken and uncertain. "My god, Hannah." I shook my head as I stalked back toward her. Fear and anxiety overcame her, causing her to shrink down into herself. Of us. Of what we would do or say in response to her honesty.

"Knox." Brody's hesitation rocked me as I neared them again, but I didn't stop. I grabbed Hannah in my arms and held her to my chest so tight I was probably cutting off her air, but she squeezed me back just as tight, sobbing harder now that I was comforting her.

"You can't turn it off." I told her, smoothing my hand over the back of her head and Brody slid behind her, holding us all together as chaos still swirled. "And I never want you to. I never want you to hide your heart from us, baby."

"Never again." Brody agreed, and I was glad he did, because I would physically beat him into it if I had to. "Do you remember the night Knox came out to you as bi?" He asked, kissing the back of her head and showing his gentle side that only we saw. "The night you held him all night long, afraid that you would no longer be enough for him."

She shuddered as she took a deep breath and said something too muffled to be understood.

"Try again." I said, pulling her face back enough to speak freely of my shirt.

"I was so scared you'd leave me. Or stay with me out of obligation." She admitted and then buried her face back into my chest.

"And instead, what did I do?"

"Fucked your best friend." She murmured, and I heard the tiniest bit of a smile in her still muffled voice and Brody snorted.

"She's not wrong." He winked at me.

"Kept open lines of communication with you as I explored my sexuality." I corrected her. "With you by my side."

She shook her head, negating that idea. "I don't want to explore. I don't want to do anything ever again to feel like this.

"Hannah." Brody warned. "Your sexuality can change as you get older. There's nothing wrong with that."

"And if I said I was full lesbian and never wanted to see your penis ever again?" She scoffed.

"Hit me in the nuts next time, babe. I think it will hurt less." He deadpanned and then picked her up, pulling her out of my hold to sit down on the bench before nodding for me to join them. Which was no problem, because I needed to be close to them both right now, too.

"I'm afraid you're going to hate me." She admitted. "And I never want that to happen. Just because I'm attracted to females doesn't mean I ever have to act on it."

"Just take a deep breath and hold on. You're putting the cart before the horse." I reminded her, wiping my thumbs under her eyes to clear the last of the tears. "Let's start with when you first noticed something was up."

She groaned and laid her head on Brody's chest, soaking up his gentle affection, because he usually wasn't one to cuddle. "I don't know, a few months ago I noticed I was *seeing* other women more often. And not just the normal way, like their outfits or styles, but them." She took a deep breath, "Their bodies and builds."

"And why didn't you say anything?" Brody probed.

"Because I didn't know it had to do with my sexuality." She cried, sitting up. "I thought I was just more observant or something. I don't know."

"What changed?" I asked, pretty sure I already knew the answer to the question.

She bit her bottom lip and dropped my gaze, avoiding the topic.

"You can't hide things from us, Hannah, because then you make us insecure and fear that you're going to leave us." Brody told her, doing a pretty good job of expressing the fear in my chest as she avoided the question. "That you don't want us anymore."

"I've never cheated." She said firmly, reassuring him. "I've never touched anyone else." She looked at me. "Not in my life."

I confirmed what she needed me to. "I believe you." When we were fresh out of high school and wrapped up in this weird love triangle between the three of us, she was a virgin and gave herself to us first. On the same night, so it would be 'fair'. Since then, we all had only been with each other. And knowing no other man had ever touched her, calmed something inside of me. But if I was being honest, the idea of another woman touching our sweet, loving Hannah didn't appall me either.

"Then what changed?"

"I met Lex." She confessed, "And from the first second of being in the same room as her, I felt tension building."

"Is she a lesbian?" Brody asked, having not met Lex.

"Yes. She didn't say anything about it until tonight, when we were talking about my relationship with you two. But it's not something you can miss with her. She just has—" She hesitated, trying to find the words.

"Big dick energy." I stated, for the third time, because there was no other way to describe the air about Lex. "Some lesbians have that alpha dog mentality, though, they're usually the masculine ones."

"And Lex isn't?" Brody raised his brow at me, but I let Hannah answer.

"No." She shrugged, "I mean, there are things about her that give off masculine vibes, but I think that's more in her personality. No, she's feminine. Really, really feminine." Her eyes got this faraway look in them as she talked about the tattoo artist and I watched her closely, trying to figure out what she was feeling exactly.

"So you were attracted to her, but unsure why," Brody expertly kept the conversation going.

"It was more than just an attraction." She said, and then deflated. "I don't want to talk about it."

"Why?" I asked.

"Because it makes me feel guilty. Like I cheated."

"That's how I felt when I first started feeling things for Brody." I reminded her. "Like it wasn't fair to you, but that wasn't true at all. I realized after a while that growing feelings for him didn't detract from the feelings I had for you, not at all."

"She's not our best friend, though!" Hannah cried, "She's a stranger and on the outside of this relationship. Your feelings for Brody didn't threaten me because I loved him too." She looked at the man holding her. "I understood why you were in love with him, and to me, it wasn't intimidating."

"And you think your feelings for Lex or any other female will threaten us?" Brody scoffed, like it was absurd.

"You didn't see Knox at T's." She shook her head, "He was feral."

Brody looked over at me, and I tried to think back to that exchange through Hannah's eyes. "I admit, I felt threatened," I said. "But only because I didn't know about it. I felt like I was walking in on a secret."

"I'm sorry." She stared down, and I hated seeing her so beaten by her feelings. And mine, because I didn't handle everything right.

"Come here." I lifted her out of Brody's arms and placed her in my lap, straddling me so she was forced to look at me directly. Holding her chin with my thumb as my fingers wrapped around the back of her neck to make sure she didn't hide. "I won't lie to you and say I'm not scared of this change. Because I'm human, and any change that might threaten this relationship is terrifying to me. Since I was a teenager, I knew I wanted to spend the rest of my life with you. And once Brody and I stopped trying to get you to choose between us, I knew he was going to be a partner in this life too, right next to you, for life. So the fact that you potentially want something else outside of this trio is unsettling, but it's not impossible."

"I don't want anything else." She slid her hands up my chest and around the back of my neck. "I just want you and Brody." She grabbed his hand and held onto him as she leaned forward to kiss me. "Forever. Just like this."

I yielded to her need to find a balance in life again, even though I growled in frustration at her obvious attempt to backpedal and bury everything she had unearthed about herself. "Although I don't believe you, I'm willing to set aside the conversation for now. Because I've been gone for thirteen days, and I miss you both more than I thought was possible."

A friend of ours was opening a custom shop in Ohio, so I went out to help him get it set up and organize the opening. But being separated from Brody and Hannah for that long was the worst thing in the world, and I hated it more than anything.

"I missed you too." She kissed me again, and this time she ran her tongue over my bottom lip, teasing me with just the simple touch. Anytime our girl used tongue in a kiss, meant she was needing something more than just a kiss. It was always her tell, and my body reacted instantly to her call for love. "Our bed was empty without you."

Brody snickered next to us and leaned in, kissing her neck while putting his hand on the back of my mine, massaging the muscles. "Don't act like I didn't keep you warm in his absence."

She pulled back and smiled at him. "You gave me many wonderful orgasms too, but you know what I mean."

"I do." He kissed her, biting her lip in his dominating way and making her whimper as her body rocked forward in my lap before he turned his face to me and kissed me. "I know exactly what she means."

Brody's affection was always rough and needy, where Hannah's was always sensual and erotic, and I was so fucking torn about what way I wanted them at that exact moment.

"I need to fuck." I stated plainly, "One of you is going to take it tonight and I can't guarantee that I can be gentle. Because I haven't had a single orgasm in thirteen days, and I'm aching for release."

I watched the stress of the day melt out of Hannah's eyes as my girl let her desire to please take over her thoughts. "I can help with that."

"Can you?" I questioned and then protested as she slid out of my arms. "This seems counterintuitive."

"Give me a few minutes, then join me in the bedroom." She winked at me and blew a kiss to Brody before running into the house and up the stairs.

I lost sight of her when she turned the corner at the top of the stairs, and I glanced at Brody. "You think she's going to use sex to distract us into thinking she isn't missing something?"

"Of course she will." He sighed, leaning back on the bench and adjusting his already growing erection. "But that doesn't mean we're going to let her deflect." He looked back at me. "If she wants a girl, are we going to give that to her?"

"I'd give her the moon if she asked for it." I replied confidently, meaning every single word.

"And if she asks for Lex, will you let her have that?" He raised his brow at me. "Because that's the part you seem to be hung up on."

"There's something about her I can't put my finger on."

"Lex? Like what?"

I groaned, rubbing my hand over my face as I admitted something that crossed my mind on the way home while my world spun out of control. "Like she may be the absolute best mix of you, me, and Hannah, all wrapped up in one sexy as fuck package." I hated admitting that she was sexy because it felt like a betrayal to Hannah.

"That doesn't sound like a bad thing." Brody shrugged, trying to imagine it.

"It does if she can give Hannah everything she needs. Eliminating her need for us." That was my biggest fear, to be honest. She was feminine and sensual, able to give Hannah that womanly style of touch. But she was also dominant and alpha, and if she could give Hannah that as well, what would she need us for?

Brody scoffed, standing up and holding his hand out to help me up, pulling me to my feet. "There's one thing that girl can't give Hannah, even if she tried." He stated, and I raised my brow questioningly. "Dick. Even the best strap-on won't replace the way we feel when we're buried deep inside our girl."

I snorted and shook my head, trying to find peace in his confidence. "Maybe." I opened the screen door and went inside. "I hope we never have to find out."

"Oh, boys!" Hannah's sweet honey voice called from upstairs, replacing any doubt with need inside my brain. "I'm ready if you are."

"Oh, I'm fucking ready." Brody grinned, rubbing his hands together as he started for the stairs.

I leaped forward, cutting him off and taking the stairs two at a time as he started chasing me. "Get in line, fuck wad. I'm first."

"Asshole." He cursed, grabbing my shirt, and trying to shove me into the wall to get past me on the way to the bedroom.

Hannah's girly giggle sounded from the bedroom as we crashed into the door frames and walls lining the hall on our way to her. "No fighting, or I'll make you both sit in the corner and watch."

We made it through the door at the same time, nearly getting stuck with our wide shoulders wedged. When we cleared the frame, we both froze, transfixed by the sight before us. She lay in the center of our bed, propped up on the pillows, wearing a pink nightgown. It pushed her breasts up and I could see her nipples through the thin lace covering them. Licking the pads of her fingers, she spread her legs, bent her knees, and then ran her fingers over her clit.

"Hannah." I growled, stiffening to a rock in my jeans as I watched her show.

"Care to join me?" She licked her lips as she ran her dainty fingers through her wet pussy lips.

"Bet I can get her to scream my name first." Brody challenged, pulling open the button on his jeans and shoving them down as he walked to the end of the bed.

"Game on." I agreed, pulling my shirt off over the back of my head and tossing it at him.

Chapter 8 – Brody

I wasn't an idiot; I knew Hannah was trying to distract us from her big revelation with sex. We were men after all; it was easy to see why she'd try. But she forgot that Knox and I had spent the last decade being not just lovers, but best friends with her.

We knew that girl inside and out, and we knew exactly what she needed, too.

Honesty.

With herself. Since a young age, her parents taught her to protect her image. To be a good little girl, with the best grades, the bright future, and the perfect life. They hadn't meant to make her feel that way, but her father's position of power essentially left him no choice but to expect perfection from her.

Which was why the idea of wanting something that stepped outside of that realm of normalcy terrified her.

When we had started our throuple years ago, she hid it from everyone for the longest time. Unable to admit that she had fallen in love with two men, like it was bad somehow.

Maybe that was on us for demanding that she chose between us originally. I think in a way, Knox and I could tell there was something deeper between the two of us as well, and making Hannah pick took the pressure off of us to admit it.

But the thing about Hannah was, she was honest and fair to a fault.

And when we had tried to force her hand in choosing between us, she did the exact opposite.

She walked away.

Which was what she was trying to do now. She was running from the thought that she wanted something different again and tried to hide behind the *normalcy* of our relationship now that she was used to it.

Not a chance, darling.

And I knew just how to get her to be honest with herself.

"I don't know whether to be mad that you seem so needy, even though I've kept you satisfied in Knox's absence." I kneeled on the end of the bed and grabbed her ankle, pulling her legs wider.

She tilted her head and palmed one of her breasts through the lace with a pretty little grin on her lips. "I missed taking you both at the same time."

"Fuck." Knox groaned, pushing his jeans down and fisting his hard dick. "Are you going to let me into that tight ass tonight, baby?"

Knox was obsessed with taking her at the same time, but we rarely did it anymore.

"I'm going to beg that you both slide into me at the same time." She crawled to her knees, keeping them spread as her fingers circled her clit as the other one played with her tits. "I'm desperate to feel connected to you both like that tonight. I need it."

"Hannah," I growled, pulling her lace nightie down to reveal both of her perky tits. She hated them, always saying they were too small, but they fit her petite frame perfectly. And they fit in my palm just right too. I leaned forward and flicked my tongue over one of her hard nipples before sucking it into my mouth, making her moan. Knox pulled her face to his, kissing her silent as he put his fingers on her clit, taking over her pleasure. I knew the second he pushed one deep into her because her nails dug into my neck where she was holding me to her chest.

"You're soaking wet, darling." He pumped his fingers into her, and I could hear how wet she was, making my cock pulse harder, knowing it was going to be so silky pushing into her. "Tell me something, is every drip because of Brody and I?" He questioned, and I grinned, catching where he was going with it. "Or were you wet before you got home?"

"Knox." She moaned, but didn't answer him.

Evading.

Her favorite tactic alongside running. Not tonight, Darling. I ran my hand over her hip and down to her ass, shaking one of her plump ass cheeks as I went and then to her wet pussy and slid one in flanking Knox. She gasped and arched her back, pushing back on our fingers as her knees widened. "Answer the question and I'll let you come like this." I bit onto one of her nipples and hummed on it, making goosebumps break out across her skin. "Keep hiding behind your fears and I'll make sure you don't come for hours. "

"Brody, please." She cried, begging for more as she swung her hips.

"Does our pretty girl want to come?" Knox asked, wrapping one hand gently around her neck to hold her in place. She wasn't into breath play, but I knew he was. Yet he was never anything but gentle with her, knowing her boundaries and respecting them. "Answer my question and you can come all over our fingers."

She didn't answer instantly, and we both withdrew from her greedy body, and she whimpered, digging her nails into my neck. "I was wet!" She all but yelled in frustration. "I was already soaked before you even arrived tonight!" she exclaimed in frustration. "Is that what you wanted to hear?"

"Yes," I responded, not trusting Knox's control over his insecurities, not to mess the whole thing up. "I especially wanted to hear *that*, in fact."

"Why?" She shook her head, still held by his hand around her neck as I brought my lips to hers. "Why would you want me to get wet for someone else?"

"It turns me the fuck on, believe it or not." Grabbing her hand, I wrapped it around my thick cock, stroking myself into her palm. "I'm imagining things, baby." I thrust into her hand and returned my fingers to her pussy, covering them with her wetness before rubbing them over her asshole. "Dirty, erotic things that make me want to blow right here in your hand. But I'm going to save it for your pussy."

"What things?" She challenged, needing to hear them out loud.

"If I know Brody," Knox interjected, "He's imagining what noises you'll make the first time you have another woman licking your pussy."

Her body tensed under my hand as I pushed into her ass, and her eyes rolled into the back of her head.

"Will you moan and beg to be fucked like you do for us when we're making you come on our tongues?" I wondered out loud. "Or will you take control and flip her over when you're ready for more?"

"I can't." She shook her head, squinting, her eyes closed as she fought against the sensation that idea gave her. "I wouldn't know what to do."

"We'll teach you," Knox growled, biting her ear as he started thrusting into her pussy with his finger, rubbing against mine through her body as I pushed into her ass. "Lex will teach you. She'll tell you exactly what to do and how she likes to be touched. And Brody and I will watch you lose your mind repeatedly as you give her your body."

"I'm coming." She gasped as if we couldn't tell by the vice grip her holes had on us, pulsating as her orgasm ripped through her. "Fuck!" She screamed, arching like her entire body took an electric shock.

"Our girl likes that idea." Knox grinned, licking her neck and biting her ear before letting go of her and crawling between her legs on his back. He positioned her so she was straddling his face, as I all but held her upright while she came down from the high of her orgasm. He grabbed two handfuls of her ass and pulled her down onto his mouth, going straight to work as she fell forward, resting her hands on his hips and flexing hers against his mouth. "I haven't tasted you this creamy in so long, darling. And it's from the idea of having her between these thighs."

"It's from the idea of having her between my thighs while you watch." She snapped back and then glared at me angrily, even as she rolled her hips again, grinding on his face. "It's from the idea of you taking pleasure in it, too."

I raised my brows at her and pushed her down toward his cock. "You want us involved?"

"I said I was bi." She snapped, letting her frustration free, "Not lesbian. Of course I want you there."

"That would make you polyamorous, love." I reminded her, even though that's what we already were, it was different. "And I've never known you to be keen on the idea of sharing us with another woman before." I thought back to the few times she'd shown her jealous side over the years. While it had been incredibly sexy to watch her get possessive of us and claim her territory when another woman had come looking, the idea of us all sharing another woman sent off warning bells in my head.

"I'm not." She gasped, licking the head of Knox's cock as he slapped her ass from behind, face still buried in her pussy. "It can't be with just *any* woman. It has to be the right woman."

I gathered her hair back and pushed her head down gently as she started sucking Knox off and watched her. She was telling the truth, I could tell by the tightness of her body, and it wasn't just from her orgasm. "But with her, you're okay?" I questioned, "Why?"

I had no idea if we'd ever welcome another woman into our bed, even for a night. Especially not the troublesome woman that had already caused such tension in hypothetical situations that Hannah couldn't seem to get off her mind.

"You haven't met her." She moaned, holding still as Knox shook his face back and forth, rubbing his five o'clock shadow over her pussy lips. "She's so sexy." Stroking his cock, continued. "I can't describe it, baby. I just know that if I'm going to watch you put your cock into any other woman, it has to be her." She gasped, throwing her head back as Knox spanked her ass over and over again, no doubt on edge from her sexy words. "And I want to be right there, holding her legs open for you when you do it."

"Jesus fuck." I growled, pulling her lips to mine and crashing down on them. She tasted like Knox's pre-cum and her sweet sensual honey flavor I'd gotten addicted to as a teenager. "When did you become so naughty?"

She giggled and bit my lip. "I told you." Her bright eyes stared up at me moments before they rolled as she started orgasming again. "There's just something about her."

"Enough talking about hypotheticals." Knox pushed Hannah forward as he crawled out from behind her and lined up with her pussy, pushing up into her. "I need to fuck someone."

I chuckled as Hannah cried out in ecstasy, taking him deep in the middle of her already powerful orgasm. "Seems like you've got yourself a willing participant." I didn't mind that they were using each other for pleasure, and I was spectating. Knox had been gone for almost two weeks, and while I did my best to keep our girl happy in his absence, I felt the distance with him gone as well.

"I want both of you." She whined, pulling me by the cock and stroking me. "I want to feel you both pump me full at the same time."

"You want us both?" I smirked at her and pulled her forward for a deep, passionate kiss. "Then you know how we want you."

"Damn." Knox panted in frustration as she scurried off his lap and across the bed to mine. "I was so fucking close."

"Grab the lube and shut the fuck up, ass wipe. I want to feel your dick rubbing against mine inside our girl." I glared at him, and he licked his lips as his rock-hard erection bobbed at the idea.

"When you put it like that—" He jumped up the same time Hannah all but threw me down onto the bed and straddled my cock. "Damn girl." He praised, watching the show from the foot of the bed on his way past.

"I need you." She pouted so prettily as she pinned my cock between our bodies, grinding on it. "You're being far too agreeable to my midlife crisis, Brody. And it makes me want to sugar you up and keep you distracted so you don't back down."

I tipped my head back and scoffed as I grabbed her hips and really pushed my cock against her clit as she rocked back and forth. "What a naughty little girl you've become tonight." I mused and then wrapped one hand around her throat, pulling her down to me as I growled into her ear. "I fucking like it."

"Yes." She purred, as Knox crawled up behind her, lubed dick ready to go. "Do it." She panted, "Fuck me together, please."

I nodded to him and pulled her forward to release my cock from the vice grip she held it in between us and lined up with her dripping pussy. I pushed in slowly, feeling him holding her tight as he pushed in at the same time.

She was a fucking dream, taking us so perfectly, even though we didn't do it nearly enough anymore.

"Oh my god," She gasped and pushed back onto both of us, "That's it, don't stop."

"Ask us nicely." I demanded, sliding into Dom role, and insisting she give me her obedience. "Beg us."

"Please fuck me." She licked her dry lips as her unfocused eyes stared into mine while Knox pushed deeper. He felt so good rubbing against me like this, and to be honest, I didn't know how either of us kept control of our orgasms. "Please baby, I need you both to pound into me. I want to feel you deep inside for days. I want it to ache where you are."

"Jeeze." Knox grunted, and I watched his neck muscles tense as his grip on her waist strengthened. "That's it baby, take those cocks like our good girl."

"I am." She purred. "I'm your good girl. Oh fuck, I'm coming again!" She screamed, and that was all I could take.

"Take it." I grunted. "Milk that cock Hannah."

"Brody." She dug her nails into my pecks as I orgasmed, filling her pussy with come and it set Knox off behind her.

"So fucking good." He groaned, slowing his thrusts down to match mine, filling and emptying her body at the same time until she was incoherently begging for reprieve.

She collapsed on my chest and Knox pulled free of her body before standing at the foot of the bed, staring at where I still impaled her.

"Give her every drop, man." He cupped my balls and massaged them, making sure there wasn't anything left inside of them before kissing her back, gently. "Such a good girl you are, Hannah."

"Mmh," She moaned and smiled against my neck as he went for a wet washcloth to clean us all up. "I'm a naughty girl." She whispered when he was gone.

"It's not naughty if we give you permission." I told her, rubbing my hands up and down her spine, relaxing her body as it got limper and limper against me. "There's no forgiveness to ask for after if we tell you that you can."

"I don't want you to just tell me I can." She sighed. "I want you to be a part of it." I could hear the stress in her voice, and I cut her off from talking any more.

"We'll continue this tomorrow." I lifted her and slid free as Knox cleaned her from our orgasms. "We don't have to do anything in any kind of rush."

"Hmm." She hummed, curling into her spot in the middle of the bed. "I'm too satisfied to argue anymore." She had a dreamy smile on her face as her eyes stayed closed.

"Good." Knox returned to the bed, and we took our spots on each side of her, curling around each other. "Because I have an alarm set for two hours from now. And when it goes off, I'm waking you up with more of that."

She giggled and sighed. "I like that idea."

Chapter 9 – Lex

I chewed on my inner cheek until there was a hole while I worked.

She didn't show.

I thought she would, even though I told her not to. Hell, I guess a part of me had hoped she would. But she didn't. I worked through three clients, anxiously keeping my ears turned toward the front door in case I heard her airy, sweet voice at the reception desk.

But she didn't show.

Like I said, I told her not to, but fuck if it didn't mess with my head. Her boyfriend was exactly the type of man I'd imagine for her. He was tall, muscular, and handsome, giving off those dominant and protective vibes with just the look in his eye.

Then there was the look he aimed my way when he found us together at dinner.

He was onto me, even if she didn't have a clue. His territorial instincts flared as she introduced us like everything was normal and platonic between us, because to her they were. But not to me, not anymore.

Not since that dream.

And he knew it, with just one look at us. He said nothing about it, but he didn't have to. I read him loud and clear.

She was his.

Theirs.

Straight.

Got it. So I respectfully bowed out and left her life.

So why did it fucking suck so badly? She was just someone I met a few days ago in a professional setting.

But she was also someone I spent hours upon hours with, talking about everything under the sun. Someone who asked me things about the bits and pieces of my life that mixed to make — me.

She didn't ask about my makeup. Or my style. She didn't ask about the tattoos or the piercings on my face.

She asked about my dad.

She asked about my childhood.

She asked about the reason behind my passion for my job.

She asked about the clients that touched my life every single day.

She took part in a special project for K-9 Arlo.

She cared, even if it was just for a work assignment.

I wasn't used to that kind of interest in me. The real me. And I believed that was why I was so fixated on the entire thing.

Dallin interrupted my thoughts, "Why did you cancel on Hannah?" I made sure my mask of indifference was in place as I turned to look at my boss, standing tall and wide in my doorway like some dark monster.

"She had everything she needed for the piece." I picked up the last of my things that I was gathering to go home for the night before he cornered me.

"She doesn't." Dallin squinted at me as he crossed his arms over his enormous chest. "She has a photo shoot scheduled here next week." He tilted his head toward me. "For pictures of you in this space."

I cringed, forgetting she wanted to do pictures here at the shop. "She can take pictures of the shop," I sighed, "I don't need to be in them."

He watched me closely, like he was trying to read my mind. And I felt sweat form on the back of my neck as he stared. Out of everyone I knew, if someone could read minds, it was Dallin Kent.

The man knew everything. Just like Parker said, he was always five steps ahead.

"I trusted you to take care of this." He finally said, "Through to the finish. I've never known you to throw in the towel on a project before."

"I didn't." I pulled my bag over my shoulder. "She got the information for the piece, D. I gave her what she needed."

"She needed you." He snapped.

My brows pinched over my eyes. "What does that mean?"

He just stared at me, and I suddenly felt like that fourteen-year-old girl back in my dad's house when he busted me with some shitty homemade ink job on my leg. Dallin's disappointment in me made little sense, as I couldn't fathom why it mattered to him.

"Never mind." He sighed, backing up out of the doorway. "You have a flat tire on your car. I already called for a tow. They should be here soon."

"Seriously? Again?" I groaned, suddenly remembering what the grumpy neanderthal from the side of the road the other day said about getting the spare changed right away. What was that, two days ago now? Three? Damnit. "Thanks." I whispered, watching him walk away as guilt threatened to push me down into the dirt. I walked out of the shop, ignoring everyone else as my thoughts of the perfect little girl next door overwhelmed me on my way to the parking lot.

It was as if my thoughts conjured the real thing, though, leaving me wondering if what I was seeing was an illusion.

"Hannah." I slowed my pace as she stood up off the bumper of her car parked in front of mine. She wore a pair of cut-off shorts and an oversized band tee she had knotted over her belly button, and I felt overwhelmed with the desire to see what she looked like wearing just that shirt and nothing else. Did she wear Knox's shirts at home like that? With nothing else on underneath of it?

Why the fuck was I imaging her wearing his clothes in their home?

"Hey." She put her hands in back pockets and tilted her head slightly. "I didn't want to come in and disturb you at work."

"So you lurked in the parking lot?" I questioned, glancing around. "How long have you been waiting?"

She shrugged, and a blush crept up her cheeks. "A few hours. I didn't know what time you were done for the day."

"Hannah." I sighed, hating that she sat out here that long because she was afraid to come inside.

"I just wanted to let you know the article will publish in two weeks." She licked her lips, drawing my attention there like I hadn't wondered what they tasted like all on my own. "I'm coming back with a photography team next week and doing a shoot of the space and then it will all get formatted."

"You wrote it already?" I opened the back door of my car and set my bags inside. "How bad did you make me look in it for ditching you?"

She chuckled and kicked a stone on the ground. "Maybe only slightly villainous."

"Fair, I do have a reputation to uphold." I sighed and shut the car door, before leaning against the hood and facing her head on. All day long I ached to see her again, and now that she was here, I didn't want her to leave. I didn't want this conversation to end. "I'm sorry, it was wrong of me to cut things short like I did."

"Can I ask why you did it?" She questioned, blushing further as the setting sun matched her skin tone. "I know I can be a lot and over the top sometimes. You had every right to decide when you were done, I just—" She pursed her lips, "I thought it was going well."

"Do you want the truth?" I asked, holding her stare.

"Yes."

"I took my cues from Knox." I admitted, and her eyes widened. "He made it clear that he wasn't comfortable, so I left."

She groaned and rubbed her hand over her face. "I'm so sorry. I don't know what got into him, I've never seen him act so—" She stopped.

"Possessive." I guessed for her.

"Yeah," She deflated a little, "Brody, sure. But not Knox. He's the level-headed one—" She rambled and then stopped. "It was my fault, and I'm sorry for that."

"It's not your fault." I shook my head, stopping her from going any further with that blame. "He was right to read the situation the way he did. And he was also within his right to put a stop to it." Her lips parted as she listened to me. "Within his right as your partner, not to let someone else sneak in unnoticed. He was right to claim his territory." There, I told her I was interested. Not that it made a lick of difference to a straight girl in a relationship with two men.

"Lex," she whispered, locking her bright eyes onto mine. "I think I'm bisexual."

The air sucked itself right out of my lungs as my body hummed in response to mere words. Words that changed so much. Yet also, nothing at all. Even if she was into women, she was in a committed relationship with men.

And I was a lesbian.

None of that even began to pair well.

"Say something." She took a step closer to me and I hated the fear and hope that were mixed in those sexy bedroom green eyes of hers.

"What do you want me to say?" I fought with my own emotions as a stupid thing that felt a lot like hope bloomed in my gut.

"I don't know." She blinked, like she was breaking out of the spell weaved between us. "I guess I thought maybe you'd have some wise piece of advice to give me."

I could see her defeat through the slump of her shoulders and the tiredness in her eyes.

"Don't break what's already perfect for the idea of something better." I stated, not having a clue where the words came from. She scowled at me, not liking the advice I gave her, but she needed to hear it. "Don't ruin your happy home, Hannah. Because the grass is rarely ever greener on the other side."

"What if I'm not trying to choose sides?" She challenged and stood up taller. God, she was sexy as hell when she got feisty. "Isn't that the point of being bi and polyamorous? Not choosing one or the other. The guys want me to explore."

Arousal ignited inside of me.

Was there hope of tasting her lips on mine after all? No. It couldn't be. Knox had made it clear last night that he didn't want to share, yet Hannah was standing here telling me they wanted her to experiment.

"So what?" I walked forward until we were face to face, the same height since I wore sneakers to work. "Your boyfriends are going to loan you out for a night, so you know whether you're into women? And you want me to be your first?"

Her throat tensed as she swallowed in trepidation at my crudeness, "I don't know. But they're not opposed to the idea."

"They're also not simps." I challenged, "They're going to be in control of the entire situation if or when it happens, Hannah. And I'm not one to take orders from someone else." Why was I fighting it? I was always down for a strings free hook up, and it sounded like just that. She had her relationship to fulfill her emotional needs and was offering me exactly what I was into. Sex.

Could she do strings free?

Could I do it with her?

Being this close to her, I could smell her floral perfume just like the other day when she stood over my shoulder while I worked. Everything inside of me wanted to kiss the sensitive skin under her ear that day to see if it smelled as sweet there in her neck.

But today, I wanted to spread her thighs and see if she tasted that sweet too. I was on edge, barely holding onto restraint.

"Then just say you aren't interested." She tilted her head back and swallowed, "It's as simple as that." She took a step back, and I barely stopped myself from grabbing her by the front of the shirt to keep her near. "I'll just find someone that is."

Fuck it.

I didn't stop myself. I grabbed that shirt I fixated on when I first walked up and pulled her to me, roughly until her chest bounced into mine. She gasped and panted as I stared directly into her eyes. She was so close I could kiss her. Just a few inches of lean would give me what I wanted most.

"I didn't take you for a brat." I leered, dropping my gaze to her lips. She took the bait and licked them, "You want a kiss to find out if you'll like it, like it's any question at all." I looked back up at her eyes. "We both know you'd like it, simply because it's me."

"Prove it." She whispered, and I smirked at her boldness. Sometimes she surprised me with her assertiveness and other times I craved it.

I grinned down at her and licked my own lips as her eyelids fluttered closed as I leaned in.

"Someone call for a tow?" A deep voice interrupted us, calling out from a few spots over.

I curled my lip in frustration as Hannah gasped and pulled back, stumbling over her feet to put space between us. And I let her go, because when I whipped my head toward the voice responsible for interrupting us, agitation like no other filled my entire body.

"You!" I hissed, cocking my head to the side, taking in the tall, cocky, asshole biker from a few days ago as he leaned against the hood of his tow truck. "You have to be kidding." He had a white tee shirt on that hugged his torso with dark smears of grease across his stomach and a pair of worn light blue jeans, and even as annoyed as I was, my eyes lingered on him for too fucking long.

"She's the tattoo artist?" He sneered, just as annoyed as I was, but he wasn't aiming it my way. He focused his attention on Hannah, and she twisted her head back and forth between us.

"You know him?" I snapped at her.

Her mouth opened and then closed as her brows furrowed. "I'm so confused."

He scoffed and shook his head. "Didn't look that way from here, Han," he said, giving her a disappointed glare. "Looked like you were about to cross a line."

Her shoulders deflated as she looked over at me cautiously. And then it clicked.

"Brody." I felt sick to my stomach as what I thought was finally within reach slipped through my fingers at the last second. "You have to be fucking kidding me."

Of course, her other boyfriend was the jackass that changed my tire the other day, expecting me to fawn over him for his manliness in helping me. Even though I never asked for the help.

"How do you two know each other?" Hannah asked, looking back and forth still.

"It doesn't matter." I ran my hand through my hair and sighed, already feeling the resolve inside of me turning to concrete. "I can't do this."

"Wait." Hannah reached for me fleetingly as I evaded her touch. Moments before, I was ready to take her right there on the hood of my car, but now I couldn't stand the thought of doing anything with that man's girlfriend.

Unless it was out of spite just to show him, I could do it better than he could.

"She's right, wait." Brody, the neanderthal, sighed and glared at me before turning to Hannah and it was odd watching from the outside, but he softened his gruff demeanor for her. "This is what you want?" He nodded to me. "Her?"

Hannah peeked back at me, "Well, we were just getting to that part."

"I'm not a zoo animal." I snapped, shaking it off. "I'm not going to perform so your guys can watch and get off on two girls together."

"We wouldn't treat Hannah that way." He bit back, "You have no clue what you're talking about."

"Maybe so," I shrugged, taking one last fleeting glance at Hannah, as regret washed over me with each step away that I took. "But I'm not going to stick around to find out, either."

"What about your car?" He called out as I grabbed my purse from the back seat and headed back toward the shop.

"I'll call someone else for a tow. Someone that doesn't have to loan his girlfriend out to make her come!" I yelled over my shoulder and then flipped him the bird as I walked across the parking lot.

God, what I wouldn't give to be wearing a pair of red bottoms so they could both drool as I cat walked away.

Was I twisted in the head and placing blame on Hannah's shoulders when it wasn't her fault?

Yes.

Was I healed enough in my mental health journey to be better than that.

Nope.

She picked the biggest douche canoe in the world to be in love with, really.

It was dark in the shop, everyone had gone home hours ago, yet I still sat in my suite, pouting like a teenager. I pretended to be busy with sketches, which I was, but I also didn't need to pull an all-nighter to get anything done either.

No, in reality, I was just sulking.

And stewing because the prick-ass bastard actually towed my car with my fucking lunch bag in it, and it had all of my snacks. So that led me to be hangry and salty as the hours ticked on, leaving me wondering what to do.

I could have called an Uber and gotten home, or at the very least, ordered dinner to be delivered, but I was punishing myself by making myself as miserable as possible.

"Hey, Barbie." I looked up for the first time in hours and found Trey leaning against my door. "I thought everyone had gone home by now."

I nodded to him, not even remotely interested in sparring verbally with him like usual. "Everyone else has."

He tilted his head to the side in that eerie Trey mannerism that always gave me goosebumps. I had no clue how Reyna gave him the time of day in the beginning, with his abrasive weirdo tendencies and her sweet, good-girl nature.

"So Hannah, huh?" He asked, and I felt myself gaining the energy to tell him to fuck off, barely restraining. So instead, I ignored him. Which I knew Trey hated more than anything.

I looked back down at my tablet and tried to focus on the design for a client next week, like he wasn't hovering.

After all of two seconds, he sighed dramatically and came in, throwing himself down in the chair for my client's guests, and went on. "Okay fine." He held his hands up, "I'll be nice."

"Why?" I questioned, not trusting him for a second. I didn't hate Trey, quite the opposite, really. He reminded me a lot of myself, which was why we butted heads so often. We knew the other could take all the blows and keep coming back for more without actually being offended. But I just didn't have the fight in me at the moment.

"Because Reyna told me she wouldn't let me into bed tonight if I came down here and razzed you."

I snorted and rolled my eyes. "You're so whipped."

"One hundred percent." He nodded his head like a bobblehead doll. "I'm prize motivated, and my prize is sex. All day, every day."

"And all three of them know it, don't they?"

"It's cruel, really." He sighed, leaning back in the chair and looking around. "You ever feel like designing interiors?"

I scoffed, "Huh?"

"The vibe," he waved his hand around my room and shrugged, "It's pretty cool."

"Thank you?" I questioned, "What alternate universe did I land in?"

"Meh," He looked back to me, "One where it looked like Hannah and Brody beat you down enough earlier, so I'm trying to be a nice person to you." He shuddered, "I won't lie, it makes me feel icky."

"Then stop." I deadpanned, "For the love of god, just stop." I held my hand up as he opened his mouth, cutting him off, "And I'm not going to talk about it. Not with you."

"I told Rey that Parker should be the one to come down and check on you." He sighed, "But he's off with Dallin at the gym and Rey could only stay out of it for so long." He held his hands up, "So here I am."

"I don't need someone to intervene. Or check on me."

"So what happened?"

"Nothing."

"Liar." He fired back. "I saw you nearly throw that sweet girl down on the hood of your car before her big oaf showed up and interrupted. I won't lie, I was pretty bummed that he broke up the show."

I rolled my eyes so far; I saw my brain.

"Oh, come on," He droned, "I'm a happily married man, but I can spot sexual tension a mile away. And that little show—" He wagged his finger back and forth, "Screamed hot lesbian sexual tension."

"She's straight," I said, regretting it a second after it left my mouth. Because I did not want to talk about it at all, especially with him.

"Is that the problem?"

"That, and the fact that she's in a long-term relationship." I shuddered, "I can't stand messy relationship drama."

"That's not a denial of being interested." He raised his brows suggestively, and I groaned at how he caught me. "Sounds like you want her."

"I want to ruin her," I replied, setting my tablet down on the side table next to me and then leaning forward with my elbows on my knees. "Given how similar you and I are, I'm confident that *you* know precisely what I mean by that statement. I don't want to hold her hand and coax her through her first girl-on-girl moment while Tweedle Dee and Tweedle Dumb watch to get their jollies off." Sitting back in my chair and running the back of my fingers over my lip, "I want to ruin her for them and then walk away without a backward glance simply because I shouldn't."

"But you won't." He challenged, his voice a deep timber I only heard when he was in the dark place that he hid in sometimes. "You won't hurt her. She's too pure. And you're not as big of a monster as you want everyone to think you are. It's the same reason I couldn't hurt Rey with anything more than words when she was mortal enemy number one for stealing Dallin all those years ago. I could have seduced her, tricked her into choosing me over D and Parker. Then I would have destroyed her and left her with pieces of who she used to be, alone and broken, to serve as some sort of moral retribution for my pain." He stood up and towered over me, so I had to look up at him in the dim light. "But I didn't. The same way you won't. Because she didn't hurt you to begin with. Someone else did."

"I want to though, and that's reason enough to steer the fuck clear."

"Then stop pouting about it." He scorned, sliding back into the usual Trey role I recognized. The one I longed for after nice Trey ripped open my insecurities and laughed at them. "Grow the fuck up. Go out and find some willing pussy to lose yourself in for a few days and forget about her."

"Fuck you." It was a brittle comeback, but I had nothing else.

"Yeah," he grinned sadistically, "See, that right there," he pointed to my weakness, "Is exactly why I don't believe that you don't want the good you could gain from letting her in."

"She has nothing to gain from letting me in," I replied, admitting the truth to someone who could easily turn it around and use it against me.

"A bleeding heart." He tsked and walked toward the door with his hands in his pockets. "I always knew you were a softy deep inside all of that ALT Barbie exterior."

"Don't tell anyone." I mused, giving up on even trying to refute it.

He winked and then tossed me something that I caught a half a second before it hit me in the nose.

My keys.

"Knox dropped your car off an hour ago. But I figured you needed a little longer to stew on all your girly feelings before you were fixed."

"Gee, thanks." I rolled my eyes, spinning the keys around my finger.

"Night, Barbie."

"Night, Ogre."

Chapter 10 – Hannah

I cleaned the counters until they sparkled. Then I scrubbed the oven and the baseboards in the entire living space of the house. After that, I shampooed the rugs and dusted the ceiling fans.

And I still wasn't calm.

Which was abnormal for me, because cleaning was my therapy, my meditation. Yet tonight, I was still raw and on edge and in need of something I couldn't quite put my finger on.

Brody and Knox hovered, lurking in the doorways, and watching me silently work through my mile-long spring-cleaning list, but they didn't intervene.

I *almost* kissed Lex.

So close. Inches between our lips, that was all there was. The way she grabbed my shirt and pulled me back to her, God, it was hot. The way she knew I'd like the kiss because it was with her. After all, I was quickly becoming obsessed with her, and it spoke of that connection I'd felt from the start.

She looked so good tonight.

Her tight black ripped jeans hugged her thighs like those leather pants did the other day, the ones that made me wonder what her skin felt like underneath them. She had on a tight white tank top that stretched across her breasts, showing off the fact that they were fake, and she didn't need to wear a bra.

What would they feel like in my hands? Would I like them the way Brody and Knox always seemed so enthralled with mine?

"Han?" Brody's deep voice cut through the fog of arousal threatening to pull me under and I gasped, jumping from being caught daydreaming about breasts.

"What?" I snapped, looking over my shoulder at him with the duster in my hand, cleaning the empty air in front of me.

"We have to talk about this." He said, and I could sense the thin veil of restraint over his words.

He was furious.

He didn't say how, but he knew Lex and openly disliked her. Which just made me angrier because it felt like his dislike for her was keeping me further away from what I wanted.

Her.

Them.

All of us.

I didn't want to choose. I didn't want to define the dynamics, I just wanted to—have my cake and eat it too, if I was being honest.

Was it selfish? Maybe. Was I completely willing to include Knox and Brody in my imagery of perfection by letting them be with Lex as well? One hundred percent.

I wasn't an overly jealous or possessive person before, and perhaps it was because Brody and Knox never entertained the idea of wanting anyone else. They always made me feel secure in knowing I gave them what they needed and weren't looking for it anywhere else. So the idea of sharing them with Lex didn't bother me, but she wasn't interested in them.

She was a lesbian.

She didn't want them, she just wanted me.

Damnit.

The realization of it all kicked me right in the stomach. The reason none of it would work the way I had mapped out in my fantasy.

She didn't want them.

They couldn't have her.

Therefore, they got nothing out of the move to expand my sexual partners to include her.

"Fuck." I sighed, sinking to my knees in the middle of the carpet of the living room.

"What?" Brody asked, walking into the room but keeping his distance. "What is it?"

"It's never going to work," I whispered, staring at a speck of dust floating in the air in front of me. "The Lex thing was just a fantasy I conjured up in my head in a desperate attempt to make it real. But it's not."

"Why?" Knox asked, having followed Brody in. But I still stared at that small dust mite, floating aimlessly in the air.

"Because it isn't equal." I tilted my head, lost in thought. "Someone who doesn't want you is not what I desire. I want to find someone that you want as much as I do."

"This isn't about us." Knox sat down on the couch across from me, but Brody still lingered. Knox was always the understanding one, the one who would sacrifice if it meant making Brody and me happy. "If you want to be with a woman, we'll make it work."

"I don't." Blinking, I focused my eyes on anything but that speck of dust, and looked up at him. "I don't want to just be with a woman." My body flushed at saying the words out loud. "I want to watch you be with a woman, too." Normally I would have buried the desire building inside of me, or not even spoken it into existence at all. Because I was a good girl, with good men who loved me, and I needed nothing more. But now? After the whirlwind of a week I'd had, I ached to experience what I fantasized over. Getting to my knees, I crawled to him, watching his eyes squint in confusion as I stopped at his feet. "I don't think I've ever wanted to see something more than you having sex with another woman." I licked my lips as his nostrils flared. "Well, that's not true," I ran my hands up his thighs over his jeans, "Watching you slide into Brody's body the first time will probably always sit at the top of my list."

"Hannah," Knox growled, clenching his teeth. But I turned to look at Brody over my shoulder.

"Do you want that, baby?" I tried my best to seduce him into the room with my tone, but I wasn't sure it would break through his mood. "Do you want me to help you fuck someone else? Like I did the first time you fucked Knox?"

"You're playing with fire here, and I don't think you're going to like the outcome." He replied with that fierce dominance that always made me ache to submit to him.

Purring, I lifted my shirt off and tossed it across the room. "I think I am." I didn't have a bra on, and both of their gazes fell directly to my tits as I shimmied out of my sweatpants. "I think I want to feel the burn of the fire as we all dance in it."

Knox slid off the couch onto his knees in front of me and kissed me. "You know me, Sweetheart, I'm always down for a little danger."

"Show me." I whirred and slid my hands up under his shirt to feel his warm skin.

"Your wish is my command." He knocked my legs out from under me and caught me mere inches before I hit the carpeted floor, cradling me down as he followed my body down.

He pulled my panties off and spread my legs, as I laid naked for him and ready. I was always so damn ready lately.

He kissed his way down my body, pinching my nipples and feasting on them as I rubbed my bare pussy against his abdomen, trying to get him to move on.

All the while, Brody watched silently from the doorway.

"Baby." I held my hand out to him, inviting him in, but he still didn't move. Knox lowered himself to my pussy and went to work, fucking me with his tongue and sucking on my clit as I lost focus on trying to get Brody to join. "You make that feel so good."

Knox hummed against me and pushed two fingers in deep. "You taste so good, I could do it for days."

"You know what tastes even better?" I curled up and rested on my elbows so I could see him. "Brody's come dripping out of me while you lick it up." He growled and put more pressure on my clit as I glanced back at Brody. "Are you going to leave me hanging here?"

"Yes." He growled, and I gritted my teeth in frustration.

Brody wanted to play hardball, so I'd play right back.

"Fine." I hissed and sat up, forcing Knox onto his back as I straddled his face. I faced Brody while I rocked my hips, rubbing my clit all over Knox's talented mouth. I felt kind of bad using him, but I needed Brody to join, or it'd all be for nothing. "God, yes!" I moaned, palming my breasts and playing with my nipples as I stared directly at the infuriating man. Even so, he didn't budge. I screamed in frustration. "Fine!" I crawled off of Knox when all I wanted to do was sink down onto his cock and fuck my frustration away, but Brody was cock blocking me by simply existing in his grumpy state. "Never mind!"

"Fucker." Knox cursed in annoyance as I grabbed my clothes, intent on leaving the room and sulking somewhere away from them both.

As I stormed out of the room, Brody's eyes were on fire, ignited by his own irritations, and I snarled at him as I went to pass.

He moved so fast, I never saw it coming, though I should have been wiser than to challenge his darkness at that moment. He grabbed me by the throat when I went by and pushed me into the wall, covering my naked body with his boiling one. His rage was clear as he put pressure on my neck, holding me but not restricting my breath. The blood pooled in my face though, as he held down the critical arteries and veins pumping blood in and out of my brain. I shoved at him, angrily wanting to tell him where to shove his dominance when he pushed my thighs apart and rubbed his jean-covered thigh against my pussy.

"Careful Darling, you're forgetting who's boss around here." He warned, and I whimpered when he pulled his leg away.

"Then be my boss." I challenged. "Being my boss means taking care of my needs, and right now, you're neglecting them!"

He clenched his teeth together so hard I heard them creak as he pulled me off the wall and threw me over his shoulder. I kicked my legs and swung my fists into his back for good measure, but he spanked my ass so hard with one powerful slap that I froze in shock.

Spanking had always been playful between us, but that one felt like a punishment.

"You were rude to Knox." He said, sliding me down his body and then forcing me to my knees. Knox leaned back against the couch on the floor where I left him, watching silently, though I knew if Brody went too far, he'd step in. But judging by the darkness in Knox's eyes as Brody turned me to face him on my knees, it was going to take a lot to snap him out of the headspace they were both in. "Say you're sorry."

"No," I argued, not because I wasn't, he was right, I was rude to poor Knox, using his face and body to tease Brody. I refused simply to piss them both off.

"Brat." Brody hissed, and I had a flashback to the way Lex had called me a brat in the parking lot. My pussy dripped at the name. He grabbed my messy bun and pulled it tight, angling my head to the side as he held the back of my neck until I was leaning directly in Knox's personal space. "Say. You're. Sorry."

"Sorry," I whispered to Knox, but the darkness didn't leave his eyes as his lips turned up in a sinister smile.

"Show me." Knox repeated my words from earlier as he undid his jeans. When his cock was free, he stroked it lazily, with a dirty grin on his face. "Show me how sorry you really are."

I swallowed and fell forward when Brody let go of my neck and landed in Knox's lap, cock already poised at my lips. "Careful what you wish for." I hissed before running the tips of my teeth over the crown of his cock.

"Right back at you, baby girl," Knox threatened, "You give pain, you take pain."

I hummed, sinking my mouth down onto him and running the flat of my tongue up the underside of him seductively as he placed his hand on the back of my neck, guiding me. I didn't want to fight with Knox at all, actually. But fighting with Brody made me angsty and Knox became a target for it as well. They were ganging up on me, but I didn't hate it. I actually kind of liked it.

I liked the fire in their eyes and the burn of their touch. Rarely did they show this side of themselves to me, afraid of hurting me. I'd seen it when they were with each other; the unrestrained hunger and power they used. But rarely did I *feel* it.

I craved it.

I widened my knees under me and bent at the waist, presenting my bare ass and pussy to Brody, who kneeled behind me as I turned on the charm. I sucked Knox's cock like a whore, desperate for his come, and it worked. He relaxed and softened his hold on my neck as I sucked him.

And then I struck.

With the next bob up I sank my teeth into the base of his cock and dragged them up, not hard enough to break the skin, but enough to elicit a deep growl from his chest as he pulled me off by my neck and pushed me back into Brody's arms.

"Fucking hell." Knox panted, stroking his cock and looking at the red marks I left. "I did nothing to deserve that."

"You sided with him." I nodded over my shoulder where Brody lurked, "Maybe next time you'll choose wiser."

"Brat." Brody growled in my ear. "I've never seen this side of you before. There seems to be more about you than we knew, after all."

"Maybe it's because you've treated me like a princess all these years."

He grabbed the front of my neck and pinned my back to his chest, "What else would we have treated you like?"

"Like a slut." I moaned, pushing back into him where his cock throbbed like a piece of branding iron in his jeans. I couldn't remember a time I felt it that hard before. "Like your bratty, spoiled, little slut who thinks she can just have whatever she wants."

After I said it, I realized my insecurities were talking, taking me out of the sexy high I had been riding until that point.

I felt selfish.

I felt slutty.

For wanting someone that wasn't them, and expecting them to be okay with it. And then throwing a fit when I didn't get it.

"You aren't our princess." Knox got to his knees as tears filled my eyes, angering me further. "You're our fucking Queen, Hannah." He could see the truth on my face, and Brody could feel it as I shrunk at Knox's declaration.

"We worship you, because you deserve it." Brody softened, and I hated the gentleness taking place in his hold.

"No." I shook my head, gritting my teeth as more guilt built in my chest. "I'm not. I'm a liar and a cheat."

I shrieked as Brody's grip tightened on my throat, bending me at the waist and forcing my face into the floor between Knox's thighs. Brody's hand landed on the same cheek he'd spanked over his shoulder and the burn ignited tenfold. "Is that what you want?" He spanked me again, as Knox took hold of my neck, keeping me bent over between them. "Do you want us to tell you that you're a bad person?"

"Yes." I cried, pushing back against him as he spanked me again.

"You want us to punish you for being bi?" *Spank. Moan.* "For wanting Lex?"

"Yes!" I shivered when he switched sides and peppered my other ass cheek with his palm. "I fucked up!"

"Naughty." *Spank.* "Little." *Spank.* "Spoiled." *Spank.* "Brat." *Spank.*

"Yes!" I screamed into the carpet, digging my nails into Knox's thighs over my head.

"Say you're sorry." Knox growled, pulling my face out of the carpet to look at him without letting me sit up. "Say you're sorry for being bi."

"I'm sorry." I cried, staring up at him as the tears broke free and I sobbed. "I'm so sorry!"

Brody's cock was already deep inside me before I could even finish my sentence. I screamed bloody murder from the invasion and the overwhelming emotions he was bringing out of me at the same time. "Good girl." He groaned, pulling out and sinking deep.

"Take my cock, slut." Knox held his cock at the base and smacked it against my lips, "Swallow me down with no fucking teeth, and show me you can be our good girl after all."

I took him deep, without a second of hesitation, and swallowed his cock as Brody's thrusts pushed me forward. I gagged uncontrollably but refused to pull off, punishing myself and begging for forgiveness with my mouth.

Knox and Brody both groaned in tandem, thrusting in and out of my body, and I simply knelt there, taking what they gave.

Shame burned in my gut and I desperately wanted to prove to them my remorse for acting up.

"That's it." Knox tightened his hold in my hair, "Open your throat and let me fuck it."

I stuck my tongue out, drooling all over both of us as he thrust in over and over again. Now and then he'd hold himself deep, cutting off my ability to breathe and panic would swirl in my gut before he pulled out and allowed me to gasp before pushing in again.

I was crazed for them, pushing on and off their cocks, moaning, drooling, and begging for more of their intense pain and punishment.

My entire body snapped. Darkness clouded my vision, and I screamed around Knox's cock while slamming back onto Brody's as my body started convulsing in ecstasy. I didn't deserve the pleasure, though I greedily took it, reaching under my body to rub my clit to prolong it. Brody pulled my hand away, pinning it behind my back, and replaced it with his own fingers. He rubbed my clit painfully as he laid over my back, "That's it, come for us."

I moaned and mewed as he forced another catastrophic orgasm from my body and, as soon as it was done, they both stopped moving. Knox pulled out of my mouth and Brody stayed fully buried inside of me, but pulled me upright to sit on his thighs.

My head lolled to the side as I tried to watch Knox as he kneeled forward and gently kissed me, uncaring of his raging hard-on swinging between his thighs. "No." I cried softly, reaching for him. "You didn't come."

"I can't." He shook his head against my face as he ran his hands over my face and my arms, gently petting me as Brody's fingers gently played with my swollen clit between my spread thighs. "I'll never be able to come while treating you like that."

It made little sense; I shook my head. Forcing my eyes open as Brody started kissing my neck and slowly thrusting his cock into me, grinding me on it just how I liked. I knew it wasn't giving him what he wanted. "That was to teach you a lesson, Darling," Brody whispered in my ear. "That wasn't real."

"No," I cried, as the feeling of devastation filled my chest. I needed to atone for the grief and I thought I did that by letting them use me so crudely, but they were telling me it wasn't real.

"You owe us nothing." Knox kissed one ear while Brody kissed the other, asserting, "You are not spoiled. You are not a slut. You are perfect."

"No, no, no." I rocked my head back and forth.

Brody palmed one of my breasts and rolled my nipple seductively in time with how he played with my clit. "You wanted us to treat you like that because you think you deserve it. But you don't."

"I'm ruining us!"

"You're bettering us." Knox countered, leaning down against my lips, "You did nothing wrong."

"Then why does it feel so broken in here?" I slapped my chest directly over my heart and cried.

"Because you're scared." Brody reasoned. "You feel guilty, but you shouldn't. There's no reason to." I opened my mouth to debate that, but Knox pushed his tongue into it and kissed me, silencing it.

"We love you." Knox pulled back and added his fingers to my pussy, playing with me around Brody's fat cock, still impaling me. "We love you so fucking much, we can't breathe when you're upset like this."

"I love you!" Crying, clawing at them both and rocking myself against their hands, I unraveled. "I want to make you happy."

"You do." Knox lifted my hips and then dropped me back down onto Brody's cock, making us both moan. "Even as a bi woman, Hannah. You make us happy. And we want to explore this with you."

"I don't deserve you."

Brody thrust hard the next time Knox lifted me and slammed deep. "I never want to hear you say that again," He commanded. "Do you understand me?"

"But I don't—" I cried when he pinched my nipple in his hand and gasped when he pulled out of me, pushing me into Knox's lap. "No!" I grabbed for him. "Please!"

"Just wait." Brody walked out of the room as Knox lifted me onto his cock, distracting me from Brody's absence and making me moan as he sucked on my nipples while fucking his cock up into me.

Seconds later Brody returned, and I clawed at his arms as he pressed his naked body against my back. "Don't leave me," I begged, staring at Knox and then looking at Brody over my shoulder. "Never leave me."

"Never." Brody slid his hand down my back and through my ass crack to my empty hole, pushing two silky fingers into me. "We're never leaving you. This doesn't change our love for you, Hannah." He worked lube into my ass and then I felt the tip of his cock nudging against my me as Knox started thrusting up into me again. "Just like it didn't change our love for you when Knox and I fell in love."

"Oh god," I moaned as he pushed his cock into me, overwhelmed by them as always. "I'm so scared."

"We know." Knox licked my neck and sucked on my ear, holding me still as Brody gave me his entire cock. "We know, baby, we remember how we felt all those years ago. And your unwavering support got us through it. Through the darkest, scariest hours. You were the light that kept us safe."

"I love you." I moaned, grabbing Brody's arms and wrapping them around me, as Knox did the same, both of them holding onto me as I shattered for them again. "Please, fuck me. Please, show me just how badly you want me still. Don't hold back."

Brody growled against my ear and put his hands under the backs of my knees, lifting them into the air so I was squatting between their bodies with my knees pressed to my chest, and then they both started fucking me hard. "Be careful what you ask for, Darling. Because I kind of enjoyed fucking you like a slut."

I moaned and Knox added, as he started rubbing my clit with his fingers. "Our dirty, spoiled, little, slutty Queen."

"Fuck!" I cried. "That's it."

"Our girl has a degradation kink," Brody grunted. "Who knew?"

"I have a *you* kink; both of you." I moaned, "Any fucking way I can get you."

"Oh, you'll get us," Knox smirked before kissing me and biting my bottom lip. "My hand is dying to redden your ass for fun now, and I can't wait to feel your teeth on my cock again, little minx."

"Mmh." I moaned, already close as pressure built inside of me. I recognized the pressure from the angle of Knox's cock, but I didn't tell him what was coming. "Harder," I begged like their perfect little slut, and clenched their cocks tighter as I neared my orgasm. "Harder!"

They both snapped, fucking me hard and giving me everything I needed, and it erupted inside of me. I screamed and Knox cursed as I flooded his cock with my juicy orgasm, having only squirted three other times in my life thanks to the two massive men sandwiching me and fucking me senseless. Brody growled, a primal sound as Knox pulled out and rubbed my clit furiously as I drenched his thighs.

"That's it." Brody bit my shoulder. "Squirt for us, whore."

"Fuck!" I screamed as my orgasm kept rolling through me as Knox hammered back into me. Within a few more thrusts and a lot of incoherent pleas and begging, both men roared as they orgasmed, filling me up in both holes until it dripped out of me.

We fell into a pile of tangled limbs and twitching muscles right there on the living room floor. As the post-nut dazzle, as Knox liked to call it, faded from my body, I didn't feel as overwhelmed with guilt as I had when I started processing my feelings, thanks to Brody's firm hand.

My men knew me, inside and out, and even when I felt like my entire world was crumbling down inside of my brain, they were always there to hold it all together for me.

"We're going to be alright, aren't we?" I broke the peaceful silence that had blanketed us. Brody took my hand in his, and Knox rolled over, pressing his lips to my cheek.

"We're always going to be just fine," Brody reassured me, squeezing my hand and Knox agreed, pulling me into his warm embrace. "We can make it through any big change in life, as long as we do it together."

Chapter 11 – Brody

I busted yet another knuckle on the exhaust I was trying to replace. Distraction and manual labor hardly ever went well together.

But distracted was all I'd been for days now. Since Hannah came clean about her sexuality.

Knox had been afraid when he found out that she would want to leave us for a woman, but I didn't doubt her commitment to us. Not for a second. I also wasn't dumb enough to think that if we didn't allow her to explore this newfound interest, it would fester inside of her like a disease.

Causing harm to the only woman I've ever loved, which was the last thing I wanted. So I pushed in favor of letting her explore. I wanted her to have the chance to test the waters with herself and her desires.

I'd be lying if I said I didn't want to at least be a witness to it, and not for the creepy, typical perverted male reasoning most would want to watch.

I was Hannah's first kiss.

After she was done kissing me, she turned and kissed Knox.

I was there on the day she found out she was accepted to her dream college four hours away from our hometown. I held her hand and reassured her she would be okay without us for a few years. Even though she backed out and stayed local to stay near us.

The night she lost her virginity, I lay next to her when Knox slid inside of her for the first time. And then I took my turn.

That was how it had always been.

For all the big moments in life, all three of us were together before we even understood what that made us.

I needed it to be that way for this too.

But then, I found out who the mysterious Lex was, and everything tilted out of balance inside of my head.

Hannah thought I knew Lex from some important part of life when, in reality, I'd only ever interacted with her for twenty minutes on the side of the road once.

But that was all it had taken for me to realize; we were oil and water.

We'd never mix. We'd only ever battle each other for our rightful space.

Two Doms couldn't share space within a relationship; not completely. Never mind the fact that Lex was as lesbian as they came, and Hannah wanted a woman that we could all share. It had a destined failure before it even started.

But that didn't mean we couldn't give Hannah what she wanted for her first time with a woman. Even if it was only for one time.

"Hey, anyone home?" I ducked out from underneath the hotrod I was working on and found Dallin standing at the open garage door.

"Hey, man." I wiped my hands on a rag and then shook his. "What brings you out here in the middle of the day?"

"I had a meeting a few blocks over, I thought I'd stop in and say hey." He put his hands in his jeans pockets and rocked on the balls of his feet. He was up to something.

"Spit it out." I sighed, leaning back on the car lift post, and settling in for whatever bombshell he was here to drop on me. I had known Dallin for a few years now, and the man never ceased to surprise me.

He chuckled and relaxed a bit. "I want to apologize." He ran one hand over the back of his neck. "I may have stuck my nose somewhere it didn't belong, and I hear it may have backfired."

"Lex." I surmised, raising one brow at him, and he shrugged with a small smirk. "I should have known you wouldn't have bailed on Hannah like that for the article unless you were up to something."

"Actually," He chuckled, "I genuinely had to reschedule it at the very least because of the expo next week. And then Reyna told me some things that Hannah had been asking her—" He faded off.

"Good god," I groaned, "You knew my girl was into girls before I did?"

He laughed and shrugged again, "In my defense, you not knowing, sounds a lot more like a problem within your relationship communication than it does about my wife's over-communication."

I scoffed and nodded in agreement. "We got comfortable," I admitted. "We stopped seeing her and reading her the way we used to. She said she wasn't sure until she met Lex, but we should have seen the signs that she was curious, at least."

"I agree." He nodded, "But I'm not perfect either and can admit that sometimes in my marriage we've all gotten too relaxed as well. We stopped dating each other and making time to learn more. There's always more to know."

I headed over to the large lounge area and grabbed a bottle of water out of the fridge, handing him one and then taking a seat in one of the leather chairs. The area was for clients and us to talk about builds and details, but the garage was empty, giving us the privacy for the conversation I needed. He sat in one of the other chairs and watched me closely.

"What did Hannah say to Rey?" I asked after a while.

"It was more of what she asked, Rey." He mused, "She asked her things about how Reyna was confident enough to add Parker and Trey to our relationship after we'd been together for so long, just the two of us."

I nodded, knowing exactly what Hannah had been searching for with that line of questions. "Because she wants to add to ours."

"Does she?" He asked, leaning forward on his knees to stare at me. "Because Reyna thought she was only curious about her feelings for women, not adding another to the relationship full time."

"She wants us all to add a woman to the dynamic, not just for her."

His eyes rounded a bit, and he sat back in his chair, "And she thought that woman would be Lex?"

"Fuck if I know." I scoffed again, frustrated with the whole thing. "Hannah knows Lex isn't straight. It doesn't add up."

"What about you?" He asked, "Everything else aside, are you and Knox down to add another? Lex or someone else completely."

"I have no clue, man." I replied honestly, "I can't imagine having someone else in our life full-time."

"I get it." He nodded, "It was a big change when Parker and Trey moved in, I think in a way it was harder for Rey than it was for me since I lived with all of them at one point or another in life. But for Rey, they were both brand new."

"It seems unobtainable." I took a pull off the water, remembering the way Lex looked, grabbing the front of Hannah's shirt and pulling her in like she was about to kiss her. She *had* been about to kiss her, and I interrupted her. On purpose. "Too good to be true, in a way."

"Does Hannah want to just explore or date?"

"She wants someone we can all—" I tried to find the right words, "*Play with*, I guess. God, that sounds so fucked up."

"It doesn't, actually," Dallin assured me. "Polyamory is a part of the *lifestyle*." He explained, "The lifestyle uses the word 'play' to encompass so many things. It doesn't have to be demeaning or belittling to the person you're playing with."

"Why'd you involve Lex in the first place?" I leveled him with a stare and hoped he'd give me something straight. Something solid to find a footing in through all of this upheaval.

"To be honest with you, it was more for Lex than it was for Hannah." He tilted his head to the side. "More for you."

"Me?" I scowled, shaking my head, "How does adding a lesbian help me out?"

"I'm diving way deeper into your relationship than I ever imagined I would here," He chuckled lightly, "But that's my doing at his point. Nevertheless, I think someone like Lex is exactly what you could use to level out your relationship dynamic."

"She's a Domme, D." I barked, "Don't you understand what that means? She'd never fold for me. A Dom will always need someone to submit to them, male or female, it doesn't matter. And I'll never kneel for someone else. I can't."

"Funny." He twisted the bottle of water in his hands as he regarded me. "I thought that was exactly what Knox and Hannah were good at doing."

"I can't." I shook my head and stood up, eager to end the conversation because I didn't like how it was making me feel. Like I wasn't enough for Knox and Hannah as I was without adding someone else in. "I don't want to share them that way."

"Fine." He stood up, holding his hands up in surrender. "I didn't mean to overstep your boundaries."

"It's fine." I paced as the anxious energy built inside of me. "I just can't."

"I'm sorry, Brody." He said evenly, and I believed him. I don't think he set out to step on my toes. "But I didn't come here empty-handed either."

"What do you mean?" I asked, on edge.

He pulled a black envelope from his back pocket and held it out for me. I took it and flipped open the flap.

"An invitation." He explained as I read the vague script on the matte black card. "To the Sinners Soiree house party this weekend." I looked up at him when I recognized the name of the elusive sex club I'd only ever heard about in whispers. I knew Dallin and his spouses had gone to a few of their events, but never imagined taking Hannah and Knox to a place like that. Granted, that was before Hannah's revelation. "It can be intense and over the top, especially this one since it's the biggest one of the year. But I think it would be a great safe space for you all to dive deeper into this world. Even if you just spectate for the evening, it may answer some questions you all have about yourselves and your partners."

"Why do I feel like if I take them to this place, we'll be crossing a line in the sand that we can't go back over at the end of the night?" I asked, feeling both dread and excitement at the prospect of going to the event. Lifestyle parties had always intrigued me, but I never had a purpose for them because I wasn't interested in sharing either of my partners with anyone else. At least, that was how I had felt before. Now, I didn't know what I felt.

"Because you can't." He replied evenly, like he was giving some significant words of wisdom to me, and in a way, I guess he knew enough with first-hand experience to do just that. "But that's not always a bad thing. Maybe you all go and watch from afar all night long and take what you learned back to your house to discuss and open communication up further with afterward."

"Or." I mused, knowing there was another option far more likely given the temptation inside of those kinds of places.

"Or maybe you give yourselves the freedom to explore the fantasies you didn't even know you had until the buffet of desire is laid out in front of you." He smirked knowingly, "My only piece of advice is to set clear and firm boundaries before you walk in, about what you're individually comfortable with as well as what you'd like to explore as a throuple. If you do that, then you can only learn from it positively."

"Yeah," I looked back down at the invitation as my head swam with all the possibilities the night could bring. "I'll think about it."

"Good." He nodded and backed up toward the open garage bay. "Reach out if you have questions." He winked, "Maybe we'll see you there."

"I hope not." I joked, "The last thing I need to see is Trey's naked ass running around."

Dallin tipped his head back and laughed boisterously, "I'll see you around."

"Thanks." I held the invite up and watched him get onto his bike in the parking lot and then ride off.

If I thought I was distracted beforehand, Dallin's surprise visit completely surpassed it.

Never mind the raging hard-on I was sporting from imagining all the new things Hannah and Knox could learn in a place like that. The object of my fantasy pulled into the parking lot a minute later, jumping out of the tow truck and coming inside. "Was that D leaving?"

"Yeah," I nodded, staring at him in thought.

"What?" He squinted speculatively. "I don't think I like that look."

"Shut the door." I motioned to the overhead door and turned toward the staircase.

"What?" He scoffed, "Why?"

"Shut the door." I looked at him directly. "Lock it. And put the closed sign over the window." I took my shirt off over my head and started up the stairs.

"Unless, of course, you don't want to hear about the kink party he just invited us to."

"Oh, fuck." He sprinted into motion, hitting the button for the door and then locking it, turning off the lights as he ran back across the shop.

It may have been the middle of the day, but I needed to satisfy the urges I was having. Being the boss of the garage meant I could close in the middle of the day for sex if I wanted to.

Knox ran up the stairs two at a time and slammed the door shut behind him, panting as I adjusted my cock through my jeans, palming it as he watched. "Details." He demanded hungrily.

"Dallin got us an invitation to Sinner's Soiree this weekend. It's a kink party, the biggest one of the year."

"We're going?" He raised a brow, "Why exactly?"

"The goal for going could be many things. It could be to watch and see what we're into, and what we're not."

"Or." He growled, taking a step closer.

"Or it could be to let our sweet little Hannah free to play with another woman or two."

He moved in and crowded me into the desk, "You're going to take Hannah to a kink party and let those predators free on her?"

"No." I grabbed him and flipped him around so he was the one pinned to the desk. "We're taking her to the kink party and we're going to help her find a woman that excites her and makes her feel comfortable enough to want to fuck her." I kissed him, knowing he was just as excited by the prospect of it all as I was. I was the kinky one out of our group, but he was always down to add some flavor to our life. "And then we're going to sit back and watch our girl have her first girl-on-girl experience, so she can see if she really wants it or not."

"I thought she wanted Lex," Knox growled and thrust his hips into mine. "I thought that was the end goal, even if it meant we never touched her."

"It is." I admitted, "But Hannah needs to decide what she wants more, Lex all by herself, or a female partner for all of us." I slid my hand between us and stroked his hard cock where it grew down the leg of his jeans. "Besides, I'm not convinced that word won't make it to Lex that we're going to be at the party in the first place. Considering Dallin is the one who meddled with our love life to begin with."

I bit his neck and opened his jeans.

"You like that idea, don't you?" He moaned when I got to his cock. "You want Lex to be there."

"Fuck yes," Fisting his cock I stroked him, aching to make him lose his mind over it all. "I want her to realize what she's missing out on and save Hannah from being touched by anyone else." I kissed him again and then paused, "I want Hannah's first girl-on-girl to be with Lex. I *need* to see them together, even if I can't stand her personally."

He chuckled and then pushed me backward into the office chair conveniently behind me and opened my jeans and freed my aching cock before falling to his knees at my feet. "You know what I want to see?" He teased, grabbing my cock and licking the tip.

"Hmm?" I moaned, unable to form words as he spit on the head and then stroked his palm up and down it.

"I want to see Lex, fucking Hannah, and all the while dominating you." His eyelids drooped as he sucked my cock into his mouth, teasing it before letting it pop free again, "And I'd be happy to sit in the corner with a raging hard-on, never to get pleasure again, if it meant I saw you bottom for someone else besides me."

"Won't happen." I wrapped my hand around the back of his neck and pulled him down onto my cock again, making him gag. "You're the only person in the world to control me, and even that's rare these days."

"Lies." He hissed, baring his teeth and threatening me until I let go of his neck so he could look up at me while using both of his hands on my thick cock. "You think you're in control of everything all the time." He pulled my jeans down and ripped them off, pushing my knees apart so he could get to my balls and taint, "But you're about to let someone else fuck our girl because she asked you with her pretty pouty lips and fluttering eyelashes while she rode your cock."

I grunted and clenched my teeth at his accusation, but he kept going.

"You're just a simp, willing to do anything to keep our girl happy, even if that means letting someone else touch her."

"Fuck you," I growled, but he didn't reply because he went back to sucking my cock, and I didn't fucking care about anything else. "That's it," I thrust up into his mouth, desperate to relieve the ache in my balls. "I need you, Knox." I groaned, pushing him back and standing up.

"Desperate for it, are you?" He smirked before kicking his boots and jeans off and pulling his shirt up over his head, giving me the full view of his naked body. He knew I was just as obsessed with him as I was with Hannah, there was no competition there, we just didn't indulge as often as we used to because we got complacent.

But no longer. I learned my lesson recently with Hannah's changes in tastes; I would not neglect Knox's needs too.

"You know I'm always desperate for you," I kissed him, stroking his cock and backing him up to the leather couch, pushing him down into it. "How do you want to take me?"

"Just like this," He knelt on the couch and spread his legs, presenting his perfect ass. "I want it hard, Brody." He groaned as I grabbed a bottle of lube from the toiletry bag we kept in our attached office bathroom. Some days, the urge struck even while we were at work and we needed to be prepared. "Fuck me like you used to."

"You mean back when you were obsessed with me." I coated my cock and then started lubing up his ass, pushing my fingers in as I worked it deep. "Before you forgot all about how desperate you were for me to fuck you that first time."

"I'm always desperate for this." He moaned, reaching underneath himself to stroke his cock. "You wouldn't be a good boyfriend if you didn't know that."

With a growl, I pushed deep into him. "I'm the best fucking boyfriend, I give you whatever you want, whenever you want it." I kept going until I was completely inside of him and sighed at how badly I wanted to just rail him into the couch. But I wasn't heartless, and my cock was too big to be rough right away. "I gave you Hannah when you decided you wanted her, even after

I told you I was interested." I pulled out and slowly pushed back in, grabbing the front of his throat to pull him up against my chest as I bottomed back out. "I laid next to her and distracted her from the pain the first time you pushed your long fucking cock into her, taking her virginity." Thrust.

"And then I took yours, too." He growled, throwing it back onto my cock when I pulled out. "God, I remember it like it was yesterday, too."

"Tell me." I let go of his neck but wrapped one arm over his shoulder and around to his side, so he had to stay close. I wanted him so close as I fucked him.

"You'd been fucking me raw for days." He scoffed and moaned when I rolled my hips, "As soon as you got a taste for it, you couldn't stop."

"I was addicted to making you come undone."

"Fuck." He groaned and pushed on, "Hannah helped prep your ass for that first time. The same way she helped me get ready to take your fat cock. She was so fucking perfect, waiting her turn for us."

"She still is fucking perfect." I mused, grabbing onto his cock and stroking it as I kept fucking his ass.

He gasped and started thrusting his own hips, pushing his cock through my hand and then backing up onto me in fevered need. "You bent over just like this the first time." He moaned and kept going. "Right in the center of my bed for me like such a good boy." He teased, and I slammed in hard, making him gasp as he kept going. "You begged so perfectly, too. I worked you up for hours before I finally gave it to you."

"I was nearly cross-eyed with need." I remembered how desperately he made me beg that night.

"God," He moaned, remembering too, "Hannah crawled under your body and took your cock while I gave you mine. She was fucking wild that night. It was the first time we'd all had sex at the same time and then we never stopped."

"Not until recently." I shamefully admitted. "I didn't realize how badly I missed feeling you both at the same time until she took us both the other night."

"She's perfect for us."

"And that's why I'm going to do whatever it takes to give her what she wants." I slammed into him repeatedly as we both chased ecstasy. "We have to. She'll never leave us, but she'll never be fully happy if we don't."

"I know." He grunted, fighting my hold and bending at the waist to rest his forehead on the back of the couch. "I'm desperate to give it to her. I want it as well, though."

"A woman?"

"Yes," He cried, "I know that's fucked up, but I want to fuck another woman with Hannah. With you."

"Me too."

I slammed into him as his admission forced my balls to pulse and pump come into his ass, but he held off.

I barely stopped thrusting when he pulled off my cock and pushed me down onto the couch, straddling my waist while he stroked his cock. "Yes." He moaned, tipping his head back when I crouched down and took him into my mouth, swallowing him as he started coming. "Fuck, yes!"

I sucked him down and watched his whole body jerk and twitch from coming so hard as he fell onto the couch beside me, panting and gasping for air.

"I hate you." He teased, peeking at me from one eye. "I wanted to cover you with my come."

"I know." I slapped my hand down on his bare thigh and then teased one of his balls, making him jump in agony because of their post-nut sensitivity. "But I didn't want to be sticky the rest of the day." I leaned over his face and kissed him, dominating him with my mouth. "And I make the rules of where the come goes around here. Not you."

"Fucker." He cursed as I stood up and walked to the bathroom.

"What do you say we surprise Hannah at work and go for a ride?"

"All of us?" He questioned, standing up to follow me. "I don't remember the last time we just went for a ride like that."

"That's the point," I smirked, running water and getting cleaned up.

"Hmm," He hummed, pushing me aside to get a cloth wet. "Regardless of what happens with or without Lex, maybe she wasn't the worst thing to happen to our relationship after all."

"Only time will tell."

Chapter 12 – Hannah

The red stain that I painted on my lips reminded me of her.

Lex.

I picked it out because of that, but I wouldn't admit it out loud. The guys didn't care; they kept trying to reassure me they didn't hold my obsession with her against me. Even Brody, and that was proving the power of a good fucking helping in my case. She intrigued him, and that excited me.

But tonight wasn't about her. Tonight was about me.

About the guys.

About seeing if I was really as into women as I thought I was. I spent the last few days searching lesbian porn like my life depended on it, hoping for a sign.

And all I seemed to get out of it was an incredibly high sex drive and then a tender pussy after Knox or Brody answered my pleas to be pleasured.

I was into women. Sexually, I was aroused by them, especially in sensual and erotic scenes like the ones I'd found on a few high-class sites. It wasn't raunchy or cringy. It wasn't even over the top.

It was passionate.

It was erogenous.

And I wanted that more than anything else I could remember in my recent adult life. I wanted to feel the softness of a woman's touch on my body. I craved it.

I craved seeing the guys witness that moment and then join in, giving me that mix of masculinity I ached for when I imagined sex with a woman. I wanted both.

And I guess that's what helped me realize I was bisexual. Or at least into the femininity of sex.

So tonight, I would put it to the test.

I had to know if another woman could live up to the fantasies I'd crafted in my head of Lex and the guys together with me. I had to put up, or shut up, because living in this perpetual limbo was killing me.

It was bringing me and the guys closer in ways. Physically, one or both of them had been inside of my body at every waking moment the last week. Last night, I even woke up to Knox licking my sore clit with a dirty little grin on his face while Brody fucked him from the end of the bed.

We were all ravenous. I felt starved of something I'd never tasted, but could think of nothing else.

So we were going to a house party in the hills. The group hosting it was called Sinners. It was a lifestyle club, featuring a plethora of attributes including memberships, discretion, and a never-ending pool of willing candidates to play with.

Thanks to Dallin and Reyna's connection with the founding members, we received an exclusive invite to their biggest party of the season. I didn't ask questions when Knox presented me with the thick black cardstock invite yesterday. I simply looked at him and felt settled in the finality of it all.

We were going to play.

I'd never been to anything like it before, and I should have been nervous. But I wasn't, I was voracious for the opportunity laying at my feet.

The guys were humming with an energy I'd never seen before, either. It was as if they morphed into dark and dangerous monsters of the night, waiting and watching to make their move on some unsuspecting soul. They were predators, and they had needs that they were going to fulfill tonight.

I squeezed my thighs together as I rubbed lotion over them one last time to make sure they were perfect.

The entire evening was going to be perfect.

"Mmh." A deep voice rumbled from behind me at the door. "My, my, my, what do we have here?" Knox teased.

I seductively looked over my shoulder and found both of my dapper men staring at me, dressed in their matching black suits and dangerous smolders. God, they were divine. I had always been attracted to their hotness, but seeing them in those suits, knowing our destination for the night, made me want to sink to my knees on the cold marble tile of the bathroom and show them just how appreciative I was for their support.

The road to the evening ahead wasn't always smooth, but we'd made it.

"A goddess." Brody ran the pad of his thumb over his bottom lip as he stared at me. "Worthy of our worship."

"Boys." I warned, tilting my head to the side as arousal and excitement buzzed inside of me from all of it. "The car will be here in less than five minutes."

"We've made you come in far less time before." Knox winked, and I nearly melted. "We brought you something." He pulled a black box out from behind his back.

"Two somethings." Brody revealed a matching one from behind him and they stood there, holding them out to me as if they weren't the best prize in the entire situation. "Pick one."

"I only get one?" I teased and walked across the floor of our large master bathroom. The slit of my dress flared open, revealing my leg as I neared them, and both of their gazes zeroed in on it.

The moment they told me where we were going, I went shopping for a gown, and as soon as I saw it in the boutique, I knew it was perfect for tonight.

It was made for me.

It was a slip dress of white satin, with gold chains for straps holding up the barely there fabric that covered my breasts in a plunging neckline. The back was wide open, pooling just above my tailbone before cascading down into a delicate flare. The slit sold me on it, though. It went clear up to the waist above my left hipbone, leaving panties impossibly irrelevant. The gold strappy heels I paired with it, and the way I left my long strawberry blonde hair down in elegant waves, made me feel electrified.

I felt like a goddess wearing it all, though I wondered what it would make me feel like when I took it off at some point in the evening.

"Pick which one you want to open first." Brody clarified, shaking his box a little in suspense.

"Are their rules to your presents?" I hesitated, feeding off of their predatory energy.

"Yes." Knox grinned wolfishly. "You must wear both, all night."

"I'm intrigued," I mused, and then pointed to Knox's first. "I want that one first."

"Good choice." Knox pulled the black ribbon off of it and opened it, revealing a silver masquerade mask that would cover my eyes and nose. It was encrusted with shimmering stones and glitter, shaped in a bold cat eye that I knew would accentuate the dark eye makeup I spent hours perfecting.

"It's beautiful." I whispered in awe. They said we would wear masks, as many others would be, but hadn't asked for details on them since the guys took responsibility for everything outside of my dress and heels for the night.

"My turn." Brody leered at me, and goosebumps rose across my skin, making my nipples harden to painful peeks from the threat in his voice alone. The dress was so thin, I knew they could see the evidence of his words, but I didn't care, because tonight I wasn't Hannah Kate; journalist, girlfriend or daughter to powerful men.

Tonight, I was Hannah, the recently revolutionized sex goddess.

"Should I be scared?" I asked, raising one brow at him, already knowing the answer.

"Probably." He licked his lips as he pulled the ribbon free. "But you'll be too busy to notice."

As he opened the box, he revealed a black silicone toy. Though to be honest, I had no idea what it was for exactly, other than recognizing it to be for sex.

"Care to elaborate?" I reached for the toy, and then shrieked as Brody snapped the lid shut, nearly catching my fingers.

"Be a good girl and do what you're told, and maybe we'll show you instead of tell you." He enticed.

"I'll be your good girl," I played along, giving him a flutter of my eyelashes before winking at Knox, who watched on hungrily. "Or I can be your slut. Tell me what you want."

"Turn around." Knox nodded before sliding his fingers over my hip and turning me away from them. "Grab onto the stool."

My vanity stool was low, and my blood raced through my body as excitement bloomed.

"Spread your legs as you bend baby," Brody hummed.

"Yes, Sir." I teased, slowly taking a step to widen my feet before gracefully bending at the waist with straight legs until my hands were flat on the seat. I looked over my shoulder at them, "Like this?"

"Perfect." Knox growled, sliding his hand through the slit at my hip that gaped open in this position and flicked my dress over my other side, baring my entire bottom to their hungry eyes. "So fucking perfect."

"Spread your legs further, darling." Brody put his foot against the inside of my right one and pushed, forcing me to widen my stance even more, which arched my back and pushed my ass higher into the air. "Perfect."

"Now what are you going to do to me?" I looked back down at the stool and felt one of them sink to their knees behind me. I could smell my arousal in this position and the cool air made the wetness that had already formed on my pussy tingle and stimulate me further.

"Patience, baby." Knox said from his knees, and I moaned as the deep timber of his voice vibrated against my aching clit, milliseconds before his tongue swept across it. "We need to make sure you're nice and wet for our present."

"I'm wet." I panted, lightheaded, as he grabbed onto my hips and buried his face against my pussy. "Oh, my god." I moaned.

Brody chuckled and moved to my side, running his hand over the swell of my ass like he was holding me still for his best friend to feast. "Tonight we're far more sinful than that."

Knox pushed his tongue into me and twirled it how I liked and then pulled back, blowing on my clit before giving it a gentle love tap. "You taste like us, yet I know you're wet for someone else." He growled, tempting me to go down that mental hole I wanted to avoid. "But I'll forgive you for it the second I see you touch a woman for me tonight."

"Knox." I moaned, rolling my hips and then freezing as something cold slid through my wetness. "Oh god." I hissed as Brody coated the toy with it and then started pushing it into me. It wasn't that big in reality, but it wasn't their bodies either, and the sensation of it all made it feel over the top. It was phallic shaped, with a tail at the end that seemed to stay outside of my body, based on the way it lingered against my lips.

A sharp slap of a palm resounded through the room before the sting of the motion registered in my brain. I gasped and lurched forward before Knox's firm hold on me pulled me back and Brody replied, "I already told you, tonight you're far from holy. If you want to praise someone, praise the devil, because everything you do tonight will be downright wicked."

"And perfect." Knox added, kissing my ass cheek over the sting from Brody's slap before sliding the cool satin of my dress back over my ass and standing up. "All done."

"That's it?" I whined, rocking my hips, testing out the feel of the toy and wondering what exactly I was supposed to enjoy about its presence inside of me.

"Not quite." Brody chuckled and then an electric pulse of pleasure shot through my body as the toy started vibrating inside of me.

"Oh my g—" I gasped, stopping short of using the lord's name again, considering the sting still lingering on my ass from the last time. "Fuck!" I gasped, turning off my filter and used the dirty words he wanted. "Fuck, fuck, fuck." I moaned, standing upright and letting my head loll to the side.

But as quick as it came on, the toy stopped and I whipped around to face my men, who were enjoying the show if the thickness bulging the front of both their pants were any sign.

"You're going to have to earn your pleasures tonight, Darling." Brody noted, as Knox brushed the backs of his fingers over my hard nipples through my dress. "Every single touch." Brody clarified as Knox teasingly pulled away, before leaning in against my face, "Every single kiss."

"Brody." I whined, tightening my fists on his lapels, desperate for him to understand the hunger he was building inside of me with his invisible control.

"Every single orgasm." He finished and then stepped backward. "Our car is here. It's time to leave."

"Damnit! I'm going to make both of you throb so hard this evening, I wouldn't be surprised if one of you ends up coming in your pants," I said, huffing and then grinning at them. "You don't know what you've just started, boys." I shook my head slowly.

Knox pressed his forehead to mine, brushing his fingers through the slit in my skirt and then, with the lightest touch ever, circled my swollen clit until I whimpered for him. "The only place I'm coming tonight is in one of your holes." He warned, and I melted with excitement. "Your behavior determines which one."

"I'll be good." I whispered. "But just for you."

Brody growled from beside us, hearing my attempt at pitting them against each other. "If you're not, you won't be coming at all." He warned and then held his arm out to lead me to the car like he was a proper gentleman and not some sexual deviant that told me to worship the devil tonight while we hopefully found someone else to fuck.

"Yes, Sir." I hummed, high on the excitement of it all.

Chapter 13 – Lex

The masked man at the door looked at my invite and then moved aside. He was as tall as he was wide, and impressively intimidating.

Exactly what a party like this needed as the face at the front door to keep things safe. Well, what we could see of his face, anyway. I didn't wear a mask, fuck anonymity, I didn't need it.

I was recognizable by my ink alone, add in my bold red dress and I was a standout. Which may or may not have been the point. I wanted to be seen; I wanted to be noticed, at least by one person, preferably three.

Two days ago, Parker told me in the middle of a conversation like it was the most casual thing in the world, that Dallin had gotten Hannah and her guys an invitation to tonight's event.

The Sinner's Soiree.

A blood red inferno ignited inside of me as I imagined *my* sweet, innocent Hannah in a place like that, ripe and ready for the taking.

What the fuck were Brody and Knox thinking by allowing it? Didn't they understand that men and women alike would hunt her fresh scent like sharks in the water? Desperate to feed on her innocence and take all she had to offer.

Stupid imbeciles.

I couldn't understand what they hoped to gain from attending. And that was why I showed up.

For no other reason.

As I moved through the crowd, eyes roved over my curves, fully on display yet just out of reach. I loved a good game of cat and mouse.

My dress was inspired by Jessica Rabbit's; it was vibrant red with a high slit and the strapless bodice barely covered my tits. My dark hair was smooth and long down my back, skimming across the top of my ass with each step.

It all oozed sex appeal, but I had no plans to take anyone home tonight.

As I made my way through each room, I found myself drawn in by the spectacles and allure of it all. Party goers partook in sex at every turn, across every available surface. Some even suspended midair in a rope rigging meant to keep the participant immobilized and open for others to enjoy.

It was erotic, and simply being in the presence of it all made me hum with need. I wondered what Hannah thought of it all. What would it all look like through her eyes?

Would she be so incredibly overwhelmed by it? Or would a part of her settle with the excitement like she belonged amongst it the whole time?

I ached to know.

I scanned every room, waiting to glimpse her perfection. She was near; I could sense her.

Feel her.

I just had to find her.

"Come here, little rabbit." I whispered to myself as the thrill of the hunt excited me.

It took about ten more minutes of searching before I spotted the warm glow of the lights reflected off her strawberry blonde hair. She was in the casino room, seated at a poker table surrounded by other guests as she cheered and giggled. I stopped along the edge of the room and watched her, tipping her head back and laughing as she played hand after hand.

She deserved to be on the big screen with her larger-than-life happiness at that moment. Her energy was so captivating that she reminded me of Audrey Hepburn, attracting everyone around her. She was magnificent. Not even her two brooding, dark bodyguards behind her could scare off her admirers.

One admirer in particular, I'd rather wring by the neck than allow Hannah to be in her presence for a moment longer.

Sydney Jones.

The woman who single-handedly taught me how to blacken my soul to excite hers.

The worst villain there ever was.

And she was sitting directly next to Hannah, who did not know how much danger she was in from simply breathing in the same air as the viperous woman.

Sydney was a socialite with a trust fund big enough to buy her all the toys and entertainment she desired. And once upon a time, I thought that money was something worth losing myself for.

Wrong.

And I'd be damned if I let Hannah fall victim to her slimy games.

My stilettos carried me across the room like they were walking down the runway of Milan's most esteemed fashion show. I didn't care for the attention my walk garnered me, because I moved with one end goal in mind.

Remove Hannah from the disaster she was headed full steam ahead into. Before I made it halfway, Sydney leaned over and whispered something in Hannah's ear, pressing her chest against Hannah's arm in a classic seductive move. My teeth clenched as Hannah tipped her head back and laughed, gaining even more eyes as her melodic call drew them all in.

Brody clocked me first, twenty feet from the table, and he stiffened where he stood behind Hannah. Knox wasn't far behind him, though he didn't look as menacing as he stared at me.

Fire burned in my belly as I held both of their stares momentarily before ignoring them completely as I reached the table. There were two other players, besides Hannah and Sydney, which left one seat open on the end, two down from Hannah.

Perfect.

"Good evening, fellas." I winked at the two towering men, drawing a glare and a smirk from them as I pulled the chair out. I felt Hannah's eyes on me, as I gracefully slid into the chair, setting my glass of champagne onto the felt tabletop. "Deal me in, please."

"Lex." Hannah's breathy voice carried across the space like a gentle caress, and I fought the urge to close my eyes and bask in it for just a moment. I didn't know how, but I'd bet my paycheck that her touch in the bedroom felt just like that. Soft. Gentle. Provocative. "What are you doing here?"

I finally turned to her, looking around the old simp seated between us who glanced back and forth like he was eating the entire conversation up with a spoon, and let my eyes travel over her done up face and hair, down to the plunging neckline hardly covering her perky breasts.

They were the kind of breasts that I always fell victim to.

"I could ask you the same thing." Raising a brow at her boldly, I laid down chips for the dealer, "I wouldn't have pegged you for a life-styler." I didn't use her name, given she had a mask on to withhold her identity, but I would if it would make her leave this place and never look back.

She swallowed, bristling lightly at my smart tone, before taking a large sip of her champagne.

Knox cleared his throat and came to my side, leaning down to my ear. "A word?"

"Not now, sweetie." I patted his cheek patronizingly, "The women are busy here." I grabbed my nearly empty glass and finished it before passing it to him. "But be a gem and get me a refill, would you?" I winked at him over my shoulder and had a vivid image flash through my mind as his blue eyes stared down at me.

An image of him looking up at me from his back in the center of my bed as I rode him like a prize-winning bull rider with my hand around his throat and his hands on my hips, lifting me on and off his cock.

Jesus' fuck.

The thought nearly pulled me out of the world class bitch headspace I had fallen into upon seeing Sydney with her talons in Hannah from across the room. But not quite.

I blinked it away and looked from the admittedly sexy man and turned my attention back to the card game as the dealer began laying cards out on the table.

"How do you all know each other?" Sydney asked with that velvety smooth voice that reminded me of a phone sex operator, while picking up her cards like she didn't have a care in the world.

But I knew better.

"The same way I know you, Sydney." I replied before Hannah did, glancing away from my cards as she looked over at me. "Though the roles you and I played are reversed here with this darling."

Her jaw clenched, and Hannah's lips parted in confusion. Brody nudged her shoulder, breaking her distraction as she started picking up her cards. But the entire time, he glared at me.

I wanted to flip him off. It was my first urge, yet again with that man, though I refrained. Barely.

The game started progressing, as the other two players, middle-aged men who were probably used to controlling a table, tried offering small talk to the ladies. But we had no desire to include them.

This table was only fit for the three of us.

Ruled by the three of us.

Soon to be two, if I had any say in it.

"Another." I tossed a card down and took a new one from the dealer.

I should have known better to think that Sydney would remain silent for long, "If I remember correctly, you always were terrible at poker, Alexi." She smiled down at her cards, using my full name like she had a right to as I tracked her out of my peripherals. "I could always read you like a book."

"I didn't think you knew how to read at all." I snapped back instantly, and Hannah choked on her drink as Knox laid a fresh one down for her before setting one down at my side. Looking up at him over my shoulder, I winked at him. "Thank you, Sugar."

He surprised me by grinning down at me with a look made for a playboy and nodding. "Anything for you."

I lifted the glass to my lips, hesitating briefly as I watched him take his place next to Brody. I wouldn't put it past him to poison me for all the drama over the last few weeks, but I drank it anyway.

It wouldn't be as if I didn't earn every drip of toxins they put into my drink if they did.

The round went quickly, with me winning and Sydney losing a large amount of money in the process.

Double win.

The other men at the table read it correctly and left before three of the sexiest women in the room could emasculate them any further, acting as if they didn't exist at all.

Brody and Knox took their seats, with Knox between me and Hannah and Brody on the other side of Sydney. I leaned over to Knox and whispered, "Oh, come on, why didn't you put him down here?"

He smirked as he ran his fingers up and down Hannah's neck as he leaned back in his chair before answering me. "Because I'm a much bigger fan of you than he is."

"Are you?" I raised my brows at him and then over to Hannah, who stared at us both with her mouth open like she couldn't quite believe what she was hearing. Before I could pull her into our conversation, effectively shutting Sydney and the neanderthal at the other end of the table out completely, Hannah gasped and her grip on her cards tightened until her knuckles were white. "Are you alright?" I questioned with concern.

"Yeah, baby?" Knox asked with a certain darkness to his tone, "Feeling okay?"

Her lips tightened as she glared at Knox before her eyelids fluttered closed and a red flush grew over her porcelain skin. It started on her chest, tucked between her breasts, and crawled up her neck to her face.

"Perfect." She whispered, opening her eyes, and turning her attention back to that harlot Sydney. "Continue telling me about your gala." Hannah said in a respectable voice when just seconds ago she looked as if she was about to—.

Wait a second.

I flicked my gaze to Brody, who was staring directly at me with his impenetrable stare as he brought his right hand up from his lap to rest on the tabletop. Tucked inside of his large palm was something silver, catching the light just enough for me to notice.

Dirty bastard.

I watched Hannah, while signaling for another card, without even caring what I had in my hand. Would I potentially lose three hundred dollars for being so reckless, yes. Would I potentially see something I'd only dreamed about if I kept my eyes on her, also yes.

Worth it.

"Tell me something, Lex," Knox leaned back over to me, even as Hannah side eyed our conversation while pretending to pay attention to whatever Sydney was prattling on about, but I knew better than to think she was listening to her. I knew her better. "In all of that time you spent twisting Hannah up all alone in your suite," He leaned even closer so only I could hear him, "Did you ever get to witness her orgasming?" He clicked his tongue before running it over his lips and humming. "It's hands down my favorite sight in the entire world. She orgasms with her entire soul." He turned his face, so it was only mere inches away from my ear, "Every single time."

Now it was my turn to white knuckle my cards as his words acted like molten lava on their way straight to my clit. When was the last time I thought anything that a man said was sexy? But that man, talking about that woman, had me melting in my chair.

And he fucking knew it.

"I can't say as I had the pleasure, Knox." Our noses nearly brushed as I turned my face towards his. "If you hadn't interrupted us at dinner, or if your yeti of a boyfriend hadn't been in the parking lot, I would have gotten that privilege." I licked my lips and his eyes flicked down, monitoring the motion. "But I assure you, if I had made your girl come, she wouldn't have been coming back to your bed anytime soon. She would have been hooked."

"She is." He replied, "Even without you ever touching her." He leaned back in his chair and slowly shook his head as he lifted a glass of brown liquor to his lips and took a sip. "And that has me absolutely feral."

Hannah turned to look at him head on, having heard his last sentence without context, before looking at me. I couldn't look away from her perfect green eyes as they stared at me. I didn't want to. I wanted to lose myself in them and never come up for air.

I wanted her so fucking bad I was willing to do just about anything to get a taste.

"So Knox," Sydney interrupted, making Hannah blink rapidly and lean back so the snake could talk to Knox around her, which pissed me off even more as I watched Hannah's long eyelashes flutter and her lips part as Brody once again adjusted something on the tiny controller in his hand.

They were playing with her, right in front of me and getting off on it. Bastards. Yet the idea of them enjoying her pleasures and allowing me to witness them made me feel something I wasn't familiar with. Something more animalistic.

Carnal, even.

I wanted to make her come. I wanted to give her pleasure she'd never experienced before as they watched, even though the idea of men watching me in any other situation gave me the ick. Why was it so different with them? What was so different about them?

Hannah's hand dropped to Knox's thigh and her nails dug in as Brody did another change and I wondered what the toy was doing currently to her that she enjoyed so much. It was obviously a wearable vibrator, something I owned more than a few of, and I knew how good they could feel. Especially when someone else was in control.

"This game is getting boring." I said, cutting off whatever dull conversation Sydney had been trying to pull Knox into. I flicked my cards down on the table, winning yet another round and turning in my chair to face Hannah on headfirst. "Let's up the ante, shall we?"

Hannah raised her brows and then squared her shoulders, "What did you have in mind?" Her toy was making her bold, or maybe it was just her need to come that steeled her spine. Either way, I was desperate for more of it.

"What you came here for tonight." I stated, not uttering it out loud to embarrass her, "If I win, I get that prize."

Her pupils dilated and her chest rose and fell faster as she chewed on that perfectly red lip while she contemplated it. She came here for exploration, of some sort, I was sure. And I couldn't stomach the idea of someone else doing that exploring with her. Especially not someone like Sydney.

"Ooh, I want in." The scheming cunt next to Hannah threw out, raising a brow at me. "It doesn't take a rocket scientist to put the pieces together enough to figure out what you're talking about."

"Fuck off." I rolled my eyes at her and turned my attention back to Hannah. "What do you say?"

Hannah glanced at Knox and then Brody, who both just stared back at her, but I knew there was a full ass conversation happening between the three of them with just the look in their eyes alone. They were way too in sync to not have that connection.

"What do I get if I win?" As she leaned back in her chair and crossed her legs, Hannah's movement caused her white silky dress to part, revealing a tiniest sliver of soft, smooth skin peeking out at her hip. I wanted to see more as she revealed it to me, but the table was in the way.

It wasn't in the way for fucking Sydney Jones though, who didn't even try to hide the fact that she was staring intimately at Hannah's body. She always was a sucker for women wearing no panties.

"What do you want?" I challenged, keeping her attention on me, "I named my price. Name yours."

"Yes, please. Name your price, and it's yours." Sydney added, like she was even part of the conversation. I bared my teeth at her in a snarl, winning an amused grin from Brody and a warning pat on my thigh from Knox.

"Down girl." Knox warned, and I tried to ignore the way my skin tingled where his palm rested on my thigh.

I didn't miss the way Hannah zeroed in on the contact or the way she swallowed audibly, watching it.

Was this girl into the idea of her men touching other women? Couldn't be.

Knox and Brody disliked me, that was obvious from day one when Knox essentially told me to fuck off with telepathy. So why did she look like she was quickly losing her hold on her composure the longer his hand rested on my leg? Was she jealous?

"When I win," She lifted her eyes to mine and stared deep into my soul, "I'll name the price then."

"Deal." I held my hand out, not even caring what her terms would be on the condition of her winning. I'd agree to anything at that moment, for two different reasons. One, because I was just desperate enough to humor her. And two, I had no intention of suddenly losing.

She looked at my hand and then surprised me by turning to Sydney, and holding out her hand to her, "Deal?"

Sydney's overdone face rose into a cheshire grin as she seductively took Hannah's hand and shook it. "Deal."

"Cunt." I growled under my breath and Knox squeezed my thigh, dragging my attention back to him.

"Don't fucking lose this hand, Lex." He warned firmly, and I was taken aback by the intensity in his eyes. "Or she'll fuck that woman just to spite you."

My blood raged so powerfully at the image of Hannah giving herself to Sydney just to piss me off, that I could hear nothing else but the swoosh in my ears as Hannah turned back to me with a powerful look on her face and held her hand out to me.

I examined it, as if it was tainted because Sydney had touched it, but I placed my palm into hers, reveling in the electricity that shot through it from the contact. "Deal." She smiled sweetly at me and then withdrew her hand all too soon. "Well, come on now," She tapped her knuckles against the tabletop as the dealer started shuffling cards again. "Let's play."

Chapter 14 – Knox

If that woman next to Brody won, I was throwing Hannah over my shoulder and carrying her out of there immediately. Not a fucking chance she was getting her hands on my girl.

There was only one woman at the party that was going to be Hannah's first. And my hand was warming her thigh underneath of the table. Thank god her Jessica Rabbit look alike dress had a slit on her other leg, otherwise I would have been tempted to let my fingers wander.

When was the last time I wanted to explore anyone aside from Brody or Hannah? Tenth grade? Jesus, the last time I had sex with anyone else, I was still a minor.

Unreal.

Yet, there I was. Silently praying with every single card flip, Lex would win the game. I needed it to be her who won Hannah's affection, because I couldn't count on Hannah to make the right choice and choose Lex.

She was trying to be brave and act like she wasn't all twisted up over the sexy, over the top woman, but Brody and I knew the truth. And if the way Brody's hand was mashing buttons on that controller was any sign, he was trying like hell to help Lex's odds.

He wouldn't admit it out loud, but he didn't want Sydney anywhere near Hannah either.

He also wouldn't admit that he was rock hard under the table from being so fucking close to seeing Hannah and Lex together, after all the ups and downs over the last two weeks.

"Another." Sydney waved for another card and grinned when she read it.

I could see Hannah's hand, and she had fucking shit for cards. And a shittier poker face, even without the toy, edging her closer to orgasm every minute. But at the moment, she was a lost fucking cause.

She didn't even have a pair of twos.

I looked Lex's way, but her cards were face down, as she bent back just the smallest corner to read them as the dealer kept dealing. Her expression was blank as she called for another and then discarded one.

I didn't know the fate of my girlfriend's night, and that put me on edge.

"I see your bet for our lovely Hannah here, and I'll raise you." Sydney cut in, looking past Hannah, directly at Lex.

"Not interested in anything you have to wager." Lex said without turning in her direction.

"Oh come one Lexie," Sydney teased, using a name I was sure no one got away with easily, "You used to love taking chances."

"What is it?" Hannah questioned, before looking at Lex. "Aren't you the least bit curious?"

Lex picked up my glass of bourbon and took a sip, staring off into the distance, "I learned a long time ago to take nothing that woman has to say at face value."

"You two were lovers?" Hannah mused, and Brody raised a brow at me as we both continued to stay silent and let the girls have their fun. We decided before we even told Hannah about the invite tonight that we would be at her side all night long, but she called the shots. And apparently, she was feeling bold in that decision.

"Not a chance." Lex scoffed, setting my glass down empty. "She's a user and an abuser, nothing more."

"We were lovers, alright." Sydney ignored Lex and talked to Hannah like she was telling a love story from times long forgotten. "But no one can settle Lex down into anything serious. Not even me."

Hannah didn't reply, and neither did Lex, both seemed lost in their thoughts as the dealer laid down one last card and then waited for the ladies to reveal their cards.

"I got nothing." Hannah sighed and blushed as she peeked over at Lex, waiting for her to reveal her hand.

But Sydney cut in, as usual. "Full house." She laid them down, snapping one card after another as dread filled my stomach. "Tens and eights."

Hannah swallowed so loudly I could hear the gulp amongst the other rowdy noises in the room. That was a hard hand to beat, but not impossible.

We all turned to Lex, who sat back in her chair, staring at Hannah. I couldn't tell what she was thinking. Did she lose? Did she win?

"Four of a kind." She laid her cards down and fanned them out, "Queens."

"Son of a bitch." Brody cursed from the end of the table with a telltale grin on his face.

"Wow." Hannah smiled at Lex almost shyly now that the cards were literally on the table.

"Wow indeed," Sydney stood up and pushed her chair back. "A worthy opponent," She winked at Lex who just rolled her eyes and cringed like she was physically sick to be in the other woman's presence. "Have a most pleasurable evening, Hannah." She purred, pushing my girl's hair back over her shoulder. "And reach out if you should ever find yourself curious about what Lex was so obsessed with all those years ago."

With that, she turned and left the table, leaving the four of us and a very uncomfortable dealer sitting in anticipation.

"Well," Hannah cleared her throat and finished her glass of champagne before standing up from the table. "You won, fair and square."

"I did." Lex stood as well, and Brody and I followed, leaving them to it. The tension was so thick I could cut it with my rock-hard cock. "Why don't you follow me, and we'll find somewhere a little quieter." Lex flicked a glance at me and smirked, "Your bodyguards can stay here, though."

Brody scoffed, "Not a chance." He put his hand on Hannah's waist and pulled her to his side. "But nice try."

"Can't blame a girl for trying." Lex rolled her eyes and then slid her hand around my arm, pressing herself to my side. "Whatever you say, big guy. Even I have an exhibitionism kink now and then."

He glared at her, and I grinned, enjoying the hateship that was blooming between them. She led us through the crowd, clearly having been to an event before, which both intrigued me and also irritated me somehow.

It was wild walking with her and watching how people reacted to her. I had tattoos on both arms, across my chest and back, and even down one leg, but none of it showed around the cut of my suit. But Lex's dress called for everyone's attention to notice the ink and sex appeal that she dripped with every step through the place.

Men and women alike stopped mid-sentence to stare at her, enchanted by it all. One man was mid thrust into a woman tied down on all fours on a sex bench, and he faltered and then stopped to gape at her. It was bizarre and mesmerizing all in one.

"Told you." Hannah called from behind us, and I looked over my shoulder to see her eyes travel up and down Lex's body, "There's just something there."

Lex smirked but didn't give away any other indication that she heard Hannah's admiration of her appeal as we climbed the stairs. The hallways split off at the top, and Lex walked down the dark corridor until she reached an open door. She let go of my arm and stood next to the opening, staring at Hannah.

Lex warned, "Don't cross that threshold unless you're one hundred percent ready to give yourself up to me." She looked to me, and then to Brody "I have rules for you two as well."

I grinned, "Of course you do. What are they?"

"We set boundaries beforehand, and I won't tolerate any interruptions after the door closes," she said firmly, raising her finger to prevent him from objecting. "And don't you dare touch without an invitation."

"I'm always fucking invited." Brody sneered at Lex before sauntering over the threshold into the dimly lit bedroom. "Hannah is free to do whatever she wants."

"Only because Daddy said so," Lex rolled her eyes and turned back to Hannah, completely missing the look on Brody's face as he nearly swallowed his tongue at her comment.

Did he have a daddy kink? Or just a Lex kink?

Lex zeroed back in on Hannah, who stood frozen in the hallway next to me. "What do you want, Hannah?" She asked.

I watched the girl I'd known since we were kids, and loved for nearly as long, square her shoulders and stare down the very thing I knew she wanted most. Would she be brave enough to indulge?

"I want you." Hannah replied firmly and my cock twitched, hearing her say it out loud. "And I want the men I love to be at my side the first time I have you."

Lex licked her lips, overcome with the same thing I was in that moment, and then nodded to the bedroom where Brody waited, "After you, then."

Hannah walked in and I followed her, stopping in front of Lex as she took a deep breath, like she was fighting for control over her own reaction to the situation. "Do you have any idea how lucky you are right now?" I asked, not that I expected her to reply honestly.

"More than you think I do." She stepped forward until her chest brushed against my suit jacket and looked up at me. Her brown eyes were bottomless, full of warmth and excitement and I kicked myself for judging the woman so harshly the first time I met her, because even without her affirming what I already knew, her eyes said it all.

Hannah was a gift we were all unworthy of, and Lex knew it.

"Good." I fought every urge inside of me that ached to know what her lips tasted like because it wasn't about me. The entire reason we were at the party was because of Hannah, but I couldn't deny my attraction to the leggy brunette, especially when she vocalized how important the woman I loved was. What fucking paradox had I landed in that I had the woman I loved more than anything, trying to get me to want another woman with her? "Then let's teach our girl everything she wants to learn."

Lex's pupils dilated when I called Hannah ours, but in that moment, if only for that moment, she was.

Hannah was giving herself to Lex. And I couldn't wait to watch.

The dimly lit room was a fancy bedroom, with a large king sized bed and a couple of other seating options circled around it for spectators.

"Have you been in this room before?" Hannah asked where she stood at the end of the bed, running her dainty fingers across the silky bed sheets.

I took my mask off, tossing it on top of Brody's on one of the end tables before lowering myself down into a chair directly at the end of the bed.

"Do you really want the answer to that?" Lex replied, standing at the end of the bed in front of Hannah before reaching up and pushing a lock of her strawberry hair back behind her ear.

"Yes." Hannah whispered as her eyelids fluttered closed as Lex drifted her fingers over the shell of her ear. "I think I do."

"No." Lex replied, reaching behind Hannah's neck and untying her mask, removing it so there were no barriers between them. Seeing the two of them standing so close, intent on exploring each other, had me more excited sexually than I could remember being since the first time I slid deep into Hannah's body. "I don't normally come upstairs at these parties."

Hannah's chest rose and fell, pressing the limits of her skimpy dress as she stared into Lex's eyes. They were perfect opposites. Hannah, with her glowing angelic white dress even as sexy as it was, she was a goddess of pure gold. And then there was Lex, with her dark hair and tattoos, draped in red and black, and she resembled a sexy devil of temptation and risk.

And they were fucking perfect for each other, because of their differences.

"But you fuck." Hannah moaned and her head tilted back as she grabbed onto the post of the bed. "Brody." She moaned with her eyes closed. "I can't think straight."

"Exactly." He growled from his seat on the side of the bed with that fucking controller in his hand. One look at him and I could tell how close to losing control over his lust he was. He looked unhinged and feral as he stared at the girls. And they hadn't even touched yet. "Here." He tossed the controller down on the bed at Lex's side before sitting back in his chair and palming his erection as Lex stared directly at him. "You're in control right now."

Chapter 15 – Hannah

"I'm going to come." I moaned, wanting to melt into a puddle from the way Brody had edged me all night. "I need to come."

"No." Lex commanded, picking up the controller and turning the toy off before tossing it back down. "Not for him." I mewed disappointedly as I opened my eyes and all but begged for relief. "Only for me." She purred, and I almost came from that noise alone. "You heard Brody. Tonight, I'm in control."

"Lex." I whispered, aching for her.

I nearly fell out of my chair when she appeared in front of me at the poker table. As if all my fantasizing about her conjured her in real life. And my god, she was the sexiest woman I'd ever seen before.

"Shh," She pressed her finger to my lips, silencing me. "I'll make you feel so good, baby. All in good time." I groaned, fighting for control and patience as she smirked at me. "Limits. I need to know what limits you have for tonight."

I blinked, fighting through the arousal clouding my mind as I tried to come up with an answer. "Like safe words?"

"Like how far you are willing to go." She slid her fingers through my hair again, brushing just the softest caress of her fingertips across the side of my neck.

"I don't have any limits." I swallowed when her fingers danced across the front of my neck and I moaned as she gently wrapped her fingers around my throat, tilting my head to the side as she leaned over to whisper in my ear.

"I've never wanted another woman as much as I want you." Her breath tickled my ear and goosebumps erupted over my entire body. "I've never wanted to taste anyone as badly as I do you, Hannah Kate. You're intoxicating." Her lips barely brushed over the shell of my ear, and I leaned into her, putting my hands on her waist for support as I fought the urge to melt completely. "First, I'm going to taste your lips." Her breath warmed the sensitive skin of my neck directly above her thumb, where it pushed gently on my pulse point. "I've fantasized about your lips nonstop since the first time you smiled at me."

I growled an animalistic call in warning as a feeling of desperation overtook me. "Please."

"You beg so prettily." She smiled against my jaw, "I can't wait to hear you beg the first time I run my tongue over your clit."

"Fuck." I panted, blinking back tears of anguish as I nearly succumbed to my need.

"Hmm." She hummed and then brought her lips to hover directly above mine as my eyelids fluttered closed. "Such a dirty word falling from such pretty lips." Her teeth gently pulled at my bottom lip, and I moaned, desperate for more. "Say it again."

"Fuck." I repeated it, right against her lips, fighting the urge to lean in and take what I wanted most. "Like that?"

"Just like that," She smiled and then pressed her lips to mine, instantly running her tongue across them, like she was tasting me. Just like she said she would. "Mmh." She moaned, tilting her head and deepening the kiss as I held on for dear life. No one had ever kissed me with softer lips before. The smoothness of her face against mine was alluring and so different from the sharp prickle of Brody and Knox's beards. "Your lips taste like strawberries."

I mewed like a kitten as her tongue swept across mine, and then again as she bit my lip and hovered against them. "Oh, my god." I whispered in awe.

"How was that for your first kiss with a woman?" She smiled against my lips before pulling back to look at me. She kept her hand on my neck, and I kept mine on her hips.

"I don't think I've ever experienced something more erotic." I admitted, opening my eyes and staring into her smoky dark stare. "And I don't think I got enough to satisfy the thirst."

She grinned, deepening those sexy as hell dimples in her cheeks as she glanced over my shoulder. "Look at them." She spun me in her arms and pressed her body against my back as she delicately laid kisses along the side of my neck as I faced my guys. "Look at what you did to them."

There was a fire burning in both of their eyes I'd never seen before. Not once. It was magnetic and empowering as they watched her touch me. "You did that to them, not me." I replied, revealing the secret she didn't know. "You do that to everyone you meet."

She grinned as she laid kisses on my shoulder and slid one hand around my stomach, flattening it with her fingers aimed like they were going to slide down the front of my panties.

If I was wearing any.

"I want to do incredibly indecent things to you, Hannah." She moaned, giving away that she wasn't unfazed by all of it. "I want to lay you down, spread you open, and feast on you for days."

"Please." I begged as she delicately slid one strap off my shoulder. My breast was barely covered as the fabric pooled over it, and I knew if she dropped the other strap, the dress would fall to my waist, revealing my chest to her.

And I could hardly stop myself from shimmying out of it on my own as she slowly tortured me with gentle touches and seductive kisses.

"Which one of them fucks you harder?" She asked against my other ear as she laid wet kisses down my neck to my shoulder. "Which one loses control when he's inside of you?"

I knew the answer, and so did he.

"Brody." I hummed, watching his jaw tighten as she slid the other strap free. My dress slid down, hitching around my waist and revealing my aching breasts to their eyes.

"I bet he pounds your pussy so good, doesn't he?" She slowly brought her hands up my stomach and gently brushed her thumbs over my hard nipples. Just barely. The touch was light enough I almost missed it, but the way Knox cracked his neck confirmed I didn't imagine it. "And Knox," She licked a trail up my neck to my ear as she slowly twirled her fingernails over my nipples, teasing me. "I bet he's a giver, isn't he? I bet he loves getting you off."

"Yes." I moaned, arching my back and pushing my breasts into her hands more, "He always makes sure I orgasm before he even slides in."

"Mmh." She groaned, pinching my nipples firmly and pulling them, making me gasp and cry out in ecstasy. "Walk over to him." She dropped her hands from my body completely and I shivered from the cold air taking her place. I looked over my shoulder at her, confused, and my entire body tingled when I saw the arousal in her eyes. She was so turned on by this. Just like us. "Go on." She nodded toward Knox and waited for me to follow her direction.

I indulged her, giving her what she wanted because truth be told, I ached to be near them too. I wanted them a part of this experience as much as possible. Slowly, I moved toward him forward until I stood between Knox's spread feet and then turned around to look at her, waiting for my next direction.

She pulled my strings like a puppet master and I willingly let her, aching to know what she wanted next. I'd give it to her, whatever it was. I wanted to please her.

She gently ran her fingers over her bottom lip like she was contemplating her next move, and then smirked. "Knox, please remove Hannah's dress."

She didn't ask him, and he didn't seem to mind. He leaned forward and laid a hot kiss in the center of my back before gently tugging my dress over my hips until it landed in a pile at my feet. Holding my hand to steady me, he picked it up and laid it over the chair on his other side.

Then I was naked in front of another woman for the first time since the high school locker room.

And I'd had never been so turned on before.

"You're so incredibly sexy, Hannah." Lex let her eyes travel over my naked body, and I desperately wanted to touch her. To feel her skin against mine, but she made distance between us and I tried to understand why. "Sit back on his lap."

"Why?" I scowled, wondering where she was going with it.

She smirked devilishly, and my body tingled as she stared at me with a wicked glint in her eye. "Because I want you to be comfortable when I spread your legs and find out exactly what kind of toy Brody put inside that sexy little pussy of yours."

"Oh." I panted and licked my lips, glancing at Knox over my shoulder. His cock was rock hard and tented against his dress slacks, and it was no trouble at all to sit back onto it, teasing us both as I wiggled to get seated correctly. He bit my shoulder playfully, and I moaned, leaning into his familiar presence.

"Good girl." Hannah crossed her arms under her chest as she took one step forward. "Knox, spread her legs for me."

"With pleasure." He purred like a sex hungry kitten beneath me and slid his hands under my knees, lifting them and pulling them wide, exposing my most intimate parts to the woman of my dreams. I laid back against his chest, resting my head on his shoulder as she slowly stalked toward me. She was like a lioness in the Sahara, creeping toward her prey through the brush. "Sexy, isn't she?" Knox growled.

"Yes." I panted, in awe of Lex's sexual prowess as she stared directly at my pussy.

Lex chuckled and pulled the skirt of her dress open, revealing both of her deliciously long tattooed legs before sinking to her knees between Knox's feet. "He was talking to me, sweetheart." She purred as she placed both hands on my ankles and seductively ran them up the inside of my calves, then my knees, gently curling her fingertips into the skin and dragging them as she moved to my inner thighs as she stared directly into my eyes. "And yes, Hannah is hands down the sexiest woman I've ever seen before." She slowly dropped her eyes to my spread pussy and licked her lips like she was that lioness, ready to take a bite. "And this pretty little pussy matches that sexiness perfectly."

"Lex." I moaned, grabbing onto Knox's arms for leverage as she smiled back up at me.

"I want a taste." She leaned in and blew directly onto my clit and my back bowed as I fought Knox's hold on me, aching to feel her touch me there physically. "I need to taste you, Hannah." She purred, and I moaned incoherently.

She was so close, I could feel her breath on my wet center, and I thought for sure she'd lean in and do what we both desperately wanted her to do, but she didn't.

Instead, she turned and looked at Brody, where he sat silently with his hands in fists on the arms of the chair off to the side. I watched her glide into a seductive, submissive role as she lowered her eyes and pouted her lips at him. "Can I taste your girl's pussy?"

I nearly came right there, just from watching the two of them. As Brody stared down at her, I spun my head to the side to see his face. I had no idea what he would say. I didn't know what boundaries of his she was toeing, but I could tell she was on one of them. He looked like a wild animal, even without muttering a single word to her, since he told her she was in control.

He stood up, and fear bloomed in my chest as I thought he was going to walk out on us completely.

Knox tensed beneath me too, gripping my thighs in his powerful hands as we watched the man we loved more than anything, teeter on the edge of restraint and control.

But then he grabbed the chair and pulled it with him as he turned, so he was facing the three of us directly and then slowly sat back down, spreading his legs and palming his erection where it grew down his tight pant leg. I caught the way Lex's breath hitched in her throat as she watched him grip himself before she snapped her eyes back up to his.

He smirked down at her, and I felt like Knox, and I were the spectators of the show the two of them were putting on with catastrophic sexual tension. I almost begged him to fuck her right then and there, but before I could, he nodded once.

"Lick her real good." He licked his lips as he stared her down and then looked up at me. "Make my girl come."

I sagged in relief and felt myself get wetter from just watching the two of them interact. They were like two Gods in the sky, clashing against each other and creating a world ending storm in their wake.

And it was the hottest thing ever.

"Yes, Sir." Lex purred and then turned back to me. Her brown eyes locked onto mine as she slowly lowered her full lips to my body, before gently shaking her face back and forth as she sucked my clit into her mouth.

"Oh, my fucking god." I cried, arching my back as my whole body tensed from the delicious torturous pleasure she delivered with just her lips.

She chuckled and pushed my thighs wider with her hands as she pulled back so only her tongue was touching me. She grabbed the silicone neck of the toy still buried inside of me and pulled it free, leaving me feeling empty and relieved to have it free. Like I was open and eager to take her inside of me instead. She seductively pushed her tongue into my pussy, with a rhythmic roll to it that reminded me of the way a woman grinded herself in a man's lap when she was riding him. How was a tongue so sexy?

I didn't have time to figure it out because with the next roll of her tongue, her full upper lip brushed against my clit, and I exploded.

"I'm coming." I gasped, digging my nails into Knox's arms as Lex attacked my pussy, forcing the biggest orgasm of my life through my body.

Chapter 16 – Lex

Her pussy clamped down on my tongue and her sweet cream filled my tastebuds as she cried out in Knox's arms.

I'd never witnessed anything sexier in my entire life.

Hannah coming on my face was like a world wonder, made to be seen but never believed to be true because of how spectacular it was.

"Good girl." I hummed, sucking on her clit as I pushed my middle finger into her tight pussy and curled it forward. I rolled it in the come-hither motion once, and then twice. Watching her body language for the clues I needed to make sure I was on her G-spot perfectly as her orgasm rolled on and on.

"Fucking hell, baby." Knox growled, turning his face into her neck and biting it.

Knox was a biter; interesting. I locked that information away as I lessened the pressure on her pulsating clit and then pulled back enough to just tease the tip of my tongue around it in leisurely circles as she sagged into his arms.

She stared down at me through hooded eyes with such wonder as I sat back on my heels and pressed soft kisses to her inner thigh, completing the comedown sensation for her as she fought to grasp reality.

"How was that?" I asked, running my finger over the edge of my lip and then sucking it into my mouth, savoring her taste.

"I don't—" She stuttered and panted, "That was—"

"Everything." Knox answered for her, nuzzling into her neck as he let her legs down a little into a more comfortable position. "That was everything you dreamed it would be, wasn't it, baby?"

"Yes." She moaned, licking her lips and sitting upright and staring down at me. "You didn't—" She blushed slightly, and I could see her embarrassment blooming in the aftermath of it all. "You never even got undressed."

I sat up on my knees and pushed hers apart, dominating her space so I could dominate her confidence until she was begging for it again and forgetting her embarrassment altogether. She sucked in a quick breath but quickly relaxed her legs as Knox grabbed her hips and rocked her in his lap, like he was desperately trying to keep her there while also fighting his urge to fuck her wildly.

I kissed her stomach and then up to her tits, palming them both and pulling on her nipples before flicking my tongue across them. They were fucking perfect, just like in my dream. And the noises she made while I sucked on them were far better than anything I could have imagined. She gasped, and I lifted her hands, burying them into my hair so she would finally touch me. I was barely restraining from stripping down and pinning her to that bed like I knew we both wanted me to do.

But I had other plans for the rest of her night. And I didn't need to undress to see them through.

I just selfishly wanted her attention for a few more minutes. "That's it." I praised her as she tightened her fingers in my hair and pulled me tighter to her chest. "Good girl."

"Fuck." She gasped, curling around my head until I pulled back and buried my fingers into her wild hair, pulling her down to her knees in front of me on the floor.

I kissed her as if my life depended on it, tangling my tongue with hers and rocking her body against mine. However, when her hands wandered tentatively over my shoulders and towards the swell of my breasts above my dress, I pulled back and stopped her by grabbing her wrists.

Not because I didn't want to feel her explore my body, but because I knew if she started, I wouldn't have the strength to walk away without consuming her.

"Turn around." I commanded her, leading her by her wrists in my hand to spin on her knees until she almost sat in my lap between Knox's legs. Placing her hands on each of his knees, I slowed my breathing down as she took a couple of deep breaths. "You're a very lucky girl, Hannah." I pushed her hair off one side of her neck and kissed her damp skin, dragging my tongue up it as I reached around to palm her perky tits as she moaned and leaned into me. "Don't you think you should thank your guys for letting me play with your perfect little pussy?"

She panted and stared up at Knox as I looked over her shoulder at Brody. His dark brown eyes were nearly black to match his suit as he stared at me. He flicked a glance at Hannah as she mewed and moaned in my arms, then back to me, like he couldn't decide who he wanted to watch more.

And that turned me on so much. Yet I couldn't understand why.

I put my hands over hers again and slid them up the inside of Knox's thighs until they met the monstrous erection, taking up every inch of space at his crotch.

Lucky girl.

"Mmh, is his cock as big as it feels?" I purred into her ear as she massaged it under my hand. I hated dicks, but there was something about doing it with Hannah that made me want to do more than just stroke it.

"Yes." She hummed, rocking her hips in my lap as she squeezed him. "Feel." She quickly flipped her hand out from under mine and then gripped mine around his cock and squeezed so I had no choice but to feel his absolute beast of a cock in his pants. Knox cursed and flexed his hips like he was barely restraining as much as I was from saying fuck it all and giving in to what we shouldn't want. He locked his eyes on mine as we crossed lines I had no intention of going near. I was losing my control over the situation, and I never gave over control when I was having sex.

Never.

"It's so big, isn't it?" She turned so her lips were against mine while she rocked my hand up and down his length. "It feels so good stretching me open when he fucks me."

"Hannah." I growled, matching the same one that Brody made from beside us. I'd left him out of the entire show on purpose, and I could feel how mad he was because of it. "I think Brody feels left out." She looked over at him and melted from the look of desire in his eyes aimed her way. "Be a good girl and go take his cock out."

"Yes, ma'am." She moaned cheekily and then scurried out of my arms to kneel at Brody's feet as she quickly pulled his belt free.

Knox's cock twitched under my hand, reminding me I was still holding onto the anaconda and yet I was less than interested in letting go of it.

What the fuck was wrong with me?

I dragged my nails down the length of it over his pants, making him hiss and groan, drawing the attention of the other two who watched on in fascination before I removed my hand from his lap completely.

I was in charge here.

I was the boss.

He needed to be reminded of that, as much as I did. Knox licked his lips and stared hungrily at me until Hannah's moan brought us both back to reality.

I slid behind her body again, at Brody's feet to watch as she pulled his cock free from his pants.

Fucking hell.

They were both stacked.

"Tell me I'm a lucky girl again." Hannah purred seductively as she pulled his pants down his thighs to reveal every inch of him to my eyes.

I shouldn't give in to her demand, given that it was my show to run. But she deserved it after how well she listened to mine just moments ago.

"You're a very," I nipped her neck as I slid one hand around the front of her throat, pulling her body back flush to mine, and slid the other one down the front of her body to the wet place between her spread thighs, "very, lucky girl, Hannah." I pinched her clit and made her cry out as Knox leaned over to watch us play with his boyfriend, "Stroke him, baby." I purred, biting her ear while I continued to play with her body. "Thank him for letting you play with me tonight."

"Thank you, Brody." She mewed seductively as she stroked his fat cock from root to tip.

As I played her like a fiddle for both of our pleasure, his body coiled tight while he watched. I couldn't believe he kept his mouth shut the whole time, leaving me to boss his perfect little girlfriend around, but he had. And he deserved a reward for it.

"Suck his cock, Hannah." I demanded, folding her body forward into his lap as I reached under her ass and pushed two fingers into her dripping pussy. "Suck his cock like a good girl for letting you be a dirty girl."

"Mmh." She hummed as she instantly sucked him into her mouth.

What a fucking beautiful sight it was to watch her take him deep into her throat, humming and moaning with each inch that she swallowed. My pussy throbbed, desperate for some action as I fought the urge to look up at the big brute while she pleasured him. I focused on her and her pleasure as I thrusted my fingers into her, lifting her ass into the air so I had a better angle. She squealed with delight as I pushed my tongue against her asshole and slapped her clit. She gagged and Brody lost his hold on his dominating tendencies as he praised her.

"That's it, Darling." He threaded his fingers into her hair and held it out of the way as she went down onto him.

I couldn't resist any longer, I flicked my eyes up to his face and found those dark fucking bottomless pits aimed right back at me as Hannah started coming on my fingers, screaming around his cock as she gushed into my hand. I held his stare as I tongued her ass and he went feral.

He lifted his hips and shoved his entire cock into her mouth as he used her mouth for pleasure. "Good girl." I looked over at Knox and found his cock out as he stroked it in his hand, giving two fucks about what I was planning for him. "I didn't say you could do that." Cocking my head to the side as I pushed one finger into Hannah's ass, she cried out I ecstasy again before Brody pushed her head back down into his lap.

"Punish me for it." Knox held my stare and challenged my Domme tendencies as he continued to stroke his cock. The whole thing transfixed me, as my eyes fell to his lap when he leaned back, spreading his thighs so I could have a better view of it.

I was spiraling out of control.

And something told me the guys knew it.

They were tempting me, teasing me into slipping and doing something I'd never done before. I needed to finish it and get the fuck out of the room before I let them have something no man had ever gotten.

I grabbed Hannah's hand and licked it with the flat of my tongue, surprising everyone as they watched the move. I could taste Brody's saltiness on it and barely contained the lip curling snarl that ached to break free from it.

I took her wet hand and wrapped it around Knox's hard cock as he grunted and thrust up into it. I should have pulled my hand off of hers, but I couldn't.

I didn't want to. She was distracted and unable to keep two different motions going, so I assisted her. I kept my hands wrapped around hers as it glided up and down over Knox's long veined cock. The head was nearly purple as we stroked it together and he was so on edge, every vein in his neck was bulging as he stared at her swallowing Brody's cock.

"Be a good girl and give them a perfect place to blow their load." I growled into Hannah's ear, pulling my hand off Knox and helping Hannah up onto her knees before them. "Come on her tits. Both of you." I reached around her and cupped her tits up as they both stood up and stroked their cocks looking down at us. "Coat her skin and claim it as yours."

They were both on the verge of climax; I was surprised they lasted as long as they did. Knox went first, roaring as he came all over her perfect tits, just like I told him to. He gasped and panted as Hannah smiled seductively up at them, pleased with being their trophy.

Brody was a harder egg to crack as he stroked his cock roughly, glaring down at Hannah and then at me. He wanted to come, that I was sure of. But I was sure he held off simply because I had told him to do it.

"Stick your tongue out, baby." I instructed Hannah as I pulled on her nipples, coated in Knox's release. "Take big daddy Brody's come like the perfect little good girl that you are." I nibbled her ear and looked up at him out of the corner of my eye, tempting him to defy me.

"Fuck." He grunted and tipped his head back as Hannah dove in and sucked the head of his cock into her mouth, swallowing down his come as I pushed her head further. "That's it, darling. That's fucking it."

"Good girl." I peppered Hannah's shoulders and back with slow, gentle kisses as she gasped and sank back on her heels in fatigue. The poor girl had been the perfect doll to play with for the three of us, and she did it willingly. "Such a good girl."

She leaned into my touch and then turned to face me. She was a perfect dirty mess of the both of them, wearing their pleasure on her skin and lips like her award. "Kiss me." I demanded, and I knew it was exactly what she wanted, because she leaned in instantly. Pressing her lips to mine and pushing her tongue into my mouth so I had no choice but to taste Brody's release. Little did she know that was exactly what I wanted.

I kissed her until neither of us could breathe and gasped, pulling back and pressing my forehead to hers as I tried to rein myself in. She was intoxicating before I had my first taste of her, and now I'd tasted two out of the three of them and needed more.

I felt the guys' eyes on us from above, lurking and watching us still as we all came down from the events of the night, though I was the only one who hadn't come.

And tomorrow I'd use that as my excuse for my next move, but I knew it was far more animalistic than just arousal.

I lowered my lips to her nipple, sucking it into my mouth and then trailing my tongue across her chest, gathering up Knox's come as I went until I sucked her other nipple into my mouth before biting it and making her cry out in pleasure.

"Lucky girl." I smirked at her and then up at the guys as I wiped my lip with my finger before sucking it into my mouth to savor their tastes like I had after eating her out the first time. "Lucky girl indeed."

Chapter 17 – Brody

Lex left last night after testing out the taste of Knox's come directly from Hannah's tits. She just stood up, gathered her purse, combed her fingers through her hair before looking back at us, and then walked out.

Like she hadn't just rocked our entire decade long relationship in one hour. And the three of us were trapped in some perpetual limbo where we didn't know what to do or where to go from there.

It had been quiet in the house all morning, as we all worked through our own thoughts independently as we processed the events from the party the night before.

"I can't take this." Hannah sighed, sliding a cup of coffee onto the kitchen counter and taking a seat on a stool. "We *have* to discuss it."

I turned from where I was washing dishes and dried my hands on a towel as Knox set his magazine down in the living room and joined us.

"You start." I sighed, giving her the floor since this was her midlife crisis.

"Are you mad?" She asked instantly, staring directly at me.

"No." I replied honestly. "Why would you ask that?"

"Because you've been silent since we woke up." Knox sat next to Hannah at the island and rested his elbows on the countertop. "And while silence isn't anything new from you, I think right now we need to hear your thoughts."

"We?" I raised my brow at him and looked over at Hannah.

"Yes," She agreed, "We, because I know how I feel about what happened." She glanced at Knox and then back, "And I'm pretty sure I know how Knox feels about it. But you," She hesitated, "I can't read you."

"How do you feel about it?" I countered, crossing my ankles as I leaned up against the sink and tried to give off the vibe of relaxation. But to be honest, I was anything but.

"I feel like—" She chewed her bottom lip, "Like I've never felt more fulfilled than I did last night with all three of you." I steeled my face so I wouldn't give anything away. "Which scares me."

"Why?"

"Because what if I never feel that way again?" She looked at me with those huge, trusting green eyes. "What if we never find another pairing like last night that works for us so well." She swallowed and looked down at the counter. "I thought if I scratched the itch with her, I'd be able to move on and look at other women again like I did before I met Lex."

"Yet now," Knox sighed, "All you can think about is her." He nudged her shoulder, "I know the feeling, and believe me, I feel terrible for feeling that way."

"Really?" Hannah glanced his way,

"Yeah," He admitted, "Because I should be thinking of how incredibly sexy you looked last night and how erotic it was to watch someone else run the show,"

"Yet now, all you can think about is her." She repeated his words sadly. "I don't think you should feel terrible about that. I don't feel jealously over it," Her eyes widened a bit, "Unless it means you want *just* her, and not me anymore."

Knox scoffed and wrapped his arm around her shoulders, pulling her into his side, "There is no us without you. When I say I can't think about anything but her, I mean, I can't imagine doing what we did last night with anyone else in the world. That's all."

"Same." Hannah deflated even more. "Why do you think she took off the way she did?" I could see her insecurities spinning in her head as we spoke about Lex. "Do you think I wasn't—" She swallowed, "What if she didn't like it with me?"

"Stop it." I barked, drawing both of their stares. "I won't hear that kind of talk in this house. Lex does not create or determine your worth; either of you."

I commanded, and both shrunk a little as they realized I was right. "It was fun. It was exactly what we hoped it would be, and then she left, showing exactly what she wanted to get from it. She didn't stick around because she got what she came for."

"She didn't even orgasm." Hannah squinted like I was the most obtuse person in the world. "How can you believe she left satisfied?"

I walked around the counter, picked her up by her waist, and kicked the stool out from under her. It clanged off the floor across the kitchen as I set her down firmly on the counter next to Knox. Her breath hitched as I wrapped my hand around the front of her neck and held her close to my face, so she had no choice but to listen.

"How many times have I gotten you off without taking pleasure in you physically?" I questioned, glancing down at Knox, where he shrugged with a smirk, "Or you?"

"Uh—" Hannah wondered, as she licked her lips in uncertainty.

"Too many to count, actually." Knox replied. "Come to think of it, you do that a lot."

"Because that's what Dom's do." I growled, looking between the two of them. "We see to our partners, and take care of their needs, before all else. It's not about our own sexual satisfaction. We find our satisfaction in pleasing you."

"You think she found her satisfaction in making all three of us lose our minds to lust like we did?" Hannah questioned.

"I think she went home and made herself come over and over again to just the thought of how good you tasted on her lips as she pushed you over the edge of that first orgasm."

"Or how good you tasted when she licked you off my lips." Hannah replied with a small grin. "I don't think she's as repulsed by you as she wants you to think she is."

"Darling, she derives pleasure from power." I loosened my hold on her neck, "And controlling me is the biggest flex to her when she's inside of our relationship. Nothing more."

"Maybe." Knox stood up and pulled Hannah in for a kiss, lingering against her lips as he teased her before turning to me and doing the same. "But I know without a doubt that it made her wet when she tasted me off these perfect tits." He reached over and slid his hand up Hannah's oversized shirt and toyed with her bare nipples. "And I know I want to do it all over again soon."

"Me too." Hannah admitted, grinning at him as he played with her while she was still very much in my hold. "I just don't know how to approach her without knowing exactly what she felt about it all."

"Easy." Knox grabbed her phone off the counter and opened it up while simultaneously grabbing his own phone and mashing at the screen.

"What are you doing?" Hannah asked, trying to lean over and see what our tricky boyfriend was doing, though I had a pretty good idea.

"There." Knox made a show of locking Hannah's phone and holding out his own between us to see a text message he just sent.

Tallman's Tavern. 8 P.M. Show up if you want more of last night.
-Knox

"Oh my god, you did not." Hannah shrieked, swatting him. "That's such a dude move!"

"So?" He shrugged, and looked at me, "Oh, like you weren't trying to come up with a way to get our girl round two yourself."

"I was brainstorming, though I can't say as I would have done it exactly that way." I tilted my head to the side, seeing the reason behind his impulsive move.

"You guys kill me sometimes," Hannah groaned, rubbing her forehead with her hand, "She's going to think I'm desperate or deranged. It's cardinal rule number one! Girls don't call first after the first hook up!"

"Uh, excuse me," Knox shuddered, "How the fuck would you know anything about any of that exactly?"

"And did you forget that Lex is a woman too?" I pointed out, talking reason through Knox's flare for dramatics. "Maybe she was waiting for one of us to reach out first."

"Not a chance." Hannah shook her head as panic filled her body.

Ding!

Knox's phone alerted to a new message, cutting her off and surprising us all. He opened the message, grinning like the cat that ate the fucking canary, and then held his phone out for us.

See you there.

-Xo

"Holy fuck." Hannah whispered, sagging on the counter as we all paused in a bit of shock. I didn't think Knox's plan had a chance in hell of working. Yet it did. "Holy fuck." She repeated.

"You'd better make sure you have a sexy as fuck outfit for the occasion." I drew her attention back to me, kissing her sensually until she leaned into me and gave into the trap I was laying. "Because I'm the one making the wagers tonight, and I won't fold in the face of danger."

Despite being a Sunday night, the place was crowded.

I took another drink off my beer as I watched Hannah lean over the pool table and line up her shot.

Fucking hell, she looked sexy. I wasn't dumb enough to think she wore that outfit for me, but I was sure as fuck going to enjoy the show, knowing I was the lucky cuss taking her home in it.

She wore a bright pink tank top that hugged her body like a second skin. It wasn't low cut, but it hugged her tits and every time she bent over, they swelled over the top of the fabric, and I wondered if they would actually pop out or not. So I stared, every single time. Her ass cheeks peeked out from beneath the frayed white cut-offs, and the hot pink cowboy boots she wore matched perfectly. Her hair was up off her neck in a twist and I wanted nothing more than to grab a handful of it and drag her against my body for taste.

She was breathtaking.

And she was horny. Her skin was flushed, and she glanced at the door and the old Budweiser clock over my shoulder every ten seconds in anticipation.

It was eight fifteen, making Lex officially late. But I wasn't worried, because there wasn't a person on the earth that could stay away when Hannah's sweet little body was offered for the taking.

Knox was a ball of sexual tension as well, pacing back and forth as he waited for his turn. He was normally more in control of himself than that, but I guess it made sense that he'd be keyed up waiting for her arrival tonight, given that just last night, Alexi Donovan had wrapped her hand around his cock and stroked it.

She purposely left me out last night, and she did it as a form of punishment because of how much she disliked me. But she didn't realize that while she was busy playing with Hannah and teasing Knox, I had nothing to do but watch her.

To study her.

To memorize her.

And when she wasn't paying attention, she let her guard slip just enough that I could learn some things about her. Things I bet most people didn't know at all.

Things I bet she wouldn't want me, of all people, to have figured out.

And I planned to keep them to myself until the right time to use them in my favor.

"Oh, come on," Hannah whined, as her ball banked hard to the left and bounced off the rail, missing the pocket she was aiming for. "Ugh." She pursed her lips and looked at the clock over my shoulder again.

"She'll be here." Knox tried reassuring her, as he watched her get more and more deflated with each minute that passed.

"What if she doesn't show?" She asked, looking at me for guidance. Before I could even give it to her, I noticed how more than a few heads in the bar careened around other patrons as they all tried to get a glimpse of something by the front door.

"She's here." I announced to the two of them even though I couldn't see proof of it. I could feel her.

There wasn't anyone else in the world that would cause that many bargoers to rubber neck. As if on cue, Lex's head popped out in a clearing down on the main floor as she searched the busy bar for us.

As if she could feel my eyes on her, she glanced up and the second her dark eyes found mine, my cock stirred from the electricity in the stare from fifty feet away.

"Jesus fuck." Knox groaned, sliding up next to me to catch a glimpse of her as she walked around the dance floor, grabbing everyone's attention, before disappearing into the stairwell that would bring her to the second floor. "I'm already hard."

Hannah slid her hand into mine and I looked down at her, giving the woman of my dreams my full attention, even as I felt Lex's presence as she got closer.

"Just say the word and we don't have to do this." Hannah said, squeezing my hand as she stared up at me with hesitation. "You gave me more than enough last night, Brody. I know this isn't the easiest thing for you—"

"Look who showed up after all," Knox interrupted my reply as we all looked over to Lex approaching the pool table in the corner that we occupied. "Glad you did."

Lex hitched her hip against the table and crossed her arms under her big ass tits as she tipped her head to the side, giving him one of her deep dimple grins that made it hard for me to think straight. "I like to make an entrance."

"I like your entrance." He nodded, making a show of taking in her over the top outfit as Hannah clung to me.

Lex was wearing a black and white baseball shirt, which had a rip down the front to where her bra clasped, allowing a bit of red lace to peek out over the jagged frayed edges. It reminded me of the dress from last night. The feminine lace contrasted the sharp edges of her personality and style, leaving me aching to tear it from her body. The chest piece she had tattooed from her jaw down was on full display with her shirt open that far and I spent way too much time admiring the way it covered the skin between her tits. Her black cutoff jean shorts had chains hanging from her back pocket to the front and her wide fish net stockings clung to her thick thighs all the way down to those chunky black combat boots she wore the day I first met her on the side of the road.

The ones I had scoffed at in judgment. Since then, I'd had two dreams of her with her legs pinned to her chest, wearing nothing but those boots.

And both times in those fantasies, Hannah had been riding her face as I fucked Lex like I hated her.

Which I did.

That didn't mean I didn't want to fuck the daylights out of her, though.

"Hey." Hannah gave her a timid smile and a quick wave as her hesitation made it awkward.

But Lex didn't hold it against her, "Hey, pretty girl." Lex nodded to Hannah's outfit. "I love your boots."

"Thanks," Hannah giggled lightly, relaxing a little as Lex didn't let her hesitation fester. "I like yours."

I scoffed and rolled my eyes, "You wouldn't even be able to lift your legs if you wore those things." I flicked my eyes down to the offensive things and caught the way Lex's eyes tightened slightly.

"Glad to see you're as grumpy as ever." She blew me off and turned to Knox. "Thanks for the invite."

"No problem." He shrugged, sitting on the edge of a barstool, and holding a pool stick between his legs like he wasn't as anxious as Hannah. "Figured maybe you were doing the honorable thing and giving us the chance to make the first move."

Lex's dimples deepened. "Is that what you thought I was doing?" She looked back over at Hannah and licked her lips suggestively, "Interesting."

"What were you doing, then?" Hannah asked, stepping forward to lean against the table, cutting the distance between me and the other woman. I didn't let the gap bristle at my nerves like it should have. Because in reality, I wanted Hannah to be comfortable around Lex, but more than anything, I wanted Lex to welcome Hannah warmly, without reluctance or reservation.

I needed Hannah to understand how downright irresistible she was, and that she was the prize in the situation.

Lex tilted her head to the side like a psychopathic chucky doll as she took a couple of seductive steps toward Hannah. "I deliberately gave you space and time, hoping that your thoughts of me would grow until you couldn't resist seeing me again. I couldn't take the chance of reaching out and you letting your reservations talk you out of this. So, I needed to wait until you couldn't resist."

"Well, that took all of five minutes after you left last night." Hannah sighed, opening herself up for the woman in ways I'd never seen before. "I thought maybe you didn't enjoy yourself."

"Hannah, Hannah, Hannah." Lex tsked her tongue and took one last step forward until their bodies were just barely touching. "You have no idea how many times I've played with myself since leaving that room last night, thinking about how fucking good it was with you." Hannah whimpered softly and my body tightened painfully as Lex grinned at her. "Kiss me hello, Hannah."

I watched as Hannah glanced around the busy bar briefly before throwing caution to the wind. She leaned in and pressed her lips to Lex's, and from my perfect vantage point, I got to see the way her body melted into her touch as Lex tilted her head and deepened it.

"I'm a goner." Knox grunted, shaking his head as he stared at them. "I need more."

The girls pulled back and Lex grinned over at him as she slid her free hand around Hannah's waist, pressing their hips together.

It was incredible watching Hannah giving herself so freely to Lex in ways she had never done with anyone besides Knox and I. We were used to a certain amount of creepy people watching us when we were out together as a throuple, but after so many years, it stopped catching our attention at all.

However, it was daring to kiss a woman, while the two of us watched after them with longing, especially a woman as unconventional as Lex.

But maybe our good girl wanted to be bad for a while.

And I was more than happy to let her test that theory as long as I got to watch.

"Do you want to play some pool?" Hannah asked Lex.

"I could be tempted," Lex smirked, hinting at a double meaning. However, before she explained what kind of temptation would be required to get her to play, she looked over at me and assessed my capabilities. "Think you can hulk your way through the crowd so I can get to the bar for a drink?"

It wasn't what I was expecting her to say, and I hated being caught off guard. "I can get you a drink, what do you want?"

"I'll get it." She slid her hand off Hannah's hip and quickly gave her a peck on the lips before walking backward toward the staircase she just came up. "Could just use your help to get through."

I didn't make her ask twice, considering I knew Alexi Donovan didn't ask for help often. And she hated asking me for anything even more. I nodded to Knox, "Keep an eye on our girl."

"Always." He smirked, looking off after Lex as she started walking down the stairs without waiting to see if I was following. She was the most stubborn woman in the world.

"I'll be right back." I leaned down to kiss Hannah, and she surprised me when she slid her hands around the back of my head and held me to her, deepening the kiss unsarcastically. "Don't let her rattle you." She smiled up at me after dropping back down onto the flat of her feet. "I don't know what her plan is completely, but something tells me she's going to push your buttons."

"Wouldn't surprise me if she did." I grinned and then walked off after the illusive woman.

Game fucking on, Alexi.

Chapter 18 – Lex

I made it all of two feet off the bottom of the stairs before I met the crowd, who delivered me a hard stop. I had made it up to the pool table loft when I got to the place, because I purposely skirted the actual bar, and in turn, avoided the people not interested in moving out of the way as they waited for their own drinks.

Which was why I had asked for Brody's help.

Don't think it didn't taste like acid to do it, either. The only reason I involved him and not Knox, who was just as big and dominating as Brody when he wanted to be, was because I wanted to get Brody away from Hannah for a minute.

I needed to feel him out and figure out just how far he was going to let this whole thing go. I knew he called the shots, so I'd go straight to the source.

"You're stubborn, you know that?" His deep, gravely voice tickled my ear, startling me slightly before his gigantic body engulfed me in the crowd.

"Don't act like you're surprised." I threw back at him, trying to ignore the way he smelled, as he put his hand on my hip and pulled me in behind him.

"I'm not." He shook his head, looking back at me as his fingers slid through mine and tightened, dragging me behind him through the masses. "Try not to let your visceral need to be independent get you lost in here."

I didn't reply, because my tongue was stuck to the roof of my mouth as the crowd shifted and I was pressed up against his massive back. I wasn't a small woman, necessarily. Sure, I was short without my heels on, but I wasn't fragile.

Hannah was fragile in a soft and feminine way.

I grew up in the middle of mosh pits punching punks in the dicks for the fun of it.

But pressed up against Brody as the crowd swallowed us up with every step closer to the bar, I felt—feminine. Small and protected.

And it was a fucking head trip. Luckily, talking wasn't required as the band kicked off their set and the drums began the beat to the classic rock set they started.

"Beer or cocktail?" Brody yelled over his shoulder as he pushed a frat boy looking kid out of the way and took another step forward.

"Whiskey. Maker's if they've got it." I yelled back, and he glared at me for a second before facing forward again. The crowd heaved once more, and someone shoved into my back, plastering me against Brody's.

I could *feel* his growl at the contact, and it went straight to my stomach.

Okay, not quite. It went lower than that, but I didn't need to label it to be fucked over it.

He pulled my hand, still tight in his, around the front of him to settle on his stomach as he shoved through the last few rows of people and made it to the bar. "Come here." He pulled me around to his front and pinned me against the bar with his body pressed against mine, sandwiching me.

Protecting me.

Touching me.

Burning me. From head to toe, I *burned* from how he felt against me. Not once in my entire life had I wanted a man to touch me. Never.

But Brody?

I was nearly weak from how it made me feel.

"Tito." Brody hollered, flicking his fingers up in the air, and the bartender ran right over to us.

"What can I get you, boss?" The young kid asked, leaning over the bar toward us. I didn't miss the way he looked at me in Brody's arms with question in his eyes.

"A bucket, and a bottle of Makers." Brody replied, and I shook the spell he weaved over me off long enough to find my voice.

"A bottle?" I questioned as the kid ran off to get his order.

He laid both hands flat on the bar top and leaned down to my ear. "Do you see a better way to carry a glass of whiskey through that crowd?"

"Guess not." I mused, turning to talk over my shoulder. Which left our faces really fucking close. "Why'd you invite me out tonight?" I asked before I lost the nerve.

"I didn't." He swallowed, flicking those dark eyes back over the bar to where the kid stacked bottles of beer into a bucket. "Knox did."

"Whatever." I sighed, hating how he ruffled my feathers with his touch and his words. Just once, I almost wanted it to be easy to communicate with the neanderthal.

"If it had been me who reached out, would you have accepted?" He asked against my ear, and I almost lied, just to test him.

"No." I replied and then looked over at him again.

"Exactly, that's why Knox was the one to do it."

"Why are you okay with this?" I questioned.

"Because it makes Hannah happy." He answered instantly. "And I'll always do whatever makes that girl happy. Because she is the literal fucking sun in my world, and without her warmth, I don't exist."

My chest ached at such a bold declaration from the man who seemed so gruff. As he revealed the softer part of him where Hannah was concerned, I didn't see it as a weakness like I might have with someone else.

I saw it for what it was.

Devotion and commitment. And it perplexed me more than anything else he'd ever said before.

"Why are you okay with this?" He countered, glancing around us, keeping himself aware of his surroundings in the crowded bar, before looking back down at me directly, "Why are you okay with giving yourself for just a small part of someone else in return?"

"Because that's all I want." I swallowed, trying to muster up the courage to act tough like I'd been doing every day of my life. "I want nothing more than simple fun."

"Well then," He nodded and picked up the bucket of beers and the bottle of whiskey that had materialized in front of me during our conversation, "I guess we understand each other a little better now."

"I guess so." I moved to duck around him as he gave me a little breathing room, but he stopped me with his hand flat on my stomach as he tilted his head down to be directly in my line of sight.

"Make no mistake, Alexi," He spoke my name like a lover would, and I hated it, "At the end of the day, Hannah is ours. And we're willingly sharing her with you because we know that there isn't a chance in hell of it destroying what we've spent a decade building. But if I think for even one minute that you're in this for the wrong reasons," He clenched his teeth together and the muscles along the side of his face tensed, "I'll fucking destroy every single thing you have. Understand?"

I panted under the intensity of his warning. Who the fuck did he think he was, going from the protecting oaf who declared to love his girl more than anything in the world while physically holding me to his body, to the dominating asshole I knew he really was that only cared about being in control.

"Got it." I gritted out between my own clenched teeth. Once again, he pulled the power card and put me back in my place.

Well, now I had a renewed needed to show Brody fucking Sinclair just who was in charge.

Because it sure as fuck wasn't him.

"Corner pocket." I declared, pointing to the one directly between Hannah's thighs as she leaned against the table, watching me play.

I pulled back and gently tapped the ball, sending it directly where I wanted, and the smile she gave me was the perfect reward for it.

The girl loved playing pool, and she made the game seem so sensual even though there was no physical touch occurring with each shot taken.

"Good shot." She purred across the table as she tipped a beer back against her perfect pink lips.

"Let's up the ante." Knox announced, nudging me with his shoulder as he stood next to me, "Make tonight a little more interesting."

"What did you have in mind?" I questioned, glancing over at Hannah as she turned her attention to Brody, where he sat against the wall at a table. Silently asking permission from him.

"Truth or dare." Knox grinned deviously. "If you make a pocket, you get to pick a person to go. One shot at a time."

"We're in a public bar." I raised my eyebrows at him, "I don't know what kind of truth or dare you play, but mines not very decent."

"We're on the second floor." He nodded out to the crowd below. "Stand far enough back from the edge and you can hide."

I rolled my eyes at him, down for whatever either way, and looked at Hannah. "You decide."

"I lost the last time I played a game of stakes against you."

"In the end, I think you won." Flashbacks assaulted me, and I could taste her skin on my lips and hear the noises she made as she came.

She licked her lips and then reached down the side of the table and hit the button to release the balls back to be racked. "I go first."

She wanted to play. And I wanted nothing more than to play with her.

"Game on." I whistled, walking around her, brushing her with my body as I grabbed for the triangle. "I can't wait to see what kind of nefarious dares you come up with."

"I'd be careful tempting the devil." Knox chuckled. "One time, she made me do the naked mile down Main Street of our hometown." He shook his head, "At noon."

"Cruel." I grinned at her, where she shrugged with a smirk. "I like it."

"He's hung and has a ten pack." She joked, "He had nothing worth hiding."

"Hmm." I hummed, racking the balls, trying desperately not to remember just how hung Knox was from our night together. The way his cock filled my hand when she tricked me as she moved on to Brody, tempted me.

She took the balls and set them how she liked them and then walked around the table in her sexy little pink outfit. It matched her personality perfectly, and it was alarming how much I liked both of them. Pink had never been my color before. Yet tonight, I wanted to bathe in her pink.

"Something tells me we're going to regret this." Knox leaned over my shoulder and whispered to me as she bent over the table and lined up a shot to break the balls.

"I think she'll make it up to us." She landed a solid in a pocket and grinned at us as she stood back up.

"Lex. Truth or dare?" She held her pool stick to the side of her body and stared right at me.

"Dare. For you, every single time." I replied confidently.

"Kiss me." Her voice was breathy, and I could feel the switch in her demeanor as she took a mostly friendly and kind of flirty game of pool and turned it into the gateway she needed to initiate physical contact.

"If you want a kiss," I said, my voice laced with a playful invitation, "come and get it." I would have gone to her, but I wanted to make her positively melt and didn't want the bar below to get the free show. I pulled her body flush against mine and then I guided her until Knox and I sandwiched her between us. He was a giant and shielded us from any prying eyes as I leaned in to give her the reward she chose.

I licked her bottom lip before seductively sucking on it and kissed her like my life depended on it. She moaned and ran her tongue against mine, nibbling on my lip in return. I growled and pushed forward until our hips were grinding together as I wrapped my hands around the back of her neck, kissing down the side of it as she leaned against Knox for support.

Once again, I left Brody out for the fun of it. It didn't appear Knox minded as he started kissing the other side of her neck, each of us teasing her until she gasped and held onto me like she was teetering on the edge of a cliff and needed support.

Needed us. I never wanted to share a woman with a man before. Yet with Knox, it intensified everything, knowing he was making her feel good at the same time.

"The noises you make when I touch you drive me wild." I bit her earlobe as she buried her fingers in my hair, holding me to her. "I want to make you come again. It's all I can think about."

"God, Lex." She panted and pulled my head back and kissed me. It was one of the first times she'd been assertive with me, and I grinned like a fucking fox against her lips as she went wild for me. "I want to touch you." She purred, "I need to touch you."

"You have to be a good girl to get that." I teased as I slowed down my touches and Knox pulled back with pupils the size of saucers as he fought to contain the need inside of him, too.

Hannah drove her men wild, that much was clear.

And I was jealous of that ability, if I was honest.

"So is that it?" Brody called from the same stool he sat in the whole time. "One shot and the game is done?"

"You actually want to play?" Knox scoffed as he palmed his erection and adjusted it. "We all know where we're hoping this goes."

Brody's scowl darkened, "My turn." He rose and grabbed his stick as he leaned over the table.

Hannah sighed as she detangled herself from between Knox and me with an almost sad look on her face as she grabbed her beer and took a long drink off it.

I knew she wasn't sad because our little game got disrupted. She was sad because Brody had a problem with it.

And that made me angry.

He was dangling the freedom in front of her and then getting pissy when she took it.

Knox sat down on a stool and pulled Hannah between his legs, wrapping his arms around her and resting his chin on her shoulder as she snuggled in. He was reassuring her without using words.

Their entire communication style was wordless most times.

And it was fucking infuriating as an outsider trying to understand the rules.

Brody lined up and sank a ball with no hesitation, before it finished spinning in the pocket, he pointed his stick at me. "Why do you pretend to be a lesbian when it's clear you're bisexual?"

"Brody." Hannah gasped.

"*I* get the choice between truth or dare." I countered, fighting off the urge to break the stick over his head. "And I choose dare."

"Fine." Brody countered, "Kiss Knox."

"Dude." Knox groaned, standing up and sliding around Hannah to warn his boyfriend. "You're stepping out of line here."

"No, I'm not." Brody shrugged, all the while staring right at me. "She wants a dare, that's the one I choose." He swallowed, and I already knew what was going to come out of his mouth before he opened it again. "Unless you're too scared to play a simple game."

"Fine." I threw back at him and grabbed the front of Knox's shirt, pulling him down to my height, and kissed him.

Chapter 19 – Knox

Holy fuck.

    She kissed me.

She kept her lips pressed against mine and held the front of my shirt, keeping me pulled down against her as she kissed me. Sure, I could have broken her hold and pulled away, but why the fuck would I do that?

She didn't move her lips against mine, but I felt the way they softened after a fraction of a second, like she wasn't sure what to do with herself after making the initial contact.

So I decided for her.

I tilted my head and opened my lips, giving her time to pull away and let go, but she didn't.

And I didn't hold back. I ran my tongue over the seam of her lips before sliding my hand around the back of her head, anchoring her to me. She softened even more, and her tongue met mine, tentatively teasing me before pushing its way into my mouth.

I growled, unable to stop the primal reaction to feeling her accepting the kiss and reciprocating it.

Brody's declaration about Lex's sexuality a minute ago caught me off guard, but it was making more sense the longer she kissed me back.

"I can't." She pulled back and stared up at me with wild eyes and swollen lips. "I'm not—"

"I know." I replied, understanding just how much she believed what she was about to say. "It's just a game." I smiled down at her, trying to give her the permission she was looking for to relax and blow it off.

I looked over her shoulder to where Hannah still stood, and my cock hardened from the look in her eye as she stared directly at me. "Hannah." I called, trying to break her from the spell she was under.

She blinked and looked at Lex and then back to me before marching forward. "I want to taste her on your lips." She all but climbed up my body in one jump, wrapping her legs around my waist and kissing me with everything she had.

"Fuck, baby." I growled, walking her to the wall and pinning her against it. She clawed at my back and bit my lip as she kissed me, and I couldn't remember the last time she'd been so worked up. "Easy, Hannah." I warned, pulling my lip out of her teeth, and holding her arms out wide in a T, using her hold on my waist to keep her pinned to the wall. "Down girl." I teased just for her to hear.

"I don't think I've ever wanted to be in the middle of a kiss before as much as that one." She panted.

I shook it off, knowing we needed to keep the game going, or we were going to get lost on the way to the bedroom. "My turn." I slid Hannah down my body and grabbed my pool stick from the wall before lining up for an easy shot. It clanked its way into the pocket, and I grinned at Lex across the table. She wouldn't quite meet my eye, but I could tell she was fighting to control her emotions. "Lex, truth or dare?"

Her nostrils flared a bit, and she took a deep breath, squaring her shoulders. "Truth."

"What do you want to happen tonight?"

"Sex." She replied instantly. "Isn't that why we're all here?"

"Yes," I nodded, "Then why don't we cut to the chase and get out of here?"

Lex squinted her eyes slightly and cocked her head to the side, and I swallowed in trepidation. She was up to something. "No." She grabbed her pool stick and slid up next to Hannah. "I've played your game, now you play mine."

She wasn't talking to me, though. She was staring directly at Brody. And he was staring back like they were about to fight. Or fuck. I couldn't quite tell.

Lex grabbed the chalk and started dusting the tip of her stick as she walked to the end of the table and hit the button to dispense the balls again. "The game is simple." She put the triangle down and started racking the balls. "Brody and I each set and break the balls. The one with the most to go in off the break wins."

"What do I win?" Brody interjected and walked forward. I slid my body around Hannah's tightly coiled form, fearing she might snap under the pressure of watching Lex and Brody duke it out.

"When *I* win," Lex went on, as though Brody hadn't tried to take the power from her. She stopped arranging the table and looked right at him. "I take Hannah home. Alone."

"No." I answered instantly. That was never part of our arrangement, and she knew it. I also knew she was only making the moves to regain control because of Brody's stunt with our kiss. "Lex, that's not going to happen."

"Why?" She looked over at me, "Scared she won't come back to you?"

"Lex." Hannah almost pleaded with the woman who was toeing a line so close to destruction, it wasn't even funny. Brody had been on board with the arrangement for the most part, but he'd walk away, effectively pulling Hannah and me with him, just to spite Lex for trying to get one up on him.

"Deal." Brody interrupted, drawing everyone's attention back to him. "But when *I* win," He leaned forward with his hands on the opposite end of the table of her and squared off. "I take all three of you home. With me."

She clenched her jaw as she contemplated it. "Why? So you can sit in the corner and watch me fuck your girl?"

"Guess we'll see in a few minutes, won't we?" He rolled the last ball on the table to her and stood back up. "Ladies first."

Jesus, Mary, and Joseph.

I grabbed Lex's bottle of whiskey off the table behind me and tipped it back, inviting the burn of the liquor as she set the table how she wanted.

"What do we do?" Hannah whispered, sliding her arms around my waist, clinging to me. "I mean, I'm not opposed to either option, but I'm scared as hell about what they'll do to each either, regardless of who wins."

"We have to let them battle it out." I nodded to the pool table. "I don't think either of us is going to talk any sense into them."

She sighed and laid her head on my chest. "I never wanted this."

"I know." I kissed her temple and sat back onto a stool, pulled her between my legs so I could pretend I was holding her when in reality, I was holding *onto* her for dear fucking life. Changing the dynamic of our relationship was going to be tough on everyone, but I didn't envision this. "Just say the word and I'll end it for them." There were enough scars on my knuckles to prove I could put Brody in his place if I had to, didn't mean I wanted to though.

Lex glanced over her shoulder at us and winked at Hannah before lining up her shot. My eyes instantly fell to the way her lush ass filled out those cut-offs and the ink that disappeared just beneath the frayed edge.

Did Hannah's mouth water to take a bite like a man's did? Like mine did?

That kiss left me with the lingering taste of Lex's whiskey, and I found myself at a loss, searching for reasons to resist doing it again. I knew she was a lesbian. But she didn't act like one when she looked at Brody and I. She looked like a woman torn. Indecision and confusion clouded her brown eyes when she thought we weren't watching.

God, I was a fucking goner for her.

Lex pulled back and let a shot off at the cluster in the center, choosing a side aim to get the most penetration into the pack.

And it worked, because I watched and listened as three of the balls landed in pockets around the table.

Three on a break shot.

Incredible.

She stood up, slowly unfolding her body seductively as she stared at Brody with a shit-eating grin and a top dog attitude.

I could almost feel how badly Brody wanted to pry that mentality out of her brain and show her what it felt like to be a good girl.

And I also knew how fucking hot it would be to watch her do the same to him. They matched each other in every way.

"Shit." Hannah hissed, playing with her lips nervously. "That was good."

"If you go home with her, remember where your home really is." I whispered into her ear.

She turned in my arms as Lex walked around to Brody's spot as he took hers, racking the balls with sheer determination in every muscle. The tighter the pack, the more movement when the ball hits.

More movement meant more chances of sinking the balls.

"My home is in here." Hannah said, drawing my attention away from the dance happening around the table, and pressing her hand to my chest, right over my heart. "That's not something I can forget, Knox."

"I know." Smiling down at her as she stared up with those big doe eyes, "I want you to enjoy yourself either way."

"I'm going to, because Brody will win." She winked at me. "He's never going to give someone else control over my body without a fight."

I snorted at her confidence and nodded behind her as Brody lined up for his shot. He took aim from the opposite angle that Lex did, even though it was out of his routine, and I knew he did it only to be different from her. I wouldn't have taken such a risk with such a reward on the line.

But to each his own.

He pulled back and then took his shot, effortlessly sending every single ball crashing around on the table with his strength.

One sank.

Then two.

"C'mon," I furiously watched them bounce off the rails as they started slowing down.

Three down.

"Oh, fuck." Hannah whispered.

Chapter 20 – Hannah

F our!

He did it. Brody got four to drop into pockets.

Winning the bet. Winning me.

Winning Lex.

But what did that mean for her, exactly?

"I win." Brody declared, tossing his stick down onto the table with a loud clank.

It felt like my heart was going to beat straight out of my chest and flop onto the floor as I watched them both just stare at each other. Knox's body was so still behind me I wondered if his heart had done what mine wanted to.

"Now what?" I asked, breaking the stare-down between everyone.

"Now," Lex tipped back the last of her drink before looking at me. "You get to show me what you look like sprawled out in the center of your bed." She acted as though the events did not rattle her.

"You're okay with it?" I walked forward until I was right in front of her, gazing directly into her warm brown eyes.

"Baby," She grinned and leaned forward to trace the shell of my ear with her tongue, "The where doesn't matter, as long as I get to feel your body on mine again tonight."

"Okay." I stammered, leaning into her false bravado, even though I knew it was fake. "If you're sure."

"Come on," Brody announced, sliding his hand into mine and pulling us toward the stairs. "No sense wasting time here when she wants to see you in our bed."

I didn't miss the way he said *our bed*, and neither did Lex. But the hunger I saw in her eyes was true, even if the words she was using were lies.

I let Brody pull me through the crowd, using his body to shield mine in ways that always warmed my heart. In that moment, though, I felt something more than that in his touch. It looked the same, but there was something darker there, just beneath the surface.

Something more carnal and needy.

He wanted her. Yet he fought that urge because of their personalities. Which made me wonder, did she want him as well? Did he pick up on that and was that why he called her out? Was there hope for the fairytale image in my head of all four of us being together equally, after all?

We got to the bikes on the busy street and Brody made it clear that I'd be riding with him. Which was safer for all parties involved in the long run.

"I'll follow you." Lex nodded toward the parking lot where her sexy classic red muscle car was parked.

"Or you could ride." Knox tempted her as he eyed his black bike right in front of us.

"Or you could let me drive and you could ride bitch." Lex challenged, sliding her hand over the handlebar seductively.

Knox chuckled enthusiastically before darkening his stare completely, and I shivered watching the exchange. "Baby, you want to take control in the bedroom with our girl, that's a-okay with me. You want to tell me to be a good boy and do your bidding, I'll play along. Hell, you want to wear one of those sexy strap-ons and fuck my ass; ask me nicely and I'll let you." He towered over her, and her lips parted as she listened intently, "But the only place I sit on my bike is in front. Feel free to wrap those mile-long legs around mine and hold on though, because she purrs better than a Sybian and I bet I can make you come before we hit our driveway."

"Tell me you think that's as hot as I do," I whispered to Brody and tore my eyes away from the heated exchange happening down the sidewalk from us and looked at him. "Tell me you want that as much as I do."

Brody's dark eyes moved from the others and looked at me. "I do." He replied quietly as he threw his leg over his bike. "I'm just not sure it's going to happen."

I missed what Lex replied to Knox, but hope bloomed in my chest as she put her small purse into his saddlebag and waited for him to get on and get ready for her.

Watching her slide her sexy body against his and then wrap her arms around his waist made me positively ache with need. I had been anxiously waiting all day for another taste of this foursome, and now I was finally going to get it.

"Come on, Darling." Brody held his hand out to me as Knox started up his loud bike. "Bet I can make you come before we leave the downtown limits." He winked, and I relaxed into the familiar comfort of his care and love.

"Same." I winked back at him and slid onto the bike behind him. I wrapped my hands around his waist as I plastered myself onto his back and slid them down to the already evident bulge in the front of his jeans. "Remember that one time—" I gripped him and stood up on the pegs to bite the back of his neck as we both remembered that time I jacked him off as he drove us through the winding hills on a long ride one day.

It was dangerous, invigorating, and irresponsible.

Much like every decision I'd made the last few weeks.

"Wait until we get out of traffic, and I'll pull my zipper down for you myself." He replied and then started his bike, revving her engine, so she purred between my thighs just how I liked.

We tore off through the busy streets, weaving through traffic and ignoring every law and rule of the road as we drove away from the lights and towards the darkness of the hills around the city.

I didn't wait for Brody to give me the permission he had already granted, and I pulled his pants open as soon as the speed limit and the empty road opened up ahead of us. His cock throbbed in my hand as I pulled him free from his jeans and stroked him from root to tip.

He leaned back against me, arching his hips forward so I had better access, and grunted so deeply I could feel it in my chest, pressed against his back as I circled my fingers over the pre-cum that leaked from the tip.

Knox had been following us through the city, but as we started winding our way through the country, he pulled up alongside and I watched as he caught on to what I was doing. The devious grin that covered his face as he watched me stroke our guy toward the release we both knew he needed made me tingle with excitement.

Lex watched too with just the glow of their headlights illuminating her dark face as the wind blew in the space between the bikes as we got closer to our house. Her stare flicked back and forth between my hands and my face as I stared back at her, loving the way she watched me pleasure Brody. I wanted to feel her hand wrapped around him with me as we both stroked him, but I would settle for having her eyes on him.

Knox had his hand wrapped around her calf above her boots as he drove, and his devious grin made more sense as he drifted toward the middle line and placed both of his tires right down the center.

That rumble strip line, which I had experienced firsthand, had the power to push a girl to the edge of sanity on the back seat of a vibrating motorcycle, when the craving for release surpassed the need to preserve dignity.

Was Lex there? Was her need to come higher than her need to keep Knox and Brody at arm's length?

I tightened my hold on Brody's cock as Lex's eyes fluttered closed and her head tipped back in ecstasy.

"Look at her," I yelled into Brody's ear, and he looked over as Lex's nails dug into Knox's shoulders as she shifted forward.

I could almost feel the way the seam of her jean shorts must have felt pressed up against her clit while Knox assisted her chase of pleasure.

"A secondhand orgasm is still better than no orgasms." Brody mused, glancing over at them as Knox stayed true down the center of the deserted road.

"I can't believe he's going to make her come before I do." Brody chuckled as I pouted dramatically, flexing his hips when I reciprocated with an extra tight squeeze over the tip of his cock. "I can make *you* come, though."

"You could." He wrapped his hand over mine and picked up the pace of my stroking. "Or you could be a good girl and watch Knox get what he desperately needs." He nodded back to the bike next to us and sure enough, Lex was falling over the edge of an orgasm.

Her lips were parted, her eyes still closed as she rocked her hips back and forth on the seat, pleasuring herself with Knox's help before sagging against him as her high crashed. Just in time too, as we slowed for our hidden driveway through the woods.

When Brody stopped his bike, I slid off as he slowly put his hard cock away while Lex got off Knox's bike.

"How was it?" I teased, and she surprised me by grabbing me and kissing me, burying her fingers in my hair and biting my lip. It was the most aggressive she'd been with me and I ached for it, especially because I was still one orgasm behind her for the night. "Lex." I moaned, sliding my fingers under the hem of her shirt and testing out the smoothness of her skin. "I need you."

"Take me to bed, baby girl." She pulled back and grinned with those deep dimples. "I'm done playing hard to get."

"Fuck." I moaned and then pulled her after me towards the door. "Come on boys," I called, grabbing the front of Brody's still undone jeans as I passed. "Time to cash in on your winnings."

We made it to the bedroom in a tangle of limbs and lips as I went from kissing Lex to kissing Brody and back. Knox followed close behind, just as eager as we stopped at the foot of the bed.

"Rules for tonight?" Lex paused the game, looking from me to the guys. "You're the boss, once again."

"You have to vocalize what you want and what you don't, Lex." Brody asserted dominantly as he pulled his shirt over the back of his head and revealed those sexy as fuck washboard abs. "Lines are getting blurry."

"I know." She replied and for the first time, I could feel the honesty aimed toward him. "I want Hannah." She bit her bottom lip as she looked at me.

"And I want you both to watch and to make her feel good with me." She took a deep breath. "We'll figure the rest out as we go."

"Okay." Brody nodded once and then let his eyes rove over the two of us standing side by side and then looked square at her, "Lead the way."

"With pleasure." She grinned and turned to me. "Can I undress you?" She purred, and I groaned in sexual frustration.

"If you do it quickly." I toed off one boot and then the other, kicking them aside. "Because if you don't hurry, I might burst into flames and perish."

She slid her hands under my shirt and tore it off over my head, "Eager?"

"Frustrated." I cried and then moaned as she reached behind me to unclasp my bra. Right before she released it, she paused and sensually kissed my shoulder and then to my neck. "I'm aching."

"Then let me help you get that release you need so badly." She nibbled on the lobe of my ear as she unclasped it and pulled it down my arms. The weight of my breast dropping free made me moan, and she took it further by palming them both.

Last night had been sensual and slow as she explored my body and allowed me to get used to the feel of a woman's touch. But tonight, I didn't need slow or hesitant. I needed confidence and assertiveness.

Knox sat down on the foot of the bed right next to us and leaned forward like we were the most puzzling thing in the world that he wanted to figure out, while Brody continued to lurk from the wall. Just as he had last night when she touched me.

She kissed her way down my chest and sucked on my nipples as I fumbled with the button on my shorts. As I fought with them, calloused hands slid over mine seconds before a warm chest pressed against my naked back. "Let me help you," Brody growled in my ear as he undid the damning clasp.

"Fuck yes." I moaned, leaning into him as Lex kissed down further while they both pulled my shorts and panties down my legs.

"That's the teamwork I like to see." Knox hissed, leaning back on the bed as he rubbed his cock through his jeans.

I couldn't reply because as I stepped out of the clothes, naked from head to toe, Lex lifted one of my legs and gently laid kisses on the inside of my thigh as Brody slid his large hand under my knee, holding it up and open for her.

"Oh, my god." I cried, reaching up to dig my nails into the back of his neck for support as she kissed me closer to my pussy.

"I wanted to hold you like this last night when she licked your sweet little pussy." Brody squeezed my leg, "Knox was a lucky bastard."

"I was." Our boyfriend shrugged good-heartedly, "Yet now I sit all alone with nothing to do but watch the single hottest thing I've ever seen in my life." I moaned as Lex sucked my clit into her mouth, ignoring the guys completely in her task to drive me mad. "Scratch that," Knox leaned forward again, "That's the hottest thing."

"Oh, Lex." I gasped, resting my hand on her head as she pushed her tongue into me and stared up as she withdrew it and teased lazy circles around my clit. "Fuck."

"I want you to come on my face, Hannah." She stated, "And then we can really tease these men of yours."

"Please." I panted as she pushed her fingers into me and stroked me perfectly from the inside. "Please, please, please."

Brody growled as he slid his fingers over each side of my pussy in an upside-down V and pulled my lips wider, opening me further for Lex to tease my clit. "You're so close, Han." He brought my leg higher, "I can feel it in the way your body is trembling."

"She's so good at that." I shook my head. "I'm—" I gasped and arched as blinding pleasure took over, "Yes!"

"Good girl." Brody praised as Lex hummed against me. I felt Knox stand up and join in as his lips latched onto my nipple, sucking it deep while Lex mirrored the motion on my clit.

"Fuck!" I screamed.

"You're such a good girl." Brody continued, "Our good girl doing exactly as we say." He bit my neck as I crashed into another spontaneous orgasm before the first one was even completely done.

"Jeeze Hannah." Knox groaned, moving to my other breast, "Come on Lex's face, just like she said."

I went weak in the knees as I came off the cliff of orgasm and down the other side in a free fall of relaxation, but all three of them were there to catch me.

Worship me.

Praise me.

Please me.

I didn't understand why they all three were so obsessed with making me feel good, because I felt so unworthy of it. Yet they didn't waiver in their drive to make me come, not even allowing their competitive natures to get in the way when things got serious.

"I need you." I pulled Lex up as Brody let my leg down. We all stood in a small space; bodies pressed together. "My turn." I moved to the outside, so she stood in the center of us. "I need to see you naked, Lex. You never took a stitch of clothing off last night, and I feel cheated."

She pursed her lips as Brody hitched one hand on her hip while they all looked at me. They were touching! I wanted to scream but kept my cool so as not to spook the wild animals in them. Lex interrupted my runaway mind, acting as if his touch didn't burn her skin, but I knew better. "You feel cheated? How?"

"Because I don't just want you for what you can give me." Flicking open the button on her shorts, I slowly, tooth by tooth, pulled her zipper down as her pupils dilated. "I want to show you exactly how good it can be with us." I slid my fingers down the front of her silky panties just an inch. "Even if I don't have a clue what I'm doing. I know you'll teach me."

"You know what you're doing." She shimmied as the guys started pulling her shorts down until she wore just a silk thong and her fishnets on her lower half. "If you like it, I'll like it."

"I like everything you do to me," I whispered and pulled on her shirt until she lifted her arms and let me take it off.

Her red lace bra was so sexy, but I took it off without spending time appreciate it, because my real prize was underneath. Her breasts were perfect as my gaze fell on them for the first time. "Do you like when I touch you like this?" She cupped her hands under my breasts and lifted them as she rubbed her thumbs over my nipples.

"Yes." I panted.

"Show me." She lowered her hands to my waist and stood still, waiting so prettily for me to mirror her movement.

I didn't give her a chance to change her mind. I gently placed my palms against the lower half of each breast and tested the feel of them in my hand. They were massive and beautiful, and I wanted so badly to just play with them forever. "Is this why men are so obsessed with tits?" I licked my lips, gently rolling her nipples around under my thumbs.

"Yes." Knox cleared his throat as he stared at what I was doing with my hands. "Do you like that, baby?"

"I do," I replied, Lex's eyes were on mine as I played. Her lips were parted, and she clung to my waist for support. "Can I taste them?"

"Mmh." She moaned, "They're yours tonight, Hannah. Do whatever you want to."

I kissed her lips first, lingering there as she sucked on my tongue and lips while I gently pinched her nipples. Judging by the way she panted and pushed them into my hands further, I knew she liked that.

I loved getting to know another human's preferences again for the first time. Reading her body language and listening for cues to know what she liked and didn't, as it reminded me of my teenage years with two fumbling boys, trying to figure sex out.

I felt far more confident in the moment than I did all those years ago, so I kissed a trail down her neck and over one collarbone before kissing the swell of each breast in my hands. "Use just your tongue first." Brody chimed in from behind her, looking over her shoulder. "Swirl it around like on top of an ice cream cone."

"Jesus." Lex sighed and tipped her head back, inadvertently resting it on his chest as I leaned down and did exactly as he instructed.

She tasted like my favorite sweet treat. Strawberry with salted caramel sauce on top. And I fucking devoured her.

The noises that left her mouth as I experimented, kissing, licking, and sucking on her nipples made my pussy throb.

"Knox." Lex gasped, rocking against my face as she fought to take a deep breath. "Do you think this trial run is making our girl wet?"

I bit her nipple, and she moaned a deep guttural sound as I briefly felt movement behind me.

"I don't know. Maybe." Knox chimed in, "Let me check." He dropped to his knees behind me and pulled my cheeks apart, "Fuck. She's dripping for you."

I groaned as Brody slid one hand over my cheek and pushed his thumb into my mouth, which was still around Lex's nipple. "Present that ass, darling. Give our boy what he wants."

"Mmh." I arched my back and spread my legs wide as Knox dove in, licking from my clit up to my ass. "Fuck."

Lex chuckled and covered my other cheek with her hand so both she and Brody were holding me. "Such a dirty word falling from such pretty lips." She repeated that same statement from last night and I felt like I was in a sensual déjà vu and I never wanted to leave.

"Say it again." Brody finished for her and I nearly came from how in sync they were when it came to controlling me. They wanted us and each other to believe they only had room in their minds for hate towards the other. But in that moment, with both of them dominating me and Knox while taking nothing and giving us everything, I saw them for what they were.

Identical.

"Fuck." I moaned as Knox rimmed my asshole before sticking his tongue into it and making my eyes roll back. "Yes, baby." He hummed and rubbed his chin across my pussy, using his whiskers to drive me mad. "No." I gasped, breaking out of the spell the three of them weaved around me. "I need—" I shook my head and stood up straight as Knox fell forward on his knees. "Stop distracting me."

Lex's eyebrows rose and Brody smirked devilishly from behind her as she challenged, "Since when is letting your man eat your pussy a bad thing?"

"Since it's stopping me from eating yours." I clenched my teeth and tried my best to take command of the room. "Enough trying to make this about me, it's about you."

"Every single thing that has happened between us has been about you, Hannah." Lex brushed a lock of hair over my shoulder. "There's nothing wrong with being worshiped."

"Not tonight." I shook my head and crossed my arms over my chest, hoping I looked at least a little bossy. "Not right now, at least." I pointed to the massive Alaskan King bed we had custom-made for us. "Get on the bed."

She stared at me and I could physically feel how badly she wanted to tell me no, simply to prove she was in charge.

"Please," I added a little softer, while still trying to look intimidating.

"Better do as she says," Knox stood up behind me and palmed both of my breasts, which made it impossible to look or feel in charge. "Hannah can get quite the sexy little pissed off kitten vibe going if she's disobeyed."

"The lioness." Lex corrected him, staring right at me with a look of satisfaction in her eyes. "Eager to bow down to the King when she's in the mood. But in reality, she's the most lethal in the entire pride." She licked her lips and then sauntered toward the bed, "How do you want me, ma'am?"

I swallowed down the shock of her doing what I said and praising me at the same moment and shook a disappointed Knox off.

"On your back, laying down."

Following my instructions, she seductively climbed up onto the bed and then crawled until she positioned herself at the center, laying down. The pillows gave her enough of a recline that she was staring at the three of us; I imagined with as much hunger in her eyes as was in ours.

"Knox," I called, and her pupils dilated, waiting for my command, "Help me unwrap our present." I took his hand and pulled him with me until we were crawling up the bed together. Her nostrils flared as she watched, but she didn't stop me. "Say stop, and we will."

She leaned back into the pillows, glancing at Brody, then me, and then at Knox. "This little pussy cat doesn't scare me. Do your worst, baby boy."

I bit my bottom lip at how brave she was, praying I wouldn't fuck it all up. Kissing my way up her thighs to her waist, reveling in the way her body twitched and rocked with each press of my lips until I got to the waistband of her stockings and panties. "I don't think you understand how badly I want to see you completely naked for me," I admitted to her as I nodded to Knox, who slowly moved to pull the band down, but she stopped him with her hand on his.

"With your teeth." She purred, challenging him and blurring the lines even more.

"Sweetheart, you don't want me to have my mouth that close to your *kitty*," Knox chuckled sexually, "You can't trust me around such a teasing treat."

She didn't reply, instead, she simply raised her eyebrow and rested her head back on the pillow. It was such a power move I nearly melted from it all.

I sensed Brody moving around the room and caught him pulling up a chair alongside the bed to watch. While a part of me ached to have him be as big a part of this as we were, I understood both his and her hesitation at the moment. So I allowed it for a while.

"Temptress," Knox growled and then leaned forward, using his perfect white teeth to grab the band of her stockings and tore them off with a ferocious shake of his head.

"Jesus, fuck." I fought to contain my need as Lex kicked them off the rest of the way as he went back in for her thong, repeating the process and tearing it straight from her body and tossing it at Brody with a flick of his neck.

Lex was in charge.

No doubt about it.

While she wanted me to think I was calling the shots, I knew the truth. But that didn't mean I wasn't going to have fun while I pretended. I turned away from her, completely ignoring my carnal need to spread her thighs and finally look at the pussy I'd been fantasizing about since I met her. Instead, I stripped Knox until he was as bare as we were.

Naked and hard as a rock where he kneeled at her feet on the bed, staring down at her.

When I redirected my focus to Lex, he had accomplished the desired effect. She was nearly writhing on the bed as she stared at him on display for her. So close to the wetness between her thighs, yet untouchable by her own standards.

"Time to give Brody what he won." I licked my lips. "And what I crave."

"Do. It." She dared and parted her knees as I pushed them further and finally came face to face with my prize. She was perfectly bare and exactly what I envisioned she would look like, it was unreal. I laid down on the bed, kicking my feet up above my ass as I prolonged her torture by being so close, yet not touching her how she wanted me to. I stared up at her soulful eyes as I pursed my lips and gently blew on her wet pussy. It was overwhelming to have her so exposed and so at my mercy. "Tease." She clenched her teeth as she fisted the blankets.

"Yes," I admitted before dropping one slow, sensual kiss directly onto her swollen clit and did nothing more than keeping it between my pouty lips before gently stroking my tongue over it inside of my mouth. "I believe in delayed gratification." In reality, I was savoring the taste of her on my tongue. I couldn't have imagined actually wanting to taste a woman's arousal a few months ago, but with Lex, I craved it.

"Yet just moments ago, you threatened me while I stripped you." She panted and cursed as I seductively flattened my tongue and ran it up the entirety of her pussy to that addictive clit again. "Yes," She hissed and buried her fingers in my hair, as she bit her bottom lip, watching me. "Just like that."

The badass woman was melting from *my* touch, laid out in *my* bed, begging *me* for more.

"Tell me what you like." I purred and sucked her clit into my mouth, rolling my tongue across it in a sensual movement.

"You're fucking doing it." She gasped and palmed her breasts, tweaking her nipples as her bare heels dug into the mattress next to me. "Hannah," She cried.

"That's it." I channeled Brody and Knox as I watched her unravel from my touch. The things they would say to me every time they brought me to ecstasy, just like I was with her. I ached to have them be a part of it too. I turned to Brody and smirked at him as I pushed my tongue into her. "What do you think, baby?" I asked him. "One or two fingers to start?"

I spread her thighs wider with my arm as I gently drew my finger through her sweet wetness.

"Are you asking me how many fingers to push into your girlfriend for the first time?" He questioned, driving us all wild with his dirty talk.

"Yes." I purred, glancing up to Lex, who stared at him even as he only gave me his attention.

"I don't know." He rubbed his hand across his jaw like he was contemplating it. "Do you want to tease her or make her scream?"

"Jesus." Lex panted and laid her head back on the pillow, swallowing audibly as Knox squeezed my ass cheek next to his legs as he fought to stay quiet. I could feel how much he wanted to join in.

"What do you think, Knoxy?" I looked over at him and used my fingers to open her up so he could literally see into her body. "Tease or scream?"

He licked his lips as he stared at her, "Scream." He looked away from her pussy to me, "I want you to make her scream."

"With pleasure." I went back to work, feeling braver and bolder than I'd ever felt before, as I slid two fingers into her body while sucking on her clit.

"Oh, God!" She arched her entire body like a cat until only her ass and her head touched the bed and it was so sexy that I purred against her body and drove her further towards madness. I curled my fingers like she did the other night and knew the instant I found her G-spot, even though in all of my thirty years on earth I hadn't been able to find my own. She unfurled into a mess of limbs and nails as she clawed at the bed.

"Give me more." I licked my lips and thrust my fingers quicker. "I want to see you kiss Knox again."

"Hannah," She cried in desperation as she looked at the hunk sitting so perfectly silent at my side while we explored. "Okay."

He laid down at her side and used his big hand on the side of her face to turn her to him, kissing her and muffling her cries of pleasure as I did everything she liked over and over in a rhythm that made her shiver.

I could have come from just watching them kiss while I tasted her, but I focused on her pleasure as she got closer and closer to her release.

"Touch me." She panted, digging her nails into Knox's shoulder and pulling him closer until his naked body pressed against her. "I'm so close."

"Hannah's perfect, isn't she?" Knox asked her, glancing down at me as he seductively traced his fingers over her stomach, making her twitch under them. "She's never done this before, yet she's making you crazy for her."

"It's all of you." Lex gasped, shaking her head back and forth when I dipped my tongue down to her ass and teased it. "It's fucking with my head."

I glanced over at Brody, who was staring at the two of them like they were the sun, mesmerized by them and aching to get closer. As if he could read my mind, he looked at me and then stood up, standing at the side of the bed like the boogey man in the middle of the night.

His dark tattoos and tanned skin added to the mysterious vibe, and it made me drip with excitement as he finally put himself close to the action. Both Lex and Knox sensed him and broke apart from their kiss, and stared up at him. Everyone sort of paused, waiting to see what he did next.

He leaned down slowly until he hovered over Lex's naked body with his fist on the blanket right next to her side. I was entranced as she panted, her gaze fixed on him, waiting for either of them to break through the divide they had created.

But he wouldn't move first, I knew that.

Instead, he wrapped one hand around the back of Knox's neck and pulled him in for a hungry kiss. They kissed deep and passionately right above Lex's face, and it mesmerized her.

And I wasn't going to waste the opportunity.

I started anew, thrusting my fingers into her and putting everything I had into making her come.

Whether it was my skills, the erotic scene unfolding right above her as Brody dominated Knox with his tongue, or even the way Knox's hand drifted up and cupped her breast, tweaking her nipple and playing with it, I'd never know.

But it worked, and she gasped, throwing her head back and screaming as she came on my face like the perfect good girl she really was when she let herself be.

She brought her hand up and gripped Brody's bicep as she came and he turned his attention to her. "Good fucking girl." He growled, "Just like I knew you were."

"Fuck you." She panted tiredly as she relaxed back into the bed and smiled lazily. "That was all for Hannah."

I kissed gentle kisses on the inside of her thigh and then crawled up her body until all four of us were breathing the same air.

"Whatever you say," Brody smirked and then turned to me. "Give me a taste." He grabbed the front of my throat and pulled me to him, crashing his lips down on mine and tasting her pussy second-hand, while simultaneously making mine throb. "Mmh." He growled, pulling back and licking his lips seductively, "What a pairing."

"My turn." Knox grinned and turned me toward him, repeating the same melt-worthy kiss, all while Lex lay there beneath us, watching us. "Pussy on your lips suits you." He ran his tongue over my lips once more and then pulled back.

Chapter 21 – Lex

I wasn't the kind of girl to believe in heaven or hell, but laying in their bed while they all tasted me off each other, made me think just maybe there was a place with pearly gates and eternal sunshine.

It was unnatural how right it felt to be where I was at that exact moment. With whom I was with.

Unfamiliar ideas and feelings overwhelmed me, making my head swim, and I simply wanted to rely on what I knew to regain stability on level ground.

So I did what I always did when I needed to feel like myself again.

I got bossy.

I pulled Hannah's hips forward from where she kneeled between my thighs and interlocked our legs as I flipped her over until she was underneath me, taking the spot I just vacated.

She gasped and giggled as she landed in a huff, staring up at us as I descended and hovered right over her face, using my arms to brace me.

"They call me the good girl, but we all know who that title belongs to." I rocked forward so my thigh pressed directly against her pussy and ground it there as she moaned, gripping my hips for more. "Time to learn another party trick." I flicked my thumb over one of her nipples, rolling my hips and drawing another moan from her.

"Is it what I think it is?" She bit her bottom lip.

"Depends," I shifted and brought one leg over hers, straddling it and sitting up, lifting her other leg with me until it was against my chest, effectively pressing her dripping wet pussy against mine as I rubbed them together. "Was this what you were hoping for?"

"God yes!" She moaned, with her brows pinched over her eyes as she held onto my thigh for dear life. "Oh my god, fuck yes."

Brody chuckled and stood up off the bed, removing his pants, and I tried so fucking hard not to watch that thick log of a cock swing as he kicked them off. I *really* fucking tried.

But I failed.

I swallowed, imagining the burn from it pushing into a pussy for the first time and panted from just the mental image he was giving me.

His dark eyes held mine as I fought to ignore him completely, but he made it impossible.

And I hated that.

So I gave my attention to Hannah and Knox instead.

The first man I ever kissed.

Ever.

Though I'd never tell him that.

I rolled my hips as Hannah mewed like the perfect little kitten, getting everything she wanted. And I was the one giving it to her. I was the one she wanted, and that drove me fucking feral.

"I'm going to make you come so hard," I rolled my hips like I was on a mechanical bull, "You're going to forget any orgasm either of these men have given you before."

Knox scoffed and Brody grunted as he crawled onto the bed and laid down next to Hannah.

"You believe that; I can tell." Knox drew my attention to him, where he kneeled on the other side of Hannah's leg that I was holding to my chest. "But you're not right."

"Only one way to find out." I teased and bit her calf, eliciting a screech out of her and a snarly grin out of him as he leaned forward and pressed his body against her leg, essentially making a sandwich. "The real question is, are you man enough to handle it if I do?"

"Big enough to let you find out." He reached between our bodies and slid his finger against her clit, simultaneously pushing it against mine because of the proximity between us. "Ride it."

His knuckle gave just enough pressure against my clit that I knew if I kept rocking against her body and his finger, I'd explode in no time at all, even after that earth-shattering orgasm minutes ago from her amazing oral skills.

But I couldn't back down from a challenge. Not with Knox.

Knox was safe, even if he was aligned with *him*.

Brody.

The one who terrified me.

Hannah panted, rocking her hips softly and using the pressure of his finger to pleasure herself, even though I stayed still.

"You're not afraid of a little *assistance*, are you?" He stared at me so deeply I was sure he'd see the cracks in my story.

I swallowed and looked to Hannah for her guidance, but she was so deep in the state of sexual arousal, all I saw was her need shining through her eyes back at me. So I rocked forward again, testing the unfamiliar sensation of Knox's calloused thick finger between us, and shuddered at how fucking good it felt.

And he knew it.

"That's it." He nodded his approval and leaned so close I could have kissed him without even trying. "It feels good, doesn't it?"

He was asking for the impossible, yet he already knew the answer. He could feel the answer from how my body trembled from the pleasure he was giving me, by simply allowing me to use his body.

"Yes," I admitted, fighting against my need to tell him to fuck off and shove that finger up his ass in retaliation. Why was anger and defiance always my go-to? Why did I always fight everything? "But you already knew that."

I moved again, watching the way Hannah's pupils dilated until her entire eyes were dark and needy as Brody started sucking on her nipples and playing with her body, making her writhe and shake underneath me.

I had planned to make her come, to prove to everyone she didn't need a cock or a man to feel satisfied. When in reality, here we were, using all four of our bodies to find pleasure. I was using Hannah and Knox for my release.

"I can feel how much you like it." He tempted me again, still so fucking close. "I want to make you come, Lex." He growled, "Do you have any idea how fucking wild that is for me?"

"I—" I gasped and tilted my head back, picking up speed and pressure, driving both Hannah and me into bliss. "Yes!"

"Oh my god, Lex!" Hannah cried, "Oh fuck!"

I dropped her leg and collapsed forward, kissing her and absorbing her cries as we both orgasmed mutually for the first time. And I never wanted to come again unless she was right there with me.

"You're perfect," I whispered against her lips as she clung to me. And even though the guys were lying on each side of us, I didn't feel as thrown off by that as I thought I would when I first found out she was in a relationship with them. "Absolutely fucking perfect."

She shook her head no, pushing my hair back behind my head and leaning up to kiss me, "I can't describe this feeling inside of me every time I'm near you. It's overwhelming, and when I'm with you like this, with Brody and Knox right here with us, it's *everything*."

"I know." I nodded in agreement and then sighed, knowing the moment of peace after orgasm was going to end. While I was sated and content, two hulking men with rock-hard erections were just lying in wait, barely restraining themselves. "I think you have two men to see to."

She bit her lip and looked at each side with a sexy smile before looking back at me. "You could help me."

"I'm not interested in seeing to their sexual satisfaction," I reminded her, and myself. "You know that."

"I didn't ask you to fuck them." She stared deep into my eyes, "But I think there's some gray area between fucking them and completely sitting out that you're comfortable in. Tell me I'm wrong."

"I don't know—" I hesitated, glancing at Knox and not hating the way my body tingled from the memory of his touch. Then to Brody and once again, feeling that burn of desperation inside of me every time I looked at his brooding stare. "I don't understand this."

"Me either." She smiled and kissed me again. "I think you should let go of the confusion and thought behind the desire and embrace the pleasure for what it is."

"And what is it exactly?" I sat up, letting her up until we were facing each other, with Knox and Brody lying there, silently watching us.

"Everything." She said, repeating the phrase she used to encompass the feelings growing between us. "It's everything. No labels or definitions can contain it all."

"Okay." I agreed because I had no real reason not to. "Show me how you make them lose their minds for you." I kissed her and found Brody's dark stare penetrating me when I glanced over at him. "Teach me."

"Boys." She called, scrambling and pushing them together until they were both lying next to each other. "They can't resist a good blow job." She smirked, straddling one thigh and leaning over until both of their thick cocks bobbed by her face.

"Can any man?" I deadpanned, even as I leaned closer as she fisted both cocks and ran her tongue over the tip of Brody's. She teased him like a few times, before moving over to Knox's and doing the same.

Knox was the more vocal one out of the two, groaning every time she touched him. Did she even understand the power she held over him with her body? Did she care?

She pulled back and spit on Brody's cock and then rubbed her hand over it, stroking him in long, deep pulls before she started sucking on Knox's. I watched in fascination as she worked them both up.

Brody petted her hair, gathering it to the side to hold out of her way as she sucked their boyfriend off, and I envied that kind of connection with someone. He was getting less, but eager to assist and pleasure others.

Hannah switched and started sucking on Brody's cock while stroking Knox's, and Brody's dark eyes stared at me over her head. Challenging me.

Could he tell how close I was to begging to be fucked? I wanted to be fucked hard by Hannah with a toy while they watched. Only a small part of me imagined taking one of them instead of a toy.

That small part was growing each time Hannah hummed and rocked her hips.

Chapter 22 – Brody

Teach me.

Words that Hannah and Lex uttered all night, learning more about their bodies and sexuality than ever imagined.

While Knox and I eagerly volunteered as tributes to be experimented on. Lex never touched me, and I didn't touch her, but that was fine with both of us.

She let Knox in though, occasionally kissing him and one time, even using her hand to stroke his cock before lining him up with Hannah's pussy and leading him in.

I almost nutted, watching it.

At one point, Lex laid on her back, with Hannah straddling her waist, laying flat against her chest kissing while I fucked Hannah with everything I had. When I first started, I tried to be respectful and keep as far away from Lex as possible. But when Hannah started begging for it harder and I slammed into her, my balls brushed Lex's pussy and she silently gasped, locking eyes with me over my girl's shoulder. She didn't tell me to fuck off, so I did it again.

And again.

Slamming deep into Hannah and rocking her pussy against Lex's as my balls continued to slap her soaking wet pussy lips from beneath with each thrust.

Both girls came at the same time, and I knew without a doubt that the constant impact of my body against her pussy helped push her over the edge.

Even if she'd never admit it. She didn't have to, her face said it all when her eyes rolled back in her head and she cried out in ecstasy.

I did that.

With Hannah's help. And it was the hottest thing ever. I should have known better than to think it would have softened her at all though, because as soon as I pulled out of Hannah, my come dripped out, falling onto Lex's spread pussy and she flew out of bed and straight into the bathroom like I'd bitten her.

It scared her, having us so close, and not just because she played for the other team. There was more there, deeper inside of her beneath that bad ass persona she held onto and hid behind.

The girls were in the shower, and Knox and I laid in bed, listening to the soft giggles and moans coming from the other room, but neither of us moved to join.

I couldn't get hard again if I wanted to, to be honest.

I lost count of how many times I came over the last six hours after number seven. My balls ached from even imagining it.

Knox nudged me with his hand, and I opened one eye to look at him. "You're thinking so loud even I can hear it." He said, leaving his hand on my arm and rubbing his thumb over my skin. "But thank you."

"For what?"

"For giving Hannah this." He sighed and rolled over to face me. "For keeping every smart-ass remark or chiding to yourself while she got what she so desperately wanted."

"Like you didn't want it too." I deadpanned, rubbing my hand up and down over my stomach. "It felt good, right?"

He snorted and nodded, "It felt perfect."

"No." I shook my head gently. "Not quite perfect. But good."

"What would have made it perfect for you?" He questioned, but I didn't answer. I didn't have to. "Ah," He mused, "Having Lex."

"I thought she was going to beg for it at one point." I looked over at him. "At least from you."

"To be honest, so did I, but then she—" He shrugged, "chickened out."

"She wants you," I said firmly. "I don't know why she insists on acting like she doesn't."

A loud moan floated from the shower, followed by Hannah's evil chuckle. My cock stirred against my stomach and I groaned, loving and hating how both girls could make my cock defy physics.

"I don't think she's acting." Knox shook his head. "I think she genuinely is as torn about it as we think she is."

"Maybe," I sighed, and the water turned off in the shower. "Or maybe it's all a ruse to sneak in and steal our girl."

As the girls came out of the bathroom, wrapped up in towels, Lex had her hair piled up in a messy bun and it was dry, but her skin looked fresh and clean, completely bare for the first time.

Sure, we'd seen her naked and begging for an orgasm, but she still had her *armor* on. She washed off her thick makeup and revealed fresh skin, looking far younger than she was. She then followed Hannah into bed, almost shyly. Knox and I rolled apart so there was room for them in the middle, with Hannah dropping her towel and curling into me, as Lex dropped her towel and laid against Hannah's side.

"You are at least eighteen, right?" Knox asked her with a soft nudge before yawning.

"Thirty, to be exact." She deadpanned, and he nodded his acceptance.

A silence fell around us all as sleep tried to pull me under, given that it was almost five in the morning. I had work again in a few hours that I'd gladly be late for if I got some decent sleep in exchange.

I flicked the light off on the bedside lamp and the room fell completely dark. In the darkness, Hannah broke the silence. "Tell us about Sydney."

Mention of the woman from the poker table piqued my interest, given that we knew almost nothing about Lex or her past aside from what the girls had talked about at the shop.

Lex let out a big breath and groaned, "Careful, if you say her name three times in a row, she appears like Beetlejuice."

Knox snorted, and Hannah giggled, but I just listened.

"What do you want to know, exactly?" Lex finally followed up, figuring out that Hannah wasn't that easy to brush off. Her investigative journalism nature ran strong inside of her.

"You two were together?" Hannah asked as I stared up at the ceiling.

"In a way." Lex admitted, "I met her shortly after I moved here at an—" She paused, "event."

"A kink party?" Knox guessed, and Lex groaned again.

"Yeah. I went for the fun of it, not expecting much."

"And found Syndey." Hannah finished, "What happened?"

"She sank her claws into me so far I never saw the blood until it was too late."

I could hear the pain in her voice as she spoke, but couldn't understand why exactly she didn't hide it. Maybe it was from her tiredness, or maybe she just felt comfortable sharing secrets in the dark.

Maybe there was hope after all.

"She's an abuser, isn't she?" I asked, surprising everyone, I was sure.

"The worst kind," Lex admitted. "She alienates you and keeps you all to herself until you have no one left in your life but her. The entire time you're so enamored and engrossed, that you don't see how dangerous it is until she gets bored and throws you away like trash. And by then, you have no one left in your life to pick your pieces up. I was an easy target, being that I just moved here and was all alone except for people from Twisted Ink. I made it too easy for her to get away with."

"She was your Domme?" Knox surmised.

"Yes," Lex admitted, and again, I was sure it was only the darkness that gave her the bravery to open herself up. I couldn't admit it, but something inside of me snarled, imagining that woman abusing the relationship between a Domme and a sub. "And my last. I promised I'd never give control away to anyone else, ever again. I can't."

Me. She was talking about me.

She'd never give herself to me because that woman destroyed the sacred relationship built on trust and understanding. Once again, as soon as I imagined that bond between us actually being possible, even if it wasn't sexual, she closed it. Locking herself away behind more walls and armor.

I kissed Hannah's forehead and gently got out of bed.

"Where are you going?" She asked and Knox turned on his bedside light as all three of them looked at me.

"Work." I sighed, walking into the closet. "I forgot I have something to take care of today."

"What is it?" Knox snapped. "I don't remember there being anything on the books so pressing that you can't get a few hours of sleep before dealing with it."

"Don't worry about it, Knox." I got dressed, but I could feel their eyes on me with every piece of clothing I put on. "Go to sleep, you all need your rest."

"You're running." Hannah sighed, sitting up in bed and bringing the sheet with her, suddenly hiding herself from me.

Just like I was hiding myself from her. From all of them.

Because I was the problem in the mix, keeping Lex from giving herself to them freely.

I was too dominant for her and for the second time in my life; I hated how I regretted the very core of my being. Like I should be something different.

Like I should just turn it off.

"Stay." Lex tried sitting up. "I'll go."

"No." I held my hand up, and she instantly stopped moving. "It's fine. Knox can take you back to your car later."

I didn't stick around to hear anything else they had to say as I walked out of the bedroom and through the dark house. I got on my bike and tore out of the driveway as everything weighed down on my shoulders like it had so many years ago when I walked away from everything I ever knew for something I wanted more.

Years ago, the thing I'd wanted most was Hannah and Knox. However, this time, I was the very thing standing in the way of them getting what they wanted most.

Lex.

Chapter 23 – Hannah

"This is fantastic," I whispered in awe as the film crew and photographers set up the scene for the shoot inside Twisted Ink. "I can see it coming together already."

"It's going to be amazing." Reyna rubbed her palms together excitedly as we lurked from the side as the magic came to life. "That is, if Lex ever shows. Have you spoken to her?"

"Uh—" I stammered, the conversation took me by surprise, making me feel as if I had been caught red-handed. "No, why would you think I've spoken to her?"

Reyna scowled slightly and shook her head, "Because you orchestrated this entire shoot for her—" She faced me and crossed her arms as a blush built over my face at the obvious answer she was looking for. "Unless you thought I meant—"

"No!" I shook my head, cutting her off. "The shoot. Duh. No, she hasn't reached out today about that. I told her to be here at eight." I stammered and avoided eye contact at all costs.

"Interesting." Rey mused, staring right into my mind. "You thought I meant because you were sleeping with her."

"Reyna!" I hushed and pulled her further away from the men and women I worked with all the time. "I am not—"

"Oh, don't lie to me." She rolled her eyes and opened the door to Dallin's suite, ushering me inside and closing the door behind us. "I know about the Sinner's Soiree."

"You know—" I fought the urge to crawl under the door and slink away from the entire conversation. Especially given how she left things at our house last night. After Brody left, Lex waited for Knox and me to fall asleep and then ordered an Uber and left. Waking up without Brody or Lex was like a gut punch. Once again. "What do you know?"

"I know something was happening between you guys and she wanted to pretend there wasn't. At least until Parker mentioned Dallin got you guys an invitation to the Soiree. And then she suddenly was going too."

"Oh." I brushed my hair behind my ear as she speculated past that.

"So what happened and why are you acting like a long-tailed cat in a rocking chair store?" She didn't mince words, and usually that was refreshing in our friendship, but today I didn't know what to say or how to define the last few weeks. However, if anyone was to understand what I was going through, it would be Reyna.

"I'm—" I hesitated and then just ripped the band-aid off. "I'm bi," I announced and felt my stomach drop as she just stared at me like she was waiting for the rest of that sentence.

"And?" She scoffed and waved me off when I coughed in reply, "Oh stop acting like it's 1902. You being bi is no enormous scandal."

"But I'm already in a throuple with Brody and Knox. Anything more than that is just too much. It's too far." I spoke about the fears I'd had since realizing I wanted Lex to join our relationship.

"Too far?" She leaned against the wall, "What does that mean?"

I sighed and sat down on the couch next to the tattoo bench. "Too far from normal. Too different."

"By whose standards?" She asked and then stood up straight with wide eyes. "Oh, your dad's."

"Yeah." I deflated further. "The news of me being in love with two men and intending to date them both was enough to shock and scandalize him. Imagine me trying to tell him I'm attracted to women, especially a woman like Lex, and that I want her in our relationship, too." I scoffed. "It doesn't matter, anyway. She doesn't want that. She only wants the fun."

"Okay," Rey sat down next to me. "There's a lot to unpack here, but we luckily have the time. So let's start with your bisexuality, because that's the easiest problem to fix."

I snorted and rolled my eyes at her, unbelieving. "How am I going to *fix* that?"

"Easy." She shrugged, "You're not. Because there's nothing wrong with it, you have nothing to fix. And your dad is going to agree with me on it as soon as you remind him that it is 2024 and you have no interest in allowing past generational toxicity to shape your life any further."

"Jeeze." I blew bangs out of my face, feeling overwhelmed, "You make that sound so cut and dry." I loved how accepting she was of every person in every shape and color, but I knew the rest of the world wasn't always like that.

"It is," She waved me off again and then patted her hand on my leg and moved on to the next *problem*. "Now, the expansion of a relationship can get tricky, especially if everyone isn't on the same page from the start." She rolled her eyes, "Ask me how I know."

"Trey." I smiled, remembering the way she and her husband Trey hated each other in the very beginning, after Dallin admitted to her he wanted them all to be together. "I think Lex wants us all to believe that she hates Brody and sometimes hates Knox too, but I don't think that's the truth."

"Why?" She prodded, "She's a lesbian after all, it would make sense that she wouldn't want them involved in her—" She hesitated and then just blurted it out, "Sexual exploitations."

"Ew." I cringed and then chuckled, as the weight of it all didn't seem so daunting in the presence of a friend. "I guess in a way I wanted to have my cake and eat it too."

"You wanted the guys to be with her?" She raised her brows in surprise. "You mean sexually and not just amicably as a metamour? Hmm, bravo Hannah Kate, you're a braver woman than I am."

"What do you mean? Metamour?" I laughed it off, "Now I'm imagining those flashy bullfighters with their fancy capes."

She cackled and pushed me jokingly. "Matadors are Spanish bullfighters. Metamours are essentially your partner's partner in a poly relationship. Are you really unfamiliar with the terms?"

"Yes," I admitted. "Outside of the terms triad or throuple, Brody, Knox, and I have never truly lived within the lifestyle, so we've never educated ourselves on other variations of poly relationships before."

"Interesting." She mused. "If you were to date Lex, but she didn't date the guys, they would be each other's metamour. You'd be the only common denominator between them."

"I hate the idea of that." I admitted, "And that's wrong of me, isn't it? Selfish even."

"If it's not what Lex or the guys want, then yes." She agreed, and I cringed before she moved on, soothing the burn of that. "But that doesn't mean it's not what you want. You can have hopes and dreams, Hannah. Sometimes they don't fit our current situations, though."

"The guys want her." I stared off at the wall. "At first, they both balked at the idea because of how dominant she is, but they couldn't deny their attraction to her after spending time with her. And then there're times that she—"

"She what?" Rey prodded after I faded out.

"She blurs the lines." I played with a string on my shirt. "She kisses Knox and even—" I shook my head, not wanting to give away too many details of our personal sex life.

"I get it." Rey held a hand up. "That's blurring the lines, for sure. But did you stop to think that maybe Lex is just as confused as you are about those lines and boundaries she's set? Maybe just how you were when you first realized *you* were bi."

I mulled that over in my head and tried to imagine Lex being unsure of anything. "She's so hot and cold, I can't tell."

"Listen," Rey put her hand on my arm. "I know Lex pretty well because over the years I've relied on her opinion where the guys are concerned. So while I don't know what's going through her head right now, I can guess that she's not trying to be hot and cold. That's not her normal personality. I think she's on the ride as much as you are right now."

"So what do I do?" I shook my head. "How do I help her understand what she wants? Or better yet, how do I determine if I just want a female addition to our relationship, or if I'm so fucked in my head because it *has* to be her?"

"I think you already know the answer to that because your entire demeanor changed while talking about her specifically."

"I know." I sighed, "I just don't know how to make everyone happy."

"Answer me this, if she only wanted to be with you, would you do it?"

I hesitated, though I already knew the answer to that. "No." I looked at my best friend and knew she knew exactly why I felt that way. "I don't want something outside of my home. Brody and Knox are my home."

"I know the feeling." She smiled reassuringly. "Maybe just give everyone some time to consider everything and go from there."

"I'm just afraid of her walking away in the end and taking a part of my heart with her."

The electronic bell rang from the back entrance of the shop, and I heard the crew welcoming Lex to the shoot. "I think there's only one way to find out," She stood up and pulled me with her. "But if I were a betting woman," she wagged her eyebrows and stage whispered, "which I am, by the way," she returned to normal volume, "I'm going to guess that Lex and Brody can resolve any problems in one of two ways. Either with intense power struggling hate sex, or actual adult communication." She giggled as I looked physically ill at the options laid out, "I'll let you four decide which route to take on that one, but for what it's worth, I think with a little time you'll figure it out."

"Thanks." I sighed and gathered up my strength to face Lex in the weird professional dynamic we were in at the moment. "I appreciate the sounding board."

"Anytime." Reyna slid the door open. "Once upon a time, Dallin took off to chase after Trey after he promised he would never leave me or choose the guys over me. And I'll be honest, I was far more desolate than you are right now over it because it felt like everything I had was being lost because I dared to want more. Just like you are right now."

"What happened?" I asked, having never heard that part of their story before. "How did you all come back from that to get where you are right now?"

She blew out a breath exasperatedly, "Well, let's just say there were a lot of sex toys, apologies, and blue balls included in the resolution."

Lex rounded the corner, hearing the statement from our friend, and paused with an amused grin on her face. "I think I'm late for the conversation, care to recap it for me?"

Rey gave her a quick hug and then winked at me, "Maybe I'll tell you both one day about how I managed to have my cake and eat it too."

"Can't wait." I nodded as she walked back toward the lobby, leaving me and Lex alone in the hallway.

"Let me guess," Lex turned to me and looked me up and down, heating my skin and flushing my face from a mere flick of her lashes. "That was about me?"

"In a way," I admitted, nodding to the garment bag in her hand. "I'll give you some privacy to get ready for the shoot." I smiled softly and went to step around her, following Rey out to the lobby so Lex could get changed.

But as I stepped next to her, she placed her hand on my stomach, stopping me dead in my tracks and looking over at her, like a fish on a line, waiting for my fate to be decided. I couldn't read her mood or thoughts through her dark eyes and thick makeup, and I wanted to wipe it all off and see the real her. Just like last night when she told us about Sydney in the dark.

"Or you could come with me, so I can apologize for leaving the way I did." She slid her hand over my hip and pulled me until I was flush with the front of her body and I placed my hands on her waist as I took a deep breath in of her intoxicating perfume. "Please, Hannah." She lowered her voice and closed her eyes like she was tired.

"Okay." I nodded and then stayed silent as she took my hand and pulled me down the vacant hall to her suite, closing the door behind us. It was dark in the room and she flipped a switch on the wall, bathing the room in the vibrant pink up lighting from the floor, but that was it.

I hadn't been alone with her since that day in the parking lot when I admitted I was attracted to her. Every interaction since then had been with Brody, Knox, and us. Something about being in the silent, dark room with her made everything else so much more noticeable.

The way the air conditioner cooled my overheating skin. The way the scent of her perfume felt like a blanket of comfort for my brain. The way her quiet breathing felt predatory as my eyes fought to see through the dimness. The way my stomach fluttered as she laid her bag down on the chair and sauntered toward me.

Her beauty was so incredibly captivating that I never stopped being amazed whenever I saw her. She wore a black short and tank top set, sandals, and had flawlessly done her hair and makeup. She took my breath away.

"I shouldn't have left like I did." She breathed as she continued to cross the room to me. "I shouldn't have said what I did. Brody shouldn't leave his own home because of me." She sighed gently and I could feel the sincerity in her words.

"Then why did you?"

"Because he was right." She stopped right in front of me. "And I hate that."

"He was right?" I didn't believe my ears.

She swallowed and tucked a strand of hair behind my ear, and I couldn't stop my head from leaning into her touch. I ached to feel her skin on mine as much as I did Brody or Knox. With things so uncertain between Lex and me, I longed for her touch to mend it all.

She leaned forward and gently brushed her nose against mine, closing her eyes and taking a deep breath in, like I was comforting her at the moment that I sought that same calm.

"I think I'm bi." She whispered, and I was catapulted back into that conversation between her and me not so long ago when I admitted the same. "Or I'm at least attracted to Brody and Knox, I think."

I remembered the way she tried to keep me at arm's length even after I cut myself open and revealed my dark secret to her. I remembered the way it hurt for her to be so nonchalant and tell me not to risk my happy home for something I wasn't even sure about.

And look at us now, we were in a sense of turmoil before we even gave it a fighting chance.

I was in turmoil, and so was she.

So were Brody and Knox.

"Say something." She pleaded, leaning her head to the side a fraction so her lips brushed mine. It wasn't a kiss, but more of a need to be physically closer. "Please Hannah, say something."

She needed me. "I'm falling for you," I admitted, equally opening myself up to her and leveling out the playing field, so we were both vulnerable. "And I think you're falling for me, too."

She shook her head, gripping the hair at the back of my head tightly like she was in pain. "I already have." She pressed her lips to mine again with no hesitation or seeking any comfort in the move. "I already am."

I moaned and opened my lips to hers, welcoming the way she kissed so passionately, embracing the need I could feel in her touch.

"I can't do the hot and cold anymore, Lex," I admitted, biting her lip and fighting to stay in control of my mind and body as her touch made my head swim.

"I'm obsessed with you, Han." She panted and shook her head again, "I can't play hard to get anymore. I don't want to."

"What does that mean, though?" I pulled back to look into her brown eyes, "You think you're bi, but I need to know what that means for us. For you."

She sighed and pulled back to take a deep breath, creating a space between our bodies, and while I hated the distance, I needed her words more than her touch. I knew her touch, and what it meant. But I needed her words at that moment.

"I didn't vow to always be in control of everything just because of Sydney. She was the second person who trapped me and left me broken at the end. So that's why I refuse to let anyone else have power over me ever again." She hesitated, but forged on. "I've never been with a guy before." She admitted, and I could see her vulnerability shining brightly as she spoke. "Knox was my first kiss with one."

"How?" I squinted as I tried to envision Lex never touching a man before, at all.

"I've never trusted men." She licked her lips, and I could feel her fear as a new side of her flashed through the dark makeup and bossy exterior. "When I was younger," she paused once more, and I could sense her anguish, "one hurt me."

"Lex." I gasped as tears burned the back of my nose. There was a universal language amongst women, and those words said it all. I knew what she meant. "You don't have to say it."

"I want to." She closed her eyes and took my hand like I was comforting her, and I clung to her, squeezing her back so tight I wasn't sure who was reassuring whom at the moment. "I was thirteen. I was walking home from a friend's house a few blocks away and a stranger—," She struggled but kept on, "He pulled up beside me in a car and grabbed me, right off the street without a second of hesitation." Tears welled in her eyes, but didn't fall. She had mastered hiding her pain behind her tough exterior for so long she couldn't even cry for herself. "He assaulted me in his car right there on the side of the street and then pushed me out onto the road and drove away. Leaving me in a heap."

"Baby." I cried, letting my tears fall for her if she wouldn't let hers.

"He didn't rape me, thank god." She sighed and opened her eyes, staring at me with pain in her watery eyes. "But he took away my trust in men forever."

"I'm so sorry." I clung to her, "I never would have pushed if I had known."

"No." She shook her head, silencing me. "That's the point I'm trying to make here. I have instantly distrusted every man I've met since that day. That's why I've embraced this bitchy personality and kept everyone away with my sarcasm and crass. But I can't keep Brody and Knox away when I'm being intimate with you, because you love them."

"I don't know what to do." I felt like she was about to tell me she was done.

"I want you to teach me how to trust again." She slid both hands around the back of my neck and pressed her forehead to mine. "I want to find a way to let go of my fear and let them in. Because I want them, Hannah. Jesus fucking Christ watching you with them, seeing their devotion to you, how they worship you and treat you like their Queen makes me want to worship *them*."

"Lex. I can't be the reason you cut yourself open."

"Don't you get it, baby?" She pulled back again to look at me. "You're helping me. You're giving me hope and teaching me that I don't have to do everything alone anymore. I want that." She closed her eyes and a single tear rolled down her cheek. "I've never regretted my solitude until I met you. Until Knox and Brody showed me how they treat the woman they love."

I kissed her. For the first time in my life, words eluded me and nothing I could think of captured what I wanted to express to her. So I showed her in the universal way.

The loving way.

She breathed me in as she kissed me back, pushing me against the wall and using her body to respond. I kissed her neck and bit her earlobe as she pushed her hips into mine, communicating her need as she moaned.

"I need you." She put her hand up my shirt and teased my rib cage before palming my breast through my lace bralette and rolling my nipple between her fingers. "I thought you were going to tell me to fuck off and that you'd had enough of me."

"I'm just as obsessed as you are with me," I assured her. "And so are the guys."

She huffed as she kissed my neck, "They hate me."

"No." I cried, digging my nails into her ass as I turned us and pushed her up against the wall, changing the power dynamic. "They hate the distance you keep putting between you and them, but they don't hate you." I put my thigh between hers and flexed my hips, dry-humping her into the wall. "They want you so fucking bad, Lex."

"I don't know how to do this with them. It feels so right with you, but I'm so hesitant with them and I don't recognize the woman I am when they're around."

"Don't worry about that right now." I undid the tie of her shorts and then pushed my hand down the front of them and she tipped her head back with her eyes closed and her lips parted as I rubbed my fingertips over her wet clit.

"Just feel." I kissed her neck and teased her ears as I played with her. I still felt like I didn't have a clue what I was doing when I touched her, but I just let my mind drift to the noises she was making and focused on the way her body talked to mine. "That's my good girl." I teased, and she smiled and then moaned when I pushed one finger into her.

A hesitant knock sounded on the door across the room and Lex's head snapped up off the wall and her eyes opened. "Uh, ladies." Rey's voice called out through the wood. "The crew is all set up out there."

I whispered as I pulled Lex's shorts down all the way and made her kick them off as I sank to my knees, "Buy us a few minutes and I'll reward you for your honesty." I pushed her shirt up and kissed her stomach on my way down to her pussy.

She licked her lips and smacked her head back against the wall as she stammered, "I'm just getting dressed. Ten minutes."

It was interesting to see Lex flustered because she hardly ever was. But with me on my knees pushing her legs open and pressing my tongue to her throbbing clit, she stumbled.

"Take your time." Reyna sang through the door all knowingly. "You're the star of the show, after all."

"Mmh-hmm." Lex hummed back, burying her fingers in my hair and rocking against my face. "Yes."

"You taste so good," I praised, playing with her exactly how she liked.

"Fuck." She hissed and looked down at me, holding my stare as I sucked on her clit. "Just like that Hannah. Please don't stop."

"Mmh," I teased her and kept it up, until she opened her mouth and wordlessly succumbed to the pleasure, riding out the waves of ecstasy as she kept her gaze locked on mine.

As soon as her body relaxed, she sank to her knees between me and the wall and kissed me. It was slow and leisurely, there was no rush for more or desperation to beat the clock as she prolonged our moment alone.

"I don't want to go out there." She whispered against my lips with a soft smile on hers. "I want to just take you home and forget about everyone else in the world."

"Wouldn't that be the dream?" I played along. "But there's a very needy journalist who's counting on this article to solidify her dreams and catapult her career out of small-town newspapers and into something more meaningful." I unfolded myself, standing up, and then held my hand out for her. "Chop chop, baby."

She pouted and then chuckled as she took my hand and let me help her stand. "Do I at least get to reciprocate the earth-shattering orgasm you just gave me?"

"Maybe." I hung her garment bag on a hook on the wall and unzipped it, revealing three sexy outfits. "If you're a good girl and do as you're told for the next few hours, I'll give you whatever you want."

She walked up behind me and rested her chin on my shoulder as she held me, "Be careful little one," She hummed sweetly before sliding her hand up my body to wrap around my neck. She pulled my head back until it rested on her shoulder and pushed her hand down the front of my dress slacks. "We both know who's going to be the good girl tonight." She rubbed my needy body as I sagged into her, "But if you're really good maybe I'll let you teach me how to make Knox come when we're all done."

"Lex." I moaned, imagining how fulfilling it would be to watch her overcome a piece of her fear and trauma with us. "You can't dangle that in front of me if you don't mean it."

"I mean it." She slowed her hand down and kissed my cheek. "I don't know the specifics or what I imagine it all to look like, but I want to try." She pulled her hand from my pants and loosened her hold on my neck. "You *all* make me want to try."

"Okay." I took a deep breath and turned to kiss her lips gently. "Then let's get this shoot done so we can start moving forward together."

"Look right here," The photographer instructed, "Drop your chin and lean forward a tad. Perfect!"

Lex was a natural in front of the camera and I was in awe as I watched her work. It didn't hurt that the dress she wore was her favorite shade of black lace, and the skin that it covered was minimal. It was deep cut in the front, exposing all the ink on her chest and between her breasts and the slit that opened up to reveal her tatted leg made my knees weak every time it moved with her body, showing me a little bit at a time.

"Jesus, Hannah," Reyna whispered from my side where we sat watching Lex pose, sitting on top of the reception desk with a tattoo magazine in her hands. "You've got it bad."

I sighed, unable to look away from the vixen as she stared back at the photographer with that powerful, seductive look she gave me when we first met. "No kidding."

"So I take it you two—worked things out?" She wagged her eyebrows at me and then giggled, drawing Lex's attention to us.

Lex raised one brow and then licked her lips in a way that probably looked normal to everyone else, but matched with her direct stare and the things we did in her suite before the shoot, I knew it was anything but.

"She wants to try," I admitted, blinking off Lex's power over me and looking over at Reyna. "That's more than I could have hoped for, given the way things have played out so far."

"So she's going to try—" She hesitated, "dick."

"Yeah." I rolled my eyes, watching as Lex laid back across the counter like a piece of art over a mantle. "She's going to try with all of us."

"That's great." Rey squeezed my arm excitedly.

The photographer called out a few more shots and then, with a big show of flare, announced he had everything he needed to complete the masterpiece. "Thank you so much for doing this." I walked forward and shook his hand as Lex joined us.

"Thank you for making this fun too," Lex added, "I hardly hated it at all." She winked at the man who was old enough to be our father and gay enough to be with all of our men combined. Which made him perfect for working with my girl.

"I'm so glad," He winked at her and then walked away as the crew started cleaning up.

"So now what?" Rey asked, looking around the shop being put back into place. "When will the piece be done? When can we see it?"

I chuckled, "You seem more excited than I am."

"I am!" Her eyes widened, "As soon as Dallin told me the story was going to be on Lex and then when I heard of your angle on it all, I've been salivating for it. We need more female empowerment in this world, and I think the two of you are just the two women to get it done correctly without feeling cheesy."

Lex crossed her arms, "Did Dallin tell you why he canceled on this whole thing to begin with?" She asked Reyna.

Rey's eyebrows rose, "He said you asked to do it."

"Did he?" She pursed her lips and then turned to me. "Did he tell you why he canceled, exactly?"

I shrugged my shoulders, "Just what I told you the first day, that the expo was too much work to take on at the same time."

"Hmm." She hummed.

"Why? Did he say something different to you?" I asked, wondering what was going on.

"Not at first." She rolled her eyes and then relaxed her shoulders, "But when I fucked things up with you," She cocked her head to the side, "He said he chose me because you needed me."

"Needed you?" I questioned, and Rey scowled in confusion, too.

"Yep." Lex went on, "And I'm beginning to think he set us up for other reasons outside of professional ones."

"What? How?" I shook my head, "Why?"

Reyna tipped her head back and laughed, "Oh, that meddling man of mine." She rolled her eyes, "Did I ever tell you two about how he finally got Parker and Trey to give in to their desires and sleep with me?"

"I'm sorry, what? *Get them to sleep with you?*" Lex nearly choked, "You're the real fucking prize out of all three of them, what do you mean, *get them to sleep with you?*"

Rey laughed again, "Let's just say none of us were jumping into the whole open relationship thing as quickly as Dallin had hoped for." She looked around and lowered her voice as the crew cleaned up around us. "So Dallin meddled and tricked both of them into very precarious situations with me until none of us could resist anymore."

"And you think he did that here?" I doubted it. "I didn't even know I was into women before I met Lex."

"That's not true," Lex smirked at me. "You were beginning to see the signs of it."

"Which means Dallin probably saw the signs of it, long before any of us would have." Rey added, "And we did all hang out at that barbeque for the garage a week before he called you about the interview, didn't we? The same night you asked me about my relationship with Trey and Parker."

"We did," I remembered the big cookout we had for all our friends and family at the garage celebrating all the success the guys had achieved over the three years they'd been open. "He said something weird that night."

"What?" Lex tilted her head to the side.

"He said that if we desire an opportunity for change, normalcy breeds uncertainty," I thought back and smirked at it now that it was making more sense. "I thought he was talking about work."

Reyna scoffed, "Huh?"

I shook my head, "He was telling me to not become complacent. Jesus fucking christ."

Lex snorted and then groaned, "Dirty words and pretty lips, Hannah."

Reyna's eyes rounded as she watched us interact, now that we all had a bit more knowledge of the subject. "Jesus fucking christ, indeed." She turned and walked away without another word.

"Where are you going?" I giggled as she headed toward the exit.

She waved without looking back. "To find my husband and to thank him with a blowjob for getting you laid."

"Oh, my god." I gasped and turned crimson as everyone looked at us, and Lex fell into a fit of cackles.

"I fucking love that girl." She said between laughing fits.

"Careful." I scowled at her with my best mean mug, "I'm not interested in sharing you."

She stopped giggling and gave me a wolfish grin as she pressed her chest against mine, trying to assert her dominance over me. "Jealous, kitten?"

"Possessive." I clarified and bared my teeth theatrically. "You've got three willing bodies to choose from now, but that's it. No others if you're with us."

"I'm with you." She leaned forward until her nose touched mine, "And I can't wait to see what those three willing bodies can do to a girl like me."

I groaned and took her by the hand, all but dragging her to her suite to grab her bags. "Text Knox. Either tell them to meet us at your place, or that we're on our way home to mine. And tell him to hydrate, because he's going to fucking need it."

"Pretty lips," Lex growled as I shoved her belongings in her bag while she texted Knox. "Take me home, pretty girl. I want to see what other dirty words these lips know how to say."

Chapter 24 – Lex

I followed Hannah's car through the woods to her house, and butterflies fluttered in my stomach with each mile closer. As I drove over the edge of their driveway, I forced myself to treat the experience as a fresh start.

It was a new chapter, and I couldn't help but feel an overwhelming sense of excitement and anticipation for what lay ahead.

I pushed the fear down each time it crawled up my throat, remembering the interactions I'd had with the three of them thus far, and how unthreatening they had been to my safety when my guard was down. I clung to that reality as Hannah parked her car and got out, waiting for me.

Parking Sally off to the side of the wide gravel driveway, I got out. I was still in my black lace dress since Hannah had stolen my bag of clothes in her haste to get us home to her men, and I pulled the long skirt open so I didn't trip in the darkness as I walked across the driveway in my heels to where she stood. "Why do you look surprised to see me here?" I asked, taking in her devious smirk.

"I mean, I wouldn't have been surprised if you decided to run in the other direction halfway here." She shrugged and then leaned in to kiss me.

"Take it easy on me tonight. Okay?" I meant it to be light, but even I could hear the fear in my voice. I clenched my teeth together as that brewed anger alongside the fear.

"Just say the word, and we'll stop." She weaved her fingers through mine, stood there holding my bag, and waited for me to get a grip on my emotions. "I want you to know how much you even being here means to me."

"Then take me inside." I kissed her again, forcing a smile onto my lips as I gazed up at the romantic front porch with swings and rocking chairs. "Show me how it feels to be with you. For real this time."

"Come on," She smiled sweetly and led me up the front porch stairs. When we walked through the front door, she turned a lamp on that sat on the side table and then paused. "Weird."

"What is?" I shut and locked the door behind us.

"Well, I would have thought that they'd be knocking each other over to get to us." She looked back out the window to verify their trucks and bikes were both parked in the driveway. "Hmm."

"Maybe they're asleep?" I questioned, though I would be lying if I said I wasn't a little let down by that idea.

"Not a chance." Hannah kicked her shoes off and tossed my bag down on the bench before lowering herself to my feet and unstrapping my heels. Instead of acknowledging the domesticity of the action, I simply smiled in gratitude, recognizing that her mind was preoccupied. Then a loud bang echoed through the ceiling, and a sly grin played out on her lips.

"What was that?"

"That," She giggled and pulled me toward the stairs, "Was one of our guys getting fucked." She climbed the stairs in record time. "I'm going to guess that Knox is giving it to Brody, hoping to calm him down and take some of the fight out of him." She looked over her shoulder at me as we made our way toward the noise in the bedroom. "But either way, one of them is taking it hard right now."

"Why is that so—"

"Hot?" She giggled.

"Incredibly so." I raised a brow at her as she paused with her hand on the door handle. I could distinctly make out the noise of sex through the wood. Hard sex. And my body tingled, eager to see exactly what was happening on the other side of that door. "Open it."

"Yes, Ma'am." She licked her lips and pushed the door open, revealing the act happening inside.

"Fucking Hell," I whispered. Hannah giggled again, leaning into my side. "Hmm, maybe it's me who needs to see what other dirty words your pretty lips can say."

"Fuck!" Brody roared, taking any giggling out of the equation as we walked into the bedroom. The smell of sex permeated the air and the sound of skin slapping echoed under the sound of Brody's call of ecstasy.

He was on his knees on the bed, with both arms stretched out straight, gripping the footboard as Knox fucked him. They fucked with such intensity that every muscle in both of their bodies tightened, and I found myself absolutely enthralled.

Before meeting this triad, I had never seen men in the action of sex before, and these two men were absolute perfection.

Their muscles and ink were on display as they ignored the rest of the world in pursuit of their ecstasy.

"What's the matter," Hannah quipped, walking forward with her arms crossed under her breasts as she stopped at the foot of the bed, "Couldn't wait for us to get started?"

"Fuck no," Knox grunted as he slammed deep again. He reached around Brody's neck and grabbed the front of his throat, pulling him up even further. "This bastard here went absolutely feral over Lex's text, so I figured the responsible thing to do was to fuck the animal out of him." Knox winked at me over Brody's shoulder and then blew me a kiss. "Maybe then he'd be able to act civilized."

Hannah grinned at me, "What did you say in that text?"

I shrugged, embarrassed by it now. "In my defense, your pussy was on my fingers and your taste was on my tongue."

With wild eyes, Brody stared at me and growled, "She admitted I was right, and she was done fighting this attraction. That she wanted to give it a real shot."

Knox grinned and let go of Brody's neck as he sagged forward on the footboard. "It did the trick. We were both hard within seconds and you had at least a thirty-minute drive home. So we entertained ourselves."

"I'm entertained," I admitted, biting my bottom lip as Brody groaned and pushed back into Knox with the next brutal thrust. "I can't tell if you're enjoying yourself or not."

"Baby, look here." Knox reached around and grabbed onto Brody's hard cock that was swinging between his thighs with each thrust and stroked it, making Brody form an animalistic groan and tighten his hold on the footboard even more. "He's fucking enjoying it."

"Come here." Brody reached over the wooden barrier, grabbed the front of Hannah's shirt, and pulled her until she bent forward over the end of the bed and he kissed her roughly. "Fuck, you taste like her. Did you have a taste before you got home?"

"I did." Hannah licked his lips and reached down to grab his cock where Knox let go of it to grab Brody's hips for leverage. "I licked her pussy until she came on my face before the shoot even started."

His dark eyes flicked over to me, and his jaw clenched. "You fuck up and you get rewarded."

"No," I sauntered across the room until I stood next to Hannah and stared directly into his eyes. "I admitted my faults and apologized for them." I leaned toward his ear and whispered seductively, "And then our girl sank to her knees to show me just how much she appreciated my honesty."

"Damnit." Brody groaned, "You make it fucking hard to hate you sometimes."

"I am aware." Looking at Hannah, excitement burned in her bright green eyes as she started getting what she wanted from us. "I'll admit my faults and apologize to you when you're a little less preoccupied." I cocked my head to the side, "Can't wait to see what reward I get from you two."

"Hannah," Knox growled. "Get him off before I lose my fucking mind and leave him worse off than when we started." Knox's neck was red and tight as he pumped into his boyfriend, clinging to the edge of sanity by a thread and wanting to make sure Brody found the release he needed before it was too late.

"Hmm." Hannah pulled her shirt off over her head and then peeled her sexy white lace bralette off. "I think I can help." She grabbed my hand. "Want to learn how to make Brody lose his mind?"

"Always." I nodded eagerly as Brody cursed.

Hannah pushed on Brody's chest, "Back up, make room for us."

Brody shook his head and stared me down. "Get undressed. Both of you."

"With pleasure." I purred and turned my back to Hannah, "Unzip me, baby." She giggled again and then undid the dress and pushed it off my arms, I let it fall off my body completely, landing in a fluff of lace on the floor. I wasn't wearing panties, so within a second flat I was naked in front of them all again. And I fucking loved the way I felt when I was bare and exposed to them. "Your turn." I undid the clasp on Hannah's slacks, pulled them and her panties down, and added them to the pile. "*Teach me.*"

She took my hand as we both climbed over the footboard and kneeled on the bed in front of the men. "Brody's weakness is head, I already told you that." She sank onto her belly and then scooted underneath Brody's body. "He loves a good wet and sensual sucking."

Knox grunted, "Han. I'm going to blow if you keep dirty talking like that."

She grinned and ignored him as she grabbed Brody's cock and ran her tongue over the tip of it seductively before sucking on the tip. On her belly the way she was, she couldn't move up and down his cock. But Brody was already three steps ahead of her.

He jerked his hips forward, letting Knox's cock slide out of his ass, and pushed his cock deep into Hannah's mouth.

"Bloody fucking hell," Brody growled, as his eyes closed and he cracked his neck and moved back, impaling himself and emptying Hannah's throat.

He was so thick; I was in amazement that she could take the massive cock deep, but I suppose practice makes perfect.

"Do you like what you see?" Knox asked, panting, where he stayed still with his hands on his hips as Brody did all the moving.

I nodded, entranced by it all.

"Can I kiss you?" Knox asked with that gentle persistence he always used with me. It was light and teasing and not at all threatening, and in a way, it was exactly why I allowed him the liberties I had so far.

I nodded again, moving around Brody's body to Knox's side and leaning into him as he threaded his fingers into my hair and kissed me. With slow and sensual flicks of his tongue, he warmed me up and drew the need from me until I was clinging to him, moaning with each pass of his tongue, or the nip of his teeth.

"Fuck." Brody hissed, "That's it, Darling. Take every fucking drop."

"Mmh," Knox moaned against my mouth and I assumed Brody was tightening down on his cock as he chased his pleasure. "Jesus." He whispered against my lips.

I ran one hand over his hard abs and chest as he started coming. His hand tightened in my hair and he slammed his hips forward twice, meeting Brody's thrusts as they both cried out through their release. I absorbed every plea and demand for more that fell from Knox's lips, as I dragged my nails over his waistline and lower until the tips of my nails touched the hard base of his cock. I didn't go further, frankly; I wasn't brave enough. Instead, I dragged my nails up the length of his torso and he convulsed under my touch until he pulled out of Brody and collapsed backward on the bed.

Brody rolled to the side and crumpled onto his back as his abs flexed with each labored breath. He flung his arm over his eyes as he came down from his high.

"How was that, baby?" Hannah purred, wiping her bottom lip seductively as she leaned over his body. "Do you feel relaxed enough to be kind now?"

"You tell me." He grabbed her waist and picked her up like she weighed nothing at all until she straddled his face.

She gasped and then moaned with a dirty smile on her face as she widened her knees and rested her palms on his chest, leaning forward as he licked her pussy. "Mmh, you feel very kind." She snickered and rolled her hips, so she got the most out of his abilities. She held her hand out to me and cocked her head to the side. "I want to kiss you while I come on his face."

"I suppose I can partake." I winked at her and went to kneel at her side, but Brody grabbed my waist, without even looking up from his snack between her thighs, lifted me just like he had with her, and settled me on his torso.

I straddled his lower rib cage, essentially safe from anything dangerously tempting, but it still took my breath away when I felt his strong, hard body under mine. He didn't remove his hands from my waist either as he rocked me side to side until I had no choice but to press my pussy flat against his abs.

A startled moan slipped through my lips from the sensation of the hard ridges of his body pressed against my aching clit.

Hannah's eyes were drunk with need as she leaned forward so our faces were touching. I fucking loved feeling her face against mine like that, not kissing, not sexual, just near. It seemed like she did too, for as many times as she'd done it that night alone.

"Is this okay?" She asked, licking her lips.

I nodded, untrusting my voice to be steady if I tried to use it.

"Do you have any idea how sexy you are straddling him like this?" Her eyelids fluttered closed as she leaned back and tipped her head back as pleasure made her needy. "His hands on you." She gasped, "Seeing him touch you. God!"

Brody was eating her pussy like it was his fucking job, and she shattered on his face. "You're so sexy." I moaned, testing my new toy out as I slid forward. My pussy was so wet, his abs were silky with it as I moved. I kissed Hannah as I rocked again, feeling his hand tighten on my waist and move me faster.

Hannah bit my lip and played with my tits as she came down off her high while I chased mine.

"Knox." I moaned, holding my hand out behind me for him where he still lay on the bed, no doubt enjoying the view.

"Right here." He growled in my ear as he straddled Brody's body too, keeping a bit of space between our bodies like he was unsure of what I wanted from him.

"I need you." I took his hand and wrapped his arm around my body until his big frame covered mine on all sides.

"Jesus." Hannah moaned, watching me draw him in, and she climbed off Brody's face.

I held Brody's dark stare as I laid Knox's hand on my tit and lowered the other one to the waxed skin of my pussy. "Please," I begged, no one in particular and everyone at once.

Brody's hands tightened and moved me back and forth across his stomach as Knox's hand drifted lower, parting my lips so my clit was directly against his boyfriend's body.

"We've got you." Knox bit my earlobe as he pinched my nipple and rocked his still-stiff cock against my ass.

Hannah crawled to my side and kissed me, absorbing my cries of pleasure as she slipped her fingers between my body and Brody's.

She bit my lip, "We're going to make you come. All three of us."

"Yes." I gasped, fighting off tears as I chased the most monumental orgasm of my life. "Please."

Brody's body tensed beneath me each time he rocked me forward, and it was the perfect amount of rhythm and pressure that I needed, I cracked open, falling apart into a million little pieces.

"Fuck." A primal scream ripped from my throat and they all took it in, giving me more.

More attention.

More affection.

More praise.

"Come for us." Brody growled, "That's it, Angel Eyes."

I shook my head no, out of instinct, but he just rocked me harder, forcing another explosive orgasm through my body. Wave after wave of ecstasy rippled through my body and I felt like years of build-up washed off my bones with each swell. When it finally stopped, I felt bare.

Raw.

Free.

I collapsed, unable to sit upright anymore, and Brody caught me as I fell to his chest. His massive arms wrapped around my back as he held my crumbling body together.

He held me together.

"You're okay." He whispered in my ear, and I felt Hannah and Knox's hands on my body too, soothing and comforting me, though Hannah was the only one who knew why.

The guys didn't ask.

They just held me through it.

And I knew I'd never be the same girl I was when I walked into their house that first time.

For the better.

Chapter 25 – Knox

Lex was wrapped around my body from head to toe, with her head on my chest and her legs tangled with mine.

Hannah was curled around her back, and Brody was around hers.

And the normalcy of it all astonished me.

Hours ago, she had given herself to us.

It was the first time I'd truly seen her let herself be free. Enchanting didn't even begin to describe watching her unchain herself.

Something happened to that girl in her past, and it had shaped the woman she became, yet she let go of some of that.

For us.

We had gotten little sleep after that, yet I laid awake, weighing it all in my head like a precarious teeter-totter.

Make one wrong move, and the whole thing would tip, spilling everything into the sand.

A faint buzzing from the other side of the bed caught my attention. Brody rolled over, silencing his alarm and looking over at the two women between us.

He raised his brow at me in the dim light and shook his head. He had to be at the shop early for a customer picking up a custom-ordered hood with his trademark detailed paint job. But I didn't need to be there until ten or eleven at the earliest.

I had no intention of moving from the warmth of our bed until I had to.

He kissed the back of Hannah's head gently and rolled out of bed, walking around to me and leaning down to whisper.

"You'd better make it to work."

"And if I don't?" I asked as Lex shifted, snuggling into me further.

"I'm locking up-and-coming home after the first pickup."

"I don't see a problem with that."

He rolled his eyes and gave me a quick kiss. "See ya."

"Bye."

He walked out of the bedroom and into the bathroom and gently shut the door behind him. Thankfully, our bathroom was on the other side of a giant walk-through closet, and there was another exit into the hallway.

We all had different schedules, so when we built the layout of the master suite, we aimed to ensure that the others could sleep in and remain undisturbed.

I listened to him shower, and then putz around the kitchen downstairs for a few minutes before leaving to go to the garage. When all was silent again, I tried to settle my brain and catch another hour of sleep while I still could.

I had just drifted off to sleep when someone's shifting in bed beside me woke me up.

I cracked one eye open and caught sight of Hannah slowly kissing her way down Lex's naked side as she looked at me over the delicious curves she was tasting.

"Mmh," Lex moaned in her sleep, tightening her hold on me and hitching her leg higher, brushing against my hard morning wood.

Hannah smirked as Lex shifted, rubbing her naked pussy against my thigh, ensnarled between her legs, and my cock twitched. I thought about how good it would feel to sink deep into Lex's pussy for the first time. I ached to know what kind of noise she'd make the first time she took me.

Or Brody.

Fuck, he was so thick she'd scream when she took that cock.

"Good morning, pretty girl." Hannah sang softly to Lex as she humped my leg again. I watched Hannah's hand slide down over the lush swell of Lex's ass and then felt her fingers rub across the wet lips of her pussy. "Baby, wake up."

Lex moaned and pushed back against Hannah's fingers again before her eyes blinked open, fighting against the sleep that still held her under.

"Good morning." I teased, and she sat up stiff as a board with wide eyes and panic on her face.

She looked around and found Hannah watching her amusedly and sagged in relief. "God."

Hannah smiled and leaned in to kiss her. "Did you think it was all a dream?"

"Or a nightmare." She peeked at me, but couldn't quite hide her grin.

"Funny girl." I poked her side. "You sure talk a lot of smack for someone who clung to me all night long like a pricker bush in the woods."

"I remember falling asleep spooning Hannah."

"You did." Hannah stood up from the bed in her naked wonder and stretched. Even after all the years together, my mouth still watered every time I saw her bare skin. "But at some point, you rolled over, and I spooned you."

"Hmm." Lex quipped as I sat up against the headboard, watching the two naked women. It didn't take Lex long to notice the enormous erection tenting the sheet in my lap and she nodded to it with her chin. "Does that really happen every morning?"

"Without fail." I shrugged, "Want to help me with it?" I put my hand under the sheet and stroked myself. Her lips parted and her heart rate kicked up as she fought the urge to look away, but didn't.

"I—" She swallowed and Hannah picked up a throw pillow and threw it at me.

"Don't have time." Hannah tilted her head and put her hands on her hips. "At least not if Lex plans on joining me in the shower before we go back to the city."

"Cheater." I cursed, as Hannah slowly backed up toward the bathroom. Lex didn't need to say it out loud for me to know exactly who she was going to choose at that moment.

"Hmm." Lex slid from the bed, "Tough decision."

"Not fair." I pouted and Hannah took off laughing into the bathroom, but Lex lurked at the door, looking back at me.

"Be a good boy and I'll let you watch." She licked her lips, and I sprung from the bed, but she stopped me with a raised hand as I leaped from the bed. "I get to eat my breakfast first." She winked. "Wait five minutes."

She turned and walked through the closet to the bathroom, and I watched her ass ripple with each step the entire way.

"Four. And I'm going to make you come when I'm done with her."

She looked over her shoulder and smiled. "Promise?"

"Promise," I called back, but she was already turning the corner and shutting the bathroom door behind her. "I fucking promise."

If every day started like that, I didn't think I could find anything to complain about for the rest of forever.

I cursed once again, fighting with the same custom suspension for the truck we were building. "Just get in the hole," I muttered, pushing with all my might from under the truck to get it to line up.

"Well, get it out and I'll put it in." An angelic voice called from the other side, and I ducked to see Hannah walking in through the overhead door. She winked at me and I dropped the parts I was fucking with back onto the cart and walked out from under the truck.

She wore a white skirt that hit above her knees and a nude-colored tank top that hugged her chest like a pair of hands would. She made my cock stir from just walking into the garage.

Never mind the fact that I fucked her bent over in the shower just that morning while she ate Lex's pussy like a good little girlfriend.

I had a renewed need for her with all the changes and excitement she brought to the table lately.

"Well, hello." I wiped my hands on a rag but refrained from touching her as she leaned up on her toes and kissed me.

"Hi." She smiled against my lips and then sank back down on her heels. "How are you?"

"Suddenly hard," I admitted, adjusting myself in my jeans while she watched.

"Fiend."

"Yep." I nodded eagerly.

"Darling." Brody's deep voice echoed from the stairwell leading to the private office upstairs as he walked down. "What are you doing here?"

"Hi," She smiled up at him and gave him a much spicier kiss considering he was fresh and grease-free. "I wanted to talk to you two. Are you free?"

"No." I nodded to the truck. "But for you, I'll pretend I am."

"C'mon," Brody nodded back to the office, hollering to Tito, the apprentice who worked with us three days a week. "We'll be right back."

"Sure thing, Boss." He called before going back to polishing the rims on a Chevelle we just rebuilt.

"What's up?" Brody asked, shutting the door to the office behind us as we all sat down.

"I want to talk about Lex," Hannah said and I could feel the trepidation in her body language and I instantly went on edge.

"What about?" Brody sat back in his chair, on edge like I was.

Hannah rubbed her palms up and down her thighs, "I asked for her permission to share this with you because I didn't think she was comfortable talking about it, but I think it needs to be said. At least the cliff note version."

"Hannah." I implored her to get to the point.

"She admitted to me yesterday that she's sexually attracted to both of you. Which I think we all knew." Hannah smiled softly, but I felt like there was bad news still to come. "Lex's never been with a man before. She'd never even kissed one before you," She tilted her head to the side and dropped my gaze. "When she was thirteen, a stranger assaulted her. She confessed that her initial attraction was always toward women, but the assault led her to turn completely away from men. It's why she built the alpha personality and fought to control of every aspect of her life."

"To protect herself," Brody uttered.

"Because she couldn't back then," I added.

"Exactly." Hannah sighed, "But when she dropped that wall and told me the truth yesterday, she said she didn't want to be alone anymore. She's ready to jump in, but she's scared."

"Jesus." I sighed, "How do we tread carefully when we don't know her boundaries?"

"We let her be in control." Brody mused, looking over at me. "Last night, she called for you. She invited you in."

"That's how." Hannah nodded. "We listen, we watch, and we ask."

Leaning back in my chair, I blew out a deep breath. "I don't know how to do this." Anxiety burned my gut as I imagined causing Lex undue harm. "I don't want to do something wrong. There's so much pressure."

"What are you saying?" Brody snapped. "That she's too damaged to try?"

"No!" I bit back and scowled at him. "I just don't know how to treat her with kid gloves. I don't know how to walk around on eggshells, afraid of fucking it all up."

"Learn!" Brody stood up and pointed his finger at me. His anger came out of nowhere and took me back about ten steps. "I know you had a shiny, perfect life growing up and don't know what the fuck trauma is, but that doesn't mean it doesn't exist. The least you can do is think with your brain instead of your cock while you're around her for a while."

"Dude." I stood up, so he didn't tower over me. "I'm not allowed to vocalize my fears in *my* relationship now?"

He scoffed and turned away from me. "Whatever. Just don't fuck this up for Hannah." He leaned down and gave her a chaste kiss before grabbing his leather jacket off the back of his office chair. "I have a meeting."

And with that, he left in a huff.

"What did I just do?" Hannah whispered, and her eyes were wide as saucers and her skin as white as a ghost.

"Nothing." I scooped her up and put her on my lap, potential grease stains be damned, and held her in my chair as we both calmed down from the entire bizarre situation.

"I just wanted you guys to know, so you weren't too aggressive or pushy with her. Not yet."

"I know." Sighing, she rested her head on my chest and hugged me. "I'll check back in with him later and maybe get to the bottom of it."

"You'll be gentle with him, right?" She looked up at me with those big green trusting eyes.

I snorted and rolled my eyes at her, "No, I'm going to beat him with a sock full of batteries." She giggled and relaxed in my arms. "I'll be as gentle with him as he needs me to be. But no more."

"That's fair. You always know exactly how to handle both of us and what we need."

"I'm a gifted man." I joked, already replaying the entire thing in my head, trying to figure out what exactly went wrong and what triggered him so badly.

Hours later, Brody's bike roared back into the parking lot of the garage. It was well after closing time, but I still stayed because I knew he wouldn't go home looking for a fight. He would come to the garage and I would wait for him.

Like I told Hannah, I would only be as gentle as he needed me to be. Because sometimes Brody needed to be put into his place and he knew I would do it, damaging nothing between us.

We were solid.

So when the man door swung open and his dark scowl found me where I worked under the hood of the stingray I was tuning up, I was ready for him.

"Hey, fucker." I bit out.

"Sup, nutwad?" He lobbed back.

"You cooled down yet?"

"Not even a little."

"Want to at least let me in on why you're so triggered by someone else's shortcomings?"

"You actually admit that not being able to be respectful to Lex's needs and hesitations is a shortcoming?"

"I never pretended to be perfect, I was just voicing my concerns. It's not like any of us have had to act with kid gloves inside of this relationship before." I held my hand up, "Well, at least not when you act like an adult."

"Fuck you." He cursed and walked away.

"Do you know any other insults?" I followed him as he started up the stairs to the office. "Or are you stuck in high school today?"

"I'm not in the mood, Knox."

"Which is exactly why I'm here well past dinnertime, squaring off with your pissy ass. Don't make me beat the stupid out of you."

"Fuck off." He roared, turning at the top of the stairs and towering over me. But I didn't let him have the upper hand like I usually would have.

I forged forward, pushing him back with my chest until I stood toe to toe with him on the landing. "Try again."

"I can't do this with you." He turned and walked away, but he made a critical error in his attempt to evade me because there was only one exit to the upstairs office and, as I stood in the doorway, I blocked it.

"Try again," I repeated, unmoved.

"No." He snarled, pulling his chair out from his desk and shoving it out of the way as he paced. "I can't."

"Why?"

"Because."

"Isn't an answer." I snapped. "You owe me an answer."

"I don't owe you anything!" He screamed.

I didn't recognize the man in front of me. He seemed unhinged and on edge, more so than I had ever seen Brody before.

"Ten years means nothing?" I tried to remain impassive and unbothered by his cruel words because I knew they weren't my fault. They were stemming from something deeply rooted inside of himself.

"You don't get it." He shook his head and turned away, which pissed me off.

"Exactly!" It was my turn to yell. "Because you won't man the fuck up and tell me."

"Man up?" He bellowed and turned on me. "You have no fucking clue what kind of man-ing up I've had to do because of you!"

"Then tell me!" I pushed him with my hands flat on his chest. "You obviously hold something against me, so tell me what the fuck I did wrong to earn your fucking anger out of the blue!"

"You loved me!" He screamed with wide eyes as I stood ramrod stiff as the entire world around me rocked on its axis. "When I didn't have a fucking clue what love even meant!" He grabbed the front of my shirt and shook me. "You loved me and I lost everything because of it."

I couldn't breathe.

I couldn't form a coherent thought as his words circled inside of my brain on repeat.

You loved me and I lost everything because of it.

"What does that mean?" I whispered, too afraid to move, as it felt like everything around me was going to tumble down into the pits of misery any second.

"My dad knew." He stepped back and his shoulders fell in defeat. "He could tell you weren't just interested in Hannah. So he beat the ever-living shit out of me for it, demanding that I either let you both go or be cut off and cast out of his family! He would not *allow* his only son to be gay. It was leave you or be dead to him."

My brain tried to think back to when Brody still talked to his dad, and I remembered the night he went to Hannah's beat to piss. He wouldn't tell her what happened, so she called me, but when I showed up, he wouldn't even look at me.

It was right after we took our relationship to the next level, specifically between him and me, and the rejection had hurt.

But I never thought the beating he took was because of me, or that it had been by his own dad.

"Why didn't you tell me?" I shook my head in utter disbelief. "We asked you that night, but you refused to tell us anything."

He fell into his office chair and hung his head, once again refusing to look at me. "Because I was already too far gone to get back out. I was already in love with both you and Hannah by that point, and I didn't see a way out."

A way out.

My chest cracked, and I finally knew what physical heartbreak felt like.

Such a negative event served as the foundation for everything we had. No wonder he hated me.

He finally looked up at me, but there was nothing recognizable in his brown eyes. "You're content with your sexuality, you always have been. But not everyone else is, Knox. Not everyone wants to just move at breakneck speed."

"I'm sorry." I forced through my dry throat. "If I had known back then—,"

"Don't." He dropped his head again and looked at the floor. "It wouldn't have changed anything."

"Because you were stuck." I repeated, "In something you didn't want."

He lifted his head and scowled at me. "I didn't say I didn't want it. I just didn't fucking understand what it would cost me at the time! That's why I want Lex to make sure she wants this and isn't pressured into anything by us."

"I'm sorry," I said again, picking my keys up off my desk and walking out.

"Where are you going?" he called after me, but the frustration in his voice raked my nerves even more.

"Away," I replied, throwing my jacket on as I crossed the garage. "So you're not stuck anymore."

"Knox." He called out, annoyed. "Stop."

It wasn't the call of a man who was watching someone he loved walk away upset.

It was the call of a man who felt obligated to stop what he already started.

But I was already gone.

Chapter 26 – Hannah

Knox was missing, and I couldn't breathe.

It had been two days since he left the garage on his motorcycle without a word to anyone and no one had heard from him since.

Brody came home that night, visibly shaken and upset, admitting what happened between them and that Knox left.

I tried to keep my anger with Brody in check because it wouldn't solve anything after the fact. My priority had been to find Knox.

But I couldn't.

He just disappeared without a trace. His cell phone was off and his bank account had gone untouched.

I was dying inside with every second that passed without information about him.

Was he hurt?

Was he lying somewhere in a ditch, dying all alone?

Would I ever see him again?

"Hey." Lex came into the living room and sat down on the couch next to me, pushing a cup of tea into my hands. "You need to drink something."

"I can't." I sighed. "Not until I know he's safe."

"I know, baby." She put her arm over my shoulders, "He's going to be just fine." She put the tea on the table in front of us and pulled me back to lean against her side on the oversized comfy couch. "My guess is he's somewhere processing everything that went down."

"Why hasn't he called then?" I wiped at stupid tears that wouldn't stop falling. "He has to know I'm terrified right now."

"I think his pain is so big he doesn't have room to hold on to anyone else's." She reasoned. "And that's okay. He deserves to feel this how he sees fit, and you have to let him."

"I'm just so worried about him. He's never gone MIA like this before."

"I feel to blame." She kissed my hair and settled in, "I think my wounds opened up Brody's and then he caused some to Knox."

"What a terrible turn of events."

"I agree. But maybe he just needs time."

"Have you heard anything from anyone?" I asked, hopeful that she'd somehow forgotten to tell me that someone in the search party found him.

"No." She sighed again, "But Parker went off a couple of hours ago on a hunch. Maybe he knows something."

Brody, Dallin, Parker, and Trey had been looking for him since he left. Reyna and Lex had been holding vigil with me at home, hoping he'd just pull up the driveway and say he lost track of time or something.

"I can't believe my dad hasn't even found him. You'd think the police commissioner would have some reach."

She chuckled, "He does, but knowing Knox left on his own kind of complicates things a little. You know that."

"I know." I sat up, "I hate sitting here with nothing to do."

"You just have to have faith and give him grace when we find him. Because he doesn't need your anger right now. He needs your love."

"I can't believe Brody said those things to him," I admitted for the first time.

"I can." Lex acknowledged, "Only because it's something I'd say, and I'm pretty stupid like Brody sometimes."

"You're not. And either is he." I stood up in a huff, "I have to *do* something!"

"Oh, perfect," Rey said, walking into the room. "Because I know just what you can do to calm your idle hands."

"What?" I speculated, already not liking the sounds of whatever she had planned. Even as my best friend, Reyna's enthusiasm was a little much sometimes.

"You can go shower," She picked up a limp piece of hair that hung off my head. "Because you smell."

"Ugh!" I flapped my arms exasperatedly, "It doesn't matter if Knox isn't here!"

"Well, he's on his way home, so it does matter." She put her hands on her hips and pursed her lips.

"What?" I whispered, too afraid to say it out loud for fear she'd say she was joking.

Reyna nodded her head confidently, "Parker found him at a boondocking campsite out in bumfuck-nowhere. He was searching for solitude and found it so well that his bike battery died two mornings ago and he's just been sitting there since."

"Oh, my god." I cried with tears in my eyes. "He's okay?" I grabbed Lex's hand, and she squeezed it back, just as relieved as I was.

"He's okay." Reyna confirmed, "Parker's driving him home right now." She rolled her eyes. "I told Dallin, but he agreed not to tell Brody just yet. We thought it was best to have some time here with you before Brody showed up."

I nodded, understanding their thought but also eager to relieve some of the stress on Brody's shoulders. "I get it. Thank you."

"No problem." Rey smiled sweetly and then rounded her eyes when I stayed put, "No seriously, you smell. Shower!" She pointed to the stairs and gave me a loving shove.

"Okay!" I scowled at her goodheartedly even though I was still on edge, knowing that Knox was safe and on his way home to me, relieved so much worry.

We could work through whatever we needed to as a group. As long as he was home and safe, we'd make it all work. We had to make it all work.

Chapter 27 – Knox

The sun was dipping again over the top of the tree line as I watched it, mesmerized by how no matter what happened, it rose and fell on its own, without fail.

My life was upside down and inside out, yet the sun didn't care.

The world did not care.

I found a rural campsite that I'd heard about, a couple of hours outside of the city limits, and pulled in the other night. I did not know why, but it felt right.

It felt like the right kind of place to just—disappear. Somewhere no one would know where to find me.

Where I couldn't disappoint anyone.

Or love them.

Brody's words echoed through my head nonstop. It was haunting to hear his truth after all the years spent telling me lies.

And Hannah.

God, how I missed her. I could feel her heartache in my chest the longer I sat in the desolate wilderness. It wasn't fair to leave her as I did, but I wasn't capable of tending to her feelings and needs when it felt like my entire life had been a giant lie.

Made up like a make-believe story meant to make you feel better about something.

I couldn't see up through the fog lingering around my shoulders, and I was afraid I'd be lost to it forever.

Just when things started getting really good, too.

Lex had been the whirlwind of everything I didn't realize we were missing until she showed up and knocked us on our asses. Of course, it was Hannah to notice something in her we needed.

But it ended before it even had a chance to feel real.

She was done.

She didn't want me. She wanted to heal her pain, and I wasn't the right man for the job, like I thought I was.

Brody had been right because I wasn't cautious or considerate of others when it came down to it. I was a lover. And a giver and I just wanted everyone to feel as loved as I felt.

Past tense.

But I couldn't even do that right.

Would Hannah and Brody continue with Lex, with me out of the picture? Would she want to be a part of the relationship if it was just the two of them?

Shit.

I didn't even want to be a part of the relationship if it was just the two of them.

Not if I was the problem.

I laid back in the grass and felt that overwhelming sense of calm, and nothingness lay over my body like a blanket. I knew I wasn't very far from that light at the end of the tunnel hitting me in the face like a train, yet I couldn't see a way out.

I lay there, watching the sky turn from orange to red, then to purple as inky black infiltrated it. The stars were just starting to shine through the light pollution when I heard the crunch of tires on the gravel trail across the meadow on the other side of the tree line.

I parked my bike in the trees where it died almost two days ago. In theory, I knew I should have sat up and called out to make myself known, just in case it was a large truck towing a camper that wasn't expecting to come across a person lying in the tall grass.

But maybe that was why I didn't move at all.

I watched the stars above as headlights shone over the meadow like a lighthouse beacon flashing over the darkness as it turned around the corner and aimed for the abandoned campsite.

The engine turned off, and I closed my eyes, hating that I was going to have to admit my defeats and weaknesses to some stranger when they stumbled upon me.

Suddenly, a familiar voice broke the silence, calling out from the side of the truck across the space. "Knox!"

"Fuck." I groaned, contemplating what I was going to do.

"Knox!" Parker yelled out louder, cupping his mouth to make his voice drift further.

"You're scaring away my friends, shut up!" I yelled back, still unmoving.

"Fucking hell!" He yelled louder, "Where are you?"

I raised one arm into the air above the tall grass, waving my hand lifelessly before dropping it back to my stomach as he ran across the meadow.

"Jesus, Knox." He skidded to a stop, shining a flashlight in my face. "Are you okay? What the fuck are you doing?"

"Talking to all of my friends," I motioned to the obnoxious chatter of the crickets and nightlife waking up around us, before throwing one arm over my face to block out his flashlight, "What does it look like?"

He kicked my leg and huffed, "Do you have any idea how fucking scared everyone is? Or how many people are out looking for you right now?"

"Save it, man." I dropped my arm and looked back up at the sky, "I can't take more right now."

As he walked away, my heart stuttered in my chest, thinking he might drive off and leave me to the wild animals that got a little too close for comfort the last two nights.

But the lights from his truck turned off and moments later, he walked back over and sat down next to me in the grass.

"Okay," He patted my chest, "Talk to me."

I scoffed, but it was barely audible; I had no energy left to even be sarcastic. What a shame.

"When was the last time you ate or drank?" He looked down at me pitifully.

"I don't know," I shrugged, "I think I stopped pissing this morning. Or maybe last night."

"Jesus man." He cried out and stomped back to his truck once again. This time, when he returned, a bottle of water and three protein bars landed on my stomach.

"Oof." I groaned, curling from the impact.

"Drink first, then eat." He threw himself back down on the grass. "Or I'll hold you down and shove it all down your fucking throat."

"I didn't know you were so bossy."

"Yeah well," He looked off over the empty dark meadow, "I've never come so close to losing a friend before." I waved him off, but he aimed his finger at my face as I fought to find the energy to sit upright. "You could have died out here." He looked around, "Didn't you read the article about the hiker being mauled by a bear out here just like two weeks ago? I'm pretty sure Hannah wrote it!"

"Can't say as I did." I finally got up to my ass, and the world spun faster than normal and I fell over the other side of upright and landed in the grass. "Fuck."

He grabbed me and sat me back up like I was a blade of grass. "I'm going to kill you. I'm going to nurse you back to life and then I'm going to kill you for getting yourself in such trouble."

"Hmm." I hummed as I opened the bottle of water and chugged it. Fuck, I was thirsty. "Fair enough."

He watched me out of the corner of his eye while I attacked first one bar and then another. Okay, fine, I was apparently starving.

I mumbled, "Thank you."

"What exactly was your plan here?" He nodded to the surrounding isolation.

"Well, to be honest." I took another long drink of the water. "I wasn't running on a plan. And then my bike died. And the whole idea of no cell phone reception sounded better when I had an exit strategy." I shrugged and pointed over to my Harley parked under the canopy of the trees.

"Knox!" He groaned, "Do you have any idea how lucky you are that I found you?"

"How did you manage that, exactly?"

He grunted and rubbed his hand over his face, "You talked about wanting to check this place out a few weeks ago. When we exhausted every other option, we had to think outside of the box."

"We?" I questioned, thinking straighter, with some sugar in my bloodstream again.

He looked over his arm at me, "Did you really think he wouldn't look for you?"

I scoffed and clenched my teeth. "Would you expect Dallin to look for you after he admitted you ruined his entire life by falling in love with him?" Parker's eyebrows fell over his eyes in a scowl and I looked away, hating the way the pain burned anew from even saying the words out loud. "He told me that my falling in love with him trapped him. He was stuck with no way out and he lost everything important to him because of it."

"Damn." He looked front again. "Fucking bastard."

I smirked lightly, "See."

"I'm sorry, man." He whispered, and I shook it off, unable to let the sympathy in.

"I just needed some space. No big deal."

"I need you to be honest with me, Knox," He turned to face me and stared right at me, "Did you come out here to commit suicide?"

I rolled my eyes and opened my mouth to brush him off and assure him of the answer he wanted to hear, but stopped short. "Not to begin with."

"But you were going to just lay here in the grass and let it happen?"

I shrugged, "I don't know. The longer it went on, the less it sounded like a bad idea."

"I believe that." He put his hand on my shoulder and squeezed it as I hung my head in shame. "Brody reminds me of Trey." I nodded, but didn't look up, "And Trey says a lot of shit he doesn't mean when he's in his feelings. He was emotionally stunted at a young age, which prevented him from learning how to communicate in a healthy manner."

"Healthy or not, the words still mean the same thing."

"Yeah," He nodded, and let his hand slide off my shoulder. "Maybe."

The silence stretched through the darkness and my eyelids drooped as fatigue and emotional turmoil took their toll on me.

After a while, he cleared his throat, "So now what?"

"I don't really know."

A coyote howled off in the distance and the hair stood up on my arms. He stood up and wiped his hands off on his jeans before holding one out to me. "I can't let you stay here."

I stared at it for far longer than I should have, considering I was pretty sure he could throw me over his shoulder and carry my weak ass to his truck if he wanted to. I gave him my hand, and he dragged me to my feet, holding my elbow when the world once again tilted sideways, but at least that time I stopped from hitting the deck. "Thanks."

"Anytime." He grabbed my jacket off the ground and walked by my side to his truck.

"What about my bike?" I eyed my old trusted hog longingly.

"I'll get Tito to come grab it in the morning." He shook his head, "I doubt anyone is going to be stupid enough to come back in here tonight."

"You did." I tried to joke, but it fell flat. "Thanks."

"Anytime." He repeated, watching me get up into his truck before walking around to the driver's side and turning us back toward civilization.

"Is Hannah okay?"

"No." He admitted and gripped the steering wheel, "Lex says she won't eat anything." The shame burned in my gut. "But she's not mad at you."

I nodded, unable to affirm that because we both knew she may not be right now, but she would be when the relief wore off.

We drove for a while, and I dozed on and off in the passenger seat until I heard his phone connecting to a call through Bluetooth. I cracked one eye when Reyna's voice filtered through the cab.

"Hey, baby." She sounded tired and more guilt swam in my gut.

"Baby Girl," Parker sighed, looking over at me as I gripped the handle tight. "I've got him. He's alive. No thanks to circumstance."

"You found him!" She cried, "Where? Is he okay? Did you call Dallin or Trey?"

"He'll be okay with a shower and a meal and some rest," He turned toward the highway that led to the city. "We'll be there in about an hour. But do me a favor."

"Anything." She dropped her voice.

"Don't tell Brody yet." He replied, "It's worse than he let on when he asked for our help, and Knox deserves some peace before Brody gets wind that he's home."

"Parker." She warned gently, and I wanted to speak up and tell them to stay out of it, to keep their own sanity.

"No, Baby Girl. What Brody said was over-the-top cruel, and he deserves more than just some time to sweat it out." He said between clenched teeth. "I'm going to bring Knox home and then I'll go find Brody."

She sighed, and I knew she wanted to tell him not to do what we both knew he was planning, but I didn't have the energy to save Brody's ass.

Not that time.

I was too fucking tired.

"Okay." She finally said, "I'm telling Hannah though. She's not going to last much longer without news."

"That's fine. Just let her know that what Knox needs isn't going to be found at the end of a Brody tornado."

"You make him sound like Trey," She replied and I could hear the smile in her voice. Apparently, they were more similar than I'd ever realized. Though it made sense now that I was looking at it.

"We'll be there soon, Baby Girl." He replied, ignoring what everyone knew.

"I love you," Reyna said and then hung up.

I closed my eyes and thought back to a time when Hannah said that to me without all the complications surrounding it.

Would I go back in time if I knew then what I know now? To blissful happiness before all the changes happened?

I thought of Hannah, silently questioning everything she knew about herself and how lonely I'd been when I had been at the same point years ago.

I thought of Lex, and how her spunky fire made me ache to be more and be better because she deserved it. Especially knowing why she was so bold and independent.

Then I thought of Brody, and how for years he felt like my literal other half. When I felt like we were so in sync and open with each other. There was a raw honesty between us we didn't have with Hannah because we rarely minced words or worry about feelings.

Until suddenly, the words cut so deep that I couldn't stop the blood that ran free in their wake.

Would we recover from our fight? Did he want to? Did I want to?

I ran every possibility through my head as we neared my home and became more distraught with each passing minute.

What if he didn't want to be with me anymore, but wanted just Hannah and Lex? Was that something I could do, just cut that part of my life off and pretend it didn't happen?

What if he wanted to go on like we always had? Could I pretend he didn't regret me?

God, I was fucked.

"Hey, man." Parker put his hand on my shoulder and shook me gently as I snapped my eyes open, getting my bearings as we sat in the driveway at the house.

"Right," I nodded, wiping my face with my hand, glancing over to him, "Thanks again."

"You aren't regrettable, Knox." He said, holding my stare through the dim lights from the dash. "He was wrong. And you deserve better than to be treated that way."

I nodded and looked away, unable to speak through the thick emotion building in my chest. I opened the truck door and got out, stretching my tired body as Parker stood at the hood, watching silently.

The front door opened and Hannah ran out at breakneck speed, nearly missing every step on the way down and sprinting across the lawn to me wearing a nightgown and silk robe. "Oh, my god!" She cried, flinging herself into my arms.

Even though I was dead on my feet, I caught her and squeezed her back so tight I doubted she could breathe. She clung to me just as tight, running her hands over my head and neck as she cried into my ear. "I'm sorry." I apologized. "I'm so sorry."

"Shh," She hushed me and pulled back far enough to press her lips to mine. "Don't you dare apologize to me. Never. Not for this" She buried her face back in my neck, with her legs still wrapped around my waist.

Lex hovered at the steps, wearing an equally sexy robe with her dark hair piled on top of her head. They must have been in bed when Parker called them and I wanted nothing more than to just crawl between them and the sheets and let the darkness take me under again.

Reyna walked to Parker's side, and they silently got in his truck, backing out of the driveway, leaving the three of us in the silence and the porch light.

"Let's go inside," Hannah slid from my arms and looked up at me. "You can take a shower while I make you some dinner, and then we can figure this out."

I shook my head, giving her what I hoped was a believable smile. "I just need a quick shower and some sleep."

She pursed her lips but didn't argue, simply lacing her fingers through mine and walking alongside me toward the house.

When we neared Lex, she stayed silent, expressing so much with those dark, troubled eyes as she gave us space.

But I didn't want space. When I got to the bottom of the stairs, I stopped and leaned into her, gently pressing my lips to hers. I didn't ask or wait for her invitation, and I guess that was exactly what started the entire argument between Brody and me. My inability to be sensitive to her needs because I didn't understand them.

But she didn't hesitate for even a second before putting her hands on my cheeks and kissing me back. When I pulled back, she rested her forehead against mine, "Welcome home. We missed you." She whispered, and I kissed her again.

"Let's get you both inside before you get cold." I pulled Hannah under my arm and Lex wrapped her arms around my waist as we walked inside.

"Let me fix you something to eat." Hannah looked up at me worriedly, "You look like you haven't eaten in days."

"Parker has a large supply of protein bars in that truck of his. I just want to clean this stink off and sleep, baby. I'm okay."

She nodded to the stairs, "You can go shower if you want, but I'm making you something. You can choose to eat it or not when you're clean."

I smirked and gave in to her insistence. "Whatever you say." I kicked my boots off and climbed the stairs, ditching my clothes in the hallway so the stink didn't follow me.

I turned the shower on and avoided looking in the mirror as the water heated and walked in. The water was steaming hot and was exactly what I needed to burn the grime off my body from lying on the ground for two days.

I tried not to think as the power of a hot shower tried to spin the wheels that hadn't stopped until Hannah landed in my arms. I didn't want to worry about the what-ifs and regrets. All I wanted was to forget it all.

I placed my palm on the stone wall and hung my head under the water, letting it run over my body, trying to silence the noise in my head. A soft voice came from the entrance to the oversized shower, and I looked over my shoulder as Lex stepped in.

Naked from head to toe, with her hair still piled up on her head. "I don't want you to be alone." I held her stare, unable to speak as so much spun around in my head. "Is that okay?" She asked, stepping behind me, gently wrapping her arms around my torso and placing one kiss between my shoulder blades.

Her body was warm against mine and I put my hand over hers against my stomach, unable to fight the comfort she was offering.

"I'm so sorry, Knox." She whispered, gliding her hands over my abs and chest. "I never wanted you to hurt because of me. Never."

"Shh." I hushed her, lifting her hand to kiss her palm. "I can't think about it right now."

"Okay." She reached to the shelf on the wall, grabbed my shampoo, and kissed my back again. "Then let me take care of you."

She poured some in her hands and the second her fingers pushed through my hair and her nails scrubbed over my scalp, I groaned, tipping my head back so she could reach it all. It was heaven as she slowly and sensually massaged my head.

"Rinse." She ran her hands under the water as I stepped forward, rinsing the suds from my hair.

I didn't understand what kind of relationship was growing between us, but it felt right. It felt honest in that moment. I craved honesty amidst everything else.

She stepped around in front of me and I couldn't resist the urge to look down at her wet, naked body. She was sinfully sexy and my cock thickened the longer I looked.

Hours before, I'd been ready to end it all and let nature take its course. And then I found myself in the shower with a woman who wasn't mine and an overwhelming desire to lose myself in her body sexually when that was the very reason I found myself in the woods, to begin with.

"You say you can't think right now," She pondered as she poured body wash on a cloth and lathered it up, "But your eyes say a lot is going on in that brain of yours."

"All thoughts I shouldn't be having." I admitted, "I'm a warm-blooded man, after all."

She smiled softly and dropped my stare as she brought the cloth up to my neck and started scrubbing the dirt and grime off my skin. I closed my eyes and allowed her touch to do exactly what it was meant to do.

To make me forget.

She rubbed the cloth over my chest and arms, silently working until she cleaned my abs and pushed her hand lower. I clenched my teeth together as she pressed her body to mine and leaned up on her toes to speak against my ear. "I thought you'd be mad to see me here when you got home." She wrapped the cloth around my now rock-hard cock and stroked it up and down like she was cleaning it before sliding it down further to massage my balls. I growled deep in my chest as her wet tits slid over my soapy skin as she gripped my cock again and stroked me. "I don't know what I'm doing exactly," She hesitated, and I tipped my head down to look at her. "But I think you're enjoying it, regardless."

"I enjoy every touch you grace me with, Lex," I spoke against her lush lips as my hands lost their battle of indifference and settled on her hips. "But you don't have to do anything you–"

"Don't." She cut me off, tightening her grip on my cock and biting my bottom lip. "I don't want your kid gloves or your eggshells, Knox." She repeated my fears from my original conversation with Hannah and Brody. "I want this." She dropped the cloth and gripped my cock with her bare soapy hand, sliding it over the head and down to my balls, massaging and teasing every inch of me. "I want you and your pleasures. I want the pleasures you've given me every single time you touch me."

"Lex," I growled, on edge, and fucked in the head over the whole thing.

"Shh." She pushed me back against the wall and slid her body up and down against mine while she pumped my cock. "Just relax, baby." She purred seductively, "Let me take care of you."

"Fuck, yes." I flexed my hips, pushing my cock deeper through her hand and against her silky body.

She kissed me, wrapping one hand around the back of my head and pulling me down to her delicious lips, tangling her tongue with mine as we played.

"Where's Hannah?" I asked, desperate for both of them.

"Making you food," She smiled and then bit her lip, "She sent me up here to see to your needs. I hope that's okay."

My cock twitched in her hand and I slid my hands down over her ass to pull her closer to me as I bit her bottom lip and sucked it into my mouth. "I'm not going to complain."

She pulled back slightly, "I want to try something." She licked those pouty lips that were swollen from my kisses. "Can I?"

"Whatever you want." I held my arms out at my side, "It's yours."

She took my cock and aimed it directly at those pretty pink lips between her thighs and I froze as she placed it in that small gap between her pussy and her thighs and then pushed forward. My cock slid through that silky skin, rubbing against her clit but not penetrating her even though it felt similar to sinking deep inside of a woman because of the wet friction.

"Shit." I groaned, looking between our bodies as she slid back until the head of my cock was nestled right against her clit and then slid forward again.

It was incredible how erotic it was to watch her pleasure me with her silky thighs and pussy lips. I felt guilty for using her body at first, until I pulled my eyes away from watching my cock disappear between her legs and looked at her face.

She was staring up at me with hooded eyes and parted lips as she picked up the pace and rode my cock for the first time, even if it wasn't inside of her.

"Knox." She panted, clawing at the back of my neck for leverage as she stood on her tippy toes to be tall enough to get me where she wanted me. "Does it feel good?"

"I'm so fucking close," I admitted, gripping her hips and pushing forward to take the strain off of her legs.

"Yes." She tipped her head back and moaned. "God, you feel so good."

"That's it, baby." I turned us and pushed her against the wall so she didn't fatigue and changed angles slightly, so I was pushing my cock down and then between her thighs. It rubbed directly against her clit with pressure and she took it like such a good girl.

"Please." She begged, digging her nails into my neck and biting my chest as she chased pleasure.

"I want you to come for me, baby. I need to feel you break for me." Putting my fist against the wall to keep from hurting her, I fought to control my need for her.

"Break for *me*." She challenged, grabbing my fist off the wall and wrapping it around the back of her neck. "Give me everything, Knox."

"Yes." I hissed and slammed her into the wall harder with each thrust.

"That's it." She gasped, and then cried out, "I'm coming."

"Good girl."

"I'm coming on your cock, Knox." She cried and tightened her thighs together even more, riding out the sensation of her orgasm. "Come for me, baby. Coat my skin with it."

"Fuck!" I roared and pulled back until the head of my cock nestled directly against her clit and came, coating her with it just like she wanted.

"God," She moaned, as I kept coming.

By the time my body stopped convulsing and spasming, my legs cramped, and I sank to my knees in exhaustion. I panted and rested my forehead against her abdomen in absolute shock from how good it felt to hear her beg for my touch and my body.

She ran her fingers through my hair, petting me and soothing me while we both came down from the high. When I could breathe again, I looked up at her sexy, pouty lips and bedroom eyes. "Thank you for giving me that."

"Thank you." She smiled softly.

"I want to see something." I wrapped my hand around her ankle and lifted her foot to rest on the bench beside her. Her lips parted, but she didn't protest as I spread her legs and sank to see the evidence of my orgasm coating her pussy. I growled and gently spread her open for the very first time as she scraped her nails over my scalp. "So fucking sexy." I slid my fingers through our combined release and rubbed it in, covering every inch of her sensitive skin. "Mine."

"Yours." She pulled my hand free, sank to her knees in front of me and kissed me, slow and sensually. She ran her hands over my chest and back like she was familiarizing herself with my skin and touch. "I've never trusted a man the way I trust you, Knox."

"I don't deserve it." I hovered against her lips, "I don't have a fucking clue how to do this the right way. How to treat you right."

"It's not about right or wrong." She lifted my hand from her waist and slid it over her breast to lie flat on her chest. "It's about using our hearts and trusting them to lead the way here." She lifted my palm off her chest and kissed it while staring right into my eyes like she was seeing my soul. "I trust you."

Those words had never felt more impactful before, and I needed more of them.

I needed her confidence in me when it felt like everything else was slipping through my fingers like sand. "Thank you." I closed my eyes and kissed her again. "You don't know what that means to me."

"I don't." She smiled and ran her fingers over my cheeks, "But I want to learn everything about you." She stood up and helped me to my feet as I groaned in fatigue again. "We can start tomorrow though, after you get some rest." She rinsed off and insisted on finishing her abandoned job of cleaning me, before holding her hand out to me, "Let's get you in bed."

"Okay," I smirked, turning off the water and stepping out of the shower and finding Hannah sitting on the counter in her sexy baby blue nightgown with a dirty smirk on her face. "Han."

I don't know why, but I felt guilty, as though I had been caught with her friend behind her back.

"I don't think I've ever listened to something so sexy secondhand before." She licked her lips. "Promise me that tomorrow you'll tell me exactly what you two were doing in there that made you both so loud?"

Lex walked over and pushed Hannah's thighs wide and slid her hands up her sexy thighs, pushing her nightgown up as she went and my cock twitched to life again, watching them touch. "Did you get wet listening to us?" Lex asked as her fingers brushed the very top of Hannah's thighs, and from my view, I could see she wasn't wearing any panties under her blue gown.

I groaned as Hannah opened her thighs wider and leaned back against the mirror, revealing herself to Lex and me completely. "You tell me."

Lex leaned down without hesitation and took a bold lick of Hannah's pussy, making her cry out in pleasure before sucking on her clit. "Mmh, dripping for us."

"Fuck." I groaned, fisting my cock as I watched like a voyeur.

Both girls looked over at me and smiled seductively, watching me stroke my cock.

"Think we can make him come again without even touching him?" Hannah quipped naughtily.

"Without a doubt," Lex pulled back and slid Hannah's nightgown down, revealing her tits. "But we'd better get him into bed first, the last orgasm took him to his knees."

"Mmh," Hannah moaned as Lex tweaked her nipples before pushing her backward and jumping off the counter. "Bed, Mister." She sashayed to me, sliding her nightgown over her hips and leaving it on the floor as she slid her hand over my cock and then backed up, pulling me forward by it.

I chuckled and followed the love of my life as she dragged me to bed and then pushed me down onto it on my back.

Both girls crawled up at my feet and I groaned, unbelieving that this was my life.

They faced each other and started kissing, adding extra flare for the show as I laid back on the pillows and watched, stroking myself.

"You two are goddesses." I moaned, rubbing my balls as I stroked myself.

"We're your goddesses." Hannah winked at me and then pushed Lex down onto her back playfully.

"Put that pussy on my face," Lex demanded, pulling Hannah up to kneel on each side of her head.

"Fuck." She moaned as Lex wrapped her arms around her thighs and pulled her down flush to her face. "God!"

"Show her how much you like that," I growled, stroking faster. "Make her come on your tongue, Hannah."

Hannah fell forward with a dirty smirk on her face as she pushed Lex's thighs wide, "Like this baby?" She dipped her dainty pink tongue into Lex's lips, circling it around her clit, and sucked on it.

"Just like that." I bit my lip to keep from telling them what else to do, eager to let them explore each other in their own way. Lex's moans, muffled by Hannah's pussy, were nearly my undoing.

I slowed my stroking down and forced my breathing to slow as well as I watched the show.

"How does it feel, Hannah?" I asked, desperate to be a part of it.

"So good." She gasped, leaning up and using her fingers to push inside of Lex as she rocked on her face. "Oh my god, so good. Come have a taste."

Hannah nodded to the glistening snack laid out beneath her as she fingered Lex.

"Lex?" I asked, looking for her permission to taste her for the first time.

She hummed and spread her legs wider, inviting me in, and I didn't hesitate.

When I had walked into the house an hour ago, I was dead on my feet. Yet, with these sexy women offering me such pleasure, I felt renewed and invincible.

I sank to my stomach, aiming my cock up against the bed as I laid down between Lex's legs and kissed Hannah as she moaned while Lex did something she particularly liked.

"Lick her pussy, baby," Hannah demanded, and I smirked as I went in. I went straight for Lex's clit and sucked her hard, making her back arch off the bed as she pushed against my mouth, silently begging for more. "Fuck." Hannah moaned, watching me. "I never thought I'd be turned on by watching you taste another woman."

"It's Lex, Sweetheart." I licked my lips and kissed her again as I rubbed my fingers over Lex's clit, making her cry out. "Let me hear you, Lex."

Hannah lifted her hip and Lex moaned so loud. "Jesus fuck, Knox. Don't stop, please."

"Good girl." I went back in and Hannah screeched as Lex spanked her ass and pulled her back down onto her face. "Both of you are so fucking good."

"Make her come," Hannah begged with her eyes closed and lips parted before sliding her hand over my head and pushing me down into Lex's pussy harder. "Just like that."

I pushed my tongue into Lex's pussy as I rubbed my face back and forth over her clit, stimulating it with my unshaven face and she screamed as her entire body locked up tight and snapped.

"Fuck! Fuck! Fuck!" Lex yelled, and I wasn't sure what she was doing, but seconds later Hannah let out her own cry of pleasure and I tongue fucked Lex harder for being so good to our girl and rewarding her.

The entire time I played with Lex, I flexed my hips, grinding my cock into the bed, edging myself until I was ready to blow.

"I'm going to come." I groaned as they both panted.

"Up," Hannah demanded, jumping off Lex's body and dropping to her stomach in front of me as Lex scrambled around to do the same. I kneeled in front of them and Hannah took hold of my cock and stroked me as Lex reached down and palmed my balls, gently massaging them until I was chasing bliss within their touch. "Come for us, Knox," Hannah demanded.

I looked down at them, both staring up at me as Hannah sucked the tip of my cock into her mouth and that was it.

"FUCK!" I roared as my entire body crashed through ecstasy.

"That's it, baby," Lex purred, gripping my balls firmer as they tightened for her. "Drink him down, Hannah."

Hannah moaned and swallowed my come, but pulled off at the last second and took the last few shots onto her tongue, showing me the release in a show-off fashion. I sank back on my feet, completely blown away by the two of them.

Or I thought so until Lex grabbed Hannah's face and turned her, pushing her tongue into Hannah's mouth and taking the come.

I moaned as Lex swallowed it, groaning at the taste before licking her lips seductively up at me.

I collapsed onto my back and sucked air, trying to get the dream I was stuck in to go on for the rest of forever.

Both girls crawled up and wrapped their naked bodies around mine as we all came off the high from the insane turn of events.

Hannah finally broke the silence after clicking the light off on the stand and curling back into my side. "Never leave us again, Knox."

"You make a convincing argument." I joked, but it fell flat as reality weighed back down on us. "I won't."

"Promise?" Lex asked seriously, "Don't get me hooked on you if you're going to leave us like that again."

"I'm here for as long as you want me." First, I kissed her and then kissed Hannah, assuring them both. "I hated being away from you both. I thought of you non-stop."

"Good," Hannah whispered, settling her head on my chest as she held hands with Lex on my stomach. "Because we need you. We *all* do."

She spoke of Brody for the first time since my return, and to be honest, I'd forgotten about him and the turmoil he created in my gut while I lost myself in Lex and Hannah's pleasures. As the darkness surrounded us in our bed, I noticed how, despite the pain he caused me, our bed felt empty without him next to us.

I didn't reply to her; I didn't need to.

We just let the peace we had at the moment drag us all into sleep, content to worry about the rest of it in the morning.

Chapter 28 – Brody

I sat on the tailgate of my truck in the barren parking lot, replaying the last few days while I drank yet another beer.

I was a royal fuck up. I deserved the ache in my gut and the burning pain in my heart for what I did.

I broke Knox, and in the process, I broke us. We'd never be the same. He'd never forgive me for what I said. I hadn't meant it, but it didn't matter. I spoke in anger and with fear of my own shortcomings, and I destroyed the trust between us. Forever.

I just wanted to find him, to make sure he was okay. After ensuring he went back to Hannah and Lex, I would then leave. I'd remove myself from the relationship and the house and protect them all from my toxicity. As soon as I found him.

I'd exhausted every single idea I could come up with over the last two days, and there was still no trace of him. It felt like I was drowning with every minute that passed without a word from him. I needed him to be okay, or...

No. I couldn't think like that.

Knox blissfully lived in the good of life and found a purpose behind everything. Until I broke him with my words. Destroying him.

I was no better than my father, using cruelty and poison to control those around me.

Hannah's revelation about Lex's past and how she allowed it to darken her entire world to protect herself took me back in time to the night I lost my relationship with my entire family because of my relationship with Knox and Hannah.

My father came home one night, drunk and pissed off, swinging at anyone who stood in his way to get to me. I wasn't even supposed to be home. I was supposed to be at a drag race with Knox, but he hadn't shown up. So I went home.

And found my father's fist for being gay.

Of course, I wasn't, not then and not now, but that didn't matter to him.

He'd seen some changes in Knox, and he wasn't the only one. His friends at his garage where we all worked had seen them, too.

At that point, we both had been dating Hannah when she refused to choose between us. We were young, dumb, and so full of starry-eyed dreams, we thought it would work out to share her before our desires burned too bright to deny anymore. My dad's *friends* were all convinced that Knox and I were sleeping together, and using Hannah as a cover, and had ridiculed my dad for it shamelessly. He was a weak man, who couldn't stand the heat, so he passed it on to me.

With his fist and his steel-toed boots until I couldn't move or fight back anymore.

His conditions were simple. Leave Hannah and Knox, or get the fuck out of his house, and never come back.

So I crawled out that front door, ignoring the cries of my mom and my younger sisters because I couldn't stand the thought of not having Hannah and Knox in my life.

I chose my them over my family. I couldn't survive without them, especially not since Knox confessed his feelings for me and we slept together. Walking away from Hannah and Knox wasn't an option, because I was already in love with both of them.

I dragged myself to Hannah's, climbing the tree outside of her bedroom window by the last bit of strength I had, and collapsed on her floor.

Her dad wasn't the police commissioner yet at that point, but I did not doubt if he found me in her bedroom, at the ripe age of eighteen, he still would have kicked my already kicked ass.

So she hid me, and helped me, even though I wouldn't tell her what happened to me.

The other night in our garage, I didn't lie when I told Knox that his love for me made it impossible to walk away back then. But I didn't mean it how it came out. I meant I was just as fucked over him at that point, even without understanding how our friendship had morphed into something deeper.

Something passionate.

I had no intention of ever being with a guy, but I stopped seeing his gender when I realized that love felt the same when it was authentic, regardless of who it was coming from.

It didn't mean that choosing to stay with Hannah and open myself up to loving Knox publicly was easy.

I lost my entire family.

I lost my relationship with my siblings after the lies my father told them clouded their opinions of me. I lost the opportunity to have my mom by my side, witnessing and celebrating every accomplishment I achieved throughout my life. She never got to see what I made of myself.

I regretted that loving Knox had to be a case of having one or the other.

But that wasn't on him, and it wasn't fair of me to unload all of it onto him. Hannah and Knox knew my dad was a mean son of a bitch, but they didn't know the half of it, because I spent my entire childhood hiding it.

Hiding the darkness of my life, so it didn't darken their sunshiny ones.

Knox's family loved him endlessly and openly. They embraced him and his decisions through life without a second of hesitation. And every time we spent a holiday with them or Hannah's dad, instead of mine, they both gave me the same inquisition as to why I wouldn't call mine and try to rekindle a relationship with them, thinking we had just grown apart.

So I lied, every time.

I said I didn't want anything from my family.

I said I was happy with my chosen family.

I said it didn't bother me.

I said I'd rather spend Christmas, Thanksgiving, Easter, Mother and Father's Day, and every birthday over the last ten years with their families, instead of mine.

I lied. I lied so many times I almost fell for it myself.

Because in truth, what I wanted was to go back to my childhood and remember every single feature on my mom's face as she opened the stupid, impractical gifts I gave her for holidays. I wanted to go back and memorize the warmth in the hug she gave me before I realized it'd be my last.

Four years after leaving my father's house, Hannah came home with her face as white as a ghost, holding her newspaper in her hands. She was in charge of writing the obituaries for the paper and when she handed me the next day's issue, a part of me died inside when I saw my mother's name in black ink.

Alcoholism took her, and with it, every chance of reconciliation. I sat on my motorcycle overlooking the cemetery the day they laid my mother's frail body to rest, and they buried my forgiveness in the dirt the same day.

When Knox tried to process Lex's trauma and past and how it shaped her into the closed-off and controlling person she was today, his rose-colored glasses view of life—pissed me off.

It enraged me because he had no fucking clue how hard it was for some people. It transported me back to that scared and lonely eighteen-year-old kid trying to figure out how to take on the world when I suddenly had to start fresh, without help.

So I lashed out and did exactly what my father had done to me my whole life.

I killed his happiness because I had none.

So I sat on the tailgate and punished myself for it.

Hours passed of that, and I was well on the side of sloppy drunk when a truck pulled in and parked beside mine.

Through bleary eyes, I watched as Dallin, Parker, and Trey got out, walking toward me.

I could tell, even in my state of disorientation, that they weren't there to offer their friendship.

"Well," I took another drink of my beer. "Will it be fists or words, fellas?"

"Witty." Trey mused, jumping up on my tailgate with me, swinging his legs animatedly. "I just want it noted that I told them they had to keep their hands to themselves." He shrugged, with a grimace, "I don't know if they'll listen though, and they outvote me, so I can only do so much."

He grabbed one of my beers and cracked it open, drinking it like he was going to enjoy the show either way.

"Lay it on me." I held my arms out at the side, "I'm pretty sure I'm too drunk to even stand up to take a piss, so I'll be an easy target." Parker took a step forward and I held my hand up, "I'm assuming you found him though? Given your obvious distaste for me. So tell me he's okay before you knock my lights out."

"He's fine." Parker said, "At home in bed, nestled between Hannah and Lex."

I gritted my teeth, trying to fight the sense of envy that burned in my gut, knowing he was okay and happy in the end.

Without me.

"Okay." I nodded my head.

And then he pulled back and clobbered me straight in the jaw.

Lights out.

"Did you knock him out, or was it the beer?" Trey's voice cut through my hazy brain.

"Judging by the pile of cans, I'd say it's the beer," Dallin added.

"When he wakes up, I'll try again." Parker deadpanned, and I groaned, already dreading meeting the end of his fist again.

"It was you, big guy." I hissed, rolling over to my side, on the ground, because apparently, it was too much to have hoped that one of them would have caught me before I fell face-first into the dirt. "All you."

"Good choice." Trey stage whispered from the tailgate of my truck, still drinking my beer.

I got to my knees and wrenched my jaw back and forth, testing to see if it was broken or not, but heard no clicks or crunches.

"Well, now that we have that out of the way." I stumbled to my feet and held onto my tailgate for dear life. "He's good?"

Parker scoffed and cracked his knuckles like he was really itching to go for round two, but Dallin put his hand on his shoulder, holding him back, and replied. "He was broke down in the middle of a field, ready to let exposure and dehydration kill him."

I froze, staring at my friend in disbelief. "He said that?" I asked for clarification.

"He admitted he didn't go out there to commit suicide." Parker jumped in, "But that he wasn't fighting against it anymore when I found him."

My heart shattered in my chest, hearing the words I dreaded the most. I drove him to that low point.

"I'm sorry." I kept my head hung in shame.

"Why didn't you tell us the truth of what you said when you first asked for help?" Dallin asked, barely masking his anger.

I picked my head up and stared at him, "Would you admit all of your faults to me?"

"If there was more at risk than just my pride, yes." He snapped.

"I'm sorry," I stated again, resolved to take my lumps because, in reality, nothing I could say would make it better.

"Enough." Trey bit out. "You've both made your points. Move on."

"Why are you so invested in saving his ass?" Parker bit out, "Since this whole thing started, you've had his back. And I can't figure out why when our other friend is the one who's hurt!"

"He's hurt." Trey sounded calm and purposeful as he slid off the tailgate. "Even though he caused Knox's pain, doesn't mean he isn't hurting too!"

"Stop." I shook my head and tried to reason with Trey, whose temper had always been as short as mine. "Don't fight because of me."

"You don't get it," Trey shrugged his shoulders, "But I do. I get you." He said firmly, "And I'm not going to stand by while they kick you while you're already down. Aside from the initial punch, nothing more is on us to hand out to you."

"He's right." Dallin sighed, putting his hands in his pockets as he looked at me like he didn't quite recognize the man in front of him. I hated that look. It made my skin burn. "Let's leave him to it." He took a step back towards the truck.

"You're kidding, right?" Trey spit out, "Just leave him here?" He threw an empty beer can onto the ground and stomped it. "Like this? Who are you?"

"What's that supposed to mean?" Dallin squinted at his husband in outrage.

"It means when the going gets tough, and I fuck up," he raised his arms in the air, "Again! Are you going to just *leave me to it*? To self-destruct into an early grave."

"I didn't—" Dallin sighed, rubbing his hand over his face in frustration.

"Never mind." Trey waved his hand at him dismissively, "Go home. I got this."

"What do—,"

"Leave!" Trey bellowed, and my head pulsated from it. "Just go."

Surprisingly, both Parker and Dallin got into the truck and left.

"Wow." I hummed, trying to pull myself up onto the tailgate and failing miserably, landing on the ground. "You should have left with them." I coughed after inhaling a mouthful of dirt. "I'm not going anywhere."

"You really don't get it, do you?" He squinted at me and then picked up the discarded beer cans and threw them into the truck bed and closed the tailgate.

"I mean, on a good day I might have a better shot at following." I crawled to my feet again, "But today isn't a good day."

Trey grabbed the front of my shirt and shook me. "Broken knows broken, Brody." He shook his head in disbelief, "Don't you understand that?"

"Not really."

"And that's a damn fucking shame." He let go of my shirt and held his hand out, "Keys."

"Carjacking me now?" Fishing around in my pocket for them, I handed them over. I didn't need them in my condition. I was stupid, but not that stupid.

"You wish." He pushed me toward the passenger side and then shoved my dumb ass into the seat. "I figure you'll be a little smarter with some bacon grease and a pot of coffee in that stomach of yours."

"Mmh," I nodded marginally, "It's not your worst idea ever."

"None of my ideas are bad ones." He argued, turning the truck on and pulling out toward the diner across town. The only place open all night.

"Helping me is." I laid my head against the window. "I don't deserve it."

"Some day, someone is going to say the same thing about me after I let my past get in the way of my future *again*. And maybe this is just my way of hoping you're standing there, burdening some of the blows and reaching a hand out to me as I find my way back out of the hole I dig."

"Philosophical." I muttered, "Someday I'm going to appreciate the forethought."

He chuckled and shook his head as he pulled into the lot under the neon glow of the fifties-style diner. "You know who would say something just like that to me when I try to be nice?" He put the truck in park and waited for me to look at him. "Lex."

"Hmm." I nodded, trying to dissolve the ache in my chest, knowing I fucked everything up with all three of them for good and I'd never get to see her get the healing she deserved. "Interesting."

A couple of long hours and an obscene amount of coffee later, I was driving into my driveway at half-past six in the morning.

I dropped Trey off at his place and drove home, far more sober than I had been when he found me. And forced myself to face the fury and pain I created without hiding out anymore.

The people inside of my house deserved that much, at least.

There were no lights on inside and the sun was just barely peeking over the mountains, which meant everyone was probably still asleep. So I quietly made my way inside, hanging my keys on the hook by the door I had used for years, wondering if I would still have such privileges tomorrow.

I kicked my boots off and moved through the house to the kitchen, intent on not disturbing anyone, when I heard something coming from upstairs. The master bedroom was directly above the kitchen, yet it took my tired brain far too long to identify the sound.

Maybe it was because of the turmoil burning in my gut, or the thought that perhaps that same turmoil would be affecting those I loved, but I wasn't expecting to hear what I did.

Moans.

Skin.

Laughs.

The solidification of my future fell into place, as I fell into a chair at the kitchen table, and listened to the three people I wanted more than anything, happily enjoying themselves without me.

They deserved that. They deserved the happiness that pleasure could bring. And I deserved to be completely gutted by it.

So I sat there, listening to Knox's groans, followed by Hannah's cry of ecstasy, moments before Lex's melodic voice followed hers as she gave into bliss.

Four days ago, they would have invited me into that heaven. Today, I sat on the outside.

Rightfully so.

I covered my mouth when all I wanted to do was howl in agony as I listened to my private torment. For them, I'd endure.

And then I'd leave for good.

Chapter 29 – Lex

I walked back from the bathroom to find Hannah and Knox both passed out again. They were nearly in the same position I'd left them in when I went to pee after another, mind-blowing orgasm.

Courtesy of Knox's incredibly talented tongue. The man was insatiable, addicted to making me come with his mouth since he had his first taste last night.

Four times overnight, he woke Hannah and me up for more.

Four.

I didn't know men had stamina that high, but he continuously proved me wrong. This last time I had woken up to him sliding his hard cock through my already wet pussy from behind. Just like he had done in the shower, using that space between my lips and thighs to push through and drive us both crazy. Turns out he had been thrusting into me like that for a while, but my sleep-deprived brain had left me in dreamland, where I was imagining another man giving me pleasure instead of Knox.

Brody.

I woke up thinking it was Brody's hands on my tits and Brody's lips on my neck and as I crested my orgasm and fell off the other side of it; it was Brody's name that I narrowly kept from falling off my lips as I begged for more.

I'd been so fucking close to telling Knox to just push deep into me and give me what we both desperately wanted. But I held off.

It didn't feel right to cross that bridge without Brody with us.

Hell, a part of me even felt a little guilty for letting Knox make me come on repeat while Brody still thought he was missing. At least I thought that's what he was thinking.

I was under strict instructions from Hannah and Reyna not to contact Brody. Not yet.

But it felt wrong. He deserved to be here and Knox deserved to have Brody working on healing the pain he caused. How would they ever get past the fight if they never talked about it?

Wasn't that the goal anyway, to move past it and heal from it?

Maybe I was wrong, it was my first relationship after all.

So instead of crawling back into bed, even though I could have used the sleep after the last few days of worrying, I went downstairs to find the coffee pot to wake up with instead of Knox's tongue.

As hard as that was to admit.

I tied my silk robe around my waist and fingered my hair up into a messy bun, yawning as I walked into the kitchen.

And there he was.

Brody.

The man of my literal fucking dreams. *Shouldn't tell him that.*

He sat in a chair at the kitchen table, looking positively devastated as he stared out the window. I didn't think it was possible, but he looked worse than Knox had when he crawled in last night, and a huge part of me wanted to take care of him, just like I had his boyfriend.

I didn't pick sides in the argument they had, because it wasn't my place. However, a part of me desperately wanted them to find a way to heal those wounds. And I was going to use my neutral position on the situation to serve that purpose if I could help it.

"Hi," I called, and Brody whipped his head around, surprised by my presence.

His black eyes raked down my body, taking in my attire, and his jaw clenched.

Was he mad I was in his house? Shit. Leave it to Brody to make being on his side hard.

"When did you get home?" I walked across the room and leaned against the island a few feet away from him.

"About three orgasms ago." He bit out and then sighed, looking back out the window. "Are they coming down?"

"They're asleep." I tilted my head to the side.

He nodded, but kept his gaze outside like he didn't want to even look at me. It prickled, but my skin was thicker than that. "Coffee?"

He scoffed, "I've drunk enough coffee in the last six hours to last a month."

"Ice pack then?" I asked, and he whipped his head around at me as I pointed to my jaw. "Got a pretty nasty bruise with Parker's knuckles imprinted there." I walked to the freezer and grabbed a gel ice pack and a clean kitchen towel before going back to the table. "My guess is the swelling's only going to get worse if you don't ice it now."

"I don't need ice." He turned away, and I rolled my eyes, almost smirking at his stubbornness, but narrowly avoiding it.

"Fine." I sat down on the edge of the table and put the ice on his cheek myself. His black bottomless eyes snapped to mine and I could see fire burning in them. "I don't want to be your enemy anymore, Brody." I gently cupped my free hand on the other side of his cheek to hold him still as the ice worked on his wound. "If you don't like me, say it. I can take your ugly words better than you think. But don't fight me just on principle, because right now you could use an ally."

His gaze was penetrating as he stared up at me, and it almost made my resolve falter under the weight of it. Would he lash out because it was what he was used to, or would he give into the need for a friend?

"Do you hate me?" He finally asked, working the words through his dry throat.

"For what you said to Knox? Or in general?"

He clenched his teeth again and tried to look away, but I held his face and leaned down so he had nowhere else to look but at me. "The answer to both of those is *no*." I sighed, and tentatively ran my hand over his brow, brushing his crazy hair back off his forehead. "Was what you said to him the truth?"

"No." He closed his eyes, and it was the first time I noticed how forlorn he was. "God, no."

"I won't ask why you said it then," I traced my fingers over the faint lines in his forehead as he stayed still with his eyes closed. "Do you want this?" He opened his eyes and held my gaze, so I clarified, "This home with Hannah and Knox? With me? Do you want it?"

"I want it." He growled, "You have no fucking clue how badly I want it."

"Then prove it to them." I reasoned gently, "With more than just your words."

"And you?" He scowled slightly, "I don't understand why you're being so nice to me."

"I've never *not* been nice to you, Brody," I said, and he scoffed lightly as I smiled and ran my hand over his stubbly cheek again. "I challenge you because it's foreplay for me." His eyes rounded slightly, and I leaped headfirst, like I did with Knox last night. "I guess in a way my body knew it wanted you even before my head did. So I flirted with you, the only way I know how."

"Flirted." He growled, "I wasn't nice to you, even when you were never *not* nice to me." He used my words before.

"And here I thought maybe you were just flirting with me, too." I joked with playful outrage, and then barely restrained from shrieking when he quickly grabbed me by the waist and pulled me down into his lap to sit sideways across his legs. I gasped and ended with my face inches from his.

I rode the man's washboard abs like my very own sex toy the other night, but being this close to his lips made me nervous.

"I want to flirt with you." His gaze fell to my lips, "But I don't know how."

"Then it's a good thing for you I'm a take-charge kind of girl." I leaned forward and gently placed my lips against his, moaning the instant he opened his and deepened the kiss like he was expecting it.

His hand slid over my cheek and he tilted me how he wanted, dominating the kiss and I let him, giving him that victory after such a shitty few days as I sucked his tongue into my mouth.

"Lex." He growled, tightening his hold on my waist as I clenched my thighs together. "I don't deserve any of you. I don't think they even want me anymore."

"They need you, Brody, even if they don't want you at the moment." I affirmed, "Love is weird like that."

"Have you ever been in love?" He asked, holding me close to him, but no longer kissing me, which was a shame because Brody Sinclair could fucking kiss.

"No." I ran my hand down his chest, "But I've seen a really good example of it before, right here in this house." I held his gaze, "You love them, and they love you. Which means you can overcome this with them if you try."

"I want to try." He closed his eyes and took a deep breath. "I want to make it work with all of you."

"Then there's no better way to start than with a love-filled home-cooked meal." I gave him a small peck and stood up, though leaving his lap was the very last thing I wanted to do. I grabbed the pink frilly apron that hung on the back of the kitchen door and tossed it to him with a smirk. "Take your shirt off, it smells like stale beer." He lifted the collar to take a whiff and grimaced before standing up and pulling it off over his head.

"Now what, boss?" He asked, lurking toward me with the first inkling of a smile on his face in days.

"Put the apron on and help me make some pancakes."

He eyed the pink fluff in his hands. "I think it would look better on you."

"Yes, I agree." I shrugged, "But we're not trying to get me on their good side. And no one can resist abs and pink frills when it's holding pancakes and eggs."

He shook his head with a grin. "Whatever you say, boss."

"I like the sound of that," I teased and grabbed the mixing bowl from the top shelf in the cabinet, fully aware that my ass would hang out at the bottom of my robe. When I looked over my shoulder, sure enough, he had his eyes glued right to it, and I shimmied for him before lowering myself to my heels.

I was going to get this triad their happiness back. And I hoped that they'd have room for me in their hearts and home at the end. Because I was hooked, and I no longer wanted to be on the outside looking in.

Chapter 30 – Hannah

I woke up to the smell of breakfast and coffee cooking in the kitchen and an empty spot on the other side of Knox.

I looked up at the ceiling, trying to gauge exactly how I was going to handle the day ahead because I knew it was more than likely going to get painful. But I was hoping there was healing and happiness on the other side of that pain.

I just didn't know what it was going to look like when I got there.

Before Knox could wake up and try to bury his head in the sand by burying his cock inside of me, again, I slid from bed and freshened up in the bathroom. I dressed in a simple white sundress adorned with yellow daisies, attempting to brighten the day, and then returned to the bedroom.

Knox was sitting up in the center of the bed, with his back against the headboard, staring toward the hallway.

"Morning," I said gently, bringing him out of his daydream.

He turned to me and gave me a gentle smile. "Good morning, Sweetheart."

"How are you?"

"My balls ache, to be completely frank with you." He deadpanned and gave me his signature charismatic smile.

"My vagina does too." I crawled into bed beside him. "How's your mind, though?"

He pulled me against his side and kissed my temple as we listened to the noise of pans and dishes rattling down in the kitchen.

"I don't know." He admitted, and I admired his honesty. "Do you think he's downstairs?"

I shrugged, "With Lex?" I tried for lightness, "I think we would have heard the dishes breaking off the walls if they were down there together alone."

"Hmm." He hummed, "He's here. I can feel him."

I could too, but I didn't want to give him a reason to stay in bed all day. "Are we going down there?"

"You can do whatever you want," He tipped my chin back to look up at him, "I hold no ill will toward you and your love for him."

"I hate this feeling, Knox." Shaking his hand off my chin so I could look away, I continued. "I feel like my heart is being ripped in half."

"I know." He sighed, "Believe me, I know."

"I want you guys to fix this."

"He doesn't want me, Hannah." He pulled his arm off my shoulders and busied himself with the blankets as he tried to distance himself from me. "I can't keep going on with things like that doesn't destroy me. He destroyed me."

"He told me what he said to you, and I completely understand why you're distraught over that. I would be too if I were in your shoes, baby." I crawled up on my knees to face him. "But I think we need to hear him out and learn *why* he said those things to begin with."

"I don't know if I can." He closed his eyes in pain. "You're asking me to hand him my maimed heart and let him destroy it the rest of the way."

"I understand. I don't know how to help you through this."

He swallowed and took a deep breath. "I guess we should see if he's even here before we worry about the next step."

"I guess so." I watched as he got out of bed, dressing in a pair of athletic shorts and nothing else before turning at the bedroom door to me.

"Coming?"

"Do you want me to?"

"I always want you near me, Sweetheart." He held his hand out to me and I got out of bed and walked to him, lacing my fingers through his. I was sure he wanted my strength to go downstairs, but I wasn't sure I had what he needed.

When we got to the bottom of the stairs, I heard Lex's soft giggle and Knox's hand tightened around mine.

As soon as we entered the large space, both of them stopped and looked at us.

Lex and Brody. Working together without fighting.

"Is that my apron?" I asked, fighting a smirk as I looked at Brody's hulking frame covered with the pink ruffles.

"It is." He gave me a cautious smile, "Lex told me my shirt smelled. I hope you don't mind."

I hated the divide down the middle of the room as Brody turned his gaze to Knox, who still hadn't moved at my side.

Lex moved first, wiping her hands on a towel and coming over toward us. I met her halfway, welcoming the tension relief in the shape of her lips pressing to mine.

"Good morning." She whispered against my lips as she gently combed her fingers through my hair affectionately. "Is it okay that I'm here for this?"

"Of course." I frowned and kissed her again. "You belong here, Lex."

"Okay." She smiled and looked behind me. "Morning, handsome."

I let her go as she moved toward Knox, and I faced Brody.

He looked so unsure and uncomfortable, not a single time in our entire relationship had I seen him looking so hopeless. He was a part of my heart and I needed to soothe that part, just as I did with Knox. So I walked forward and the fear in his eyes nearly broke me.

"Welcome home." I smiled up at him and he wrapped his arms around my waist and pulled me tight to his chest, peppering my neck with kisses. He physically trembled in my arms and my nose burned with tears. "Make this right, Brody." I whispered, "I can't live without both of you."

"I can't either." He replied, pulling back and looking over my shoulder where Knox had Lex locked in a passionate kiss. "I need all three of you."

"Then prove it to him," I said, patting his arm as I moved to the coffee pot and poured myself a cup.

Brody wrung a towel in his hands as he stood there, waiting for Lex and Knox to part, when they finally did Lex looked guilty as she glanced over at Brody before joining my side at the counter.

Brody cleared his throat, "Hi."

Knox's jaw clenched, but he didn't reply, though they stared at each other.

"I owe you an apology that can't even begin to heal the pain I caused you." Brody tried again, "But I'm asking that you at least let me share something with you that I've never told another soul before. And maybe you'll understand me a little better when I'm done, and then you can decide if you ever want to see me again."

"I know you, Brody." Knox squinted, "At least I thought I did."

Brody nodded his head and then tossed the towel down on the counter, looking at me and forging on.

"Do you remember that night I showed up at your house, beaten?" My chest constricted, remembering what he was talking about. I had been so scared, he was so wounded I didn't know how to help him. So I called Knox.

"Yes." I nodded, and Knox remained silent as Brody turned to him.

"We were supposed to go to the drag races that night. But you didn't show up. Do you remember why?" Brody asked.

Knox huffed, "What does that have to do with this now?"

"Please." Brody implored, "It's important, and I'd like to know why you didn't show up."

Knox shook his head. "I don't know!" He snapped, "Someone said you had to pick up a tow in Clearstead."

"My dad?" Brody's voice was thick, and I covered my lips in fear of the whole thing boiling over and ending before they got the resolution they needed.

"Yeah, I guess. Why? What does that have to do with this?"

"My dad is the one who beat me up that night. And it wasn't the first time, but I'd been able to hide it from you guys mostly until then."

Lex's hand found mine, and she squeezed as we both watched on in horror.

"That's what you said the other night, but that doesn't make any sense to me." Knox's shoulders deflated.

"He accused me of being gay." Brody cleared his throat, "Evidently, the guys at the garage had been watching us and picked up on something changing between us and ridiculed him for it. He lied to you that night about me being on a tow, to keep us apart. And then he attacked me as soon as I walked through the door after you didn't show up at the races."

I watched Knox's defensive stance soften as the pieces started clicking for him as they did for me, while Brody continued.

"He beat me unconscious and when I came to, he told me to leave you and Hannah or leave his house, because he refused to have a gay son. I begged him not to do it." Brody's voice broke, and he held his hands out at his side in exasperation, "I begged him to love me enough not to care who I dated, but he wouldn't. So, I crawled out of his front door, and he never allowed me back."

Knox paled.

"I chose you, even without knowing what our future looked like." Brody swallowed, "When I said that your love trapped me, I meant I loved you first. And I didn't understand it, but I couldn't walk away from you or Hannah because it would have hurt just as much as you asking me to walk away today."

"You said you regretted me!" Knox shook his head in agony.

Brody stepped forward, "I regret that I have nieces and nephews I've never met who have no idea I exist. I regret all the big moments I missed over the years, both good and bad. I regret that I never got to tell my mother goodbye." His face crumbled as the emotions took over.

"Oh my god," I whispered, remembering the day I brought home her obituary and the way he shut down after that.

Brody continued on, "I regret that I didn't know my last hug with her was my last until it was too late to reconcile. She died before I felt secure enough to tell her I still needed her in my life!" He licked his lips as tears pooled in his dark, bottomless eyes. "I regret that she never saw me with you and Hannah because she never got to see how loved I was." The tears spilled over his lashes and ran down his cheeks. "I regret that she died, thinking I didn't love *her* enough to stay."

"Brody," Knox's face fell.

"I never regretted you." Brody took a hesitant step forward, pulled the frilly apron off, and put his hand over his heart where both of our names were written in permanent ink. "I regret that all I have left of her are eyes that look like hers when I look in the mirror and memories of a happy childhood that only existed because of her love amidst my father's hate."

"I'm sorry." Knox swiped at his face. "I didn't know."

"That's my fault." Brody took another step forward, "Because I tried to shelter you from that pain and grief. Your family loves you in ways you will never grasp, baby. And I never wanted you to know how bad it was for me my entire life. It all just boiled over when you seemed so unphased by Lex's triggers and acted like you weren't capable of understanding how to be cautious with someone else's heart. Because since I was eighteen years old, I've hidden this wound to protect *your* heart." Brody turned to me and I stared back with tears streaming down my face. "I just wanted to keep you both from hurting. But I turned out to be just like him."

"No." I shook my head and crossed the kitchen to him, unable to stay out of it any longer. "You're nothing like him!" I cried, wrapping my arms around his neck and clinging to him. "I'm so sorry you lost her that way."

"I shouldn't have kept it from you."

"No, you shouldn't have," Knox interjected, walking to us hesitantly as I untangled myself from Brody's arms. "You should have trusted us with your pain instead of shielding ours."

"I know that now." Brody sniffed, "I know, Knox. I'll never forgive myself for putting you through this."

"Never again." Knox grabbed the back of Brody's neck and pulled him forward aggressively, kissing him. "Don't you dare ever hide anything from me again."

"I won't." Brody clung to him, and I felt a sense of relief trying to lighten my anxiety. Were we going to be okay after all?

"And if you're riled up like that and run off at the mouth again, I'm knocking you the fuck out instead of running from it!" Knox declared, "I'm fucking fighting for this. From now on."

"Me too." Brody declared and sighed as they both took a deep breath, fighting off the emotions that threatened to pull us all under for good. "Fighting tooth and nail. For all three of you."

"I like the sound of that," I spoke up, pulling Lex toward us, who watched it all with tears in her eyes and a proud smile on her face as the guys worked it out.

"Me too," Lex added, sliding her arms around Knox's waist as Brody pulled me into his. It was like with us all together, we could work our way through whatever came up.

"So who wants bacon?" Brody joked weakly, nodding to the full spread laid out behind us on the counter. "I burned the shit out of my abs with that grease splatter, so you'd might as well enjoy it."

"I think I'll enjoy it more knowing you suffered a little," Knox smirked, and though I could tell it was a bit brittle, it gave me hope that with time we'd all be fine. Perfectly fine.

Chapter 31 - Knox

"You're killing me smalls, you know that, right?" I groaned as Hannah sashayed excitedly down the blacktop, swinging her hips back and forth as she tested the abilities of that mini skirt.

She glanced over her shoulder, blowing me a kiss with her bright red lips before turning back around.

"She wants us to break our knuckles tonight," Brody added from my side as he lowered his sunglasses to watch her plump ass cheeks peek out from under the skirt as she jumped up and down at the railing.

Lex looked at us and then laughed out loud as we caught up to them. It was drag night, and Brody had recommended it as a date night opportunity. At the time, it sounded like a great idea. But that was two days ago, and I regretted the decision with every ounce of my body.

After our breakthrough in the kitchen, we spent the next couple of days locked away, *learning*.

Learning about each other again as if I hadn't known Hannah and Brody for more than half of my life, while simultaneously learning about Lex and her incredible life. It had been easy and relaxed and while there was still tension between Brody and me; we were on the right track.

The only problem I had with the entire time spent bonding and getting to know each other was we didn't fuck.

Not once.

No one came.

And while I had meant it when I told Hannah that my balls ached from how many times I had come that night with her and Lex, they had more than recovered. Yet still, no one fucked.

No sex, even though we were all physically touching, all the time.

Cuddling. Kissing. Embracing.

We played board games and read or worked on art in the bright sunshine in the living room while enjoying the peacefulness.

It felt like we were four teenagers who didn't know how far we were going to go but were enjoying the build-up on the way.

The problem was that we were all ready to burst, and the sexual tension had been building to insurmountable levels. It was just a game of who was going to beg first.

And with the way the girls looked tonight, it was easily going to be me.

Hannah's red pleated mini skirt gave naughty schoolgirl vibes and the white lace tank top she wore with it made my knees weak because it was so sexy and low cut. It was no surprise to learn it had come out of Lex's closet when they went to her place to restock her clothes and essentials at our place.

It didn't escape my attention that she went to get more clothes, but she didn't return any of her other ones, she just accumulated more at our house.

And I fucking loved that because I wasn't ready to let her leave anytime soon.

I woke up the last few mornings with one or both of them wrapped around my body, and I was desperate to keep it that way.

I pressed up against Hannah, pinning her to the tall concrete wall as the two dragsters lined up for the next race. "You're being naughty," I growled into her ear, pushing my cock against her lush ass.

"I am." She giggled, looking at me over her shoulder as she rocked back against me, rubbing my cock with those cheeks. "I have a bet with Brody that you'll break first."

"Fucker." I growled, looking over at our guy where he smirked with Lex boxed in like I had Hannah.

He shrugged and winked. "It's going to be so good when you beg for it. I'm going to enjoy the show before I give it to you."

Lex licked her lips and turned in his arms and seductively adjusted her thin white tank top that matched Hannah's over her black leather miniskirt, drawing his eyes to her big juicy tits. "Did you know," She purred to him, running her hands up his chest, "That Knox can make me come on his tongue in thirty seconds flat?"

My cock stirred, remembering how fucking good she tasted on my tongue, even as I realized she was playing dirty with him in retribution for his bet with Hannah.

His head snapped around to me and he worked his jaw back and forth. "You tasted her pussy?"

"Oh god, did I ever." I groaned, playing it up, but my cock hardened even more as Hannah wiggled again, laughing at our predicament. "Right after I covered those pretty pink pussy lips with my come in the shower."

"Fucking hell." He growled, and he turned his attention back to her. "You're playing with fire, baby girl."

"I have a tendency to mix a little pain with my pleasures," she purred. "What did you bet Hannah to make sure Knox lost?"

"Yeah, what are the stakes?" I wondered as Hannah turned in my arms, mirroring Lex's stance.

"Whoever gives in first, has to sit in the corner and watch the other with us," Hannah answered, winking at Lex. "Hope you don't mind that I bet your body."

Lex tipped her head back and laughed before sliding out of Brody's arms and pulling Hannah out of mine, backing her into the wall with her hand around her neck.

I didn't even care that we were in public; I needed to fuck so badly I was willing to lift their skirts and do it right over the wall.

"Be careful," Lex warned seductively, "Or I'll make you sit in the corner and watch me take them both deep for the first time."

"Fuck." Hannah gasped, as Lex slid her hand up the inside of her thigh and up the front of her skirt.

Brody and I moved in, shielding them with our bodies as the wall hid the rest.

Hannah pleaded, "Please let me come. I lose, I don't even care if I have to watch them fuck you over and over again tonight. I need to come."

"That's my good girl," Lex murmured, dropping her hand off her neck and holding onto the wall behind Hannah's ass. "Spread your legs for us."

We were at the end of the drag, and the crowd was sparse, making it the perfect place for the girls to play. And for us to watch.

Fuck the drags, we were running our own show at that point.

Hannah stepped apart, and I leaned in to kiss her as Lex pulled her panties to the side and started playing with her sweet, wet pussy. "God." Hannah moaned against my mouth. "I'm so horny."

"Brody, keep her quiet." I turned Hannah's face to him and slid my hand down Lex's arm until both of our fingers were on our girl. "Damn, she's soaked."

"I bet your cock would slide right into this silky pussy." Lex purred, using her finger to push one of mine into Hannah's tight body. "I want to ride your face again while you pound into her."

"I want you to ride more than just my face," I admitted to her, sliding my hand over her ass and spanking it through her leather skirt.

"I want that." She melted into me with those big eyes. "Are you going to fuck me if I ask you nicely?"

Hannah sagged into her as she and Brody listened intently to what Lex was saying. It was a big step for us, but more importantly, it was a big step for her.

"No, I'm not." I shook my head slowly and her eyes widened, surprised by my rejection. "But I am going to hold your legs back and guide Brody's cock deep into your body."

"Knox." She moaned. Picking up speed with her fingers around mine on Hannah's clit.

"I'm going to make you come on my face first, and then when you're so relaxed and silky, he's going to give you your first real cock." I groaned, edging myself with my words. "God, you're going to come so hard with him buried inside of you."

"Home." Hannah begged, "Let's go home!"

"No." I pulled Lex's hand out of Hannah's panties and made a big show of sucking each of them clean, and then brought Hannah back over in front of me. "You're going to watch the drags you were so excited to see tonight. And the first time you come when we get home will be as Lex scissors you hard into our bed. And then you can take a cock, either cock you want. But not until then."

"I'm not going to make it that long." She cried, stomping her feet in a cute little temper tantrum.

I turned her into the wall and kissed her neck as I forced her to look forward, "Just imagine how good it's going to feel when Lex rubs her sweet pussy all over yours."

"Knox, I swear to god!" She hissed, but the dragsters igniting cut the rest off, as they were ready to race.

And so were we.

I slammed the door shut behind us, throwing the lock and kicking my boots off as Hannah started ripping her clothes off. Lex followed suit, a little more seductively, and then they both ran up the stairs.

God, tits and ass bouncing up and down stairs were my weakness, and I had double vision.

Brody put his hand on my arm as I went to follow them and stopped me. "I want to make sure we're good."

It was the first time he outright asked me if we were okay since everything happened. The man had groveled for days, apologizing, servicing me domestically with food and privileges, and absolutely spoiling me. And in a way, I fucking thrived on his pedestal. When in reality, it just meant I was above him, looking down, and I hated that.

He earned my forgiveness with his honesty that first morning at home. Everything past that had just been soothing the burn of the wounds left over from the initial fight.

I should have squared up with him well before that moment, but I was a selfish man, and being his number-one priority for a few days had been incredible.

But taxing.

"We're more than just good, baby." I kissed him, letting go of the reservations I'd had, and showed him exactly how good we were. "You have to forgive yourself if we're going to move forward because I have."

"I know." He groaned, grabbing my belt and pulling me tighter to his body, "I just regret—"

"Enough." I fisted his cock through his jeans and his eyes fluttered closed as I stroked him. "I want to fuck tonight. Hard. I'm tired of edging myself and I need to release. Which means I need you. No one else can handle the kind of mood I'm in."

He flexed his hips, and I tightened my hand on him. "Knox."

"Come on," I pulled his belt open and then the button and zipper, removing his cock from his tight jeans, leading him up the stairs by it. When we got to the top, I kissed him again. "I need you inside of me before I touch our girls, or I'll take it too far with them."

"Whatever you need." He bit my neck hard enough to leave an imprint of his teeth and I hissed, slamming him into the wall, fisting him faster. "I'll give you what you need, Knoxy." He teased, flipping us around and pushing me against the wall as he undid my jeans, freeing my cock.

Moans flowed down the hall from our bedroom and I knew our girls were playing and as much as I wanted to see it, I needed to fall into the right headspace and let him control the situation, or I'd fuck it up with Lex.

He ripped my shirt off over my head and then shoved my jeans down, helping me step out of them until I was naked, then he repeated the process on himself. "Go into the bedroom," He commanded, rubbing his thumb over the pre-cum that leaked out of the tip of my cock. "Get on your knees in the middle of the floor."

"There he is." I bit his lip and then pulled back. "I've missed him the last few days."

"Careful what you wish for." He threatened, fisting his cock and stroking it. Watching Brody stroke his cock was one of my favorite past times.

Sucking it was a close second.

The last few weeks had revolved around the girls and their exploration, and even later tonight, we'd give Lex something she had bravely worked towards.

Right now, however, was for me. It was for Brody.

It was for our decade-long relationship that had gone neglected for far longer than it should have.

"Fuck, that's hot." I sauntered into the bedroom and found Lex's ass straight up in the air, legs spread and pussy on display for me as she buried her face into Hannah's.

Hannah giggled and moaned as I watched Lex push two fingers into her wet pussy and started thrusting hard, rocking her entire body into it.

We were all looking for the feral side of each other, evidently.

I held Hannah's stare as I sank to my knees in the middle of the floor and her eyes rounded as she sat up, interested in what was happening. "Oh fuck, yes." She scrambled to her knees and turned Lex around to face me. "I have a secret to share with you Lex, watching Knox suck Brody's cock is one of the most erotic sights for me."

Lex moaned as Hannah cradled her body with hers, kneeling behind her and pushing her dark hair to the side so she could kiss her neck and play with those big tits.

Brody walked in through the bathroom, cock so hard it barely bobbed with each step as he looked at me and then at the girls. Brody walked in through the bathroom, his cock so hard it barely bobbed with each step, and instructed Hannah, "Spread her legs." The girls instantly obeyed, and he praised, "Good girl."

"Lex, or me?" Hannah teased, sliding her fingers down between Lex's spread thighs to play with that pussy.

"Both of you." Brody praised and then turned to me, "Do you want to be a good boy or a naughty one?"

I hummed, dripping cum for him already. "Whichever you'd prefer tonight."

He grinned, and I knew I was in trouble, "Face on the floor, ass in the air."

"Oh god." Lex cried, and I peeked at her, riding Hannah's hand as she stared at us before I did what Big Daddy Brody said. We rarely played like this anymore, but as I arched my back and presented the way he wanted me to, I remembered how fucking hot it was.

And it turned Hannah savage. Would it ignite something in Lex, too?

"Good boy." Brody walked around behind me and even though I knew what was coming, I still jumped when his meaty hand landed on my ass as he sank behind me. The cap of the lube opened with a deafening click, and I arched harder for him, desperate to impress him. I hissed when the cold lube landed directly on my ass and Lex moaned again. I wanted to watch her watch Brody and me together for the first time, so badly, but I followed the rules.

"Fuck." I hissed again when he pushed his finger in deep without warning. It was small compared to his dick, but still intense. "God, yes." I pushed back on him when he started thrusting it into me and then growled wildly when he reached between my legs and fisted my cock while he played with my ass.

"Arms out flat on the floor." He commanded, and I reached forward like a yoga pose. It was a power play, forcing me to be at his mercy, and I ate it up like cat nip as he replaced his finger with a toy. "Relax." He pushed the silicone plug in, burning past the ring of resistance until it sat completely inside of me.

The last time he fucked me in the office at the garage, there had been no workup or prep. Tonight, we had the toys and the time to make it even more pleasurable.

"Show me how much you like it." Brody walked around in front of me and I sat up, rolling my hips to adjust the placement of the toy, and then did exactly what he loved. I stuck my tongue out and waited for him to put his cock on it like a good little toy.

He didn't hesitate, fisting his leaking cock and slapping the thick head of it against my tongue before pushing it into my mouth. I relaxed my throat and let him take it all the way down until his balls rested against my chin and he moaned an erotic song, signaling he wasn't as immune to it as he wished he were. He fucking loved dominating me.

He pulled out and grabbed a fistful of hair on top of my head, holding me still, and started thrusting down my throat.

"Oh god, I'm coming." Lex cried, and I hummed my support to her as Brody used me. My cock leaked as he grunted and groaned.

"Get on the bed." Brody pulled out, and we both gasped, barely holding onto control.

Moving closer to the bed, I saw the girls instinctively part ways, creating a space in the middle. As I laid on my back, I pulled them down beside me. Our lips locked in a passionate kiss, and I couldn't resist exploring between their legs. Meanwhile, Brody closed in on us.

"Better you than me." Lex mused, biting my peck as Brody stroked his cock.

"I like it hard," I growled and lifted my legs as he folded my knees back onto the bed. "I need the pain so I can be gentle with you when I fuck you for the first time."

Her eyes softened, and she silently kissed me again, slowing it down and sensually coaxing me into a calmer state as Brody pulled the toy out of my ass, making me hiss.

"I don't deserve you three," Lex whispered, and then grabbed my knee and held it wider for Brody as he lubed up his cock. "I think I'm going to come again."

Hannah giggled, "Isn't it sexy?"

"So sexy." She wondered out loud as Brody pushed the tip of his cock against my ass and grabbed the front of my throat so I'd look at him and him only.

"Who's ass is this?" He growled.

"Yours."

"Who's in charge tonight?"

"You are." I hissed as he pushed the head of his cock in.

"Who's the naughtiest good boy?" He smirked and pushed in deep, making me cry out in ecstasy and pain.

"Me." I groaned.

"That's right." He rolled his hips, loosening me up as he held my throat and leaned over my body, sandwiching my cock between us. "You're mine, Knox." Even though the girls were physically holding me open for him, they disappeared under the intensity of his stare as he slid out and bottomed out again. "This ass is mine. I was a changed man the first time I took you." He grunted and thrust again, "Just like this, angry and hard. I fucked you so hard you couldn't sit down for days."

I tipped my head back against the bed as he let go of my neck and slammed in hard. "Yes!" I hissed, "Again."

He pulled out completely and then shoved it back in, making me cry out. Sweat covered my skin from the sheer willpower to lay still when all I wanted to do was bounce on that fucking cock.

"You want this cock; you're going to take this pain." He threatened, and I nearly came from his words alone, but held off. He pulled Hannah's face to his and kissed her hard as she mewed and rocked against our bodies needily. "On his face, Darling."

"Yes, please." She licked her lips as I grabbed her hips and lifted her onto my face.

"Ride my face like a bull, Sweetheart," I said as she rested her hands on my abs and adjusted herself just how she liked. The second her pussy touched my tongue, we both moaned. She was soaking wet and dug her nails into my stomach as she started riding me like a good girl. I peppered her ass with spanks, drawing primal cries of pleasure and pain from her lips.

"Come on, sexy girl," Hannah mused, patting my lower stomach and then stroking my cock and holding it flat against my stomach. "Rub your pussy on his cock while he gets fucked."

Brody grunted something animalistic and his thrusts faltered right before Lex giggled and landed on my abs thanks to his powerful arms.

Hannah held my cock still and Lex's pussy lips slid right over the hard ridge before she tentatively slid back and forth on it. "Oh, fuck." She moaned.

I found myself trapped in a vortex of touch and taste, where I lost all sense of whose touch belonged to whom, except for the unmistakable location of each pussy and the forceful penetration of Brody's cock, which was pushing me towards oblivion.

"You like riding his cock, don't you?" Brody cursed and I could almost feel how clenched his teeth were.

Lex moaned, "God, yes," and Hannah leaned forward. Their lips tangled, muffling their moans.

I wished desperately to see the show we were putting on, but resolved simply to be used for all three of their pleasure, intending to film it next time to watch afterward.

Because there was most definitely going to be a next time.

I was so fucking close I had to focus on keeping control as Lex's hot pussy stroked my cock and Brody's cock rubbed my prostate.

"Tell me, Angel Eyes." Brody growled between thrusts, "You have the sexiest little asshole, do you like it played with?"

Lex moaned and Hannah panted as I waited on pins and needles for her answer.

Please say yes.

Images of me and Brody pushing into her body side by side flashed through my brain and I almost nutted.

"Yes." She moaned and slid forward more than before as the head of my cock nestled against her pussy entrance. She rolled her hips, letting just the very tip of my cock burrow into her heat before sliding back down the length. "I love it."

"Lean forward." He commanded.

Her big tits laid against my chest and I felt her hair tickle over my arm as she bent her head around Hannah's body to show him what he wanted.

The animalistic noises she made did me in. "What's he doing?" I all but begged.

"He lubed up his fingers and is rubbing them over her pretty little hole," Hannah explained to me.

"Like this?" I took my wet fingers and played with her ass as I sucked her clit.

"Fuck!" She screamed and widened her knees to press her pussy firmer against my face.

Brody wasn't done playing puppet master, "I want to put one finger in you. Tell me I can."

"Yes." Lex cried, sliding forward so my cock pressed against her pussy, opening again. "Please, Brody."

"Good girl." He praised and she let out a deep guttural moan, "Such a good fucking girl."

I could hear sucking, and Hannah cried out as I imagined Lex started sucking on her tits. I pushed one finger into her ass, mirroring what Brody was doing to Lex, and she screamed, shattering on top of me, and coating my face in her tremendous orgasm.

"Fuck! Fuck! Fuck!" Hannah screamed again and Brody thrust into me harder yet, turned on by the sight of our girl coming undone.

Hannah collapsed off of me, laying in a heap on the bed, and Lex descended, pushing her tongue into my mouth to taste our girl's orgasm on my lips.

I was feral and desperately needed to come, or the next time Lex teased us both by letting the first half inch of my cock into her pussy, I was going to slam all the way home.

I gripped her hips and slid her down, so her pussy lips sat on my balls and slid her back to the tip, repeating the process as she started talking in tongues and clawing at my chest and neck.

"Is that your whole finger?" she gasped, looking over her shoulder at Brody, who had his eyes fixed on the spot where his finger and my cock were playing with her body.

"The whole fucking thing." He looked at me over her back. "How did we get two fucking perfect women who are obsessed with us and each other?"

"Fuck if I know," I grunted, and she bit my peck as she rubbed her wet pussy all over my cock and threw it back onto Brody's finger in desperation.

"Yes!" She screamed and her pussy gushed and Brody groaned as her body tightened around his finger. "More!"

He spanked her ass, and I grabbed a handful of her hair, clenching it as she spasmed in my arms, begging for more.

If I hadn't been in control of her hips, I knew she would have sunk onto my cock, just to fulfill her desire to be filled in both holes, but she deserved better than that. So I held her down and through the waves of her orgasm before she slid off my body to the bed beside me like Hannah did.

With both girls off of me, I had a clear view of Brody's tense body. I curled up, and he met me halfway, kissing me desperately. "You're perfect," He growled, "taking care of both of them before yourself."

I groaned and fell back onto the bed as he crouched and penetrated me from a different angle, rubbing directly against my prostate.

"Our turn to return the favor." Lex licked her lips as she and Hannah simultaneously kneeled on each side of me and grabbed my cock, that was hard and angry, desperate for relief.

They both seductively started licking it like a melting ice cream cone together and I grabbed a handful of each of their asses.

"That's it," I cried out, "I'm coming. Fuck, Brody!" I roared as he jack hammered into me with their mouths covering every inch of my cock and licking my come as it spurted out.

It was the first time Lex had tasted my cock, and it blew my mind, knowing she was tasting herself on it as she cleaned me up, moaning and swinging her hips like she was desperate for more.

Brody roared, chasing his own ecstasy, and I felt the heat of his orgasm inside of me as he pumped me full.

Seconds passed.

Then minutes.

It could have been days as we all lay sprawled out in the bedroom, some on the bed, some on the floor.

And fucking smiled. It felt so damn good to smile with my people.

Chapter 32 – Lex

It was dark in the bedroom when my eyelids opened; I wasn't even aware I'd closed them. I sat up, silently groaning as my sore body ached from lying on the floor. The carpet was thick and plush, but it was still a floor.

I glanced at the bedside clock and saw that it was after one in the morning. And I was hungry.

However, food wasn't on the menu.

I craved something far more filling than that.

We had come home, planning to take our relationship to the next level by conquering the last boundary I had originally set for the guys before I understood my attraction to them.

But then we all had a wild orgy while the guys fucked and passed out. Watching Brody and Knox together was hands down the sexiest thing I'd ever seen, and I ached for my turn.

Brody was on the floor with me, with Knox and Hannah in the bed, though I didn't quite remember how we all got there.

Brody had gone to the bathroom to clean up after fucking Knox, and I'd laid down on the carpet to catch my breath, and then I fell asleep, meaning he joined me on the floor rather than lay in the bed.

That was an act worth rewarding.

I could just make out his dark frame lying on his back with his arms stretched out over his head and his naked body on display in the shadows.

His body was magnificent, with every inch toned and tattooed, and I couldn't deny my liking of it after spending so much time staring at him over the last few weeks. We all knew the truth, I was falling for them all.

I rolled over onto my side and watched the rise and fall of his chest with the glow of the hallway light outlining his abs, transporting me back to that night I overcame a huge fear and used his body for pleasure.

There was a power exchange between us when I used him, giving him nothing in return and he knew it, keeping me comfortable and safe where I saw fit. To be honest, since the first night at the Sinner's Soiree, he had respected every single physical boundary I set, even if he pushed my emotional ones.

When he challenged me at the pool table about my sexuality, part of me wanted to admit to him then that I was questioning everything, but that felt like a failure. As if I was failing the me, I had vowed to be as a teenager desperate for control over my body and my life. There was no point in having power if I was lonely, though. I was tired of being surrounded by people every day, and random women every night, yet feeling so alone each morning when I woke up, as the high was no longer sustaining my cravings.

I gently laid my fingertips on one of Brody's abs, tracing the valley and the peak down to another one while I watched his face for disturbance. I turned my finger over, using the edge of my fingernail to trace the same line back up to his chest, and leaned over him, laying gentle, open-mouthed kisses against his skin.

Something I loved about being with women was how soft and sensual their touches were. I loved the gentle seduction, but with Brody and Knox, I found I loved giving those soft and sensual touches as much as receiving them from Hannah.

His muscles quivered under my lips and his arms moved as one instinctively wrapped around my back, pulling me closer before he even opened his eyes. I leaned on my elbow, looking down at him as sleepy eyes opened and focused on me before I pressed another slow wet kiss to his chest, holding his stare.

He didn't speak, and neither did I.

We didn't need to. Our touches spoke louder than words, expressing our needs.

He brushed his hand over my cheek and I leaned into it as he threaded his fingers in my hair and pulled me forward, kissing me. His lips moved slowly, dancing across mine before using his tongue to seduce me. I was obsessed with the way Brody kissed; it made me feel like he was touching my entire body.

"I'm sorry." He whispered, laying soft kisses over my cheeks and face.

"For what?" I bit my bottom lip when he ran his hand over my ass, hitching me closer to him until I put one thigh over his.

"For neglecting you tonight."

I snorted, very unladylike, and used my teeth on his lip. "You made me scream in ecstasy." He rocked his thigh between mine and I sighed, feeling my body respond to his instantly. "I hardly consider that neglect."

"It wasn't what we were planning, though." He licked my lip, teasing me. "It wasn't solidifying you as ours."

"Do you feel like I'm not yours?" I kissed his jaw as his fingers tightened in my hair and he pulled me back by it.

"You're ours." He growled, "But I need to be inside of you, it's in my DNA to want to possess you that way."

"Then take me." I purred. "Why do you think I woke you up?"

He growled again and rolled us over. My legs fell wide, instantly accepting him between them, and his cock wedged against my pussy as he brushed my hair away from my face to stare down at me. "Promise me this is what you want. Because the minute I feel you from the inside out, you belong here, with us."

"Brody," I whispered, overwhelmed by his commitment to me so easily. I struggled with commitment my entire life, and they all made it seem so easy.

"Say it, Angel Eyes." He kissed my neck, and I tightened my legs around his waist, "Tell me you'll stay."

"I'll stay." Dragging my nails up his back, desperate for him I gave him what he wanted. "I'm yours, I'm here." I put my hand on his throat and pulled his head away from mine so I could stare into his eyes. "I want all of you."

"Then hold on, baby." He grinned a sinister grin as he pinned one of my knees to the floor, spreading my thighs wider and sliding down my body. "Because I need you soaking wet to take my cock for the first time."

"Mmh." I moaned, running my fingers through my hair as his lips covered each of my nipples, sucking on them and making my back bow off the ground.

"Let them hear you begging me." He demanded, and I hissed.

"Hannah." I shrieked when he bared his teeth and bit my nipple, making my pussy clench. "Knox!"

"Good girl." He kissed down my stomach and folded both of my legs back, opening my pussy as he hovered right over it. Movement on the bed caught my attention, but I couldn't look away from Brody's dark eyes as his tongue wet his lips. "Do you have any idea how many times I've fantasized about making you come on my face?" He smirked and licked a slow, sensual trail from my ass to my clit.

"Mmh, now that's a way to wake up." Knox leaned over the side of the bed and rubbed his hand over his face, waking up.

Hannah peeked over his shoulder and smiled at me before jumping out of bed to join us. "You look so pretty open and wet for Brody."

Brody dove in, sucking my clit into his mouth, and the sharp pokes of his beard were just like Knox's, stimulating every inch of my skin.

"Kiss me." I panted, grabbing for Hannah as Brody's tongue slid inside of my body.

"With pleasure," She purred and brought her lips down to mine, muffling my moans and pleas as Brody rocked my world.

I sensed Knox joining us on the floor and then Brody's mouth pulled off my pussy and a colder one took its place, aimed the opposite way.

I gasped and Hannah pulled back so we could see as Knox kneeled at my side, bent over and eating my pussy upside down as Brody held my legs open for him.

"Oh, God." I collapsed onto the carpet, panting, and then Hannah started sucking on my nipples, driving me wild as Brody and Knox tag-teamed my pussy. I couldn't tell whose mouth or fingers were working me anymore, but that added to the excitement of it all. "Yes!" I grabbed hair, whose I didn't know, and pulled as I crested my orgasm in record time.

I understood the term worship for the first time in my life as the three of them worked together to please me, and the intensity of the feelings it created in my chest overwhelmed me.

My nose burned as they shifted and Brody picked me up, wrapping my legs around his waist and carrying me to his bed like I weighed nothing at all. That strength used to intimidate me, though with Brody and Knox, it made me feel protected and feminine.

Taken care of.

Revered.

"Are you still with me, Angel Eyes?" He asked, and I melted even more for his ability to use pet names that made me mush.

"I'm with you." I held onto him as he kissed me, laying us down in the center of the bed as Knox and Hannah joined us.

Hannah laid down on her back next to me and took my hand in hers, holding it as both guys kneeled on the end of the bed, towering over us. "I never knew I wanted this until I met you." She said as we both turned our heads to stare at each other.

"Are you sure you still do?" I questioned, "You're giving me something you planned to keep to yourself forever, baby."

"I'm sure." She smiled, leaning over to kiss me, rubbing her nose against mine as the guys moved in sync, lying between our legs. "I can't wait to keep you forever."

I moaned when Brody's large, fevered body laid against mine and turned back to him, even as I held Hannah's hand in a death grip.

"You have tears in your eyes, Angel." He hovered over me and I tightened my legs around his waist, wanting to avoid the obvious reaction I was having to everything. Knox looked over at me with concern in his sweet eyes, and Hannah leaned up to run her fingers through my hair.

"I'm overwhelmed by how important you all make me feel," I admitted. "Cherished." I cleared my throat as those tears multiplied.

"You're worth the effort, Alexi," Brody stated, like it was plain as day.

Knox agreed, "We wouldn't want this with anyone else but you, Sweetheart."

Hannah was right there too, "You're perfect, Lex." She kissed me and I clung to her. Hannah told me, "We were always meant to find you and take away your loneliness."

The tears broke free, sliding down my temples into my hair as I smiled at her. "Thank you for finding me."

"You're ours," Brody confirmed, and his cock jerked between our bodies as I dug my nails into his shoulders. "We're not letting go."

"Don't ever let go." I took his cock, and he pulled his hips back as I ran the head through my wetness, testing the feel of him there before pulling him closer to me. I held his stare as he pushed forward and slid the head of his cock into me.

He was so thick it nearly took my breath away with just that much inside of me. He slowly sank into me, staring at me the entire time as the tears continued to trail from my eyes.

When he was buried all the way in, he paused and kissed me with that slow perfection of his I loved until I couldn't resist clawing at him, begging him to move as I rocked my hips against him.

"Please." I pleaded against his lips, desperate for him to fuck me. While I wasn't a virgin, I had already taken care of that years ago with a toy and had since enjoyed penetration play, but this experience was unlike any other. It was him. It was them.

"Good girl." Knox moaned and then I heard him sink into Hannah, drawing moans from her lips as they watched us. I fucking loved having them at our side, making love and watching us, touching us.

"Beg me," Brody demanded, fighting that dominant side of himself for the softer side he had shown me thus far. But I was ready to have the real him with me.

"Please." I licked my lips seductively and dug my nails into his back as I leaned up to his ear, "Please, Daddy."

He growled and pulled out before slamming back into me. "Say it again."

I laid back against the bed and smiled up at him, "Please, Daddy. Please fuck me like you're as desperate for me as I am for you."

Knox chuckled as he leaned over and dragged his teeth over Brody's neck. "I knew you had a Daddy kink. I just knew it."

"I have a Lex, kink," Brody swore, thrusting into me like a man giving his woman everything he had.

"That's so hot." Hannah moaned and I looked at her, smiling at me as Knox slammed into her. Her tits shook with each thrust and I reached over, playing with my favorite toys as he fucked her. "Mmh," She grabbed Brody's neck and pulled him over. "Kiss me, big guy."

He chuckled and pushed his tongue into her mouth dominantly, and the shift in the angle of his hips lit me on fire.

I erupted without warning, screaming in ecstasy as it ripped through me. Brody groaned, pulling back to watch me. "Good girl, coming on Daddy's cock."

"Don't stop." I gasped, begging him like the good little girl he wanted me to be. "Please."

Instead of giving me everything I asked so nicely for, he backed up, letting his cock fall out of me completely as I sputtered in shock and disappointment.

He flipped me onto my side and spanked my ass with a dirty smirk on his face. "Switch."

"Mmh," Hannah purred seductively as Knox pulled out of her, "Not so fast, *Daddy*." He groaned as she took hold of his cock and pulled him to the center of the bed, and then pushed him down onto his back. She straddled his cock and took him deep, tipping her head back to moan as Knox and I watched on hungrily. "Come here, baby." She grabbed my hand and helped me up, positioning me so I was straddling Brody's face. "I want your lips while Knox fucks you and Brody licks you."

"Jesus," I moaned when Brody pulled me down against his mouth, greedily licking me while Hannah bounced up and down on him.

"That's what I'm talking about, baby." Knox kneeled behind me and kissed my shoulder and neck until he was at my ear. "You want my cock?"

I moaned, "Yes."

"I may not be Daddy," He teased, fisting a handful of my hair as Hannah played with my tits. Paired with Brody's tongue skills on my clit and I was already on edge. "But I can fuck you hard enough to make you forget."

"Please," I begged, riding Brody's face. "Please, Knox."

"Good girl." He praised and pushed me forward so my ass was popped and my pussy was exposed to him. "That's it." He ran the head of his cock through my wetness and then pushed inside, slowly giving me time to accept him and grasp what he was doing. "How does it feel?" He whispered into my ear.

"Like heaven." I cried, "Like I've been missing you my whole life."

"That's right." He said, placing his hand between my shoulder blades and pushing me forward until my head landed in Hannah's lap, "I can't wait to feel you come on my cock for the first time."

"The first of many." Hannah purred and then gasped when Brody started slamming her up and down onto him with his hands on her hips.

And I was home.

Epilogue – Brody

Two Weeks Later

I parked my bike against the curb and busied myself with taking my gear off when really I was hesitating. It was stupid, but I was nervous.

I was at Twisted Ink, randomly on a Thursday, and I wanted to see Lex. But it was unannounced and unexpected, and I didn't know how she'd react. She spent every night at our house, even though a few times she had half-heartedly planned to go to her own place for the night. I was pretty sure she was just as addicted to us as we were to her.

Which was why I drove across town after a meeting with a client, to see her. I forced myself off my bike and grabbed the takeout lunch from T's Taco Garage around the corner out of my saddlebag and pulled my big boy pants up.

The electronic chime when the door opened raked my nerves over how loud it was. "Hey, man."

Trey leaned on the reception desk with his tablet in front of him, chatting with some of the other employees, who were all staring at me.

"Hey." I shifted the takeout and took his hand for a shake. "Lex around?"

The little shit grinned devilishly as he leaned back onto the desk and I rolled my eyes, already knowing the shit storm I was about to stir up.

"Possibly." He eyed the bag. "Depends if you're sharing T's tacos?"

Parker walked out of his suite and eyed me up. "What's up?" Things weren't necessarily back to the easy camaraderie we'd had before the knuckle sandwich he gave me a few weeks ago, but they were at least civil.

"Just passing by." I nodded in greeting and then groaned when Dallin walked down the hallway with his head in his own tablet, looking up when he got to the reception area and pausing.

"Hey," He walked around everyone else and shook my hand. "Here to see Lex?"

"Yeah." I sighed. "It's a little hard to get past security these days." I nodded to his husbands standing guard.

Dallin scoffed and waved his hands, "Leave the poor man alone."

"I wasn't doing anything!" Trey ridiculed, "I just asked if he brought enough for the entire class."

Dallin ignored both of them, even though Parker still hadn't said anything, just stared at me. "She's wrapping up a client right now. Probably two minutes longer and she'll be out."

"Thanks." I backed up to the seating area. "I appreciate it."

"Wait." He stepped closer and lowered his voice. "I want to apologize for my part in the—"

I cut him off, "Don't worry about it." I looked down at my feet, incredibly uncomfortable at how my friendship with these men seemed to be over, at least the way it used to be.

"I do worry about it." He affirmed, "I worry about it a lot, Brody. Hannah gave Rey the cliff notes version of why you and Knox fought at all," He sighed, "It wasn't our place to judge you. We're the last men in the world to judge another man for their mistakes."

"Don't worry about it." I repeated and shrugged, "I appreciate the fact that you guys helped me look for Knox and ultimately found him before it was too late. That's all that matters."

"For what it's worth," Dallin tried again, and I contemplated leaving the takeout lunch with him and taking off altogether. "Lex seems to be on cloud nine lately. Which you know better than anyone, that isn't her norm."

"Yeah," I smile gently, "Things are going pretty great for us."

"I'm happy for all of you, Brody. Honestly."

"Thanks," I replied, and then movement down the hall caught my attention and no one else mattered.

Lex walked out of her suite, with her client following her to the front door. She had on a pair of light blue cut-offs and a black cropped tank top with her long dark hair in lush waves. Her signature wide fishnet stockings and chunky boots finished the look.

And I was hard in no time flat.

Her dark eyes found me instantly in the crowd of men around the front door, and she smiled sweetly. I stayed off to the side and silent as she went through her goodbyes with her client and his girl as they followed her out and waved.

When she turned to me, I knew I made the right choice to stop and see her because the smile on her face made everything else worth it.

"Hi." She walked around the guys and straight into my space with zero hesitation. I wrapped her up in my arms and leaned into her when she rose on tiptoes for a kiss. If she didn't care about the audience, I didn't care. She lingered against my lips and then kissed me again. "Are you here to see me?"

"Who else would I be here for?" I questioned, and she sank back onto her heels with a satisfied smirk.

"Come with me." She took my hand and turned, "Go away now," She shooed the men and other co-workers away who were all gawking at at us. "No free shows."

I smirked as she led me past all of them, but I paused next to Trey, reaching into the bag and laying a single wrapped-up taco on the desk in front of him before walking away.

The man saved my life that night I was intent on drinking myself into an early grave. The least I could do was give him a taco.

"I knew you wouldn't leave me out." He cheered and then stuck his tongue out at Dallin and Parker. "No tacos for you!"

Lex giggled and walked us back to her suite, shutting the door behind her. I'd never been in her suite before, though I'd seen it when I came to get ink by the guys occasionally. Being locked away in it with her instantly raised the temperature of my blood.

"You brought me lunch?" She leaned back against the freshly sanitized tattoo bed in the center of the room and, whether she meant to be, it was seductive. Every single thing she did was seductive.

"I did. I was hoping you were free."

"For you, always." She crooked her finger and motioned for me to come closer, and when I was within reach, she took hold of my belt and pulled me the rest of the way. "I'm suddenly ravenous."

I gripped her lush ass and picked her up, sitting her down on the bed as she wrapped her legs around my waist and kissed me. She was obsessed with kissing me. She had different things she did with each of us; with Hannah, she was always playing with her hair, and with Knox, she was constantly running her hands up and down his skin.

With me, her lips were always on mine, and I was more than happy to oblige.

"I missed you," I growled when she pulled my belt open.

"I missed you." She undid my jeans and pulled my cock free. "I hate waking up and finding you gone."

"I talked to Hannah this morning on her way to work." I pushed her shirt up, already knowing her tits would be free and ready for my touch. "She said something about a soapy bubble bath happening this morning."

"Mmh." She hummed, stroking my cock as I leaned down to suck on her nipples. I was pretty sure if I edged her hard enough for long enough, I'd be able to make her come from sucking on her tits alone, they were so sensitive. "She was bratty this morning. She was begging to be dominated, and you and Knox were gone."

"So kind of you to take our place." I undid her shorts and pulled her off the table to pull everything down her legs, tossing her boots and clothes into a pile before picking her back up onto it. "Tell me everything."

As I tipped her back on the bed and spread her thighs wide, she couldn't help but moan. She looked so sexy with her shirt bunched up over her big tits and naked from there down, spread open and wet for me. "She was in a snarky mood from the moment her alarm went off." Biting her knuckles to stay quiet when I licked her, she went on. "Without even realizing it, she desperately needed re-centering."

"So you re-centered her?" I pushed two fingers into her pussy while I sucked on her clit.

"Right on the kitchen counter." She buried her fingers in my hair and pulled, leading me back to her pussy and rocking against my face. "I bent her over the counter and spanked her until she was begging for more and pleading to come."

I growled and thrust my fingers faster. "Did you fuck her?"

"Laid her out on the counter, ate her pussy until she came three times, and then took a bubble bath with her for aftercare."

"You gave, but didn't take?" I sucked hard on her clit.

"Oh, she gave in the tub." She smiled, "She scissored me in the tub until we were both far more relaxed and happy."

"You're perfect for her." I stood up and pressed her hips into the bed with mine, rubbing the head of my cock through her pussy lips.

"No." She shook her head as she stroked my cock and aimed me right for her opening, pulling me in. "I'm perfect for all of you."

"Fuck yes," I hissed as I bottomed out into her. "We're going to keep you forever."

"Please." She moaned, clinging to my neck as I slammed into her. Thank god she had a high-end tattoo bed and not one of those fold-up ones, or it would have collapsed with the first thrust. "I need you, baby."

"I'm right here." Slowing my thrusts down, I stared directly at her, giving her inch by inch in slow thrusts until she was grasping at the end of her control. "I'm with you."

"Come for me, Brody." She whispered. "I want to feel you come with me."

"Yes." I clenched my teeth, "I'm there."

"Me too." She tipped her head back and tightened down on me as her lips parted in a silent moan.

"Milk my cock like a good girl," I growled, rolling my hips in circles as I came deep inside of her. "Take that come, Angel."

"God," She gasped, licking her lips, and kissing me while I stayed buried inside of her. The girl loved to fucking kiss me.

"This was not what I planned when I stopped by." I smiled against her lips, "I just wanted to feed you."

"I'm thoroughly stuffed." She clenched down on my cock and I grinned as I pulled out of her. She pouted sexily as I suddenly left her empty and helped her down onto her feet. "I have something to admit."

I groaned and fought down panic, trying to swirl as I put my cock away, "Lay it on me."

"I bought something today."

"I'm going to need some clarification here." I stared at her as she started getting dressed and prolonged my discomfort.

"In my defense, it's Reyna's fault." She said, licking her lips and rocking back and forth on her heels. "She made me take her to the sex store to stock up on new toys."

"Alexi." I snapped, raising my brow at her, "Spill it."

She sighed and laid her hands on my chest, trying to use her seductive powers to lighten the blow, I was sure. "I got a double-ended dildo."

My spent cock twitched in my jeans, and I fought an array of dirty comments to make but refrained.

Barely.

"Are two real cocks not enough for you?"

She leaned in closer and purred, "Four sounds better."

"Angel." I growled, "Explain."

"You see what I was thinking was—"

And everything faded to black as she told me her plans.

"This is about trust," Lex stated, running her fingertips over Hannah's bare back. I watched as goosebumps followed the trail and my cock throbbed in my boxers.

Knox grunted when she turned her attention to him and tilted his head to the side before biting his neck. I could tell by the way his body flinched; it was hard.

And it made him harder.

"This is about pleasure," Lex said against his ear as she dragged her nails down his chest. His cock bobbed where grew thickly between his thighs. He was in a chair with his hands cuffed behind the back and his ankles tied to the legs. "This is about control."

"I volunteer as tribute." Hannah smiled blindly behind the mask that covered her eyes, keeping her on edge.

She kneeled on the padded bench at the end of our bed, with her wrists tied to the posts spreading her arms out like she was flying, and her legs pushed open wide how Lex positioned her.

They were both naked, blindfolded, bound, and vulnerable.

And I felt like a monster, barely restraining from descending on them. I needed to consume them, the darkness inside of me was breaking down the walls of restraint, begging to be free.

"Do you even know what you're volunteering for?" I growled against Hannah's ear, and she shrieked in shock as I silently hovered behind her.

She turned her face toward me, even though she couldn't see me. "I trust you." She purred, "I want to be your slut tonight, Daddy."

Knox groaned, and I looked over in time to see Lex lower her pussy directly onto his hard cock. She didn't touch him anywhere else, just hovered over his cock with her back to him and sat down, taking him deep in one smooth descent.

She licked her lips and rolled her hips when her ass was in his lap before spreading her legs so I could see where she took him.

"What's happening?" Hannah whipped her head around, trying to see through her blindfold as Lex moaned, rising and taking Knox's cock deep again. "Tell me! Please."

"Tell her, Knoxy." Lex hummed, reaching between her legs to his balls and rolling them through her fingers as she leaned back against his chest and rested her head on his shoulder.

Fuck, she was so divine with her black ink and big tits dominating him.

Using him.

My balls ached for release, and I pushed my boxers down so I was as naked as everyone else.

"She's riding me." Knox panted, "Fuck, she's doing that thing you guys do when you roll your hips while we're buried all the way deep inside of you."

He was painting Hannah such a seductive picture, and she panted like she could see it all vividly.

Lex locked eyes on me as she rolled her hips back and forth with Knox in deep, just like he said, and circled her clit with her fingertips as she stared at me.

She was my fucking equal. Something I never imagined wanting, let alone finding.

"Is she wet?" Hannah licked her lips again, staring at them through her darkness. "Is she dripping for you, baby?"

"Soaked." Knox growled. "Like she was planning this for far longer than she let on."

"Mmh." Hannah moaned, dropping her chin to her chest. She was so distracted by listening and thinking about Knox and Lex that she never even sensed me moving behind her.

So when I put both hands on her hips and pushed forward, burying my cock in her unsuspecting pussy, she screeched first, then moaned, dropping forward as far as she could with her arms spread wide to accommodate me.

"That's it, slut." I spanked her ass, and she vibrated deeply in her chest, "Take my cock."

I thrust four times and then pulled out, stepping backward as she cried out in frustration, fighting against her bindings.

Lex stood up off Knox's lap at the same moment and walked over to me. She kissed me hard, rubbing her naked body against mine as both Hannah and Knox groaned and grunted in annoyance.

"I'm falling in love with you," I admitted out of nowhere and our restrained lovers froze, silent finally, as Lex stared up at me. "Just thought I'd share."

Lex smiled and slowly sank to her knees at my feet. "Do you have any idea what your words do to me, Daddy?" She licked her lips before trailing her tongue up the length of my cock, moaning as she tasted Hannah's pussy on it.

"I have an inkling suspicion." I grinned and moaned when she deep throated me, gagging on my cock and then spitting on it, rubbing it in with her hand.

"You're late to the game, though." She moaned, lifting my cock to twirl her tongue around my balls. "I told Knox this morning that I was already head over heels in love with both of you."

I grunted and Knox chuckled. "Perfect boyfriend perks." He chided teasingly. "She sucked my cock right after that."

I buried my fingers in her hair and pulled her down on my cock until she gagged again, holding her there as she stared at me, waiting to let her breathe. When I released her, she gasped and spit on my cock again. "I love you, Brody." She double fisted my cock and stroked me. "The three of you absolutely complete me."

"Mmh." I pulled her up to stand again and kissed her, "Good, because I would have hated to tie you down and fuck all three of you tonight for your unacceptable behavior."

"Maybe another time." She winked.

"Deal." I kissed her, "But let's get back to our task at hand."

"Oh, right." She pulled away and walked to Hannah, as I grabbed my toy of choice off the dresser on my way to Knox.

"Tell me something, Knox." I swirled the glass around right in front of him so he could hear the ice clank as I grabbed a cube out and slowly ran it down his neck to his chest. "Who's ass feels the best wrapped around your cock?"

He grunted as I slid the ice over one nipple and down over his abs. "Well," He licked his lips and hesitated the lower the ice went. "I've only had the pleasure of taking yours and Hannah's so far." I ran it up the length of his hard cock and twirled it around the head, making him gasp and fight his cuffs.

"That's not an answer."

"Hannah's." He snapped. "Every time."

"Bastard." I smirked, knowing even if it wasn't the truth, that he would have said it just to spite me.

I grabbed a new cube of ice and pushed it directly between his spread thighs until it wedged somewhere behind his balls and against his taint. I stood up as he squirmed, trying to dislodge it.

Hannah moaned, catching my attention, and I looked over to find Lex kneeling behind her, eating her ass and fingering her pussy.

"I think I'm going to fuck Lex's ass tonight, Knox." I tossed his way, and he froze, no longer caring about the frozen water against his taint. "She told me I could have it if I wanted it." We hadn't fucked Lex's there yet, though she was no novice to anal play. We just had done nothing past oral and playing with it during sex, but both Knox and I were feral for the chance to take another one of her firsts.

Hannah was even more, constantly playing and prepping Lex to take us for the first time, knowing we wouldn't be gentle when we finally got it.

"Fucking—" Knox cursed, fighting his bindings earnestly as Lex chuckled against Hannah's ass.

"I think I'm going to bend her over right in your lap when I slide into her for the first time." Fisting his cock, "I'll let her hold on, right here, to brace against my fat cock stretching her open."

"You're the fucking bastard." He cursed, working his jaw back and forth as I stroked him, using Lex's wetness still dripping down him as lubricant. "You got her pussy first."

"And you tasted her first." I tightened my hold on him. "You rubbed this cock all over her pussy and covered it with your come." I pushed my other hand between his legs to rub his cold taint, "Repeatedly. By the time I sank into her, you'd already had so many of her firsts."

"Fellas." Lex sang from her position on her knees behind Hannah, "No bickering, or I'll let Hannah fuck my ass while you watch."

"I like that idea!" Hannah cooed and then moaned when Lex spanked her ass with both hands. "Mmh, yes."

"You really want to be a little vixen tonight, don't you?" Lex stood up and spanked Hannah again.

I walked away from Knox, drawn in by the way Hannah's ass rippled under Lex's hand with each spank. Knox protested and called out, but I was transfixed.

"More." Hannah begged, "God, yes!"

Lex moved to the side, and I laid my palm down hard on Hannah's ass, making her scream and moan, pushing back and arching her back further to take more spanks.

"Fuck, that's so hot." Lex wrapped her hand around my cock and stroked me while I peppered Hannah's ass with spanks, reddening her flesh and drawing incoherent pleas for more from her lips. "Tell Daddy what you want," Lex instructed.

"Cock." Hannah gasped, "I want to come on a cock."

"Who's cock?" I demanded.

"Anyone's!" Hannah screamed and Lex smirked at me.

"Sounds like we need to break out my new toy."

Lex walked over to the closet to grab the dildo that she had spontaneously bought with Reyna at the sex shop as I dipped two fingers in Hannah's soaking pussy. "Are you ready to take our cocks, Darling?"

"Slut." Hannah purred, pushing back on my fingers as I curled them and stroked her G-spot. "I want to be Daddy's slut. I told you that."

I smiled to myself and then pulled her ties free, releasing her arms as she fell forward onto the mattress. "Then be my fucking slut and lay on your back so Lex can fuck you with her toy."

She pulled off her blindfold and scrambled across the bed as Lex pulled Knox's blindfold off on her way by, holding up her toy as she passed.

"Oh, fuck." Knox growled, "Let me out of these cuffs."

I grinned at him and flipped him off. "How many orgasms can I give our girls before you break that chair to be free?"

"Brody!" He bellowed, but it didn't matter because I'd let him free all in good time.

Lex showed Hannah the lime green dildo she bought and a bottle of lube as she crawled up the bed.

"Spread your legs, baby." Lex pushed Hannah's legs apart and held her hand out for me to join them. "Daddy's going to fuck your ass while I fuck our pussies with this."

A loud crack drew all of our attention across the room as Knox broke free of the chair, disseminating it in his wake as he stood up, shaking off the ropes from his ankles.

"Jesus Christ." I groaned, "That was a perfectly good chair."

"Then you should have thought twice before you teased me to this point." He glowered, pushing his way onto the bed and picking Hannah up and tossing her onto her stomach. "I'm done playing as the toy tonight." He took the toy from Lex and pushed her down onto her stomach so the girls were both on their knees with their asses facing each other. "It's my turn to call the shots."

Lex purred seductively, arching her back and leaning backward so her pussy rubbed against Hannah's, with their legs scissored. "I was wondering when you were going to take charge."

Hannah chuckled and rocked back and forth against Lex, pleasuring herself as she waited to get fucked. I knew our girl was desperate to be filled, and she didn't care by who or in what hole. She would come either way because she was our good little slut after all.

I snorted and spanked both girls' asses as Knox poured lube over each end of the dildo. "You love switching, just as much as he does, don't you, Lex?"

She lifted her head and blew me a kiss as Knox pushed the end of the toy into Hannah's pussy, making her moan.

"I do." Lex admitted, holding still as Knox worked the thick toy into her pussy before lubing up the center of it and pulling them both back onto it by their hair. He was in a crazed state, and I was fully prepared to let him dominate the girls. "Fuck, yes." She hissed, twerking her ass up and down to move on the toy as Hannah started rocking back and forth, testing it out.

"I'm fucking this ass." Knox poured lube over Lex's asshole and pushed his fingers into it without mercy. "It's mine."

"Mmh," Hannah moaned, "I going to come."

I gave her a spanking and took the lube from Knox, pouring some onto her ass as I pushed her face down into the bed, so her ass arched way up into the air. "Not before you take me deep."

"What?" Hannah cried in frustration, "I'm so close."

"Don't come." I commanded, squatting over her back as Knox did the same over Lex's. The toy was long enough that we could both just line up above them while they still rode the dildo. "Not until you're stuffed full."

"Fuck, Knox!" Lex screamed, and I looked over my shoulder as he pulled her head up off the bed by her hair and slammed hard into her ass. "Yes!"

"Fucking take that cock." Knox growled, pulling out and the backward momentum pushed me forward into Hannah's ass, making her moan and push back onto me.

"Oh, my god!" Hannah cried out, and I lost all restraint.

I fucked her like a two-cent whore, slamming deep into her as she threw it back onto my cock and the toy, pushing and pulling the toy in and out of Lex as Knox savagely fucked her.

There was so much screaming and begging I couldn't even focus on anything else but the pure ecstasy of Hannah's ass strangling my cock as the toy slid against it inside of her pussy.

Lex's moans of pleasure pushed me over the edge as Hannah came, convulsing underneath of me as Lex kept pushing that toy into her pussy as I filled her ass with my come.

I collapsed forward as Knox let out a roar of bliss as Lex came around his cock, begging for his come to fill her up.

When we all finally stopped moving, we were a tangled mess on the bed, all gasping and panting for air, as we came down off yet another incredible high.

Lex moved first, crawling over Knox and me to wedge her way between next to Hannah, kissing her deeply. I sat up enough to watch as Lex leisurely used her sensuality to draw Hannah's arousal back up after their orgasms until they were rocking against each other and playing with their bodies.

"Again?" I scoffed in disbelief.

Lex looked over her shoulder at me and her eyelids fluttered closed as Hannah took the opportunity to lower her lips to Lex's nipple, sucking on one while pinching the other.

"Yes. Again." Lex hummed, dragging her fingers through Hannah's long hair, holding her to her tit. "And again and again, until I can make Hannah understand just how fucking blessed I am that she fell for me and invited me into this relationship." Lex turned back around to Hannah, who looked up from her tits and licked her lips as Lex went on. "Because nothing in the world has ever felt as right as being here with the three of you. And I'm going to spend all of my free time showing my appreciation to our girl."

"That's an idea I can get behind." Knox chirped from the other end of the bed. "In about ten minutes." He threw his arm over his face as the girls giggled. "I came so hard I think my left nut completely sucked itself up into my body."

"And they wonder why I desired the sensitive and sensual touch of a woman." Hannah deadpanned, lowering her lips to Lex's nipple again to continue her fun.

"I wonder none." Laying back on the pillow to watch the girls, already feeling the buzz of need burning in my cock again. "I totally see the appeal."

Epilogue – Hannah

Six Months Later

"Ouch." I hissed as the needle ran across my skin. "How do you stand this?"

I looked over my shoulder to where Lex was bent over my ass, stabbing it a million times over with a needle and branding me with ink. Sure, I'd had to beg her to do it in the first place, but I was having doubts halfway through.

"I usually sleep through them." She responded, and I could hear the smirk in her voice. I wanted to kick her but figured the word *Daddy's sluf* tattooed instead of *Daddy's slut* wasn't worth the risk. "You're doing so good, baby."

"Oh shut up," I argued, feeling as sour as humanly possible for no reason other than I hated pain.

I should have known better than to get so mouthy, but the pain made me do weird things. Only half a second after the words escaped my mouth, she landed a forceful blow on my other ass cheek with such power that I was surprised it wasn't Brody's strength instead of hers.

"Ouch!" I hissed, covering my bare ass where she spanked me. "The latex gloves really add to the sting."

"You deserved it." She deadpanned. "Stop being a baby and think of how good Brody's going to fuck you tonight for wearing his brand."

With a whine in my voice, I declared, "I can't do this. I still have one more to go." I couldn't just wear a permanent mark for Brody when I loved three people equally, which meant three fresh tattoos.

She sighed and set her tools down and pulled off her gloves. I hated being so whiny, but I couldn't help it. My emotions were all over the place.

"Sit up." She commanded, walking over to her things in the corner and grabbing a satin bag out of it.

"What's that?" I got up to my knees, careful not to touch anything against the burning hell fire on my ass.

"Be quiet, and just do as you're told." She demanded, and I bit my lip to keep from refusing. She was my Domme at the moment, that much was clear by her tone, and I was to obey. But everything inside of me wanted to rebel. "Spread your legs and lean forward on your hands."

"Why—"

Smack.

"Oof." I groaned as my cheek lit up on fire again.

"I told you when you begged me to brand you, that you were going to follow my rules or I wasn't going to do it. So follow my rules. Leg spread, lean forward."

I was completely naked other than my red bralette because the place she was tattooing was directly where my underwear waistband rode right above my ass cheeks.

I stared at her over my shoulder as I slowly, and as seductively as possible, spread my knees as wide as the table would allow and then bent forward, popping my ass out for her as she instructed.

"That's my good girl." She praised, running her hand down my back to my cheek, currently not being stabbed to death, and shook it a little. "I like it when you follow my rules."

"You like it more when I'm a brat." I pouted and then held my breath in anticipation as she pulled something from the bag and put it on the tattoo bed beneath me.

"You like being a brat so I can tame the naughty out of you," She countered, leaning against my side so her lips were right by my face. "And if you would have told me the day I met you that you were such a naughty little slut, begging to be punished, I would have laughed in your face."

"You brought it out of me." I purred, leaning forward so my lips brushed hers. Moments ago I had been in agony, yet with a little attention and some commands, I was purring and dripping for her. It was fucking magic.

Her fingers dipped between my thighs and rolled over my clit and then to my pussy lips. She hummed as she ran my wetness over my hole before dipping one finger into me. "I love it when you're my sexy little brat." She purred back against my lips. "And I love watching Brody and Knox fuck you like a little slut when you get in these moods."

"Maybe we should have let them know what we were doing today." I licked her lips and moaned when she put another finger into me. It never ceased to amaze me how wet she could make me, and as she took my wetness and rubbed it all over my pussy again, I moaned in need.

"No need." She spanked my clit lightly, "I have everything you need for an attitude adjustment. Sit down."

I paused, and she cocked her brow at me, daring me to defy her. I slowly lowered my pussy down and felt something stiff brush against me far sooner than the table would have.

"All the way." She demanded when I froze and pushed me further until whatever she put below me slid inside of my pussy and nestled against my entire body, front to back.

I looked down between my legs and saw something neon pink and silicone lying flat against the table with something that looked like a hotdog in a bun lying atop. The piece inside of me felt like a thick plug, it wasn't deep but it was wide, filling me up.

"This toy is going to tickle your clit and your ass." She explained, and I rocked my hips to test it out. Ridges and grooves lined the entire length of it, rubbing across my clit and my ass with every move. "It's called a grinder vibe pad. I bought it just for you."

"I think I'm going to enjoy it." I smiled and licked my lips.

"You're going to need to." She mused before clicking something in her hand and turning it on. "Because I'm not turning it off until you're done with my ink."

"Oh, fuck!" I fought to contain a scream as the entire thing came to life. It danced across my clit and asshole like a million little tentacles sucking and tickling me. "Oh, God."

"That's what I thought." She hummed and then walked back around the table.

"How the fuck and I supposed to stay still?" I cried, rocking forward on the toy and grinding against it. The name suited it. "It'll look like you gave me the tattoo on a tilt-a-whirl."

Lex hummed, gloving back up and straddling the table behind me. "Figure it out, baby girl."

I gasped when she bent me forward more, which stretched out my vagina around the toy and pushed my clit down harder on the vibrating bumps. "Yessss!" I cracked my neck and stayed still as the buzz of her tattoo machine started back up.

When she pressed the tip to my back on the other side, I moaned but stayed still. The vibrations of the toy settled out the burn of the tattoo until my head felt foggy and the sensations all jumbled together.

"Such a good girl." She praised, dancing her needles of torture across my skin. Knox's tattoo was longer thanks to his fascination with calling me his sweetheart, but before I knew it, she was done. "How are you feeling?"

"Hmm." I hummed, with my head hanging between my arms and my eyes closed.

"Hannah?" She got off the table and walked around to face me. "Look at me."

I opened one blurry eye to peek at her, and she smiled. "You're in subspace."

"Hmm?" I hummed, tipping my head back and grinding on the toy again, now that she wasn't torturing me, allowing me to move against the delicious thing.

"The place where pain and pleasure mix." She leaned forward and kissed me, keeping her hands free of me since they were still gloved up. I pushed my tongue into her mouth and lifted myself up off the toy to feel the one inside of me move and lowered back onto it. "Tell me how you feel."

"I want to come." I moaned, leaning my head on my shoulder as my eyes closed again. "I want to come so bad."

I heard the snap of her glove come off, and then her fingers dipped between me and the toy as she moaned. "You're so fucking sexy."

"Yes." I cried out weakly as the fog dissipated now that she wasn't torturing me. "I need more."

"Be a good girl and ask nicely, and I'll give you whatever you want." She teased, and I watched her pull her phone out of her pocket and move behind me.

As she winked at me, she aimed the phone in my direction and pressed the capture button. It then dawned on me she was filming a video of me on the toy. My brand new ink was visible from that angle and my pussy clenched hard, knowing she was going to show Brody and Knox how naughty I'd been via text.

It made the brat in me purr like a kitten.

"Please, Angel," I moaned, using the pet name that Brody came up with for Lex because I knew it made her weak to be worshipped in a godly way. "Please make me come. I want to come all over our new toy."

"That's it, baby." She lowered the camera as I leaned forward, showing them my wet pussy impaled on the toy as it vibrated on my asshole. "You want to be Daddy's Slut and Knox's Sweetheart, huh?"

"Mmh." I moaned and then bit down on my knuckles when she clicked a different button on the toy and the thick part inside of me started thrusting. "Oh god." I cried, thankful that we were all alone in the shop after hours. "Oh, my god!"

She moved around front and lifted my bralette up, exposing my breasts and the ink that wrapped around my left side in honor of her. She played with my breasts, rubbing her thumb over one nipple before pinching it and zooming in on the words she branded there.

Alexi's Good Girl.

"She's ours for good now, boys." Lex purred into the phone before ending the video and pressing send.

She tossed her phone down on the bed and pushed her tongue into my mouth as the toy pushed me over the edge of my orgasm and I came. I screamed her name as she pushed me down harder onto the toy and forced two more orgasms from my body before turning it off.

"Let's get you home so I can watch both guys bend you over and fuck you to show you how much they appreciate your dedication to us."

I hummed and leaned into her. "Only if you ride this toy at the same time."

She gave me one more lingering sensual kiss "With pleasure baby girl, with fucking pleasure." Both our phones started vibrating off the hook and we giggled, knowing our guys were going nuts for more.

By the time my feet hit the floor, I was so completely relaxed that I didn't even feel the burn of the new ink on my skin.

It was like that every time any of them touched me. Nothing else mattered, because in the end, I felt nothing else but them.

Epilogue – Knox

One Year Later

"Are you nervous?" I asked, rubbing my hands together. "Because I'm fucking nervous."

"No." Brody deadpanned, but I knew better. He was so fucking nervous. He was just better at hiding it than I was. "If you don't stop hopping around over there, I'm going to punch you."

"Or you could just suck my cock." I groaned, "Maybe an orgasm will relax me."

He scoffed and glared at me. "I have fucked you four times today. FOUR! My cock has nothing left to give to you."

"I didn't ask for your cock, I asked for your mouth." I snapped, but before he could snap back, the sound of Lex's car pulling into the driveway got our attention. We both fell silent as we watched through the kitchen window as Hannah and Lex got out, holding hands and laughing together on their way up the stairs.

"Show time." He whispered as we backed up away from the windows.

The girls had spent the day with Reyna at the spa, having a pamper day, which had been the perfect ruse to use to get them out of the house so we could set up.

To propose.

It was fucking stressful enough to plan a romantic proposal for one woman, let alone two. What if one said yes, but the other said no? Then what?

I was a fucking wreck trying to make sure it all went perfectly, and we were out of time to change anything as Lex opened the door and walked in, laughing with Hannah and the freezing when she saw the two of us standing in our tux's, waiting for them.

"Hello." Lex purred as Hannah stood at her side with an amused grin on her face. "What's the occasion, boys?"

"Tonight," Brody stepped forward, pulling a rose off the counter for both of them, "We're taking a trip down memory lane."

"In the bathroom down the hall, you'll find your outfits hung up. Get dressed and meet us back here."

They both smiled excitedly but didn't move right away.

"Unless, of course, you don't want to go back to the Sinner's Soiree on our one-year anniversary." Brody teased, and both girls jumped into action, running down the hall to the spare bathroom to get ready. Exactly one year ago today, Lex and Hannah played for the very first time, unlocking something in all of us we never turned our backs on again. It was where it all started. And we wanted to go back and play again.

It took them a few minutes, but they were walking back out in the same dresses they wore the first night we all played together and photo flashbacks played through my mind of that night. We told the spa that morning when we called, to give them the full works with hair and makeup too. It just further played into our plan.

I was going to enjoy playing the game.

"Ready." Hannah purred, leaning into my side and kissing me. "Are you as excited as I am?"

"You have no idea." I held onto her and then leaned over to kiss Lex after she detangled herself from Brody's arms.

"Let's go." He said, motioning for the girls to go first, but when they predictably opened the kitchen door, Brody cleared his throat and stopped them. "Not quite." He walked around Lex and shut the door, locking it and turning off the outside lights. It showed we were in for the night and both girls looked at each other in confusion.

"What's going on here?" Lex squinted at me and pursed her lips.

"Follow me," I held my arm out for her and she cautiously pressed her body to mine as I led her to the living room.

Brody and I had spent all day long transforming it into the casino room from the Soiree. Red and orange fabric hung over the lamps, casting a sultry glow over the room, and we had put the furniture in the den to clear the floor for the one thing we needed for our plan to go off without a hitch.

A poker table.

Both girls gasped, looking around at the entire room, from the lighting to the fully stocked liquor bar on the console table against the wall and to the lone poker table under a warm spotlight.

"Oh my god," Hannah sighed wistfully, "You recreated it perfectly!"

Brody kissed her temple before leading her to the table. "Care to play a game?"

She squealed excitedly and took a seat as he pulled out one chair for her at the table. I nuzzled Lex's ear with my nose. "How about you, Angel Eyes?" My cock twitched when she sagged into me and moaned. "Want to place a bet?"

"It's worked out so well for me in the past." She looked up at me, "But I'm scared to chance fate."

"Live dangerously, Lex." I implored, walking her to the table and helping her into the chair. When she settled herself in the chair, I dropped my hands to her bare shoulders and grazed them down to where her strapless red dress started right over the swell of her tits.

I was hopelessly addicted to her tits, and when she moaned from my touch and leaned her head back against my stomach, I gently pushed my fingers down the front of her dress to tweak one nipple before I leaned down in her ear. "I never got to play with you the last time you wore this dress." She moaned again, and I bit her earlobe as Hannah watched on, licking her lips. "I'm going to change that this time."

"Fuck." She hissed as I stood up and walked around to the dealer's place as Brody sat in the chair between the girls.

I enjoyed the way they all looked up at me with heat in their eyes as I started the show. "One game. Winner takes all." I announced

"And what exactly does the winner get?" Lex leaned forward on her elbows.

"Winner's choice." Brody clarified. "To be announced or kept secret until it's time to pay up. The winner decides."

Hannah wiggled in her seat and slapped the table. "Deal me in Mister," She used an old-timer's thick Western accent. "I've got pussy to win!"

Lex tipped her head back and laughed as Brody and I chuckled at her joy. She was so fucking full of bliss and happiness, the entire light of our lives.

It was almost as if Brody felt that same overwhelming sense of love for her as I did because he looked at me with a heated stare, communicating silently, *"She has to say yes."*

"Well, now that we know what Hannah is playing for," I smirked, turning their attention back to the game at hand. "Lex? Brody? Care to share with the class what you're putting up for a bet?"

"I will." Lex brushed her hair over her shoulder and stared at Brody. "If I win, I get your ass." She licked her lips, and I knew Brody's cock was thickening in his pants from her declaration. She turned to me and pointed my way, "And then yours."

"I'm just the dealer tonight, Lady." I lowered my voice. "That's a very bold claim to make to a total stranger."

She chuckled and leaned back in her chair, "Like it or not, when I win, you'll be riding my strap-on and screaming my name. Those are my rules."

"Accepted." Brody intervened, answering for both of us. I didn't sweat it because it was far from a losing price to pay either way it played out.

Even if I hadn't already staked the deck to ensure that Brody won.

"And your bet?" Hannah purred, leaning into Brody's arm, "What do you get if you win?"

He turned his head and kissed her lips. "I'll tell you when I win."

"Mmh," She hummed, leaning back into her chair. "I kind of hope you do."

"Okay, let's play." I reached for the deck.

"Wait." Lex laid her hand on the table, and my pulse sped up. "Aren't you going to ask the pretty ladies to cut the deck?"

I swallowed, fighting the urge to look at Brody for guidance. Cutting the deck would mess up the cards with no guarantee that he would win.

And we'd planned this for way too fucking long to mess it up now. "What's the matter, boys?" Hannah chimed in, reading me like a book. "Worried you might lose now?"

"Cut them in." Brody leaned back in his chair with one arm laid on the table, like he didn't worry about anything in the world. "It still won't help your chances."

Lex pursed her lips and Hannah rolled her eyes as I held the deck forward. Lex cut first, and then Hannah. Leaving me with absolutely no idea what cards were where in the deck anymore.

I sighed and cracked my neck, trying to roll with it. "Let's play."

I dealt the first round and watched on pins and needles as they each looked, and then another round.

I wanted to know what was in Brody's hand, but kept doing my job. I hated feeling so useless.

They all three exchanged cards as I kept dealing. I tried watching their faces each time they peeked at a new card, but I couldn't read a single thing.

I was sweating bullets, stressing the whole time until it was time to reveal their cards.

Hannah sighed first, tossing her cards down, face up. "I suppose no pussy for me tonight." She pouted for full dramatic effect.

Lex reached across the table and patted her hand, "You can have my pussy whenever you want it, baby."

Hannah smirked, dropping her act, and then giggled. "If you insist." She tapped her fingers against her lips as she speculated. "I could lick your pussy while you fuck their asses."

"Hmm." Now it was Lex's turn to pull a full dramatic flare as she licked her lips and rocked in her chair like the idea was overwhelming here. "Now there's an idea worth collecting on."

"Win the game first," Brody interjected.

Lex laid her cards down in a flashy fashion, one at a time as they each clinked against the felt table and we all leaned forward to see them.

Four of a kind.

Fuck. It was the same hand she won with the night of the original Sinner's Soiree. The one when she won Hannah.

I clenched my teeth and watched Brody glance back at his cards. It felt like my heart was going to beat right out of my chest as I watched him, waiting for any clue of what he had.

He laid them down in a pile and slowly fanned them out, revealing his hand.

"Straight Flush." He grinned at Lex, who deflated in her chair momentarily. Hannah giggled at the whole thing, already having lost what she wanted, and I let out a sigh of relief. "Now, time to pay up."

Brody stood up from the table and I walked around, holding my hand out for Lex as he helped Hannah to her feet.

"So, Daddy." Hannah purred, "What exactly do you win?"

"Let's go somewhere a little more *private*, and I'll tell you." The same way we had that first night, we climbed the stairs to the bedroom, even though it was ours and not a stranger's this time.

We had decorated it to match the feel of the room that night, with low warm lighting and chairs spread out around the bed to watch.

Hannah bounced on the balls of her feet gently as she walked in ahead of us with Brody, and I smiled at her happiness.

Lex, on the other hand, was a little more reserved. "Sad you lost?" I asked her.

"Incredibly." She sighed, looking up at me with her deep, soulful eyes. "I desperately wanted to fuck you."

I kissed her, unable to hold back any longer from sinking into her body with my tongue when I wanted nothing else than to feel it with my cock. "Tell you what, play Brody's game like a good little girl, and you can have that."

Her eyes widened excitedly, "You'll let me?"

"Fuck, baby doll." I groaned, pushing my hips forward so she could feel my erection against her stomach. "You could have asked me for that on a random Tuesday morning in the kitchen with bedhead and sleep goobers in your eyes, and I would have bent right over and presented for you."

"Fuck." She moaned, running her hands down the front of my body to my cock, stroking me through my suit pants.

"Do you mind?" Brody cleared his throat, bringing me back to reality.

"Sorry, boss." I joked, pulling back from Lex's tempting body and biting Hannah's neck on my way past her to stand next to Brody at the foot of the bed.

"So." Hannah crossed her arms over her chest, watching us. "Spill the beans."

Lex walked over and stood at her side, matching her same unimpressed but also interested vibe as Brody dragged it on longer. "What do you want?"

"You." Brody stated plainly, turning his attention from Lex to Hannah, "Both of you."

"For the rest of our lives," I added. It felt like everyone in the room stopped breathing as Hannah's hands fell to her sides and Lex's lips parted.

"Will you marry us?" Brody asked as his voice cracked. "And vow to spend the rest of your lives with us just like this."

"Happy, dirty, and safe?" I finished.

Hannah had tears running down her face as she smiled brightly, ready to run into our arms, but paused when she saw Lex was unmoving next to her.

"Angel?" She whispered, sliding her hand through Lex's. We didn't have to say anything, for her to understand that this was an all-or-nothing situation. It didn't feel right to move forward if one of us wasn't on board.

Truth be told, I'd have waited an eternity for both of them if they asked it of us.

Lex swallowed and looked at Hannah before looking back at us, and I could feel her fear pulsing out of her deep brown eyes as she licked her lips.

"Say something, please," Brody begged softly, and I took his hand, feeling his heart racing through the pulse point in his wrist.

"Are you sure?" Lex whispered, blinking as tears dripped over her dark lashes. "About me?"

"Oh, baby." Hannah cried.

"No," Lex shook her head, "It makes sense to marry Hannah. I support that one million percent for both of you." She looked at Hannah and cupped her cheek. "You deserve that, Han."

"Do you not want us?" I asked, fighting the pain that bloomed in my chest, "We wouldn't have asked you if we didn't mean it, Lex."

"I want you." She closed her eyes and more tears fell. "I want to marry you all more than anything else in the whole fucking world. I just don't feel worthy."

Brody and I descended on them, pulling Lex and Hannah into our arms and holding them both tight as one big unit.

"I love you." Whispered into Lex's ear and then the same into Hannah's.

"We're not complete without both of you." Brody added, "We're a unit, together with all four of us." He kissed them and then I did. "Once upon a time, Lex, I told you that Hannah was the literal fucking sun in our lives, and without her, we didn't exist." Hannah sniffled and Lex hung onto his every word. "But you're our fucking moon, Angel. Without you, we can't exist either, we need both, surrounding us and keeping us upright. We need the light and the dark, we can't have one without the other."

Lex sobbed and Hannah kissed her, absorbing her pain and hesitations to replace them with assurances and love.

"Which leads us here." I pulled a small ring box from my pocket and Brody did the same. Mine had Hannah's ring, opening it up to show her. I loved the sweet, misty eyes she gave me as I pulled the ring out and slid it onto her finger. She eagerly held her hand out and gazed at it, twinkling in the light while Lex stared at hers.

"Oh my god, you guys." Hannah moaned, staring at her ring. Neither of the rings was traditional in the single-stone sense. They both matched design-wise but were different in coloring. Hannah's was four intertwining bands of white diamonds laid in rose gold bands. Whereas Lex's was four twisting bands of black diamonds in white gold. The girls were different and so perfectly alike it made no sense, but it just fit.

We all fit together.

"I've never been so happy in my entire life." Lex sighed, looking at the ring on her finger and spinning it around.

"Same." Hannah chirped in, "It feels like nothing could ever top this."

Brody chuckled devilishly, wrapping his arms around Hannah's waist and nuzzling her ear as she melted into his touch. "So you don't want to fuck my ass while Lex fucks Knox?"

"Ooh!" Hannah cried. "I *so* want to do that! I want to do that real fucking bad!"

Epilogue – Lex

Two Years Later

"Fuck, yes." I moaned, tipping my head back and grabbing the shower bar as Hannah's tongue pushed into my pussy and twirled. "I'm going to come!" Panting and digging my nails into her hair, I pulled her tighter against my pussy to ride her face as my orgasm broke free.

"That's my good fucking girl." Hannah moaned, standing up and licking her lips as she kissed her way back up my body. "I could taste you like that every single morning and still not get enough."

The truth was, she had been. Every day for two weeks, she had woken me up every hour of the night, desperate for sex. I was used to a high sex demand from my spouses, given that two of them were strong, dominant, testosterone-filled men who never seemed to get enough, but this was a lot for Hannah.

She was insatiable.

I had fucked her with a strap-on for hours last night before bed, trying to wear her down and relieve the ache inside of her so that she could get some sleep. But a few hours after finally going to bed, she woke me up, straddling me and rubbing her pussy against mine.

I wasn't complaining, but with Knox and Brody across the country on the race circuit, I was burning out. And they had an entire week left before they were coming home.

Their friend from Ohio asked them to go on a three-week race circuit across the states to promote their hugely successful hot rod garage. They had a few show cars that they'd been building for years that were perfect for the circuit and they so deserved to show them off.

When they first told Hannah and me, I could tell Brody wasn't going to go. They never left us at the same time, and usually if one had to go away for business, it was always Knox, because Brody preferred to stay home.

But they deserved it so much that Hannah and I instantly pushed them both to go. It took some persuading, a lot of it actually. And mostly in the form of sexual domination and sweet submissive begging to get them both to agree to it in the end.

I mean a lot.

I had to cancel three different appointments that week because I couldn't sit down from how hard they both fucked us on repeat right before they left. It was like they were trying to get three weeks' worth of sex in order to hold them over.

It blew my mind that even after being married for over a year and together over two, they still lusted after me and Hannah like we were shiny new toys to play with.

And I loved it.

But I was ready for them to come home, simply to satisfy Hannah's obnoxious, spontaneous sex drive so I could sleep.

God, I just wanted to sleep for four days straight in a dark cave with no disturbances to recover from the last few weeks.

"I need more." She slid her fingers through my pussy lips and rocked her hand.

"I can't." I shook my head. "God, Han. I'm so tired. I need to take a break!"

She pulled back and pouted slightly, but she knew I was right. We'd been at it all morning again already. "I'm sorry."

"Don't be." I sighed, kissing her and soothing the burn of my tone with my lips before taking a deep breath against her face. "I just need to relax."

"You're right. Let's go back to bed and we can take a nap. We don't have to go to the thing."

I groaned because she couldn't be more wrong. "It's Reyna's baby shower!" I felt like crying because of how badly I didn't want to go, but had to since our best friend deserved it from us. "We have to go."

"Ugh." She pouted, but I walked around her. "I'll be right out."

"If I hear you moaning from using the handheld showerhead, I'm cutting the water off," I warned firmly.

"Yes, Daddy." She purred, replacing Brody's nickname since I was being her boss.

I rolled my eyes and wrapped my towel around my body as I went to the vanity to get ready. I rested my hands on the cold stone and hung my head, trying to muster the strength to blow dry my hair.

I groaned, leaning down to grab my dryer from under the sink when something else caught my eye, making me pause.

"Are you wearing a dress to this thing?" Hannah called from the shower as she turned the water off. "I feel like a baby shower is a dress thing."

"Han?" I stammered, pulling a box from under the sink and turning to face her.

"What?" She asked, wrapping her towel around her body and seeing the box. "Oh, are we out? We'll just grab more on our way home." She brushed it off, but I was frozen stiff.

"Han." I tried again, suddenly unable to form words as I did the math and tracked dates in my head. "Han."

"What?" She shook her head, staring at the almost empty box of tampons in my hand. "What's the big deal?"

"We're *late*," I whispered. "Like a week and a half late."

Of course, our periods synced up within the first six months of living together, which made things interesting. So when I saw the box and realized we should have bought more before that moment, the math added up that we were both late.

"Holy fuck." She whispered, frozen in place just like I was. "Do you think—?"

"That we're pregnant?" I guessed, "At the same time? Without trying?"

"Yeah," She swallowed, "I mean it would make sense."

"How?" I cried in sheer panic.

"Well, for the last week, you've been sleeping like the dead." She shrugged. "Isn't that a pregnancy symptom?"

I nodded slowly, "So is ravenous sex drive."

"Jesus." She leaned on the counter beside me and we both stared off into the distance, processing. "I guess we need to pee on some sticks." She bent over and grabbed the *in case of emergency* pregnancy tests from under the sink. There had been times over the years that one of us had worried about certain symptoms, so we kept a box lying around just in case.

"How are you so calm?" I whispered, feeling like I was going to crawl out of my skin at any moment.

"I don't know." She shrugged, going into the toilet room and peeing on the stick. "I guess I'm just feeding off you and your vibe. Which is *not* calm at all. One of us should be level-headed about this."

She was right, normally I would be the one to be sensible and calm in a moment of stress. I took a deep breath and took my turn with the toilet, sticking my test back into the wrapper and setting it down next to her identical one when I was done.

"Tell me this is going to be okay, either way, it plays out," I begged, staring at her and she softened, holding me in her arms and soothing me.

"You're loved, Lex." She stated. "You're safe." She combed her fingers through my wet hair. "You're supported and cared for. This is perfectly okay."

We had talked about having kids someday, in the future, over the last few years. But it was always an arbitrary thought because there were so many logistics to figure out before we went down that road.

Fuck, getting a marriage certificate was hard enough. Technically, I was married to Brody, and Hannah was married to Knox, though the ceremony we had at home was with all four of us together, vowing to each other equally. The one thing we did fight about the most back then was what we were going to do about last names.

We ended up keeping our own, because it was such a point of contention that we didn't want to argue about something that was supposed to be good.

"I'm scared." I admitted, "I don't know how to be a mom."

"Me either." She admitted, "Mine died when I was ten, remember."

"I'm sorry." I sighed, laying my forehead on her shoulder as shame burned in my gut. "I'm just freaked out."

"Do you want kids?" She asked, though we'd already discussed it before.

"Yes." One big resounding yes, that was never in question. "I just thought it would be a conscious decision to make when the time came."

She giggled and pulled me back to look in my eyes. "Well, then I guess we should have made the guys wrap up, pull out, or take our pills on a more regular basis if we didn't want any chance of a surprise."

"Two surprises." I widened my eyes in disbelief. "What if we're both pregnant?"

"Then we'd better buy double the ice cream from now on." She giggled, "You know how possessive you get over ice cream." I laughed lightly and relaxed in her arms. "I want it to be positive."

I felt surprised by her statement, but I wasn't entirely against it either. "For both of us?"

"One hundred percent." She smiled. "I love you, Angel Eyes. I can't imagine a better way to go through this than with you at my side."

"Even if I'm not pregnant, I'll still be at your side. I love you so much, baby."

She took a deep breath, and I forced myself to push the fear down to let the tiny bit of excitement I felt underneath it, free to burn brighter.

"Let's look together." She picked up her test, and I picked up mine. I would have hesitated, but with the more time that passed, the more cautiously excited I got.

I pulled the wrapper off and read the words written out digitally on the screen.

Pregnant.

Hannah squealed excitedly next to me and showed me her test as she looked at mine. She was pregnant, too.

"Holy fuck."

"Two babies!" She screamed, dropping the test and hugging me. "We're going to be moms! Together!"

"Holy fuck." I repeated, but at least that time I managed to smile afterward.

She giggled and hugged me tighter. "I know it's a lot, but we'll figure it out. I promise. Love conquers just about everything else in the world and we have a lot of love in this house."

"Yes, we do." I gentled and relaxed a little. "We sure fucking do."

It had been a wild week since finding out both Hannah and I were pregnant, to say the least. We each made appointments with an OB, started taking vitamins full of things neither of us could pronounce, and spent a lot of time staring off into the distance.

We both tried to figure out what the future was going to look like for our family as a whole, but also for our relationships individually.

I fucking loved Hannah, and having such a monumental event happening at the same time for both of us made me fall even deeper in love with her. It rocked me to my very core every time I imagined her holding her little baby in her arms, who had Brody's dark eyes or Knox's sandy blonde hair. I ached to embrace her nurturing instincts and let them ease some of the worry in my heart. To be honest, I was just as excited to hold my baby in my arms, even though I was also afraid.

I had great parents growing up; they loved each other intensely and never shied away from showing that love around me and my siblings. But it just didn't feel like I was embracing the prospect of motherhood as quickly or as naturally as Hannah was.

And then there was the anxiety of wondering what the guys would say when they found out. Hannah and I agreed immediately that we didn't want to tell them over the phone. And short of packing up and flying to a random drag strip in the middle of the country somewhere to tell them face to face, we were stuck keeping it a secret for a few days.

But the night that Brody and Knox were due home was upon us, and the butterflies in my stomach were making me nauseous. I didn't think it was just the morning sickness that started the other day, either.

There was the fear of rejection in my heart, and I couldn't relax until we shared the news with them. My entire adult life, I had an exit strategy in place in case someone fucked me up. The only time it had failed me was with Sydney and I wasn't trying to compare the situations, but old scars were hard to heal.

"Are you okay?" Hannah asked, sliding her hands around my hips as I stood motionless at the kitchen sink, staring out the window toward the driveway.

"Yeah." I smiled, pulling her arms around my stomach as she rested her chin on my shoulder. "You?"

"I feel like I'm going to poop my pants." She deadpanned, "But that could have been the three billion tacos I ate for lunch."

I smirked and turned, leaning back against the sink as we held each other. "That most definitely could be it."

"I love you." She stated plainly. She'd been doing it repeatedly lately like she could feel the fears in my heart, even though I never spoke of them. Scars were a weird kind of thing to live with, and a weirder thing to love someone with them.

"I love you too," I whispered, kissing her lips lightly and leaning my forehead against hers. We stayed like that for a long time, breathing each other in and centering ourselves.

Noise from the front of the house drew our attention, and we both looked out the window where Knox and Brody were getting out of Brody's truck and stretching out their sore muscles before jogging up the steps.

"Are you nervous?" Hannah whispered, pulling me through the house to the living room, where she had a whole thing planned.

"No," I replied firmly, trying to force myself to believe it. "Because I have you. And you have me."

She beamed over at me with all of her golden perfection and slid her hand in mine as the kitchen door opened, banging against the wall in Knox's haste to get inside.

"Sweethearts!" He bellowed, "We're home!"

"In here." Hannah sang back, and they both rounded the corner, pausing when they saw us standing there together, hand in hand.

"Ooh," Knox grinned, leaning into Brody's shoulder. "Do you think whatever they have planned is kinky?"

Brody scoffed and took a step forward, but I held my hand out first, making him stop.

"Not so fast," I ordered, and they both raised eyebrows at me in surprise. "Hannah has something she wants to tell you first."

She was literally bouncing from foot to foot, and I knew she was going to burst at the seams if she didn't get it out. She raised her hands into the air and screamed, "We're pregnant!" Which wasn't at all what we rehearsed and I tipped my head back, laughing at the chaos those words were going to cause.

Both the guys' jaws dropped in surprise as they looked back and forth like they couldn't comprehend her words, so she rubbed her hand over her stomach, visually showing them.

Knox moved first, lunging for her, pulling her into his arms, and swinging her around in the middle of the room, "You're pregnant?" He cheered, laughing and kissing her all over.

And I was so happy for her. Knox put her feet on the ground and Brody moved in, kissing her deeply and smiling his rare unreserved happiness at her as she beamed up at him. They celebrated together, and I watched from the outside of it all, smiling ear to ear as happy tears pooled in my eyes.

Brody pulled back from them and crossed over to me. I could see the hesitation in his eyes as he tried to read me. "I missed you." He sighed, kissing me like he was a dying man getting his last taste of life, but it further confirmed that Hannah's words were as confusing as I knew they'd be for them.

"I missed you too," I replied, taking peace in the fact that Hannah was being celebrated so deservingly, and just let it be for a minute.

Knox finally pulled away from Hannah and rushed me, kissing me and clinging to me as I held him. "Sorry," He admitted sheepishly, "I got caught up."

"You're perfectly fine," I smiled, kissing him again and breathing in his familiar scent. "It's big news."

"The biggest." He smiled so brightly that I was afraid his cheeks were going to cramp up. "Are you okay?" He asked, and Brody leaned in, eager for my reply to the question. "It's a lot, right?"

I nodded and took both of their hands as Hannah giggled guiltily. "I see what I did wrong now."

Both guys turned to her, and she rolled her lips as she rocked on her feet sheepishly.

"What do you mean?" Brody asked.

"Well, you see what happened was," Hannah moved between the guys and wrapped her arms around my waist, leaning into me. "When I said *we're pregnant*, I meant we're," She rubbed her hand over my stomach and hers at the same time. "*both* pregnant!"

The guys froze stiff as though their brains were buffering the information together, and then they launched.

"Fuck yes!" Knox cursed, picking me up and wrapping my legs around his waist, jumping around in excitement. "Are you fucking kidding me!"

I gasped and scrambled back to the ground as the nausea churned.

"Don't!" Hannah cried, pulling Knox off me as I fought for control. "She has morning sickness!"

"Fuck." Knox froze with his hands on my arms. "Are you okay?" He gasped, "I'm so sorry, I don't know anything about pregnancy, at all."

I smiled and patted his cheek lovingly. "You're fine, just don't twirl me and we should be safe."

Brody pushed him aside and wrapped me up in a massive hug, covering my entire body with his as he breathed me in. "I can't believe this." He whispered in awe. "Two babies."

"Unless they're twins, Knox's dad is a twin." Hannah teased, "Then it could be four or six, or—" She went on and Knox's eyes got bigger and bigger with each times table covered.

"Are you happy?" I asked Brody, aware that out of the two guys, he would be the most reserved about it, just like I was.

"Incredibly." He assured me. "You?"

"Terrified," I admitted with a shy smile.

He kissed my forehead and pulled me to his side as Hannah and Knox started rambling about baby stuff in jubilation. "Me too." He conceded as we watched them.

"Thank god they have enough optimism and confidence in this whole thing to make up for our worrying." I joked.

"We're a perfect match, all of us." He gently placed his hand on my nonexistent baby bump. "And these babies are going to be the perfect addition to this family."

I stared up at him with teary eyes and nodded as the emotions of it all clogged my throat.

To think, a few years ago, broken down on the side of the road, I met a wonderful man but flipped him off for telling me he didn't like my boots. And now he was staring down at me and confessing everything I needed to hear to feel secure during the scariest moment of my life.

It wasn't love at first sight for Brody and me, but it was an everlasting kind now, thanks to Hannah and Knox's blinding support and understanding.

Without them, I never would have felt as loved as I was at that exact moment.

Soon to be multiplied by two.

The End.

Bonus Scene

Whoa, that was a wild ride. Are your legs weak? Did you drink enough water? Are your batteries charged? Is your partner on standby? Because I promised more, and I'm ready to deliver.

So without any more chatter from me, let's dive back into the spicy world of The Kent household and go back to that infamous and highly demanded playroom scene.

You remember the one, right? Where Reyna spent all day with Lex's help transforming their spare bedroom into a kinky red room of big bad wolf play toys. Right, how could we forget? We ended right as Reyna asked Dallin, Parker, and Trey one very important question.

From Twisted Ink - *"Predictable, huh?" She walked over to a set of drawers and pulled something out, hiding it behind her back as she walked back to us. "Well, did any of you expect me to buy this?" She pulled a thick strap-on dildo in a bright pink harness out from behind her as she cocked her head to the side. "Because I'm ready to make the three of you start begging me to fuck you like you make me do all the time." She winked. "So who's going to be the good boy that gets to use his toy on me first after I make you come with this cock in your ass?"*

Let's Go!

Parker's POV

"Me!" Trey erupted, throwing his hand into the air like a schoolboy. "Me, me, me!"

Reyna giggled, and I rolled my eyes.

"There's only one way to figure it out." I pushed Trey to the side from where he was crowding Reyna out.

"And how's that, handsome?" She smirked at me seductively.

"Rock, papers, scissors." I deadpanned, "Duh."

She tipped her head back, laughed, and then nodded. "I think that sounds perfect." She started working the strap-on harness up her legs. "You boys figure out who is taking this cock and I'll get ready to give it to you."

Dallin groaned, and Trey rocked on his heels, holding his fist out instantly. We all wanted to take her toy, as it was her first time showing interest in using one. But more importantly, we wanted a chance to use our selected toys on her first.

"Rock," I started and Dallin and Trey played along, "Paper," I eyed them both, "Scissors."

I threw Rock.

Dallin threw scissors.

And Trey threw scissors.

"I win!" I cheered, fist-pumping the air and turning to our wife. "That rigging is going to keep you defenseless for me, Baby Girl." She licked her lips and swallowed, "Are you ready?"

"Don't skip out on the best part," She took a bottle of lube out of one drawer, "Naked and on the bench." She nodded to a leather contraption against the wall. When Trey pulled it out into the middle of the room, I groaned when I saw it in its entirety. "Bound and helpless for me. "

"Reyna," I growled, throbbing as I eyed the wrist and ankle cuffs. "You conveniently left the bondage out of the initial proposal."

"What's the matter, baby?" She stroked her hand up and down the long pink dildo, rubbing the lube into it. "Afraid to be at my mercy?"

I silently yanked my belt open and pulled my shirt off over the back of my head. As predicted, her eyes fell to my abs, and she stared as I undid my jeans, pushing them down and kicking them aside. I was naked and rock solid for her in ten seconds flat.

"Do I look scared to you?" I challenged and walked to the bench, stopping right in front of her so I towered over her. "Tie me down and fuck me, Baby Girl. Make me beg for it. Make me scream your name. Do your worst." I kissed her hard, pushing my tongue into her mouth and she instantly moaned, "But just know that when you're done, I'll have my revenge."

I knelt on the knee pads that spread my knees shoulder width apart and then bent over the padded chest part, dropping my hands into the cuffs down by my knees. I was bent over at the waist, with my cock swinging freely between my thighs and my back was flat and parallel to the floor.

I was vulnerable, and my blood pressure rose as Trey quickly started locking the straps around my ankles as Dallin did my wrists.

He paused right in front of me and stared down at me before kneeling so we were at eye level. "I'm glad it's you taking her toy first." He smirked, "It'll warm you up to take our cocks when she's done."

"Fucker." I fought against the bindings even as my cock throbbed between my thighs.

"It's been a few years since we've run a train on you." Trey mused, running his hands over my ass cheeks and spreading them.

"Nobody's doing anything without my say so," Reyna interrupted, walking around to the front and squatting down with her legs spread wide so I could see her bare pussy under the straps of her dildo. "I'm going to make you feel so good." She purred, leaning in and kissing me deeply as she wrapped her hand around my throat and tightened it. "I can't wait to make you lose your mind."

"I already am," I growled, flexing my hips the best I could in my bent over fashion, and cursed when a hand wrapped around my cock, stroking it powerfully. "Fuck."

"Good boy." Trey leaned over my back and bit my shoulder. "You're already leaking for her." He rubbed the pre-cum leaking from my cock up the shaft and then rolled my balls.

"Stop playing with my toy." Reyna snarled, walking behind me and stepping between my feet. "Tell me you're ready, Parker."

"I'm ready." I hissed through clenched teeth, reminding myself that I volunteered for the position I was in.

"Beg me." Reyna poured lube on my ass and used her fingers to rub it in. "Beg me to slide in deep, Parker."

Those were words I'd force out of her if we switched positions. Words I would force out of her lips when we switched. "Please, Rey." I moaned when she pushed her fingers in, swirling them around the loosen me up. "God, please fuck me."

"Good boy." I could hear the joy in her voice as she pushed the tip of the pink dildo against my ass and started thrusting forward. "Mmh," She moaned like she could feel pleasure through it. "That's it, baby." She paused, "Push back onto it."

I rocked back as far as my wrist cuffs would let and she slammed forward, forcing the entire thing deep. I roared as it burned and send electric bolts of pleasure to my cock. "Yes!"

Dallin started stripping his clothes off as Reyna worked out a rhythm she liked and fucked me. Trey lingered against the wall, opening drawers and exploring the room as I took Reyna's fake cock like a good little boy.

I would do literally anything she wanted me to. And she fucking knew it.

"You take her so perfectly," Dallin kneeled in front of me again and kissed me, pushing his tongue into my mouth and silencing my groans of pleasure and pain as she fucked me roughly. "She's giving it to you so hard."

"She'll be taking it this hard too," I grunted.

"Permission to play with your toy, Madame?" Trey asked from behind me and I tried looking over my shoulder, but Dallin wrapped his hand around my throat and held me in place as Reyna giggled seductively and slammed in deep.

"Permission granted." She purred and then slowed her thrusts as I fought against Dallin's hold. "Oh, fuck." She hummed when Trey reached between my legs and massaged my balls.

"Trey." I groaned, tightening my hands into fists and curled my toes, fighting off my body's urge to come.

"Shh," He whispered, and then something tight wrapped around my balls at the very base of my cock.

"Fuck!" I roared, trying to shake him off as the tightness intensified as he slid it down over the thicker part of my balls. "Trey!"

"Shh," He repeated and then the band started vibrating, causing curses, sounds, and drool to fall from my lips as Reyna thrust faster again. "God, you're so hot taking her toy and wearing mine."

"I feel slightly left out." Dallin cocked his head to the side as he stared directly into my eyes, "They're both playing with the toy, don't you think I should get to play too?"

I clenched my teeth as I imagined all the ways Big D was going to play with me, bound up and helpless.

He smiled sinisterly, and I recognized the dark in his eyes as he stood up tall, and stroking his fat cock right in front of my face.

"Stick your tongue out for me." He demanded, and I swallowed, already knowing I would, but wanting to be a bit of a brat instead.

He chuckled, and I clenched down tight on Reyna's toy cock as he wrapped his hand around my throat, instantly cutting off my airway until I unclenched my teeth and stuck my tongue out like a good fucking boy, desperate for air.

"That's it," He growled, smacking his cock against my tongue and then rubbing it all over my cheeks and lips. "Tell me something, Park," He pushed his cock head into my mouth, releasing his hold on my neck, making me gasp for air as he pushed in deep, cutting off my airway again. "Who's cock do you like taking better?"

"Bastard." Trey chuckled from where he still kneeled behind me at Rey's side. "Tell him mine and I'll give it to you when Rey's done."

She laughed, "Already rushing me?"

"You're dripping with arousal, Kitten." He purred, "We all know you're going to end up spreading those pretty thighs and begging to take cock instead of give it before too long."

"Mmh," She hummed, dragging her nails down my back from my neck to my ass cheeks. "Fucking you turns me on, Park. How does it feel to know you make me wet without even touching me?"

I couldn't reply, because of Dallin's giant cock pushing in and out of my mouth, but I shook my hips slightly in reply and she moaned, before spanking my ass.

Usually, we reserved spankings for her lush ass, not ours.

But I didn't hate it.

Dallin pulled out of my mouth and forced my head back to look up at him as Rey pulled all the way out until my ass gaped for her pretty pink cock. "Well, who's the winner of your desires?" He asked, "Who's cock is your favorite?"

"Rey's." I gasped and roared when she slammed back in without warning. "Fuck, yes!"

The vibrating band around my balls got stronger and Trey's fingers massaged them like he couldn't help but touch me while the others played too.

"That's it." Reyna purred, "You're so close, aren't you?"

"Yes!" I was fighting my orgasm so hard, desperately wanting to hold on to my sanity for a moment longer because I knew if I fell over the edge of bliss, I'd go insane trying to repay the favor on them.

"I want you to come for me, baby." Reyna leaned over my back. "I want you to come so hard and then I want you to tie me up and fuck me like your helpless little toy." She bit my shoulder and dragged her nails up and down my back. "You want that, don't you, baby?"

"Fuck." I grunted.

"You want to fuck me like your little rag doll, while they watch you claim your prize, don't you?" She fucked me slow, with deep and electrifying thrusts. "You want me to come just for you, while they sit and watch. Tell me."

"Yes." I roared, tipping my head up to the sky as my body broke, coming on her cock and screaming when Trey wrapped his hand around my cock and stroked me through my orgasm. "Trey!" I cried from the way he pushed me over the edge with his merciless tight grip.

"You're such a good boy," Dallin smirked down at me with his still rock-hard cock bobbing in front of my lips as I gasped for breath and sanity.

"Undo me," I demanded as Reyna slid free of my body. "Now!"

"Okay," She cautioned, as she hurriedly undid my ankles. Dallin undid my wrists with a cautious look in his eyes as I stayed frozen until I was free of all four cuffs.

And then I struck.

Reyna's POV

For a big guy, Parker could move with lightning speed.

Which was something I forgot about as I undid his cuffs, worried I'd pushed him too far.

I did push him too far. But not the way I had feared when he screamed to be free.

No, I pushed the predator in him too far by taking control of him and driving him toward insanity with sexual frustration.

He turned and grabbed me by the neck, pushing me against the wall with one swift move, taking my breath away as I gripped his wrist for leverage.

"Now who's in control?" He pressed his face against the side of mine and licked it as he pulled the harness of the strap-on free, and chucked it across the room. "You're mine now."

I hummed and my pussy throbbed at the obvious hunger in his eyes. "There he is." I purred, releasing his wrist and fisting his cock that was still hard against my stomach, "There's my big bad wolf."

That was the very reason I built the playroom, to begin with. I wanted their true animals to be free at home since we couldn't play in the woods as often as we liked.

"Cuffs!" He demanded over his shoulder and I held his stare as Trey eagerly handed him a pair of thick cushioned leather cuffs from the drawers. I didn't even know half of what was inside, thanks to Lex's far more extensive knowledge of the kink world. She had ordered most of it and even arranged it by use earlier before she left.

Parker let go of my neck and cuffed my wrists together in front of me before dragging me across the room to the bed. He raised my wrists up and hooked them to a ring in the center of the top structure. It was so far up I had to stand up on my toes to reach that far.

"Stay." He ordered like I was his pet and I winked at him.

"Maybe."

"Brat." He added before grabbing the rope rigging he had picked out for his toy pick. "We'll see if you have any brattiness left in you when I'm done."

"Maybe you should try spanking it out of me." I challenged, winking at Dallin over his shoulder, who stared at me with that same familiar darkness in his eyes. "Or maybe I should offer that privilege up to D, we both know how fond he is of reddening my ass."

Trey chuckled from the side of the room, the only one still dressed, but I wasn't dumb enough to think that would stop him from joining in on the fun, if I enticed him enough.

So I poked his beast, "What are you laughing at, Daddy?" I licked my lips and shook my tits for him, in my restrained position, "You didn't win after all."

His smile fell, and he cocked his head to the side. There was my dark and dangerous beast. "Careful, Rey." He warned, "Or I won't wait my turn."

"Hmm." I hummed, "I didn't know you were a rule follower."

His lips tightened, but Dallin kept him in check as Parker wound the rope up into a weird webbing without ever looking up at me.

"Don't even think about it." Dallin warned, "Parker won this, fair and square."

Trey licked his lips and started stripping down. "I'll wait all night if I have to. I'll still make her scream for me before I'm done."

My pussy throbbed again as I riled my guys up. Parker may have won first pick, but I knew them well enough to know they would end up fucking me all together before we were done if I got my way.

And I always got my way.

Parker slid the rope up my legs and then wound the long tail around my torso and arms, silently working me into some sort of harness that matched the black leather one I was wearing as an appetizer.

"You're going to cry so prettily for me before it's over," Parker whispered ominously and my heart thumped loudly in my chest.

He undid my wrists and tied them behind my back, attaching them to the ropes around my waist. "Now what?" I purred, trying to force him to tell me what else he was going to do to me so I could prepare. I knew they'd never hurt me more than I could handle, but the fear still crept into my stomach as I turned them all feral for me.

He didn't reply, adding to the tension in the room as he started working the harness to a rigging point in the center of the room. I thought he meant to immobilize me with his fancy knots, but I should have known there were far more sinister plans in his mind that just that.

When I was hooked, he grabbed the pulley from the other side of the room and drew it, cinching the slack out of the line and creating pressure in the ropes around my body.

"Oh, God." I gasped when the pressure built so much that my feet lifted off the floor and I fell into the ropes, as they supported me like a hammock seat. They held my weight under my thighs and across my back until I was almost six feet off the ground. "Parker."

"Spreader bar." He replied, nodding to me as Trey eagerly walked forward with the infamous metal bar in his hands.

"Wait." I cocked my head to see them as I spun slowly in the air in my reclined position. "This was a one-player game."

"Enter reinforcements." Parker raised his brow at me as I spun enough to see him, "You didn't think I'd leave them out when you let them play with me during your game, did you?"

"Parker." I moaned and then shrieked when Trey's powerful hands wrapped around my ankle, quickly fastening one and then the other into his toy.

It was about two feet wide, so it held my feet apart, but not exactly how I imagined when I saw it in his hold earlier.

"How is that?" Trey looked between my knees and up my body as I lifted my head to see him. My head was unsupported, so it fell backward unless I held myself in a crunched-up position.

"Fine." I hissed and realized my mistake instantly.

He stared at me and clicked a button on the bar before sliding my legs apart so far that my hips burned almost instantly. "How about now?" He licked his lips, staring directly at my exposed pussy as I fought the contraption to close my knees at least, but it did no good.

"Perfect." Parker hummed appreciatively from the wall before cocking his head to the side, "Well, almost."

Trey grinned and grabbed a loose rope from the rigging point, attaching it to a ring on the bar. Then, Parker started lowering the entire thing, including me, until my ankles were suspended way above my head and spread wide apart.

I was effectively helpless.

And open.

And so fucking wet.

"This is called a seated suspension position." Parker tied the thing off to a hook on the wall and sauntered toward me. "How does it feel? Are you comfortable?"

"Do you care?" I scoffed, fighting to keep my head up to stare at him.

"Yes." He snapped, walking around to grab a handful of my hair and pull my head up, "Communication is one hundred percent necessary to make this enjoyable and safe for everyone Reyna. You know that."

"I don't like my head hanging upside down." I admitted, "But other than that, it's comfortable."

I knew the ins and outs of rope use since Parker had often used it to bind me up before, just never in the air suspended before.

"Tingles, pinching, or pulling." He stated as he slid something under the back of my head and attached it to the ropes above me. "You tell us immediately. Got it?"

With my head supported in a silk sling, I felt much more comfortable and nodded my agreement. "Got it."

"Good." He licked his lips and then stood at my ass, staring down at my exposed body. "Crop."

My heart rate jumped even higher as Dallin smirked, grabbing the soft leather riding crop he'd picked out of the box.

"Parker." I hissed in warning, but it was Dallin who replied.

"Did you know this rope harness makes your thick ass look even plumper?" He flicked his wrist and slapped the crop against my ass cheek, making me shriek and jerk from the burn. "Fuck, Rey." He growled, grabbing my burning ass cheek and squeezing it as he admired the mark he left there. "Be a good girl and ask for another."

"Fuck you." I hissed and then screamed when he swung it and slapped my clit. "God!"

"Be a good girl and ask for another." He repeated authoritatively like he hadn't just electrocuted me with a defibrillator through my clit.

"Please," I begged prettily, too afraid to feel the sting against my clit again without pleasure mixing with the pain. "Please, can I have another one on my ass?"

"Good girl." He praised and gave me not one, but three more on my ass until I was writhing and begging to be fucked. "That's our girl."

"PLEASE!" I screamed, finding Parker's blue eyes in the chaos. "I need pleasure. This was about pleasure, not pain!"

"You're right baby," Parker ran his hands down the inside of my thighs until his fingers slid through my wet pussy and then pushed two deep into me as I clenched tight around him. "You're so fucking right, Baby Girl. Fellas, our girl wants pleasure with her pain."

"Yes!" I mewed pathetically when he leaned down and sucked my clit into his mouth and started tongue fucking me aggressively. "Don't stop." I pleaded.

"Is that what you needed, Kitten?" Trey pushed my hair back off my forehead as he stood at my side. "You just wanted his mouth on your pussy?"

"No." I gasped and licked my lips. "Cock is what I want. I want all three of your cocks."

He chuckled and pulled his rock hard cock out for me, stripping down. "Where do you want it, darling?"

"Fuck my throat," I demanded, as Parker rocked me on his face in my suspended harness.

"Only if you ask me nicely." Trey teased, sliding the silk sling down to my neck so I could tip my head back, but I still felt supported as he aimed his cock at my lips in my upside down position.

God, he was going to rock me on and off his cock like a pendulum and I was going to come so hard from it, I could already tell.

"Please fuck my throat, Daddy." I purred, licking the head of his cock. "While Parker fucks my pussy. I want to take you both in tandem."

Parker smacked my clit with his hand and stood up, tracing my wet pussy with the head of his cock. "You want our cocks at the same time?"

"Yes!" I screamed in frustration, eager for pleasure. "Please!"

"Daddy will give you what you want." Trey groaned and lined himself up, pulling me by the ropes until his cock was pushed down deep into my throat. "Fuck yes," He hissed, "Take that fucking cock, Kitten."

As he swung me off his cock, Parker's cock stood tall and hard, impaling me without hesitation thanks to the rocking motion of my body. The hard piercings on his cock pulled on my inner body as he gave me his entire length. I discovered early on with Parker that I had to be highly aroused to comfortably handle his full length, and I was in that state and more as Trey pulled me back onto his.

Both guys grunted and groaned as I hung helplessly, taking them equally, and I loved how it made me feel. It gave me that same feeling I got when I was used by them at the end of a game of hide and seek. When I wasn't their wife, who they cherished and worshiped, but their dirty little toy to be used for their pleasures and fun.

It made me drip with arousal, each and every time, without fail.

"You take them both so good, Rey." Dallin tweaked my nipples and then rubbed my clit as our husbands fucked me.

I shattered, orgasming around Parker's cock as Trey started spurting down my throat.

There was a mix of grunts and groans as Trey pulled out of my mouth and Parker slammed in deep, filling my pussy with his come.

I hadn't even realized that Dallin had been stroking himself, but when his hot come branded my stomach as he came all over me, I moaned, knowing I could make him come without even touching him.

"Jesus." I gasped, laying there in the air as we all panted and smiled. "I think Lex was right about this room."

Parker groaned and started unraveling me from the web he tied me up in.

Trey held me as Parker loosened my bindings, "And what exactly did the queen of snark have to say about our sex life?"

I giggled, knowing he and Lex had a very tumultuous relationship because they were both so prickly. "She said it was going to get me knocked up."

Dallin growled deep in his chest as he wrapped his hand around my neck and pulled me to his face, and kissed me. "Tell me more about that." He kissed me again. "Is that something you want? Is that why you gave us a new place to play?"

I leaned into him as Parker loosened the last bit of rope and lowered my feet to the floor and all three of them circled me, rubbing my skin where the bindings rubbed and helping me as the blood worked back into my limbs.

"Maybe." I admitted, though I'd been afraid to before now. "But even if I didn't, it's a hell of a good place to pretend and practice."

"There's one kink that I think I have worse than a primal one, Baby Girl." Parker bit my bottom lip and sucked it into his mouth.

"What's that?" I dared to ask as Trey nipped my neck with his sharp teeth.

"Breeding Kink, Kitten," Trey answered, and I moaned as Dallin and Parker agreed. "Even if it's not to get you pregnant. The idea of filling you up with that chance is one hell of a prize."

"A prize I'm willing to do just about anything to win," Dallin added.

"Oh, fuck." I sagged into them, knowing I'd just awakened a new kind of beast inside of them all. "Oh fuckity, fuck, fuck."

Parker chuckled as he lifted me off my feet and walked me over to the bed, laying me down in the center as they all joined. "This playroom is going to be so much fun."

Printed in the USA
CPSIA information can be obtained
at www.ICGtesting.com
CBHW031654240724
11961CB00002B/3

9 798330 261475